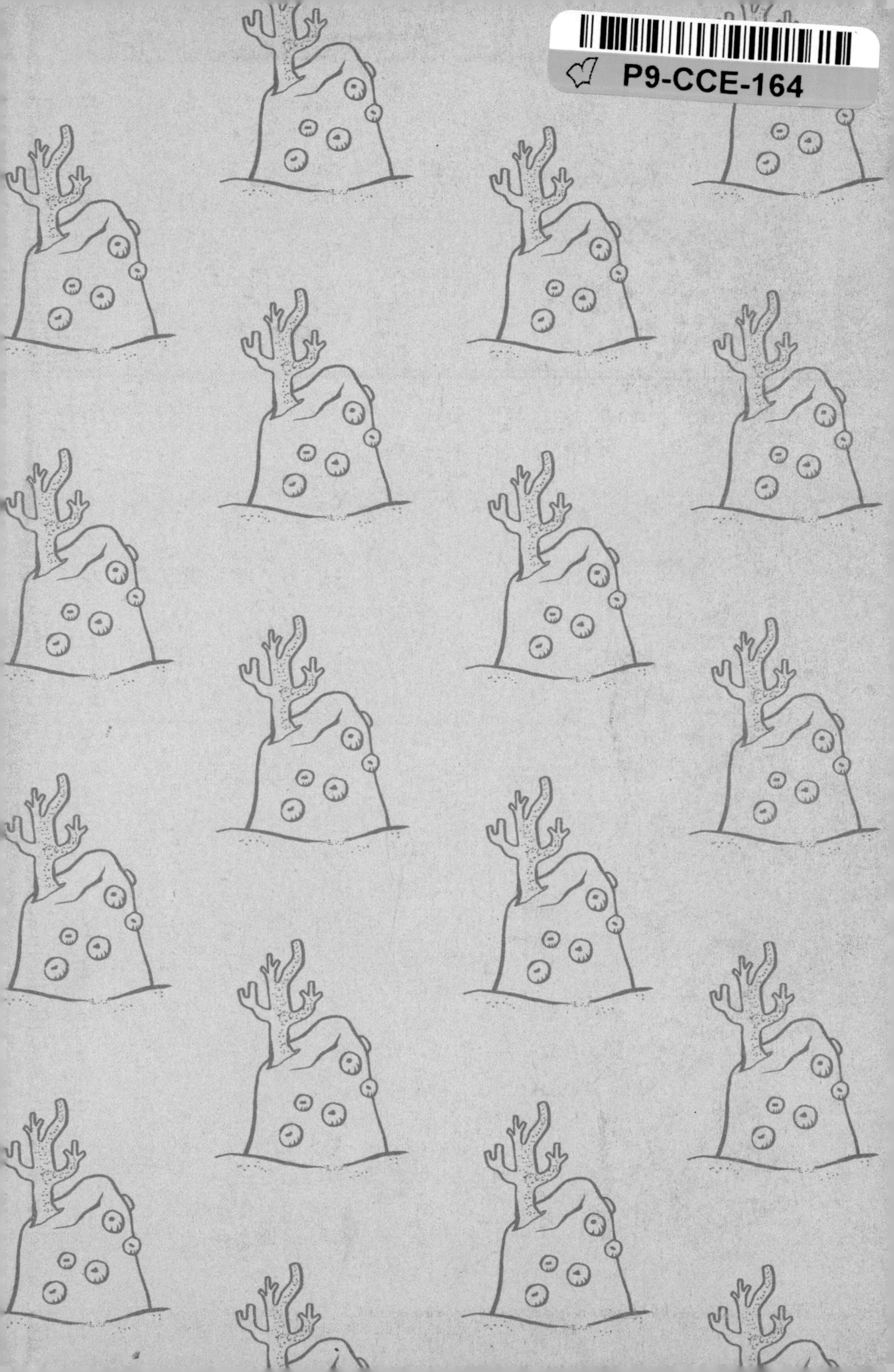

READ ALL THE PACEY PACKER BOOKS!

1

PACEY PACKER, UNICORN TRACKER

2

PACEY PACKER, UNICORN TRACKER:
◆ HORN SLAYER ◆

3

PACEY PACKER, UNICORN TRACKER:
◆ MERMAIDS VS. UNICORNS ◆

I can hardly wait.

PACEY 3 PACKER UNICORN TRACKER

MERMAIDS VS. UNICORNS

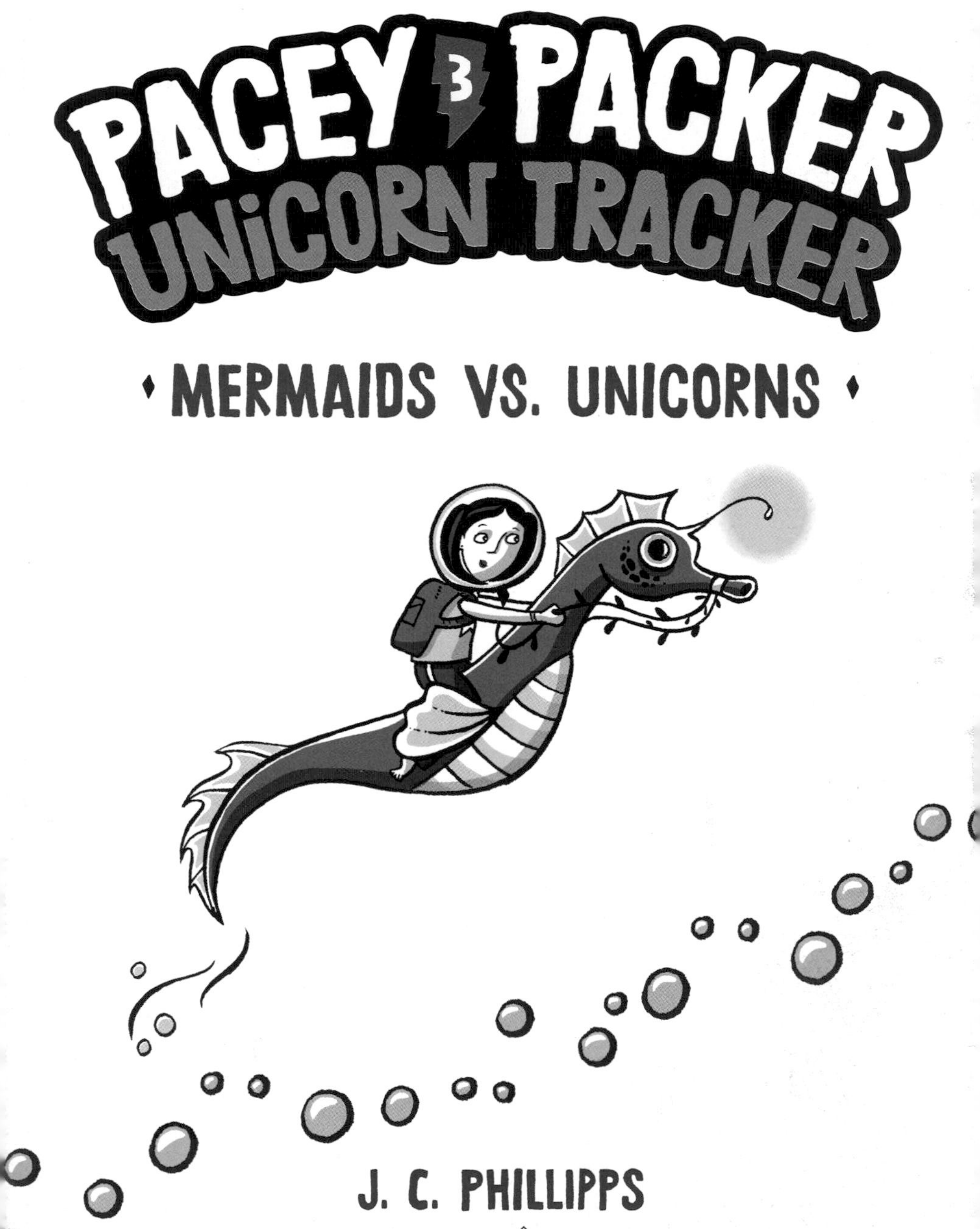

J. C. PHILLIPPS

RANDOM HOUSE NEW YORK

Copyright © 2022 by J. C. Phillipps
All rights reserved. Published in the United States by Random House Children's Books,
a division of Penguin Random House LLC, New York.

Random House and the colophon are registered trademarks of Penguin Random House LLC.

RH Graphic with the book design is a trademark of Penguin Random House LLC.

Visit us on the Web! rhcbooks.com

Educators and librarians, for a variety of teaching tools,
visit us at RHTeachersLibrarians.com

Library of Congress Cataloging-in-Publication Data is available upon request.
ISBN 978-0-593-17956-7 (hardcover)—ISBN 978-0-593-17958-1 (ebook)

MANUFACTURED IN CHINA
10 9 8 7 6 5 4 3 2 1
First Edition

To the Litwits:
Joan, Kip, and Natalie.
Best critique group ever!

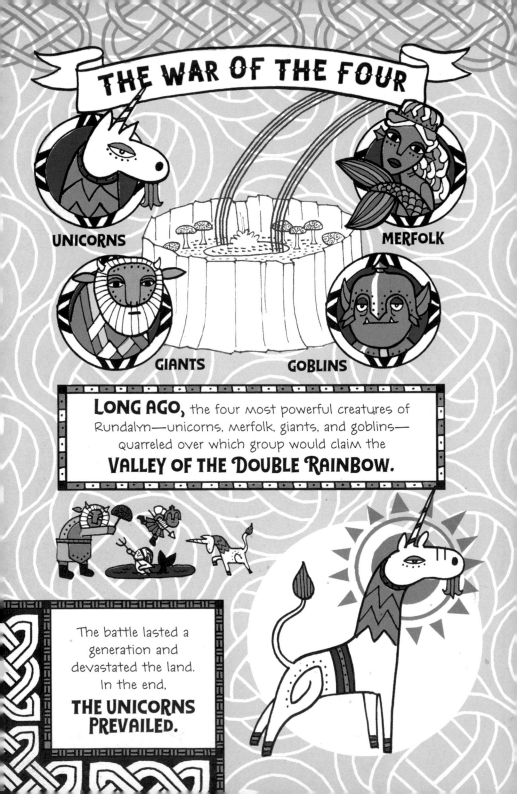

THE WAR OF THE FOUR

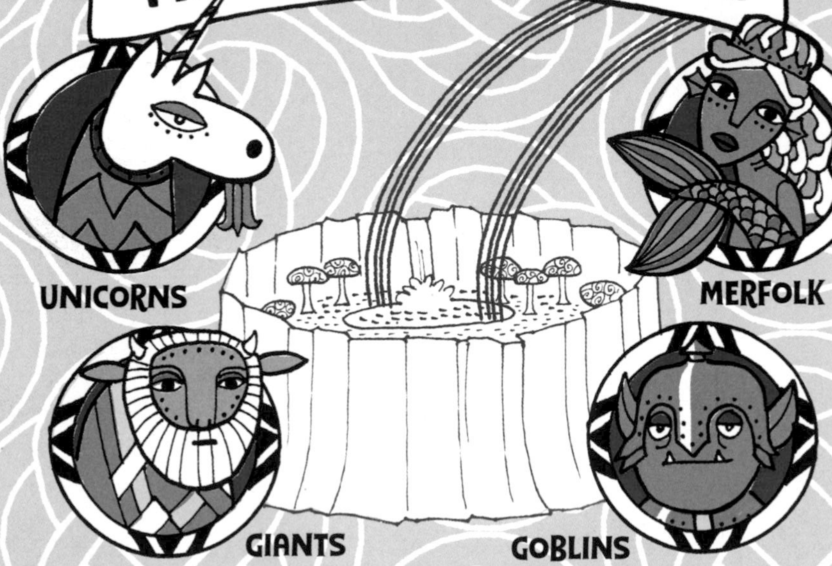
UNICORNS
MERFOLK
GIANTS
GOBLINS

LONG AGO, the four most powerful creatures of Rundalyn—unicorns, merfolk, giants, and goblins—quarreled over which group would claim the

VALLEY OF THE DOUBLE RAINBOW.

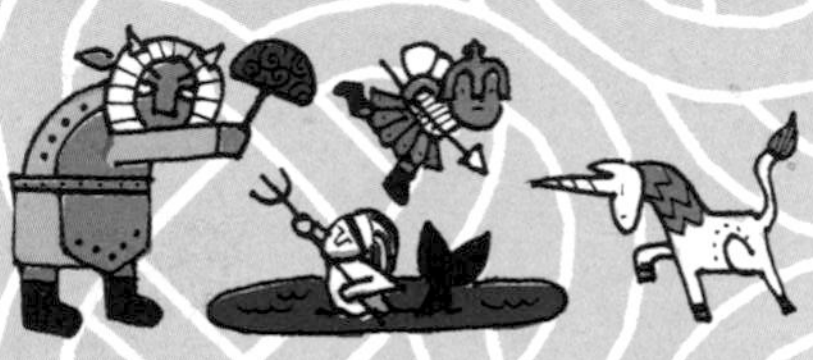

The battle lasted a generation and devastated the land. In the end,

THE UNICORNS PREVAILED.

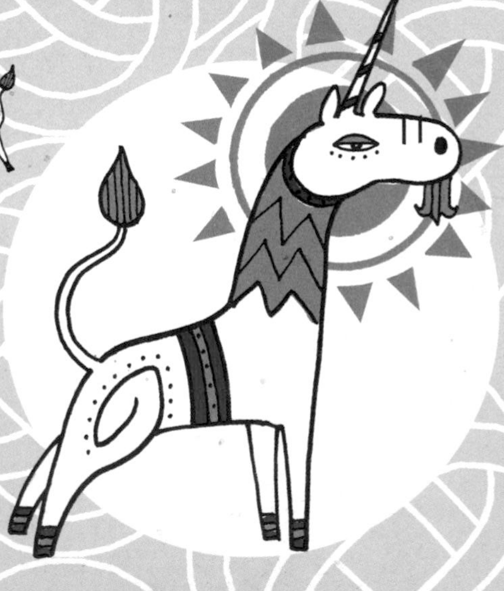

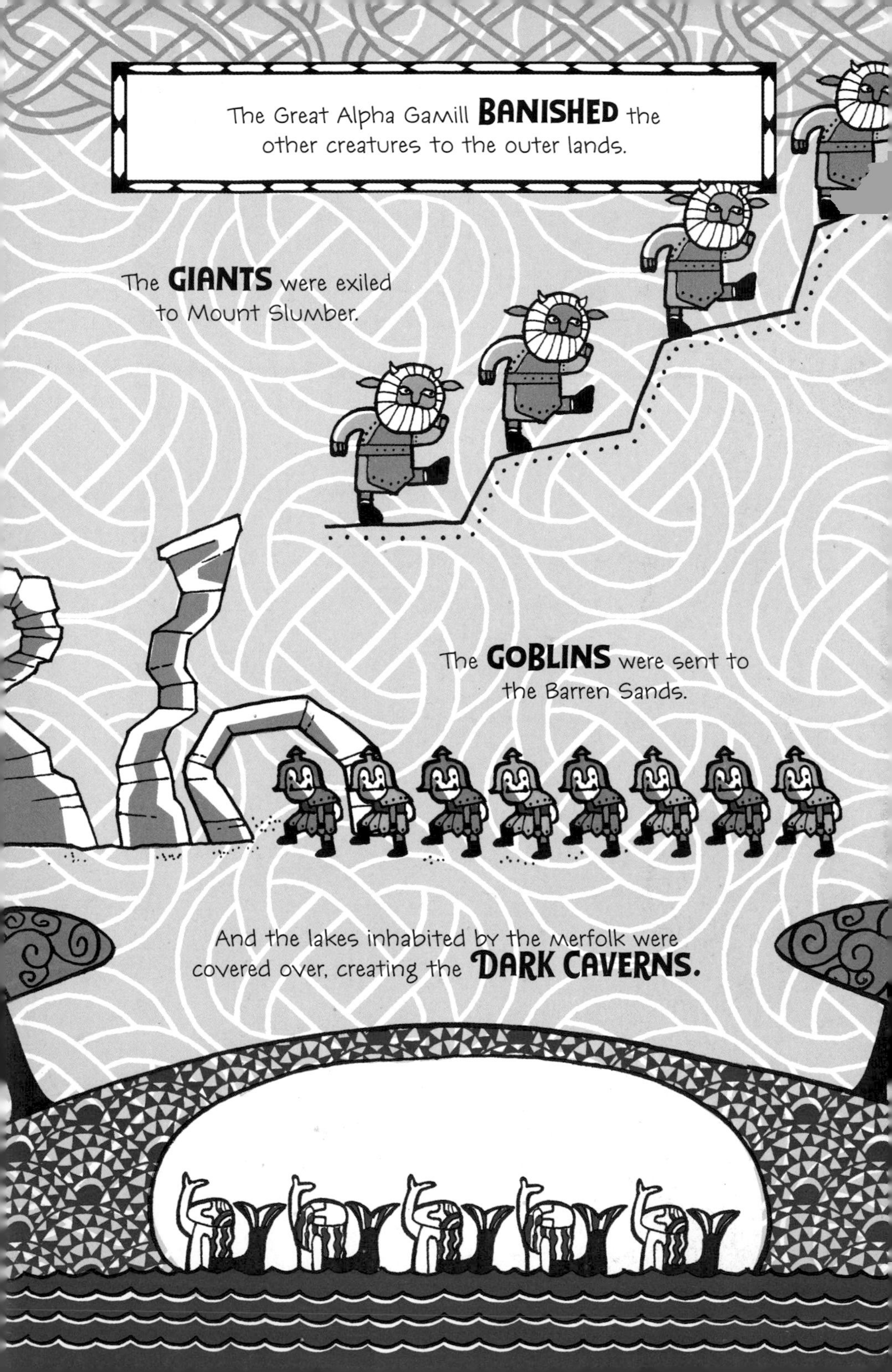
The Great Alpha Gamill **BANISHED** the other creatures to the outer lands.
The **GIANTS** were exiled to Mount Slumber.
The **GOBLINS** were sent to the Barren Sands.
And the lakes inhabited by the merfolk were covered over, creating the **DARK CAVERNS.**

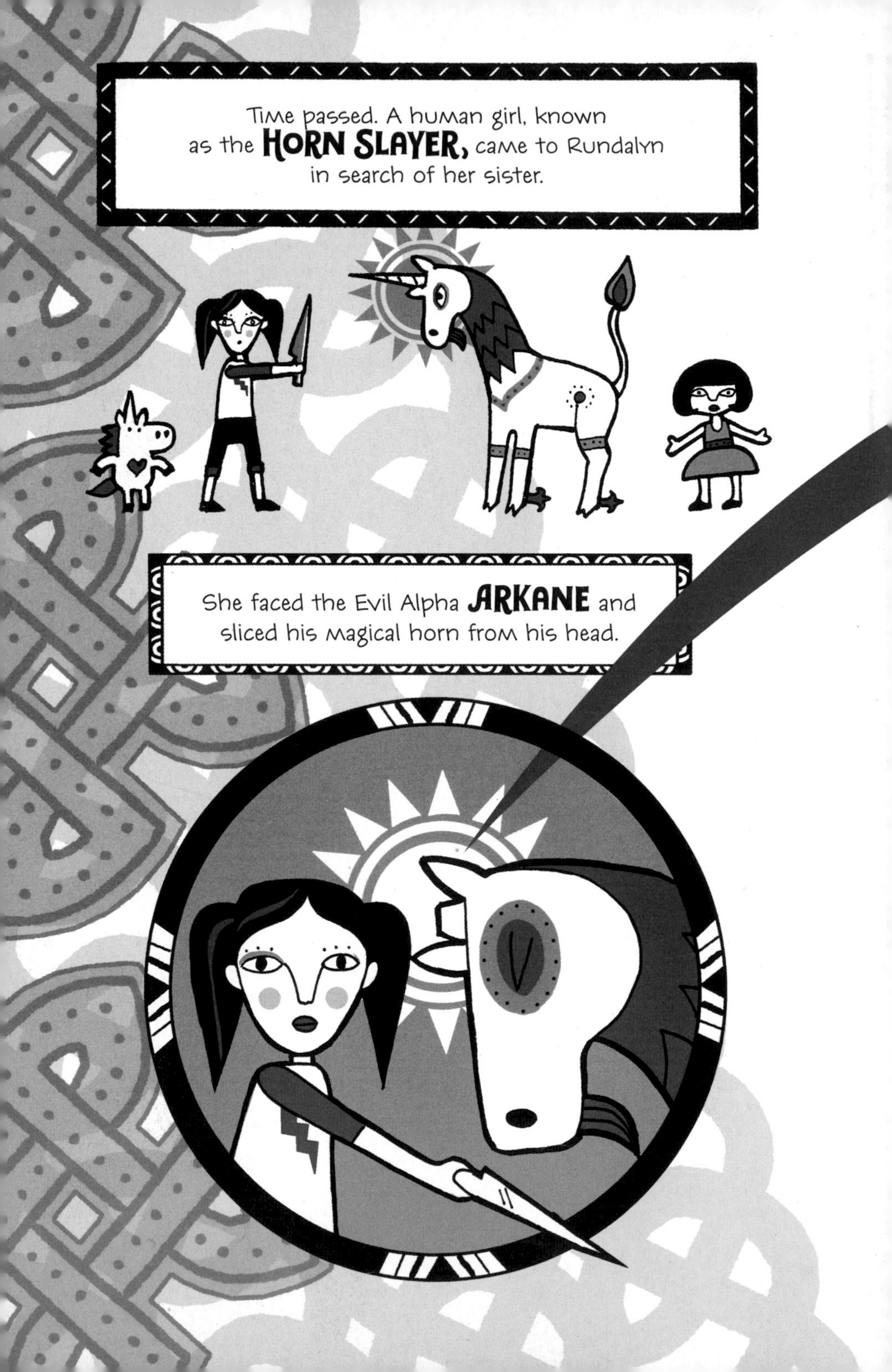
Time passed. A human girl, known as the HORN SLAYER, came to Rundalyn in search of her sister.
She faced the Evil Alpha ARKANE and sliced his magical horn from his head.

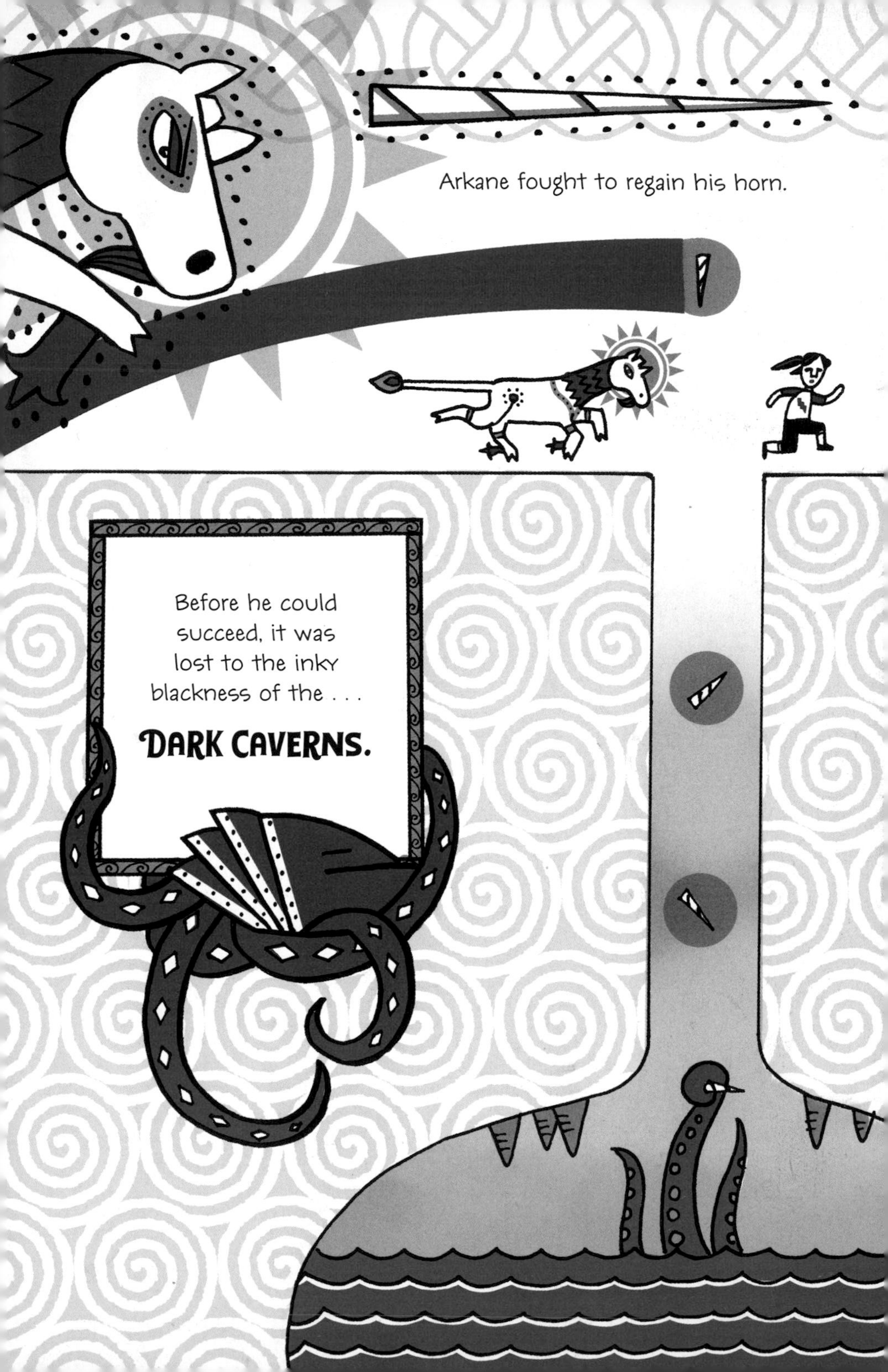
Arkane fought to regain his horn.
Before he could succeed, it was lost to the inky blackness of the . . .
DARK CAVERNS.

CHAPTER 1
PEOPLE WHO NEED PEOPLE

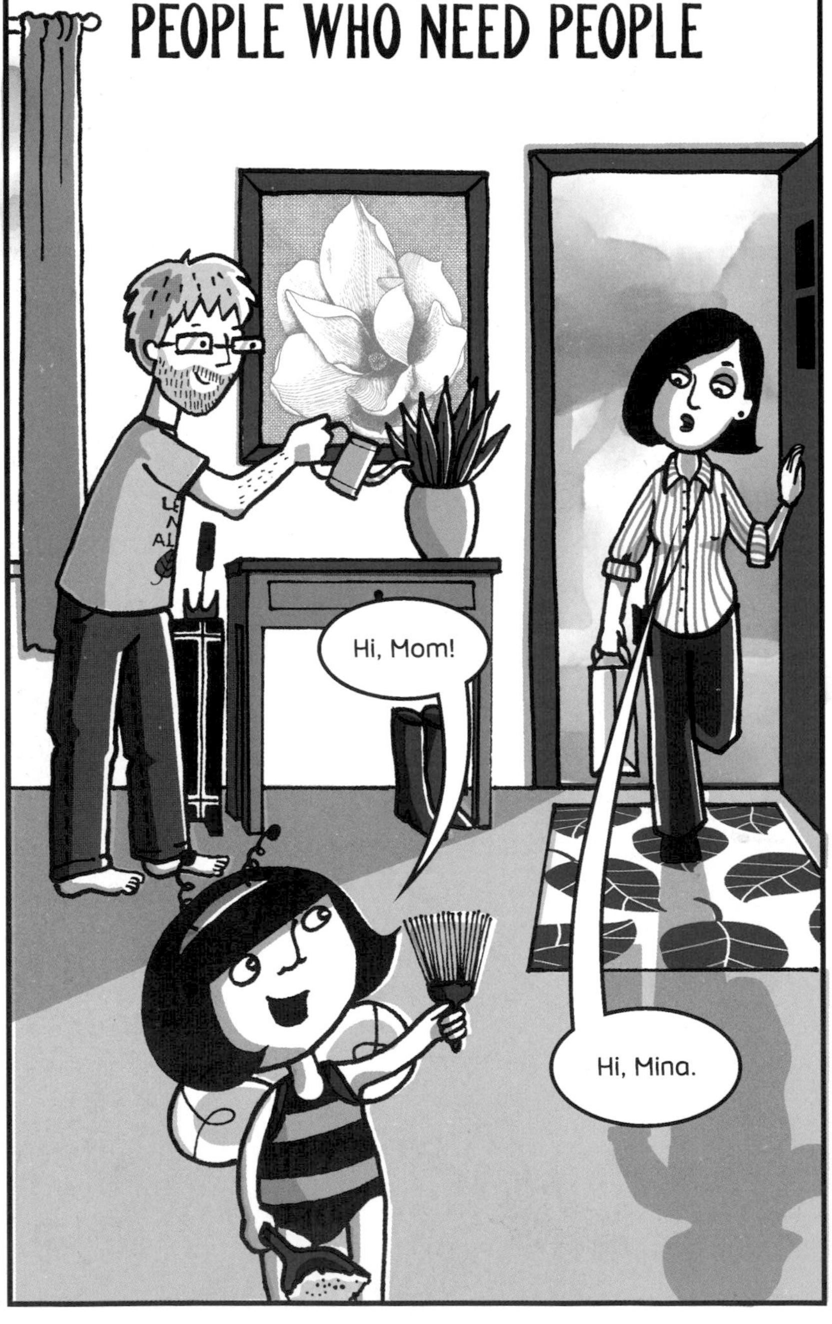
Hi, Mom!
Hi, Mina.

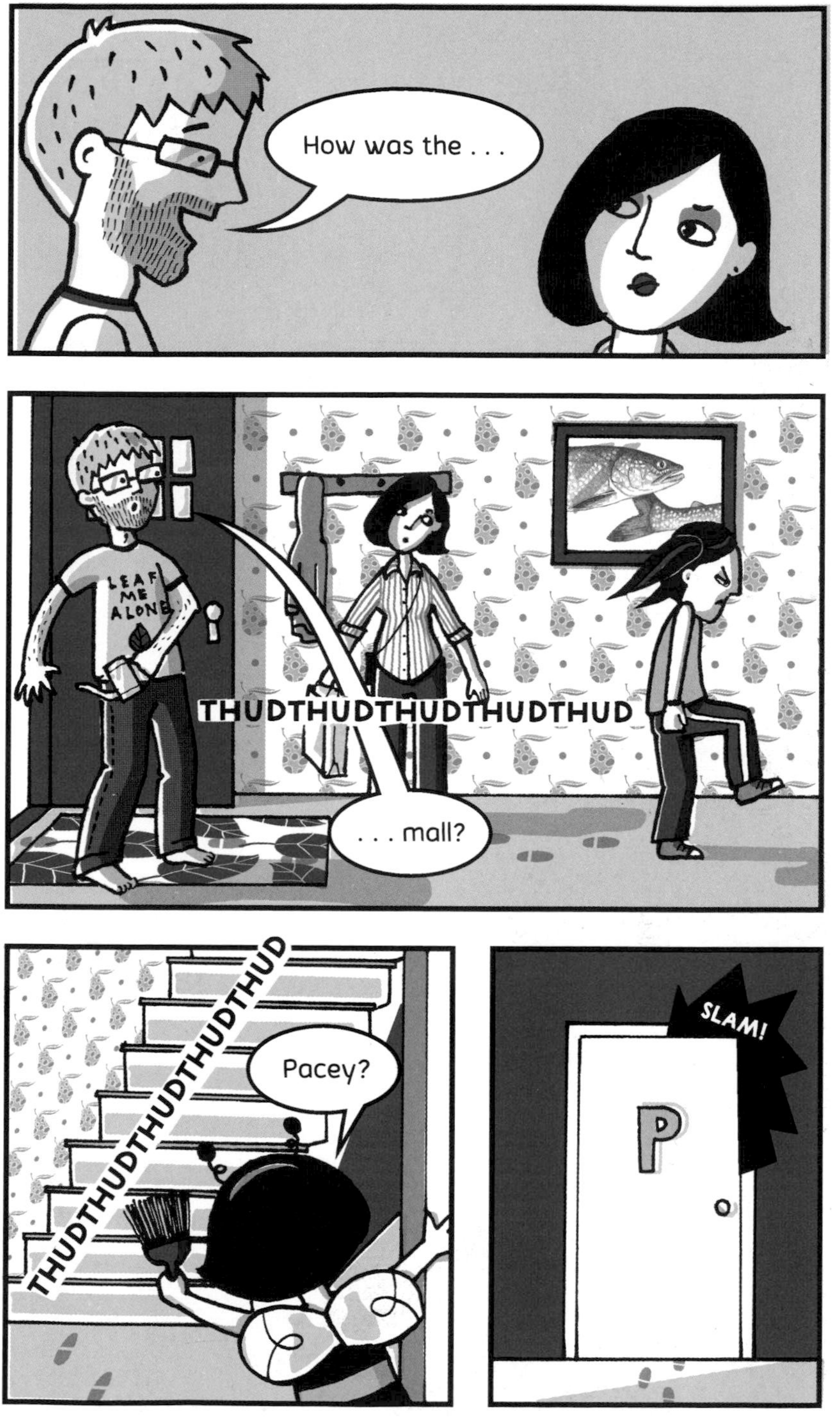
How was the . . .
LEAF ME ALONE
THUDTHUDTHUDTHUDTHUD
. . . mall?
THUDTHUDTHUDTHUD
Pacey?
SLAM!
P

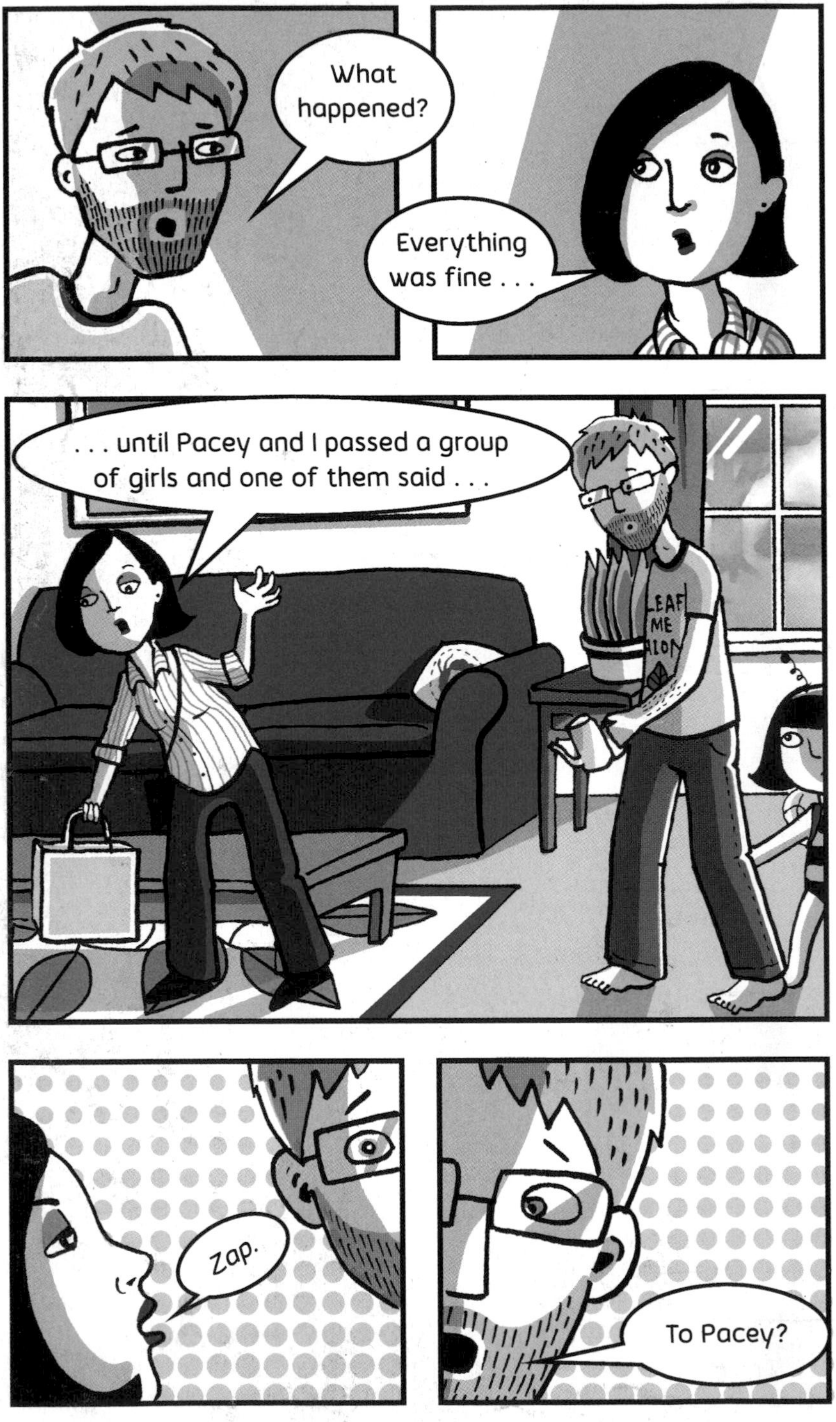
What happened?
Everything was fine . . .
. . . until Pacey and I passed a group of girls and one of them said . . .
LEAF ME ALON
Zap.
To Pacey?

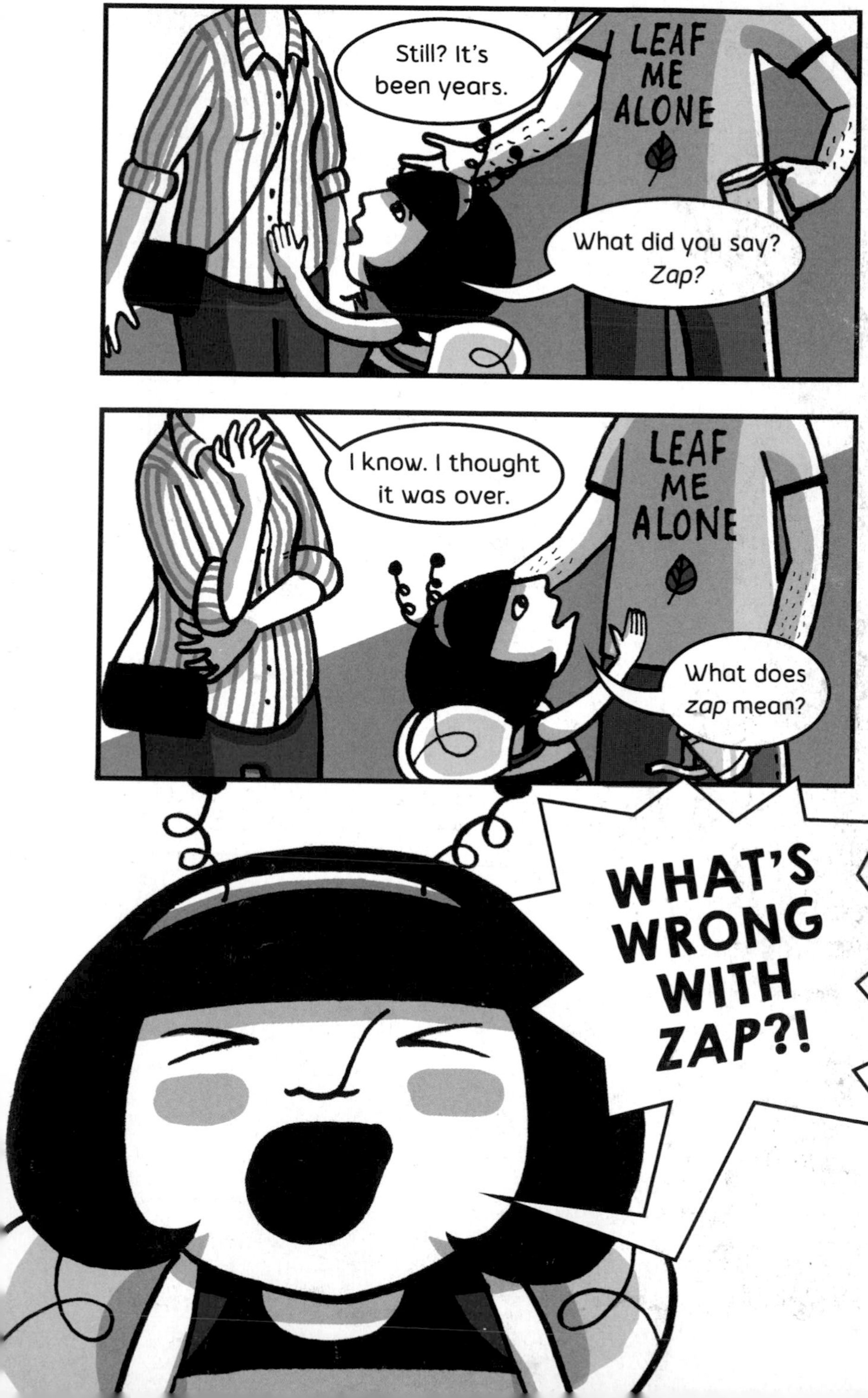
LEAF ME ALONE
Still? It's been years.
What did you say? *Zap?*
I know. I thought it was over.
LEAF ME ALONE
What does *zap* mean?
WHAT'S WRONG WITH ZAP?!

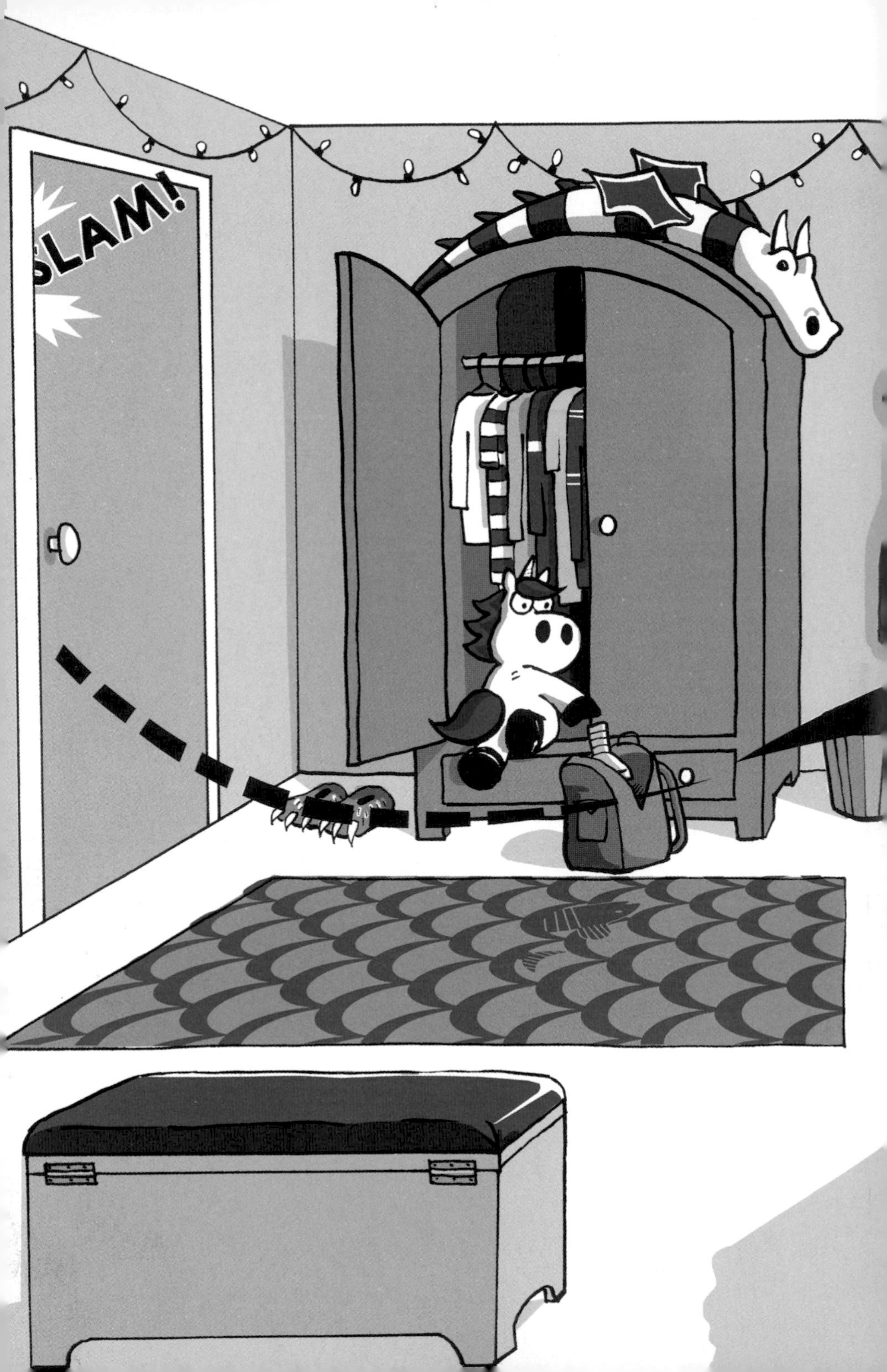
SLAM!

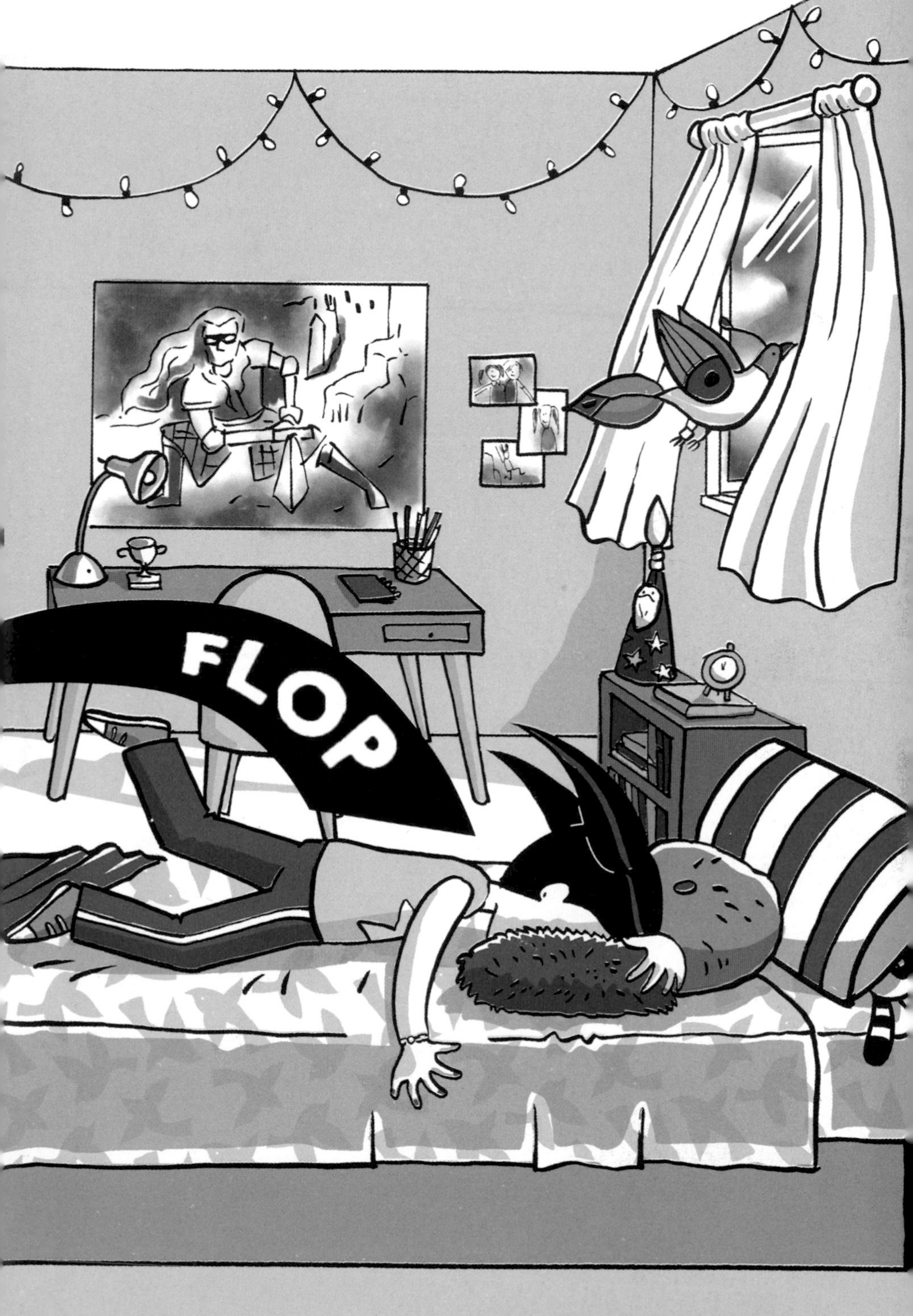
FLOP

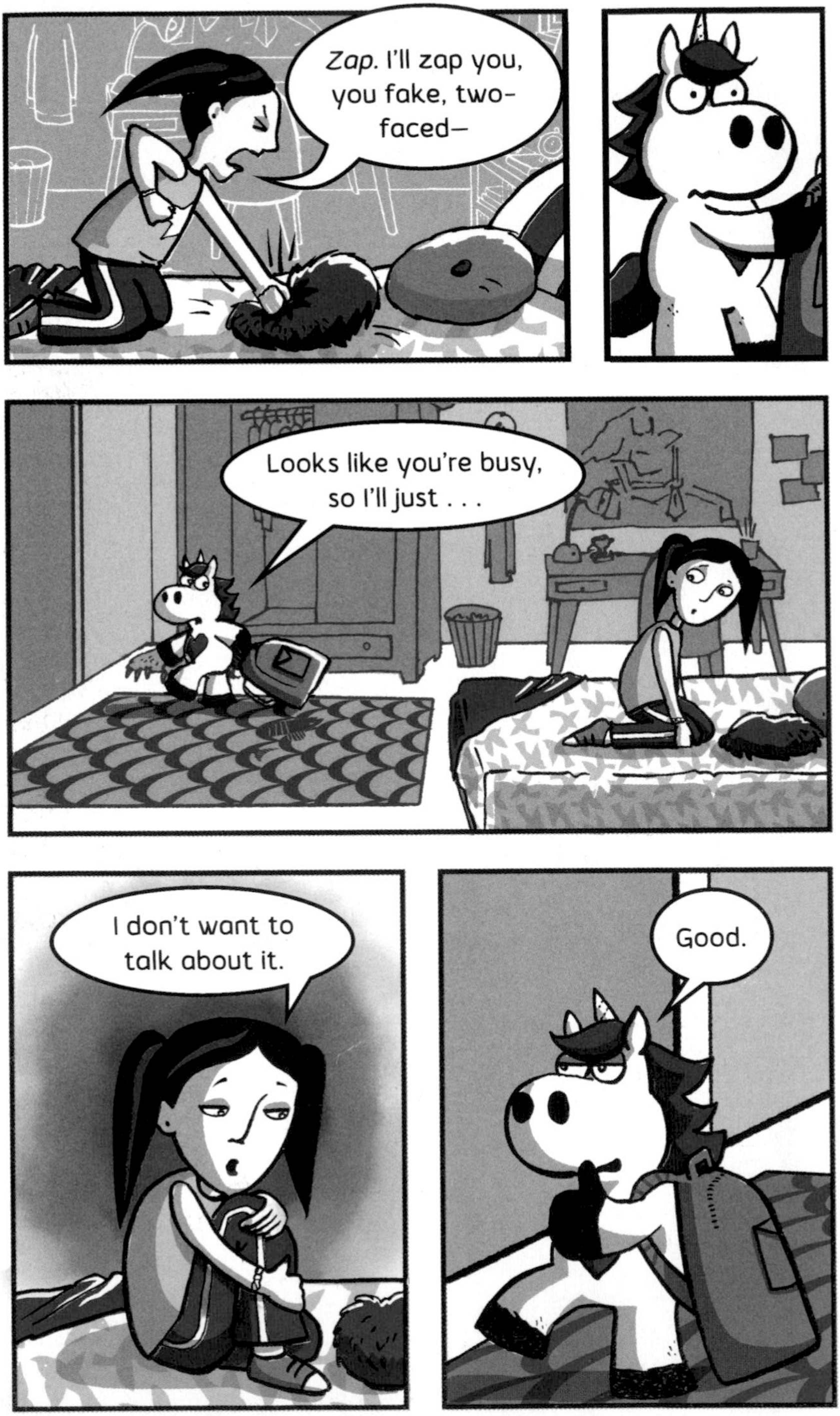
Zap. I'll zap you, you fake, two-faced—
Looks like you're busy, so I'll just . . .
I don't want to talk about it.
Good.

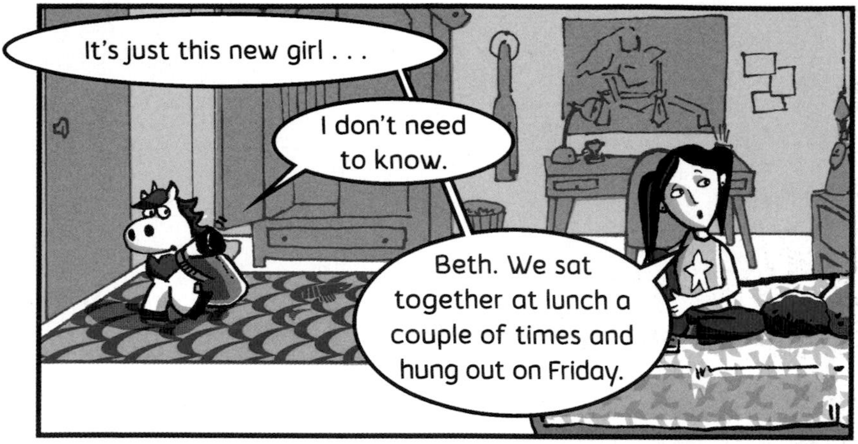
It's just this new girl . . .
I don't need to know.
Beth. We sat together at lunch a couple of times and hung out on Friday.

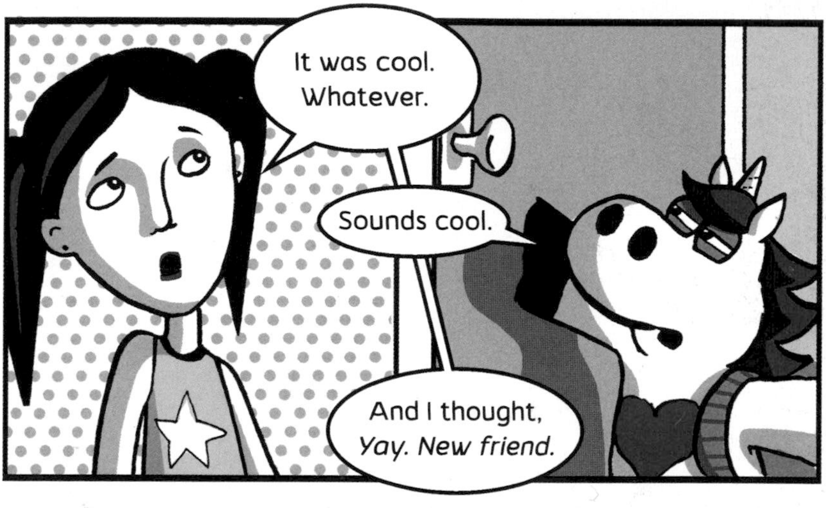
It was cool. Whatever.
Sounds cool.
And I thought, *Yay. New friend.*

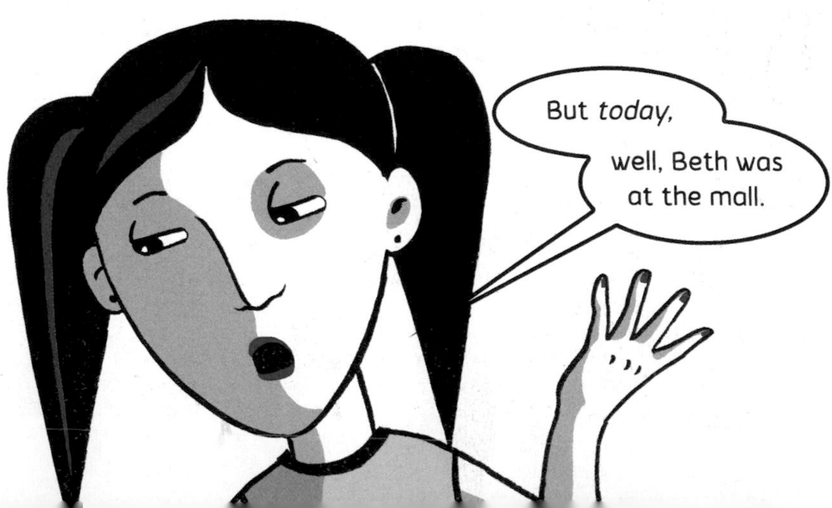
But *today,*
well, Beth was at the mall.

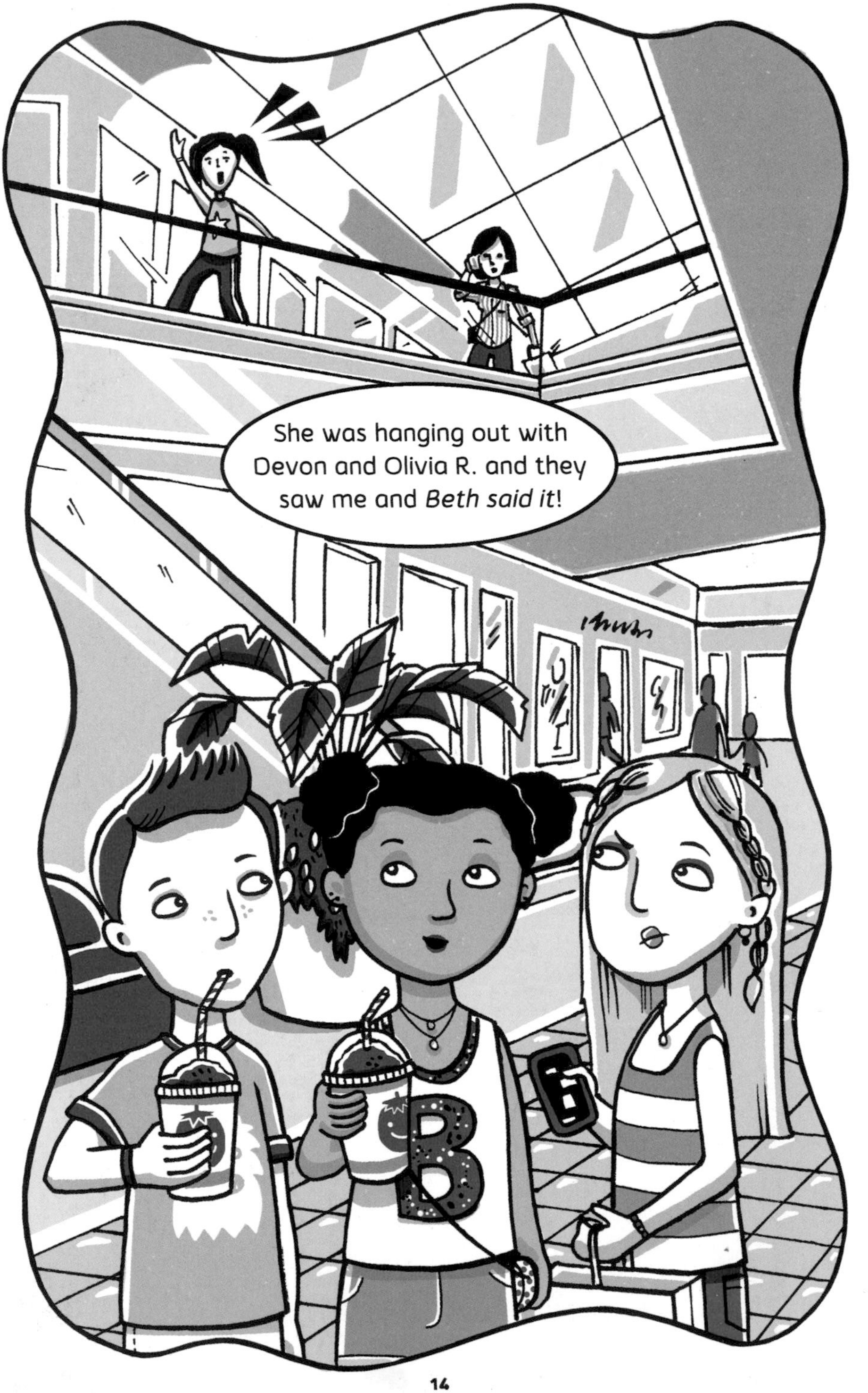
She was hanging out with Devon and Olivia R. and they saw me and *Beth said it*!

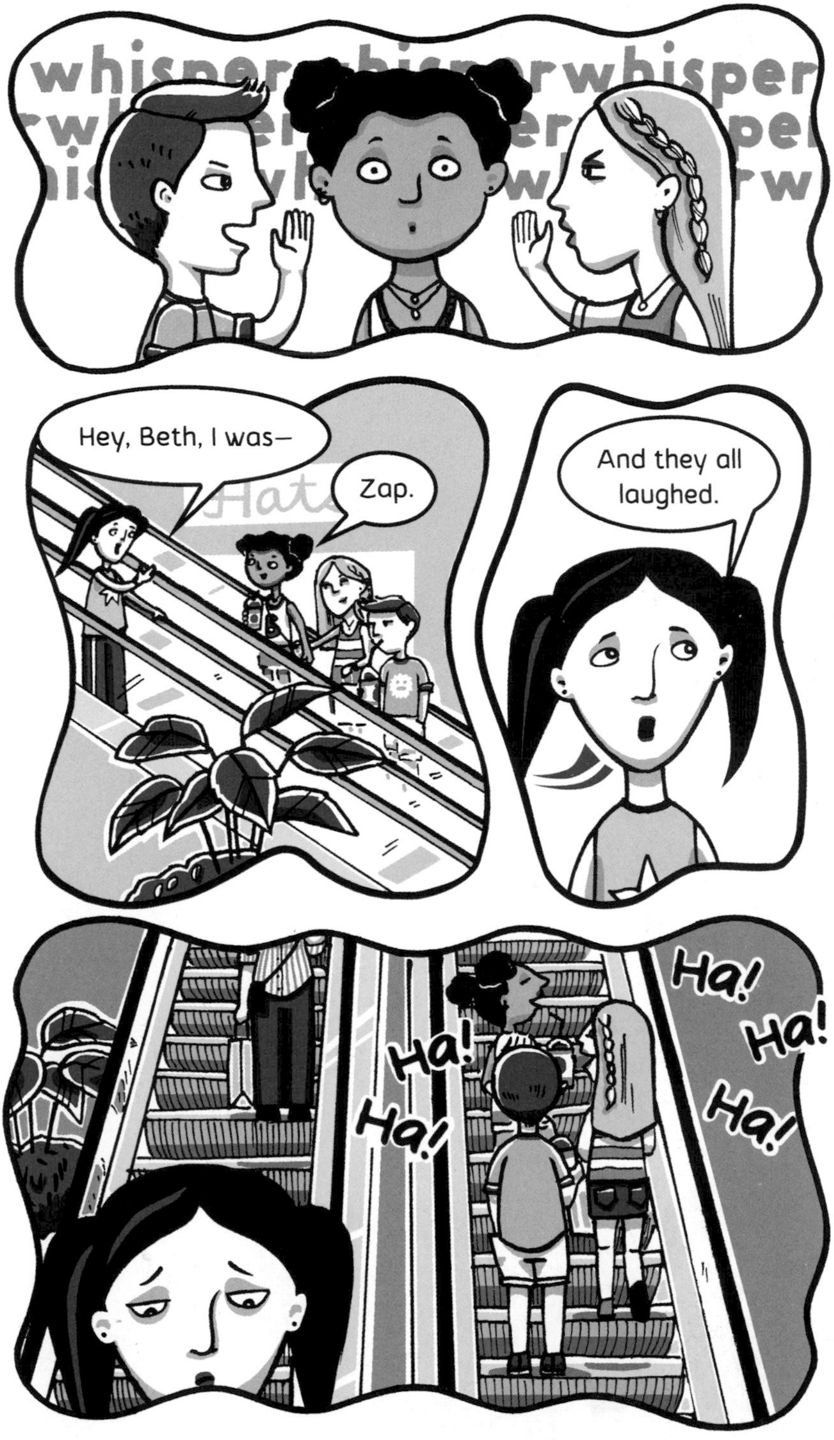
whisper whisper whisper
Hey, Beth, I was—
Zap.
And they all laughed.
Ha!
Ha!
Ha!
Ha!
Ha!

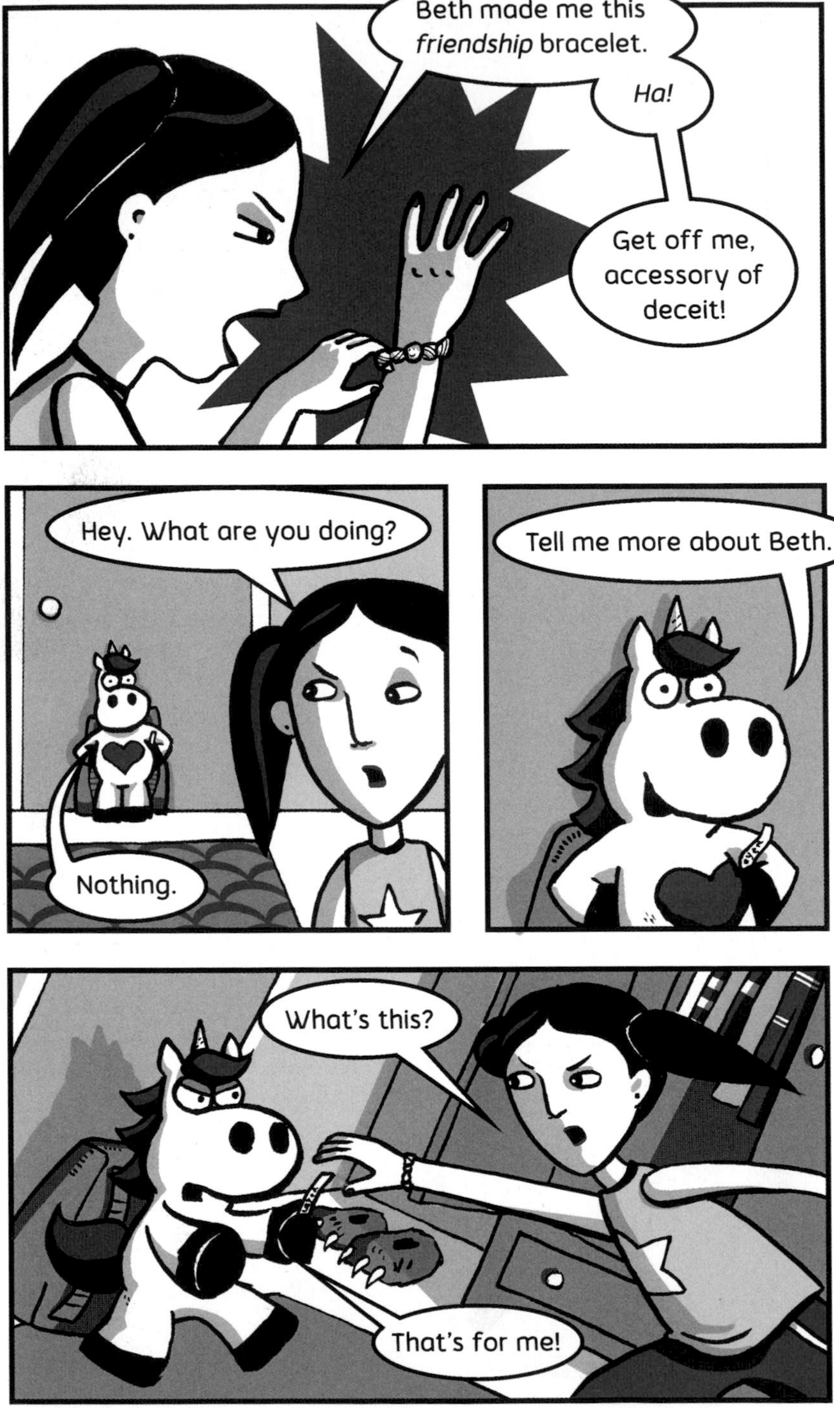
Beth made me this *friendship* bracelet.
Ha!
Get off me, accessory of deceit!
Hey. What are you doing?
Nothing.
Tell me more about Beth.
What's this?
That's for me!

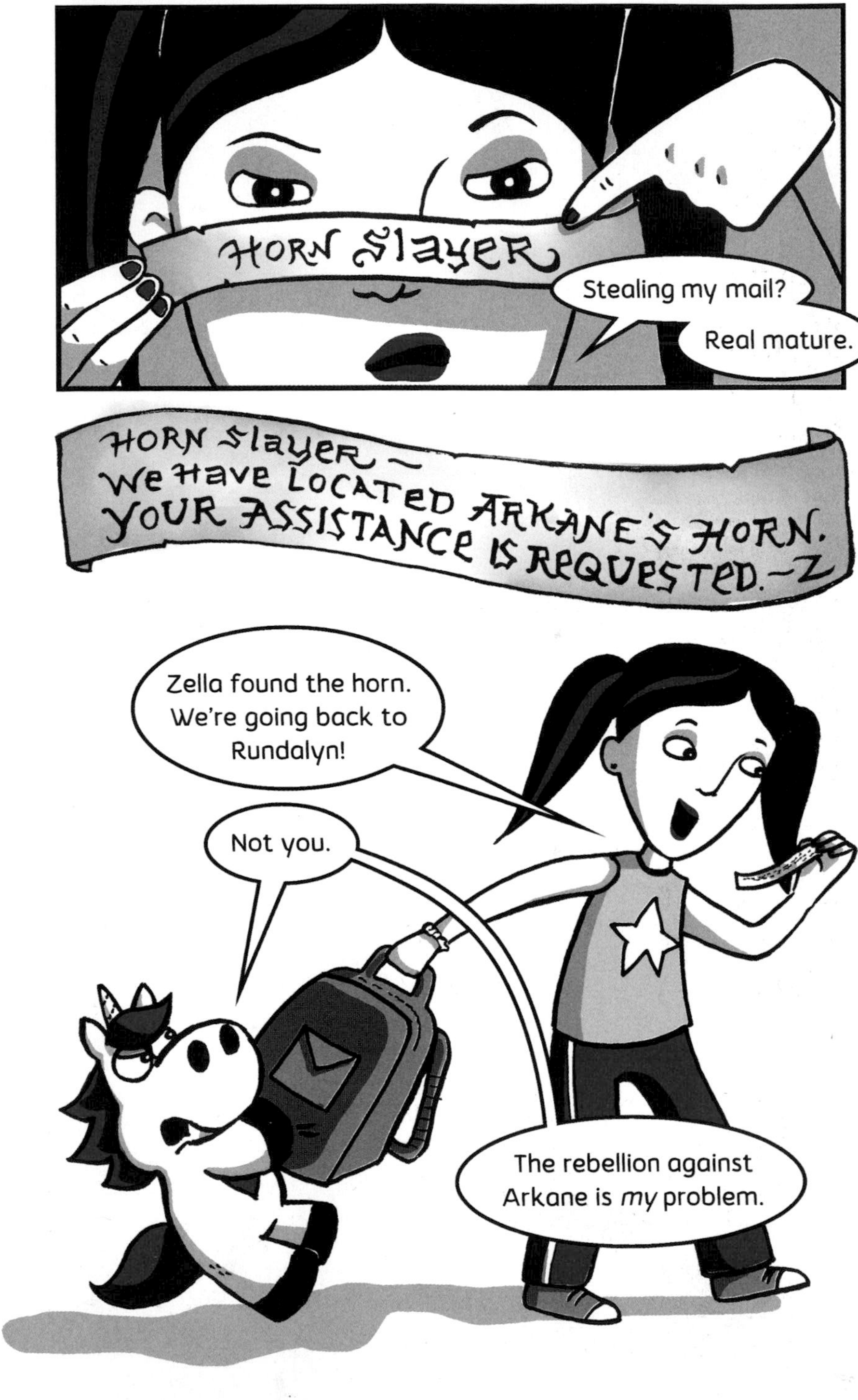
HORN SLAYER
Stealing my mail?
Real mature.
HORN SLAYER—
WE HAVE LOCATED ARKANE'S HORN.
YOUR ASSISTANCE IS REQUESTED.—Z
Zella found the horn. We're going back to Rundalyn!
Not you.
The rebellion against Arkane is *my* problem.

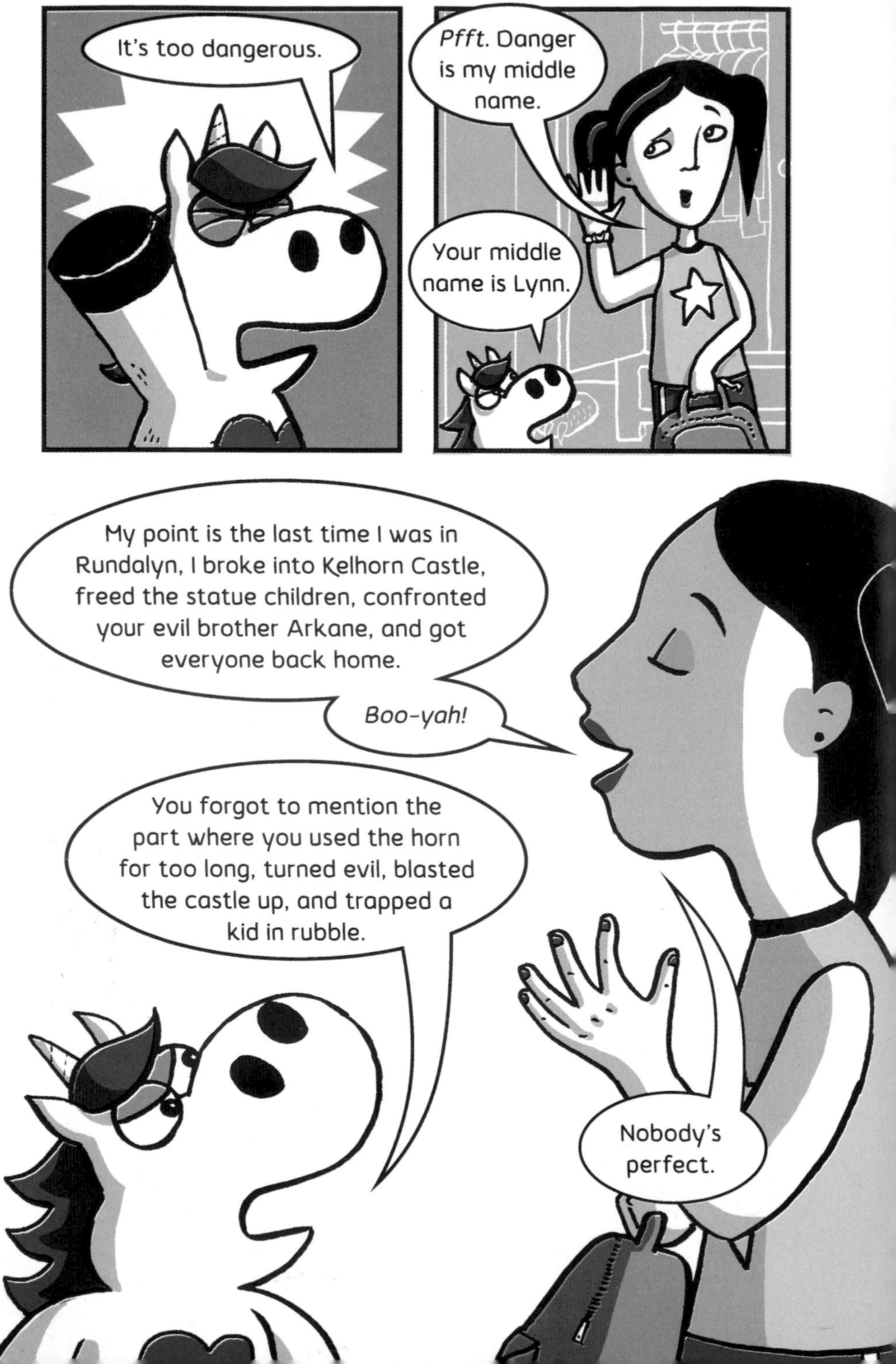
It's too dangerous.
Pfft. Danger is my middle name.
Your middle name is Lynn.
My point is the last time I was in Rundalyn, I broke into Kelhorn Castle, freed the statue children, confronted your evil brother Arkane, and got everyone back home.
Boo-yah!
You forgot to mention the part where you used the horn for too long, turned evil, blasted the castle up, and trapped a kid in rubble.
Nobody's perfect.

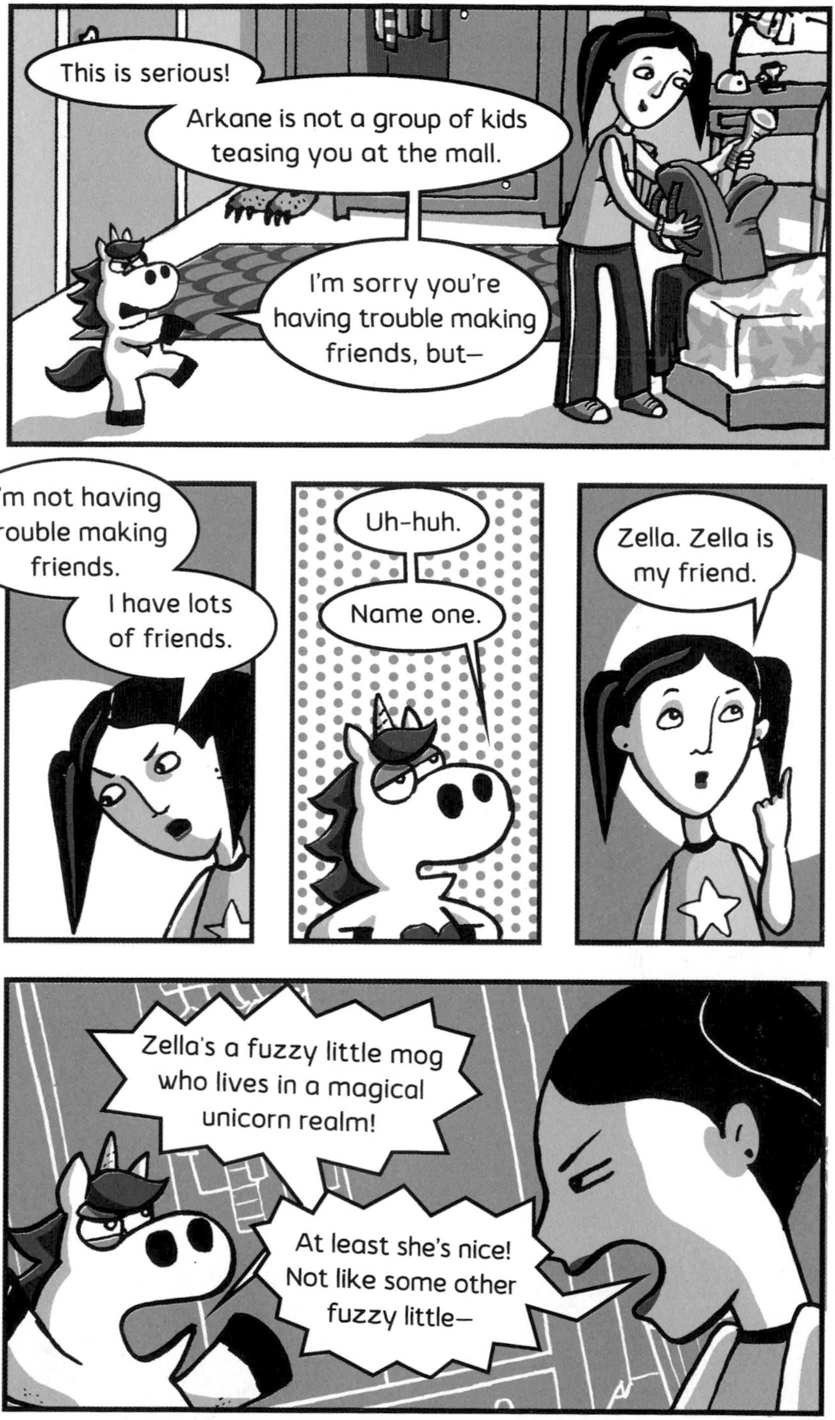
This is serious!
Arkane is not a group of kids teasing you at the mall.
I'm sorry you're having trouble making friends, but—
I'm not having trouble making friends.
I have lots of friends.
Uh-huh.
Name one.
Zella. Zella is my friend.
Zella's a fuzzy little mog who lives in a magical unicorn realm!
At least she's nice! Not like some other fuzzy little—

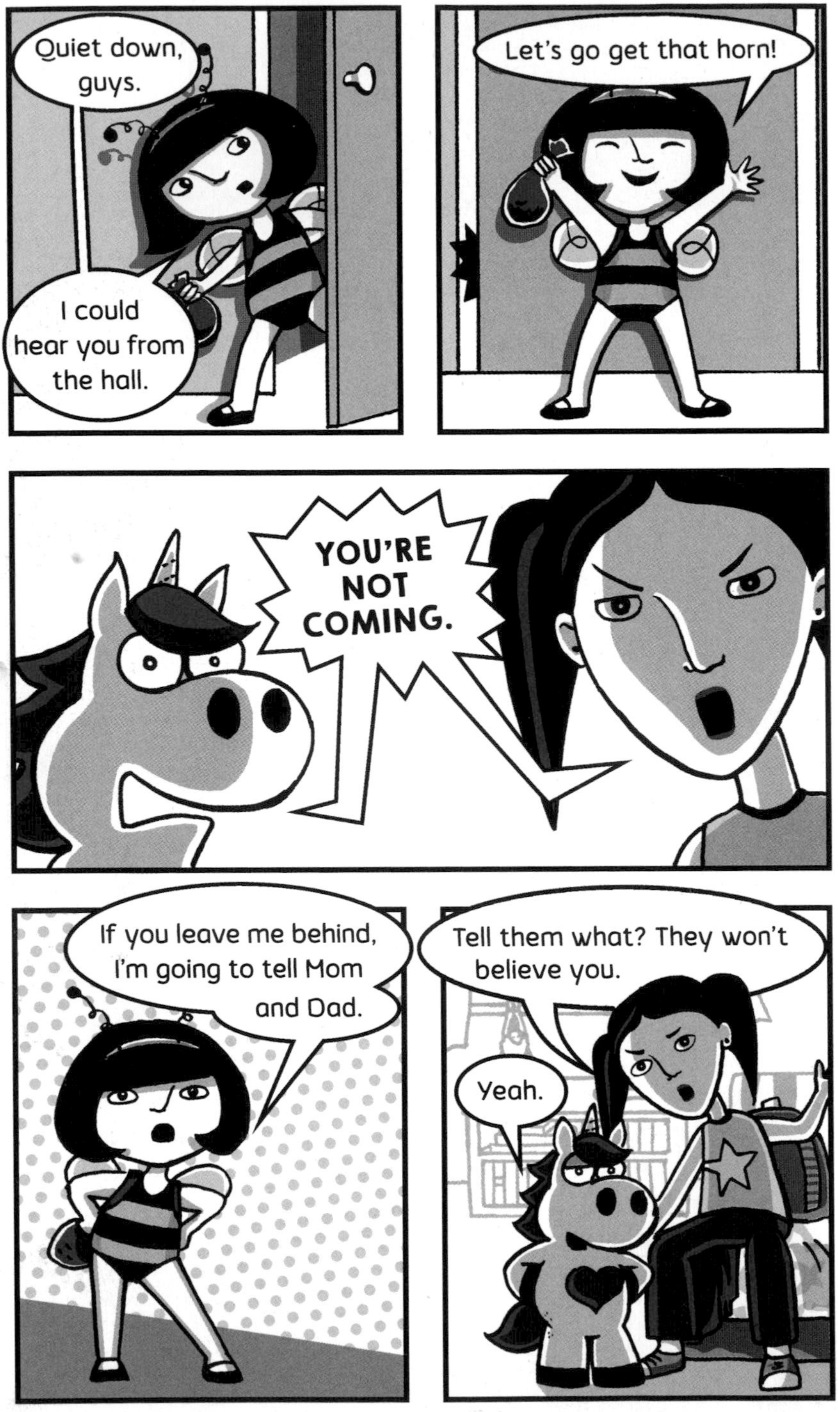
Quiet down, guys.
I could hear you from the hall.
Let's go get that horn!
YOU'RE NOT COMING.
If you leave me behind, I'm going to tell Mom and Dad.
Tell them what? They won't believe you.
Yeah.

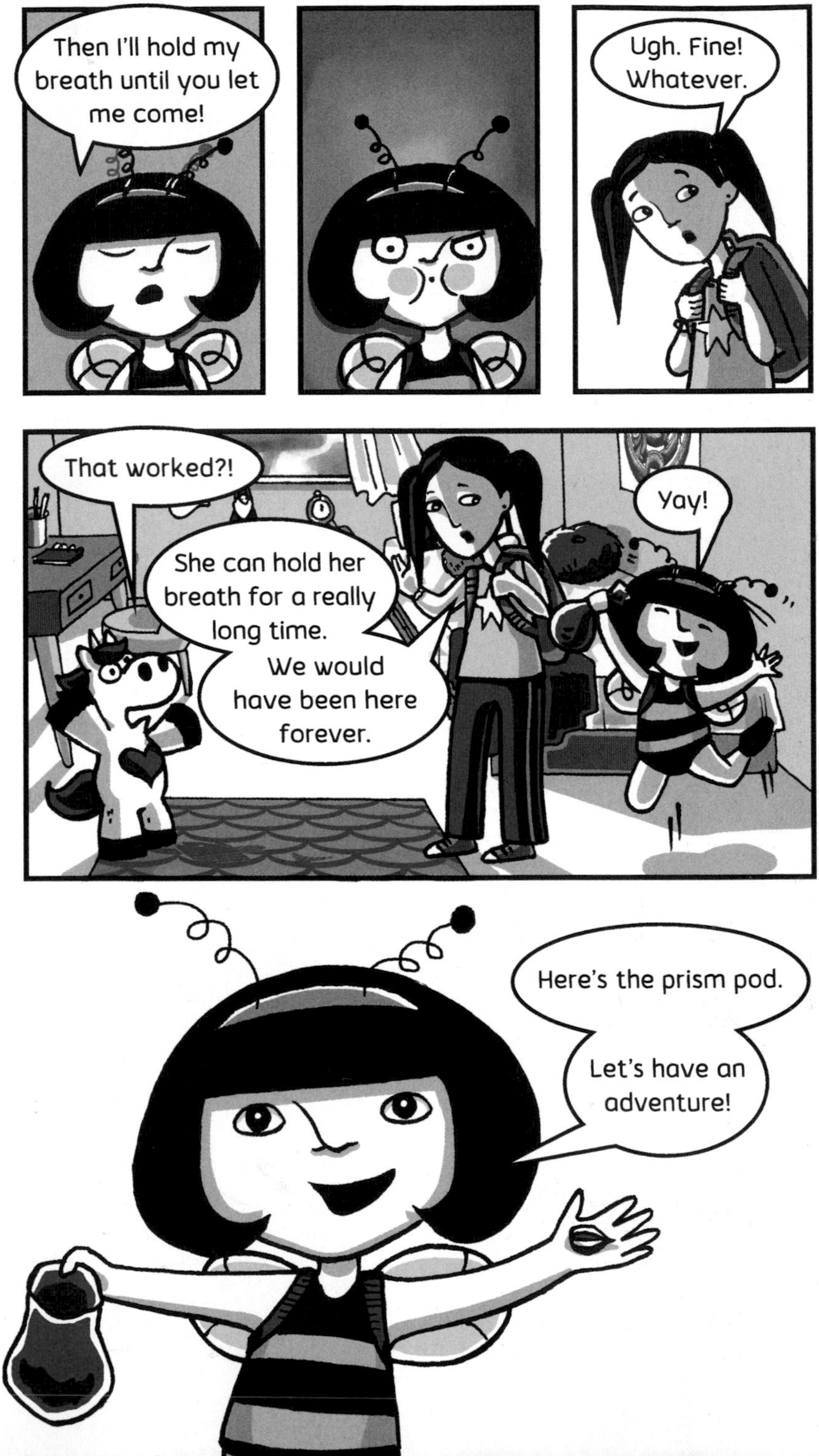

Then I'll hold my breath until you let me come!
Ugh. Fine! Whatever.
That worked?!
She can hold her breath for a really long time.
We would have been here forever.
Yay!
Here's the prism pod.
Let's have an adventure!

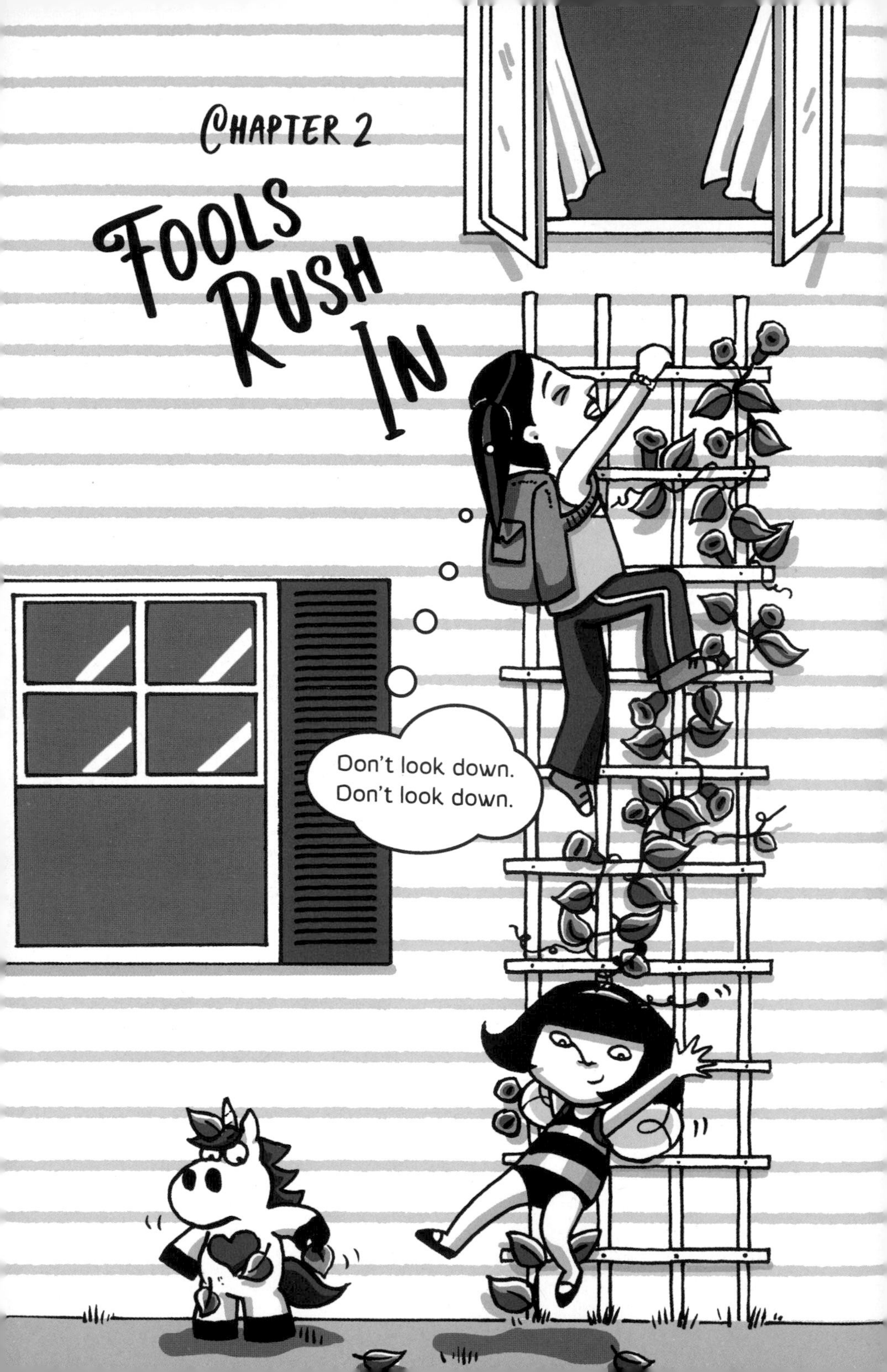
CHAPTER 2
FOOLS RUSH IN
Don't look down.
Don't look down.

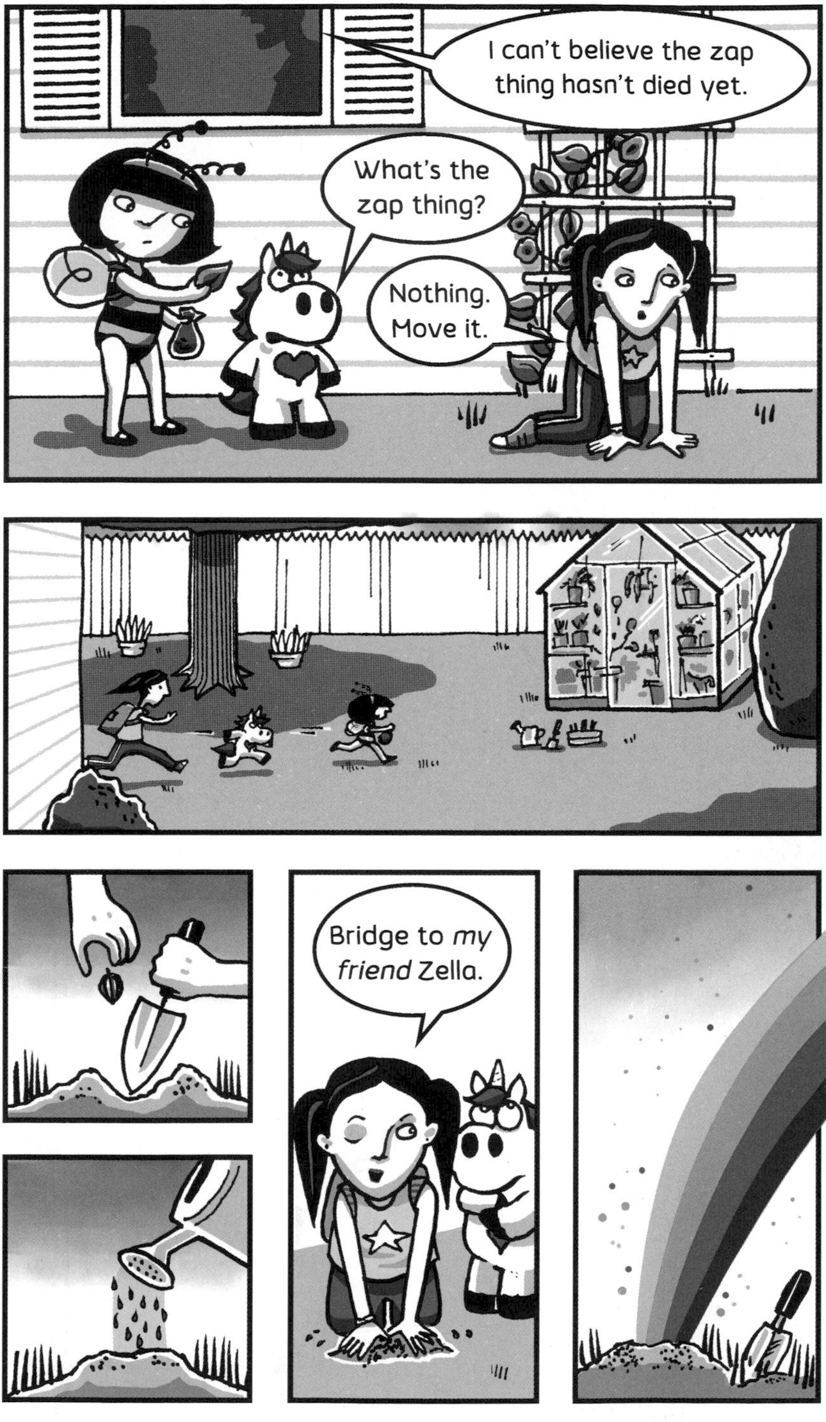
I can't believe the zap thing hasn't died yet.
What's the zap thing?
Nothing. Move it.
Bridge to *my friend* Zella.

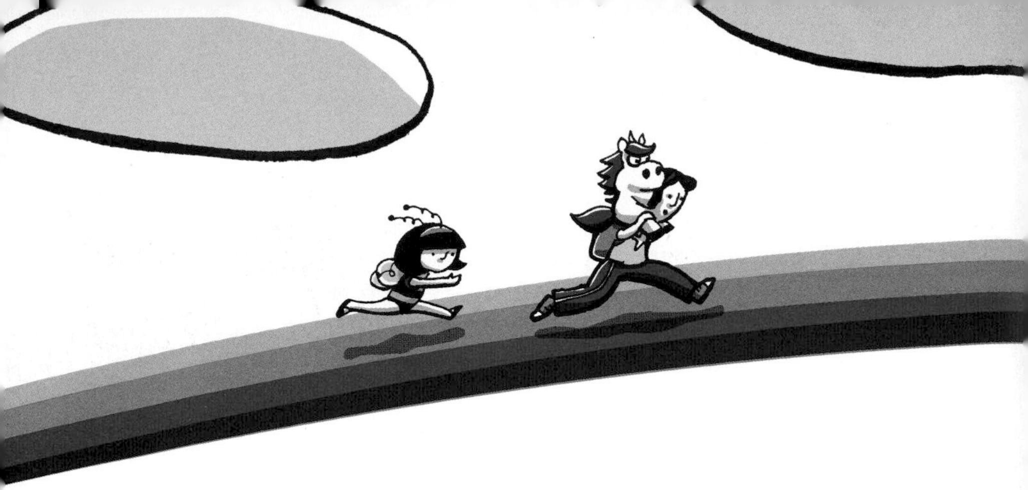

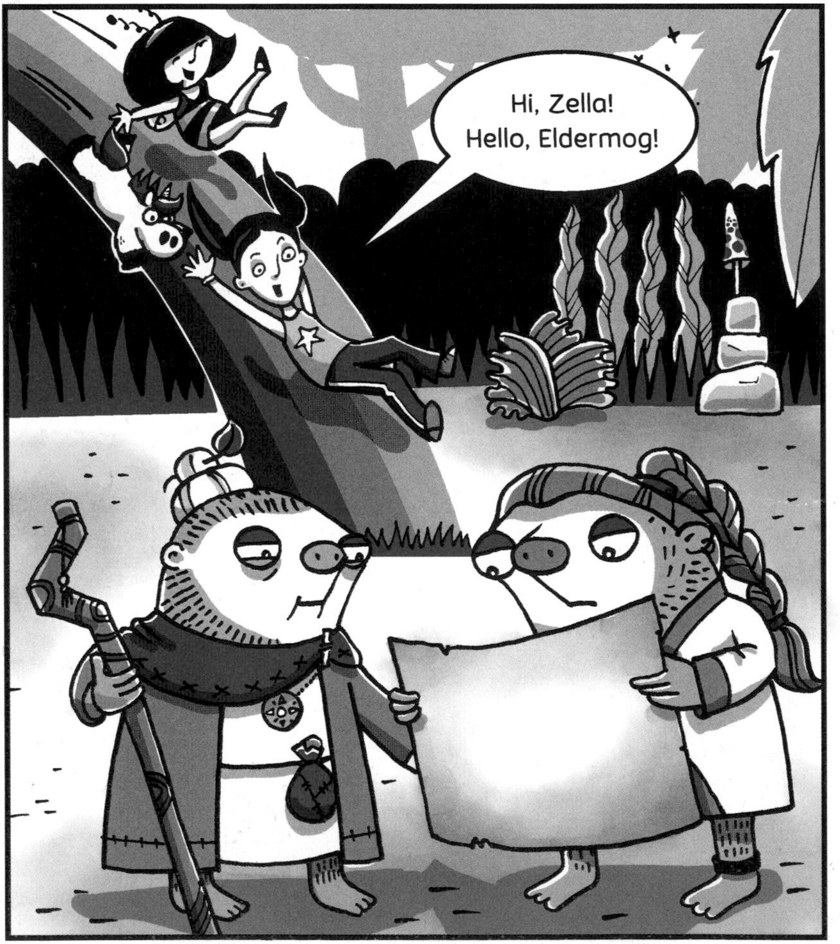
Hi, Zella!
Hello, Eldermog!

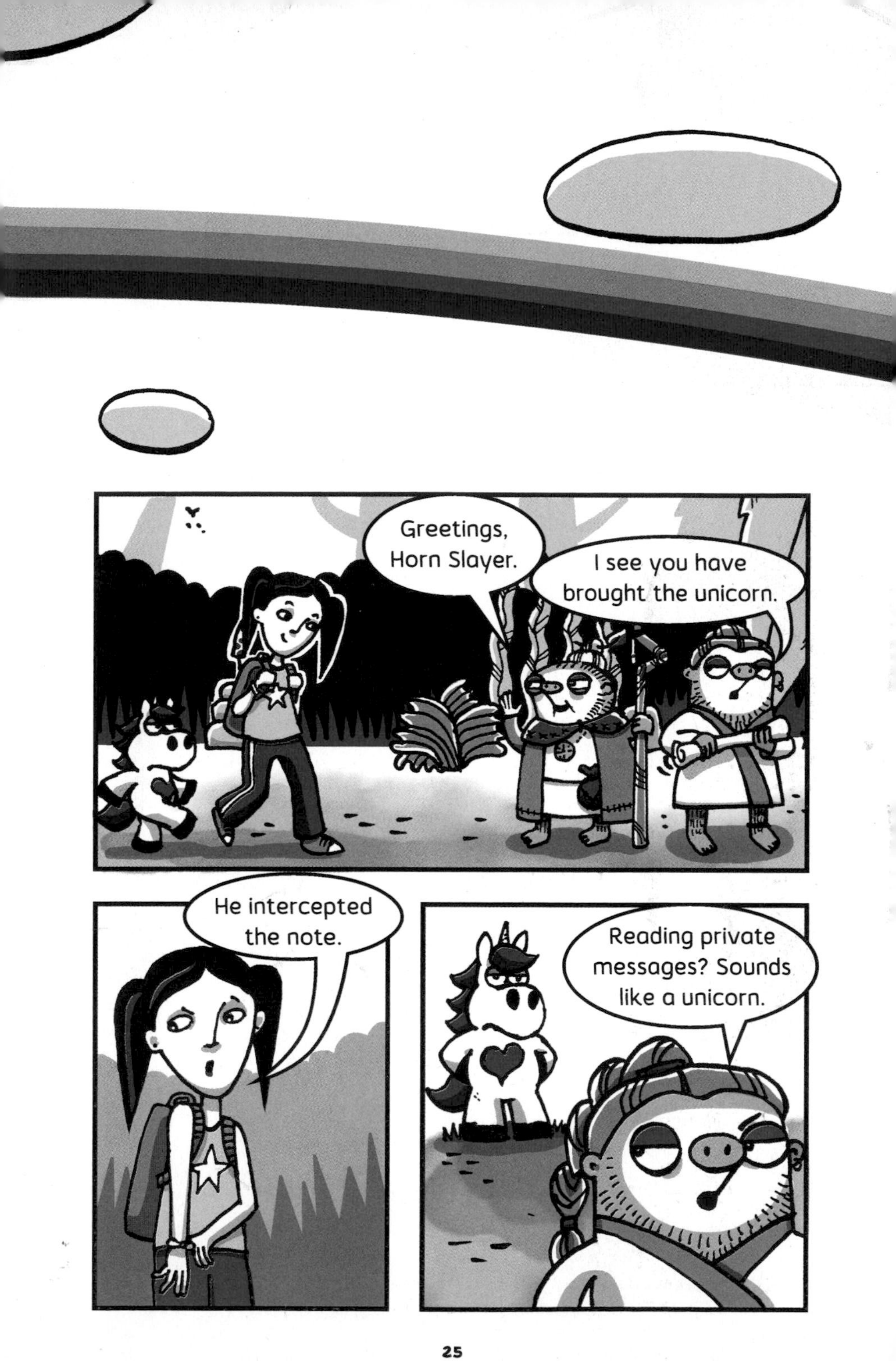
Greetings, Horn Slayer.
I see you have brought the unicorn.
He intercepted the note.
Reading private messages? Sounds like a unicorn.

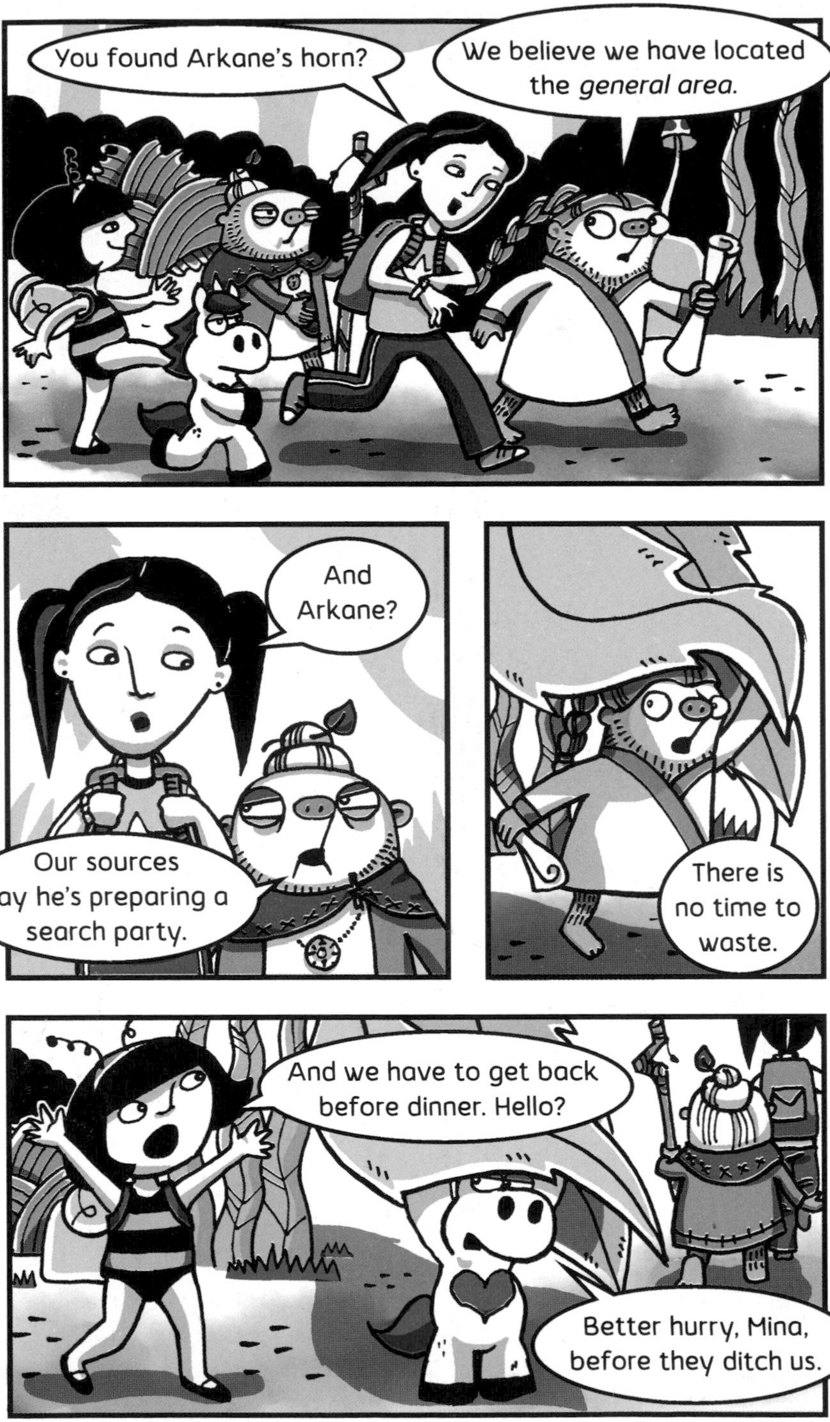
You found Arkane's horn?
We believe we have located the *general area.*
And Arkane?
Our sources say he's preparing a search party.
There is no time to waste.
And we have to get back before dinner. Hello?
Better hurry, Mina, before they ditch us.

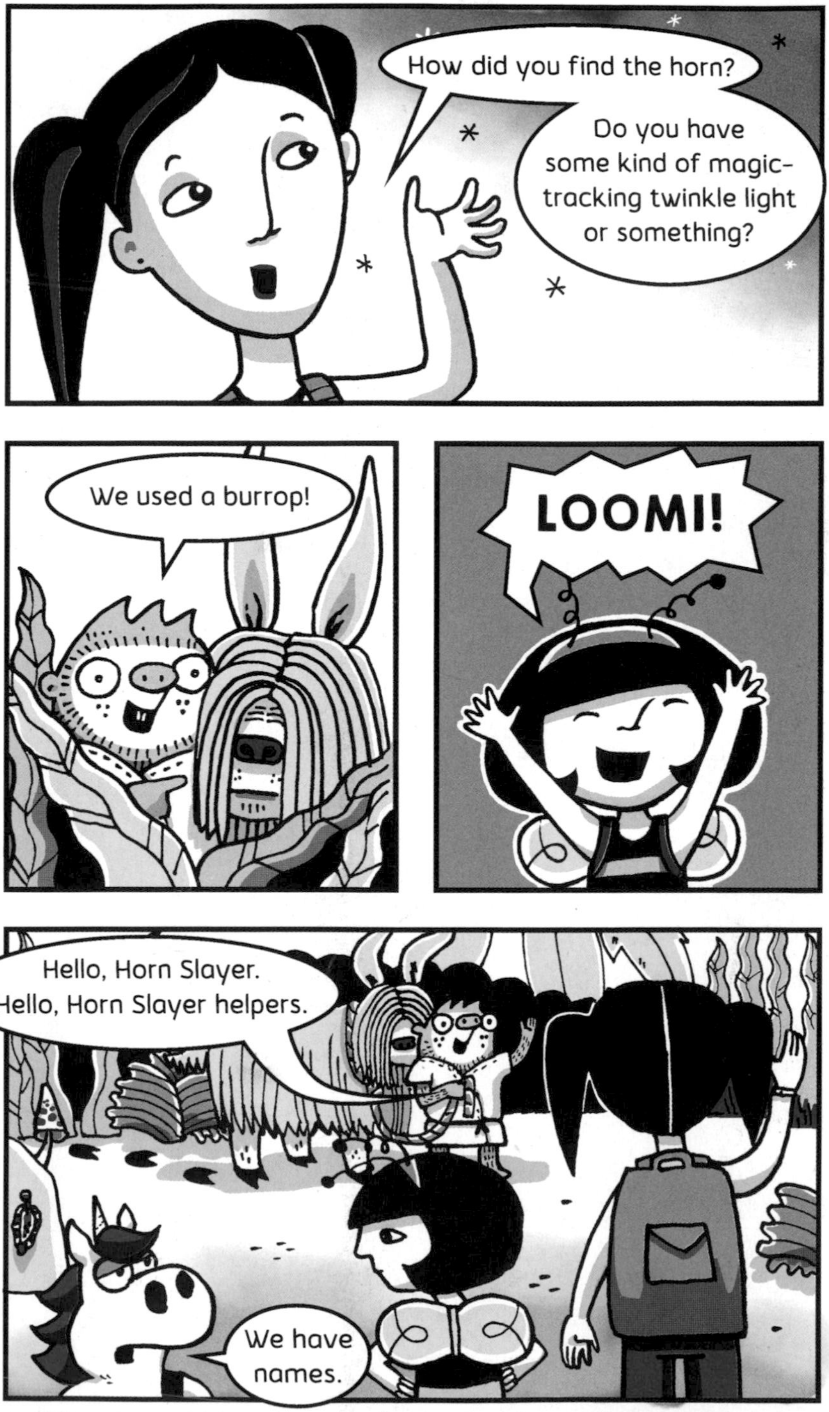
How did you find the horn?
Do you have some kind of magic-tracking twinkle light or something?
We used a burrop!
LOOMI!
Hello, Horn Slayer. Hello, Horn Slayer helpers.
We have names.

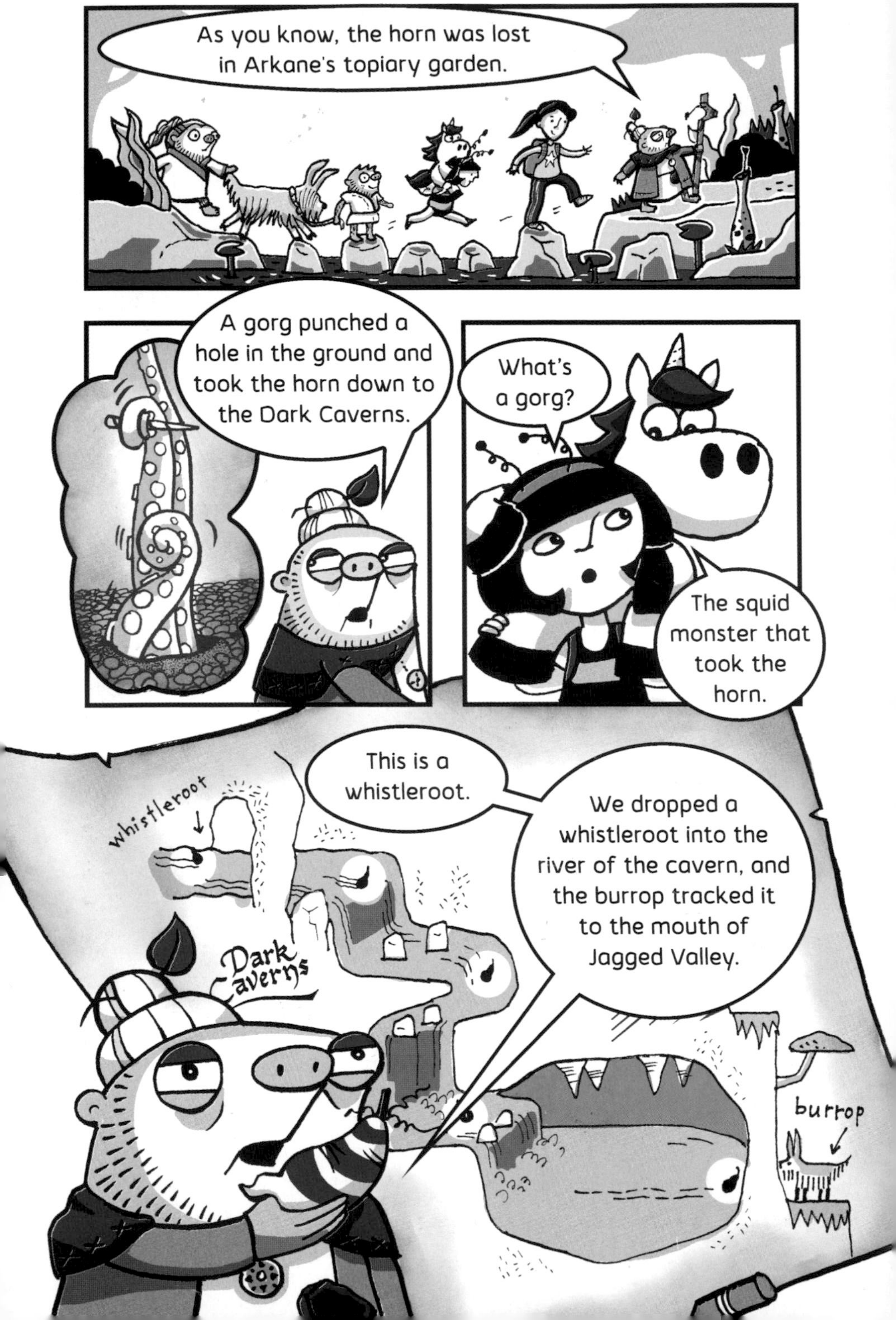

As you know, the horn was lost in Arkane's topiary garden.
A gorg punched a hole in the ground and took the horn down to the Dark Caverns.
What's a gorg?
The squid monster that took the horn.
This is a whistleroot.
We dropped a whistleroot into the river of the cavern, and the burrop tracked it to the mouth of Jagged Valley.
whistleroot
Dark Caverns
burrop

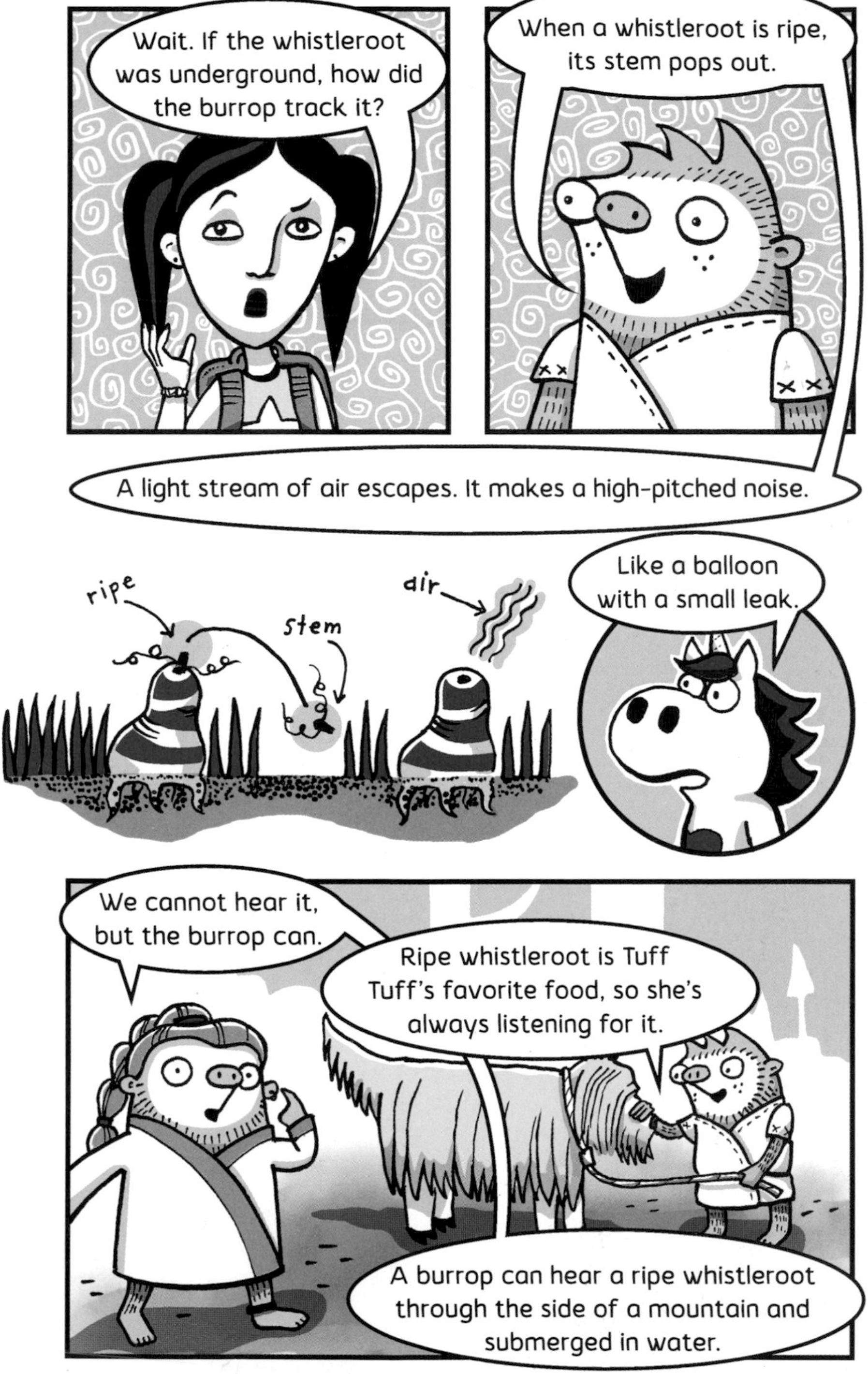

Wait. If the whistleroot was underground, how did the burrop track it?
When a whistleroot is ripe, its stem pops out.
A light stream of air escapes. It makes a high-pitched noise.
ripe
stem
air
Like a balloon with a small leak.
We cannot hear it, but the burrop can.
Ripe whistleroot is Tuff Tuff's favorite food, so she's always listening for it.
A burrop can hear a ripe whistleroot through the side of a mountain and submerged in water.

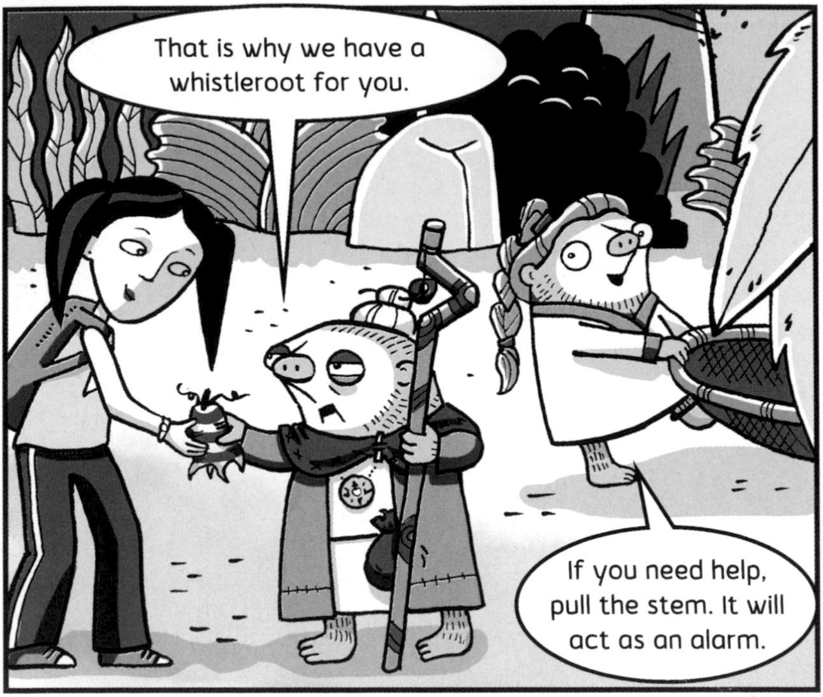
That is why we have a whistleroot for you.
If you need help, pull the stem. It will act as an alarm.

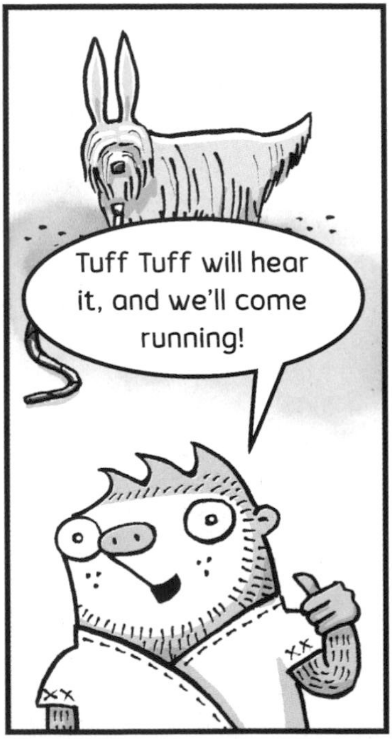
Tuff Tuff will hear it, and we'll come running!

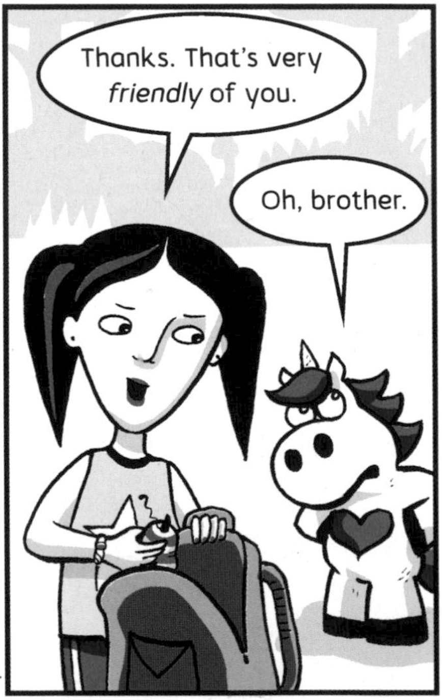
Thanks. That's very *friendly* of you.
Oh, brother.

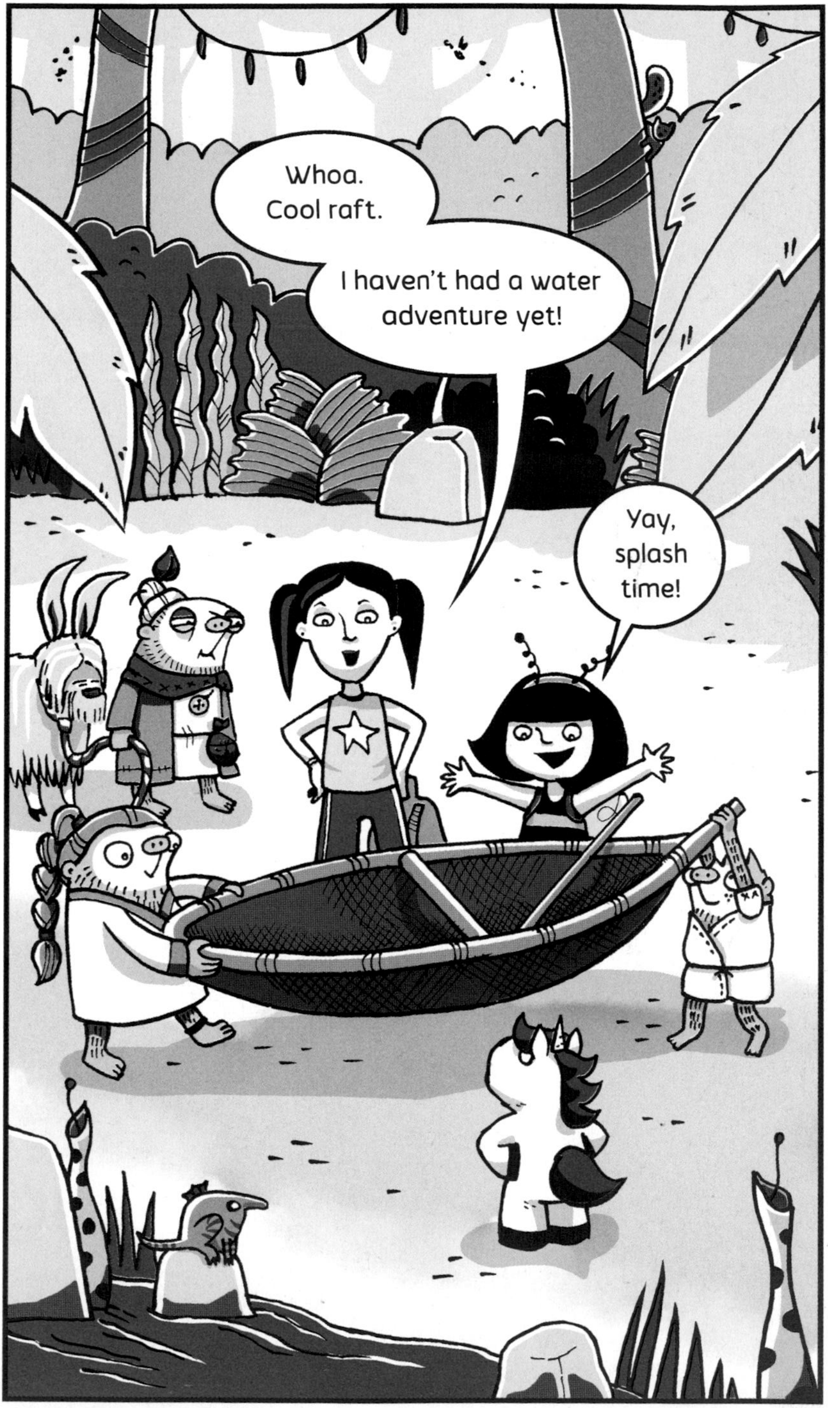
Whoa.
Cool raft.
I haven't had a water adventure yet!
Yay, splash time!

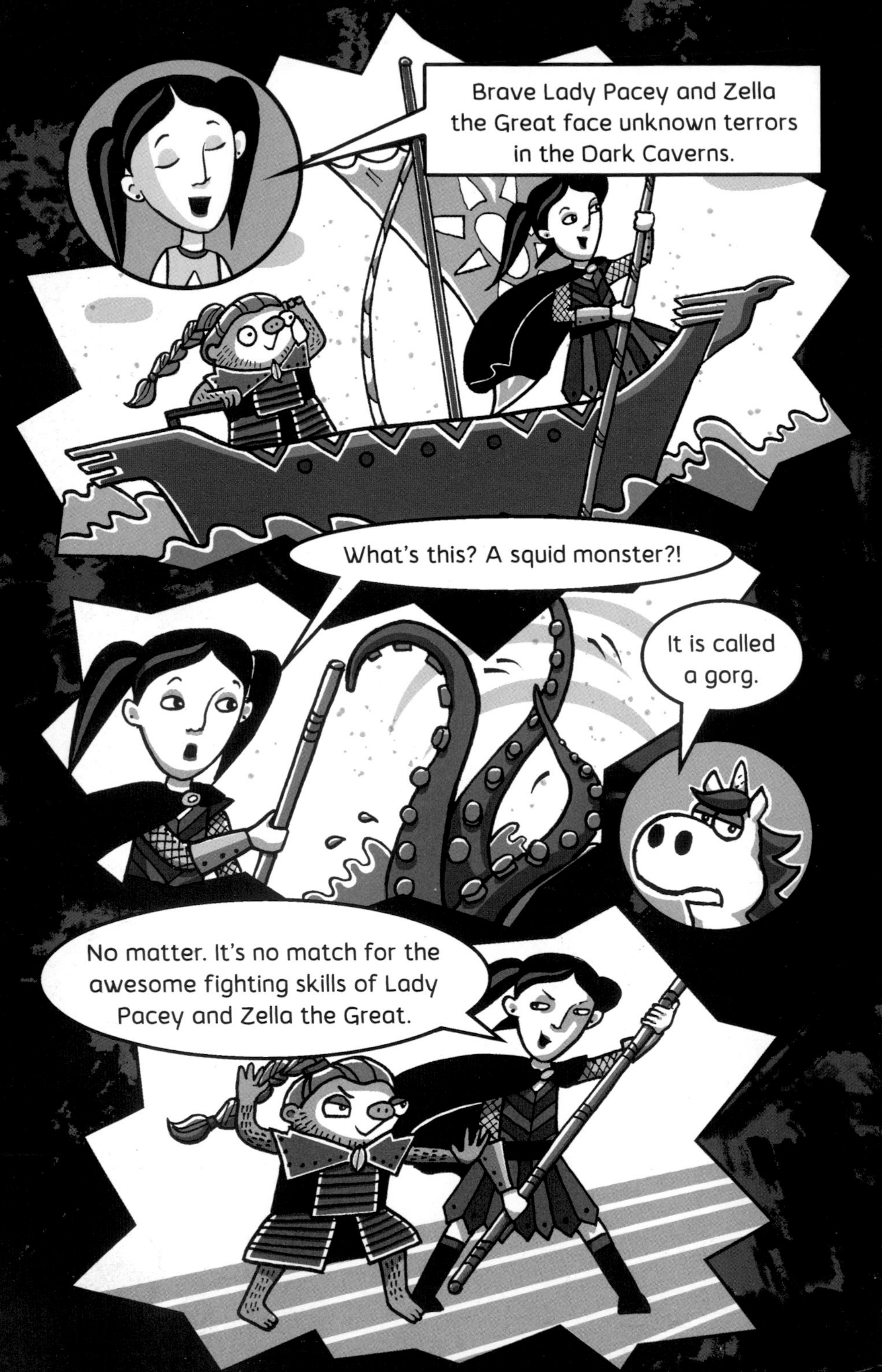
Brave Lady Pacey and Zella the Great face unknown terrors in the Dark Caverns.
What's this? A squid monster?!
It is called a gorg.
No matter. It's no match for the awesome fighting skills of Lady Pacey and Zella the Great.

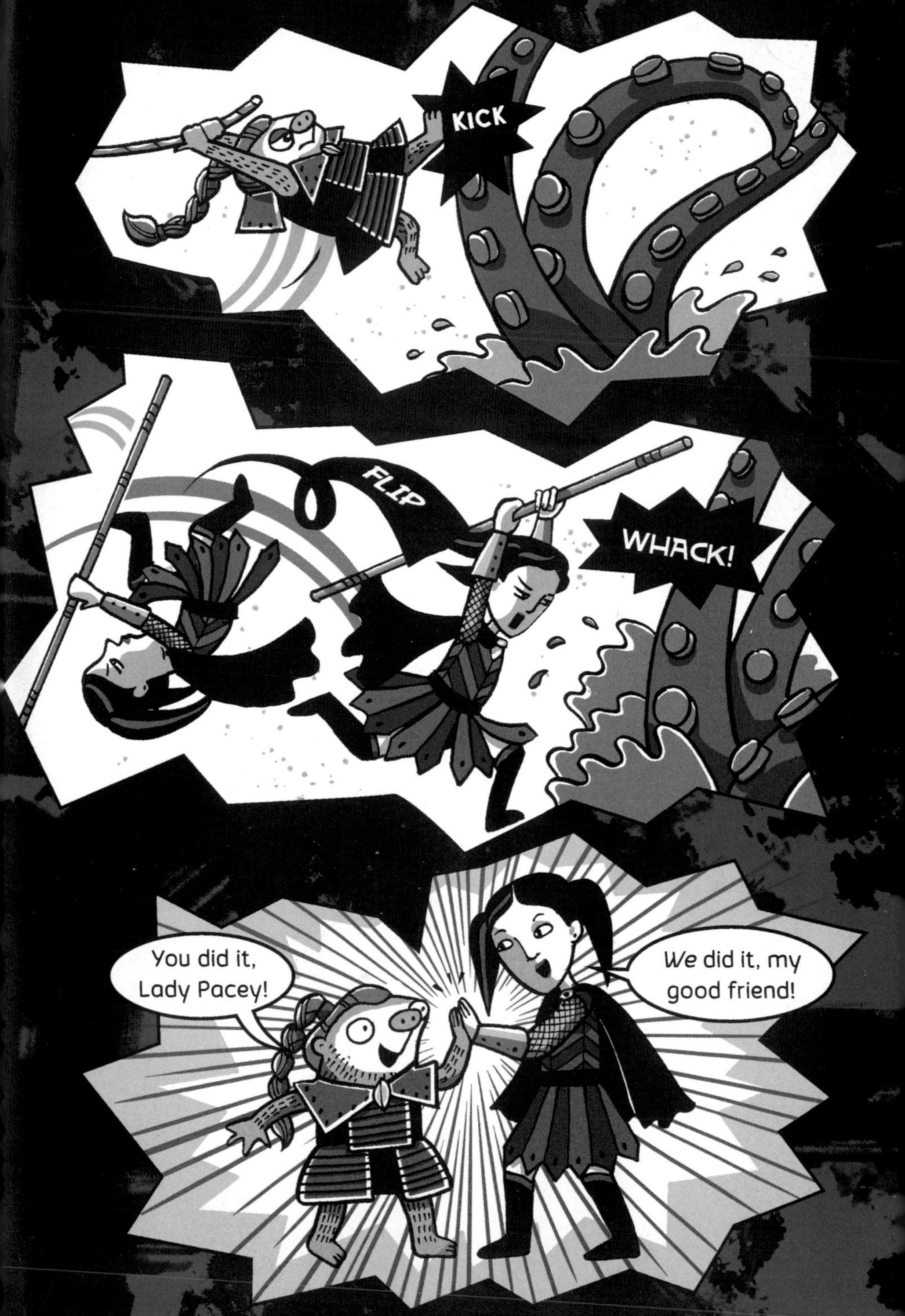
KICK
FLIP
WHACK!
You did it, Lady Pacey!
We did it, my good friend!

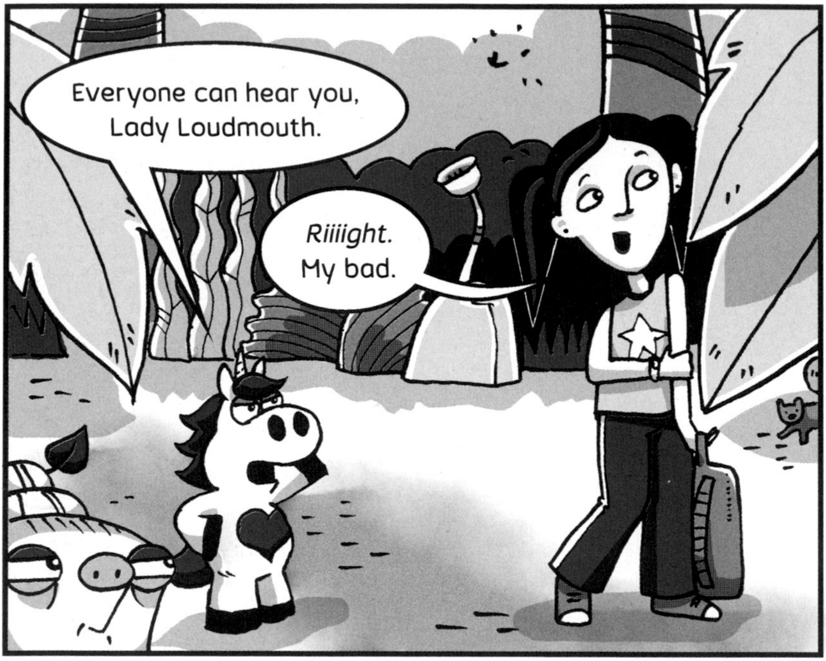
Everyone can hear you, Lady Loudmouth.
Riiiight. My bad.

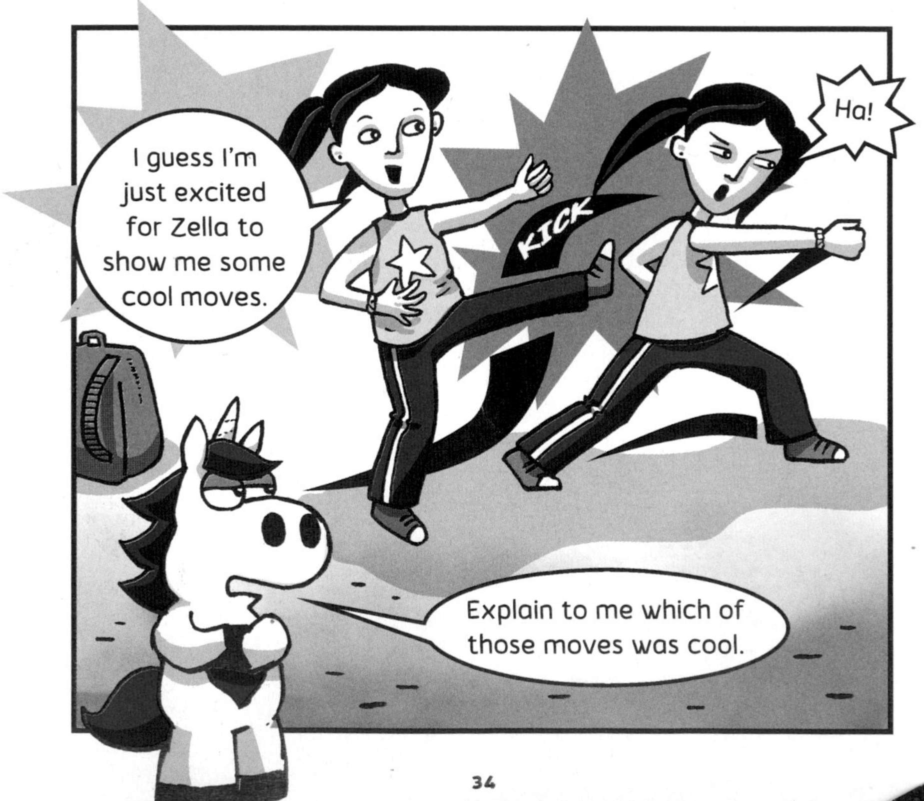
I guess I'm just excited for Zella to show me some cool moves.
KICK
Ha!
Explain to me which of those moves was cool.

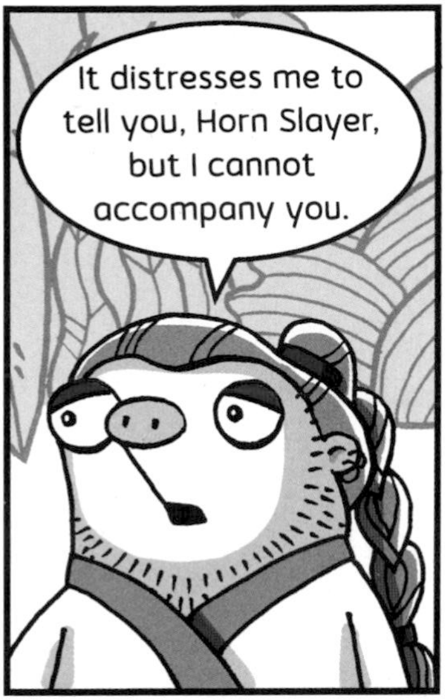
It distresses me to tell you, Horn Slayer, but I cannot accompany you.

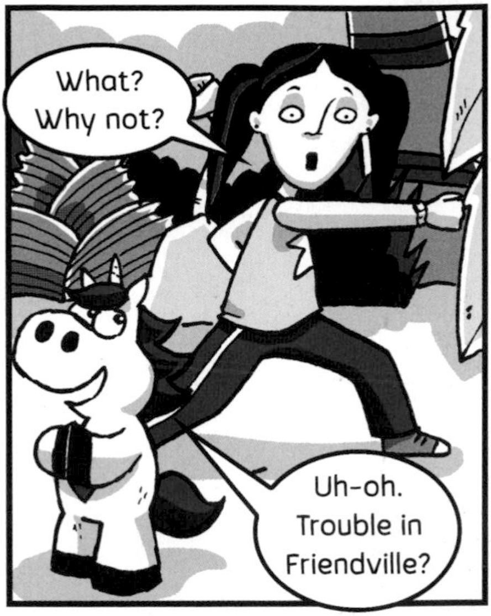
What? Why not?
Uh-oh. Trouble in Friendville?

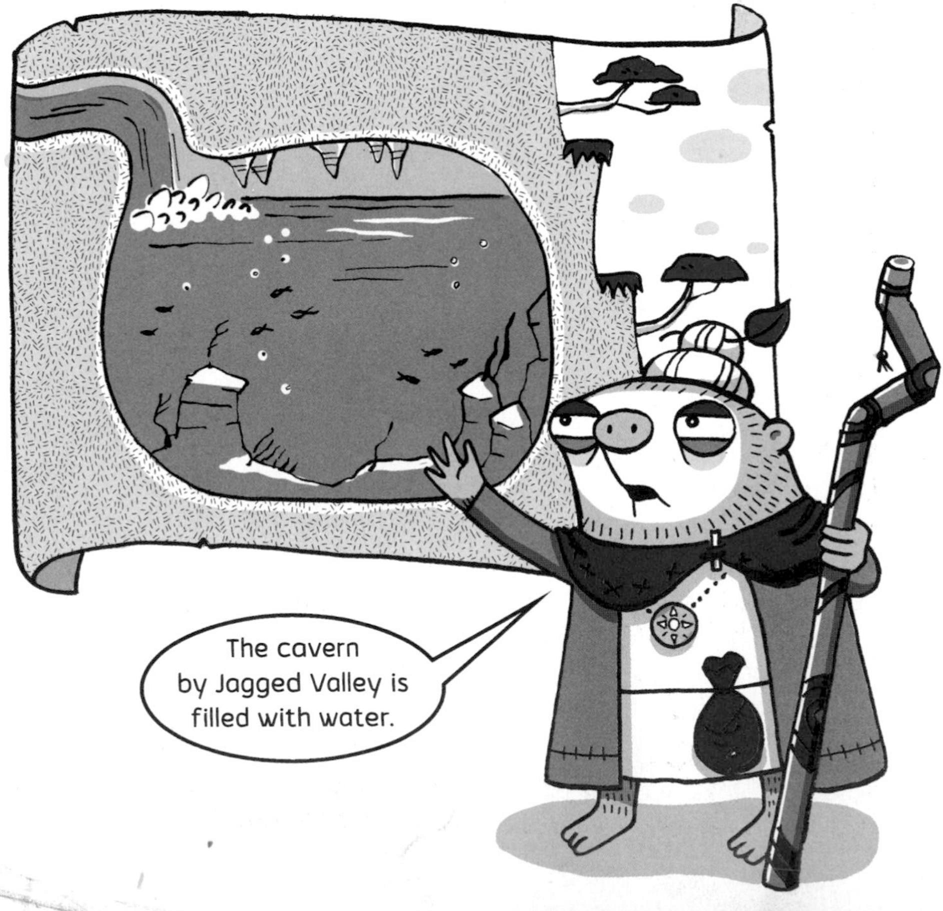
The cavern by Jagged Valley is filled with water.

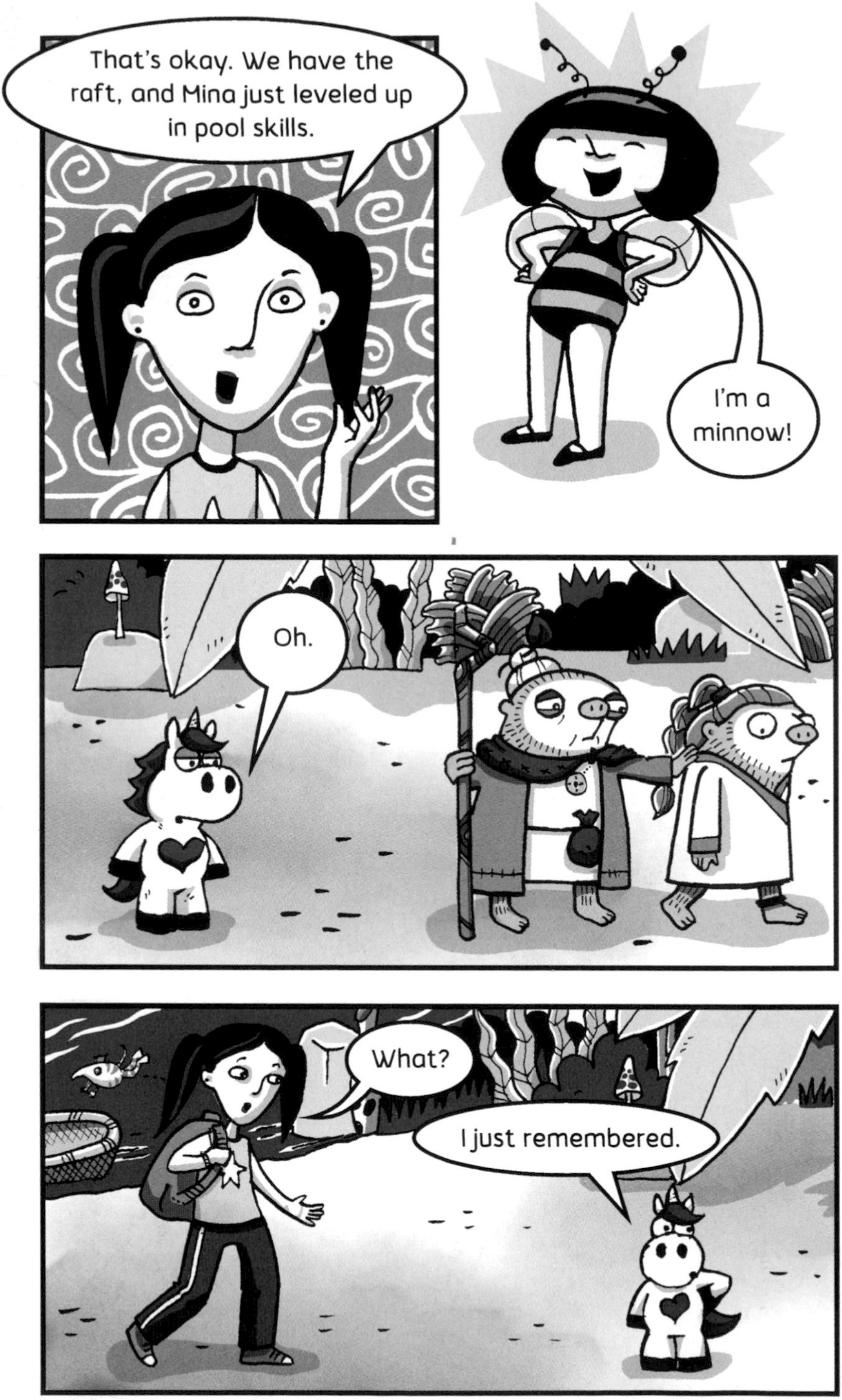
That's okay. We have the raft, and Mina just leveled up in pool skills.
I'm a minnow!
Oh.
What?
I just remembered.

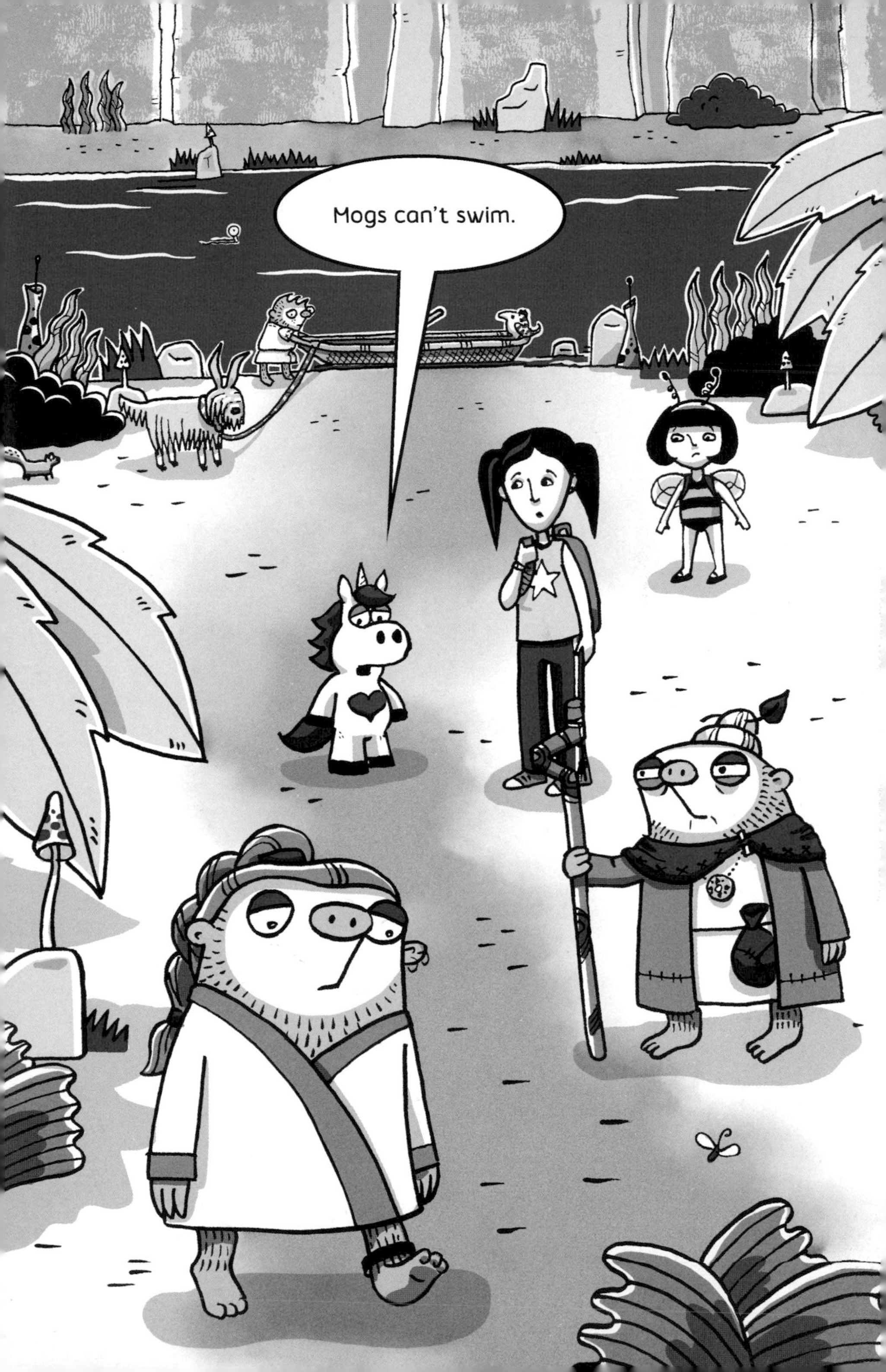
Mogs can't swim.

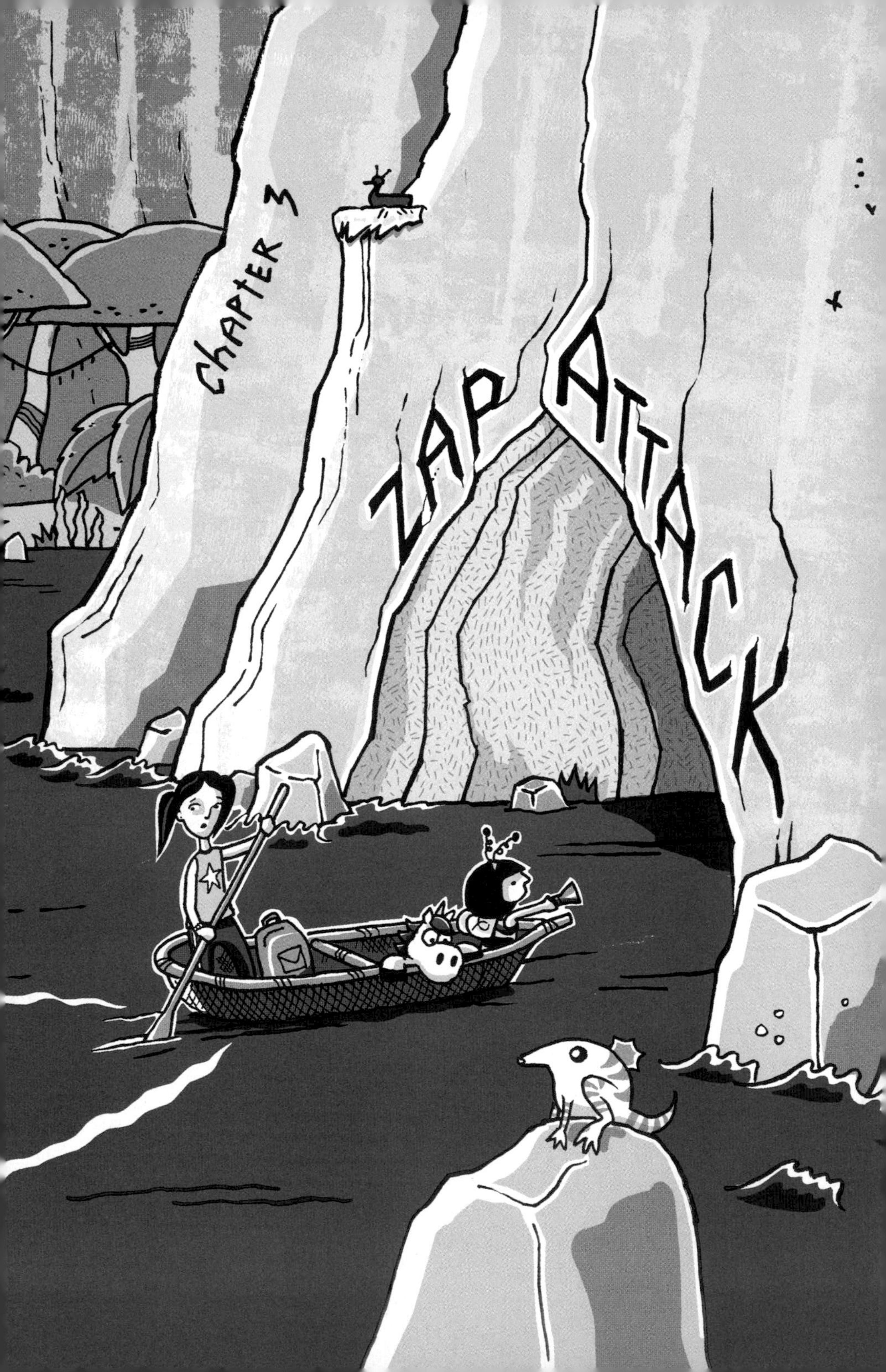
chapter 3
ZAP ATTACK

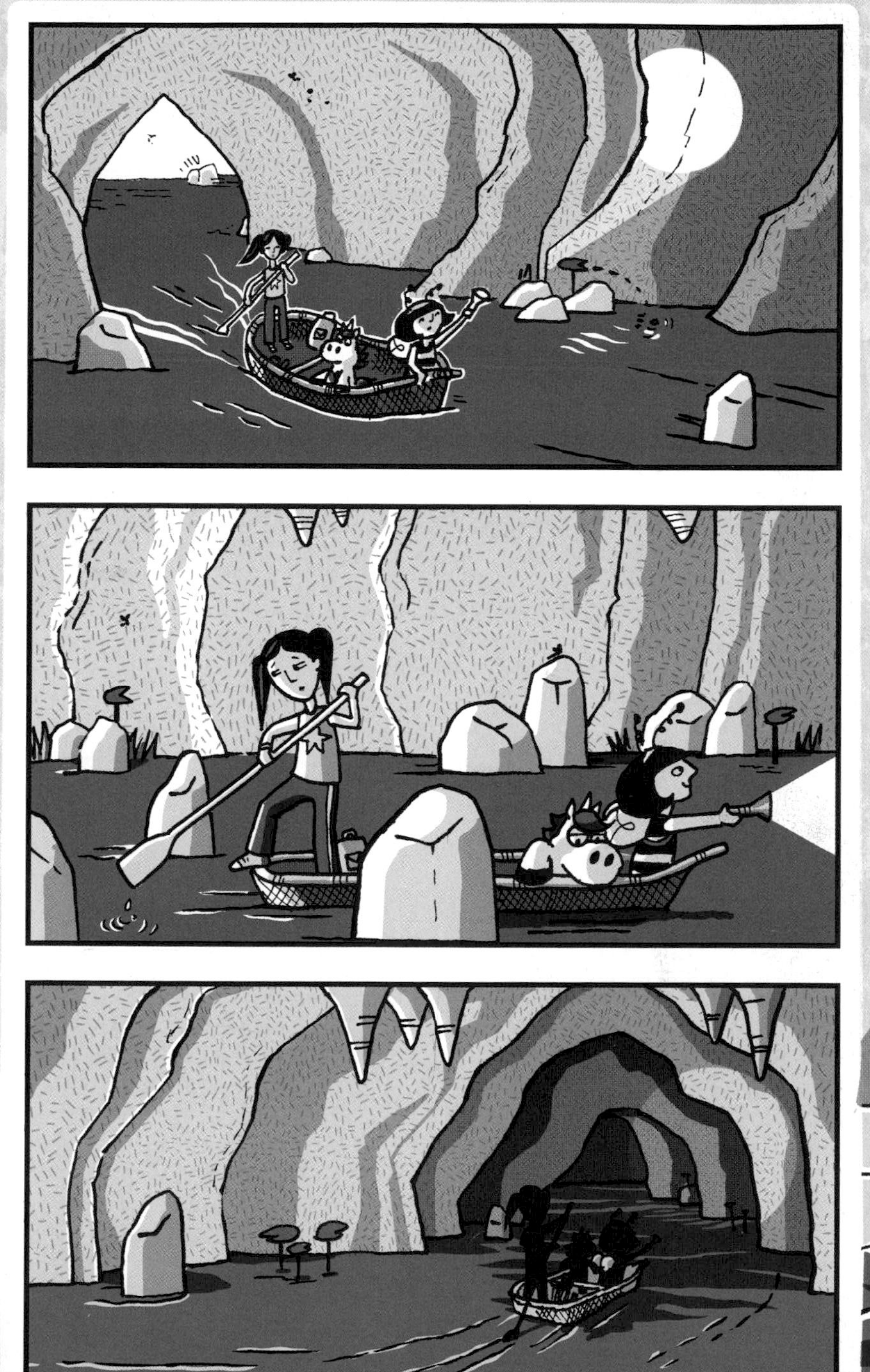

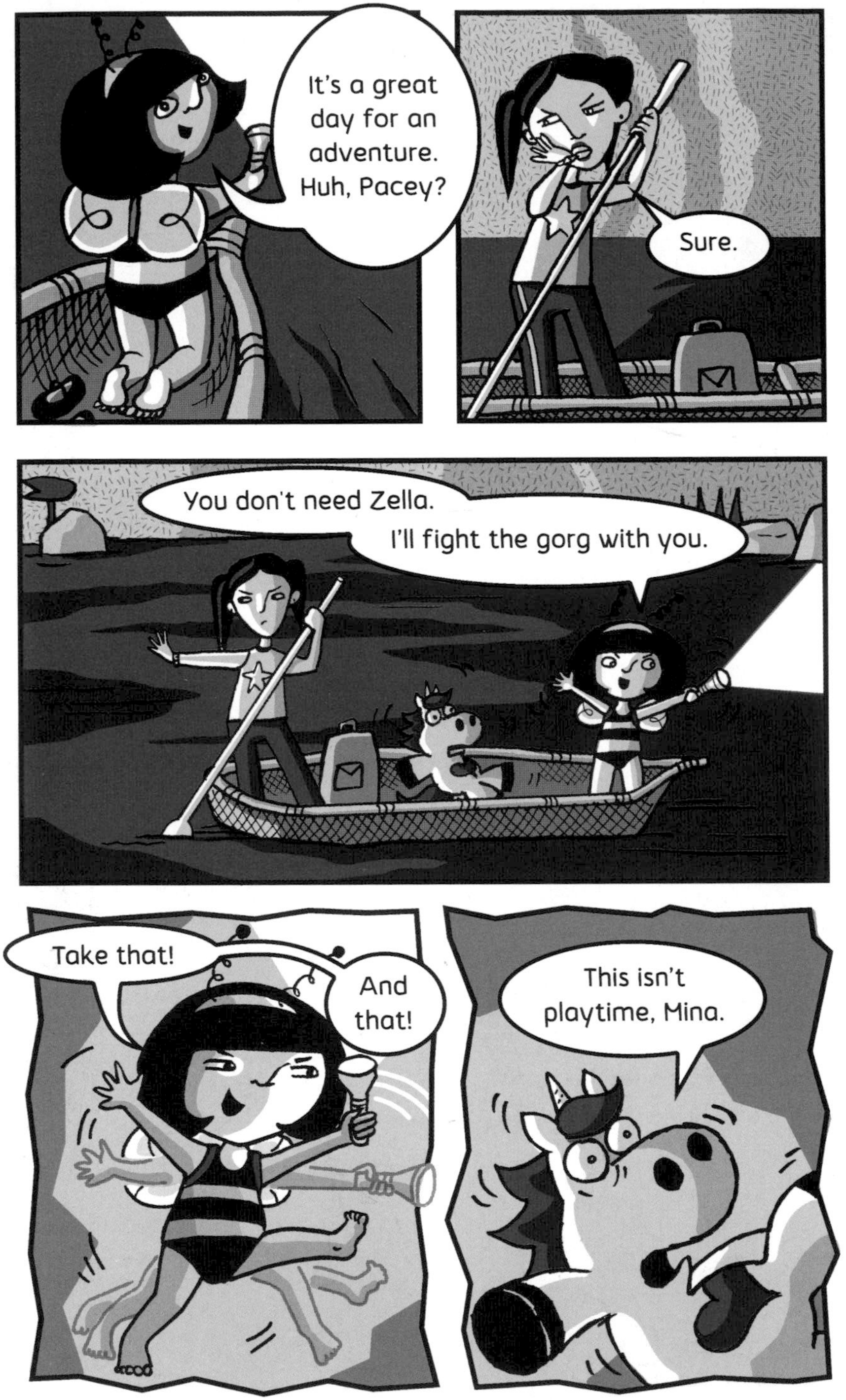
It's a great day for an adventure. Huh, Pacey?
Sure.
You don't need Zella.
I'll fight the gorg with you.
Take that!
And that!
This isn't playtime, Mina.

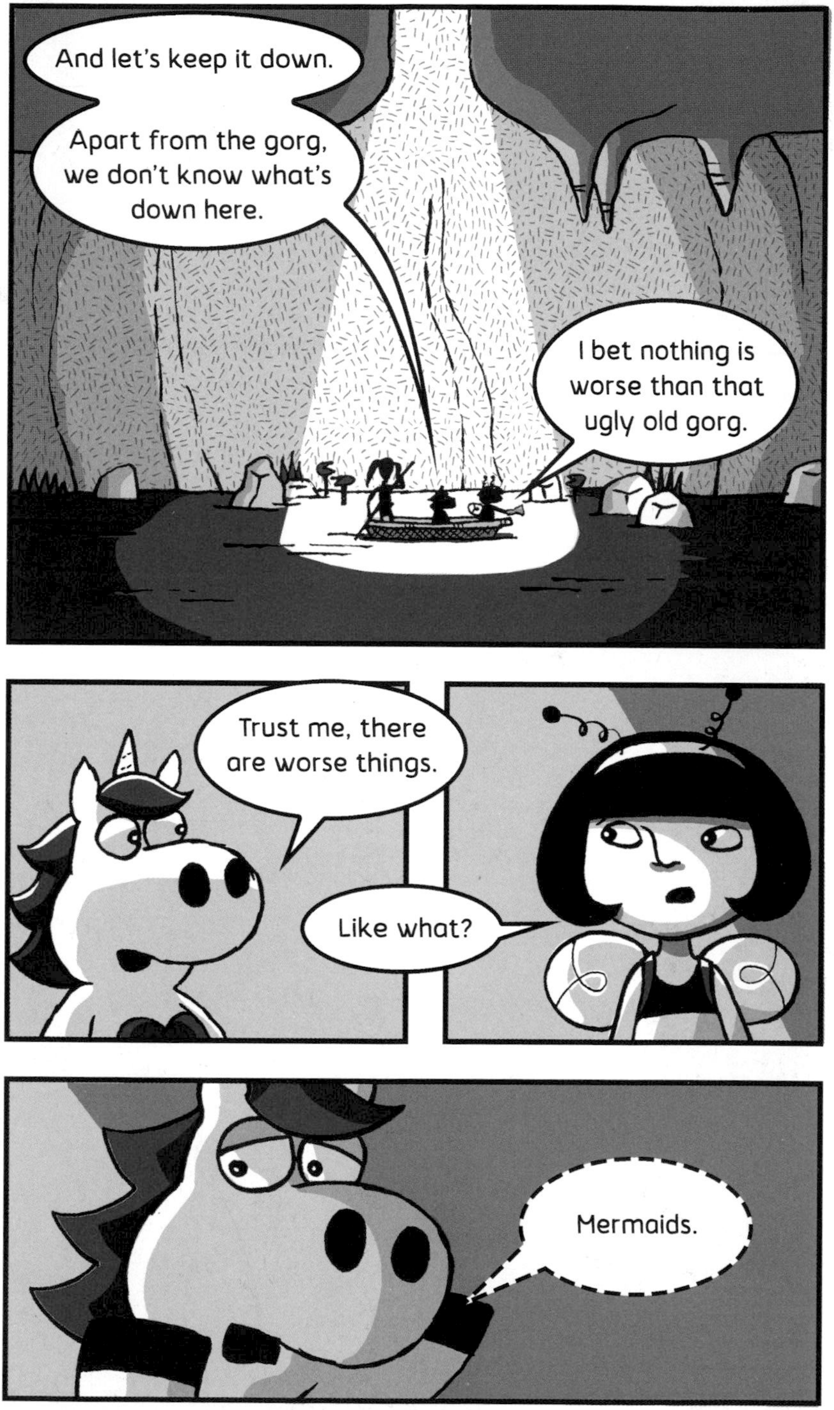
And let's keep it down.
Apart from the gorg, we don't know what's down here.
I bet nothing is worse than that ugly old gorg.
Trust me, there are worse things.
Like what?
Mermaids.

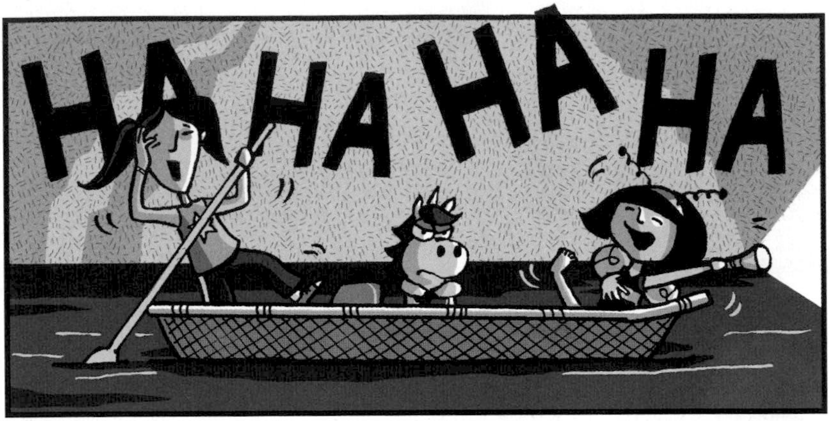
HA HA HA HA HA HA

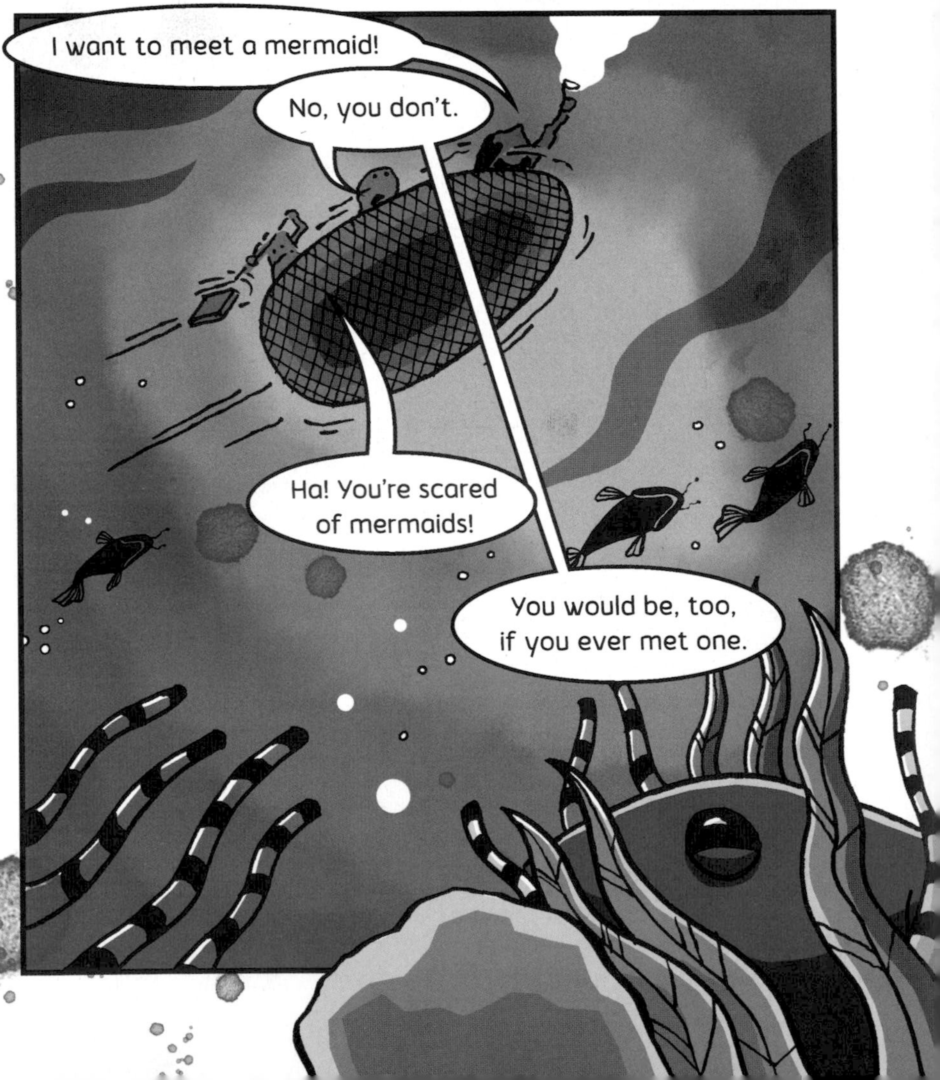
I want to meet a mermaid!
No, you don't.
Ha! You're scared of mermaids!
You would be, too, if you ever met one.

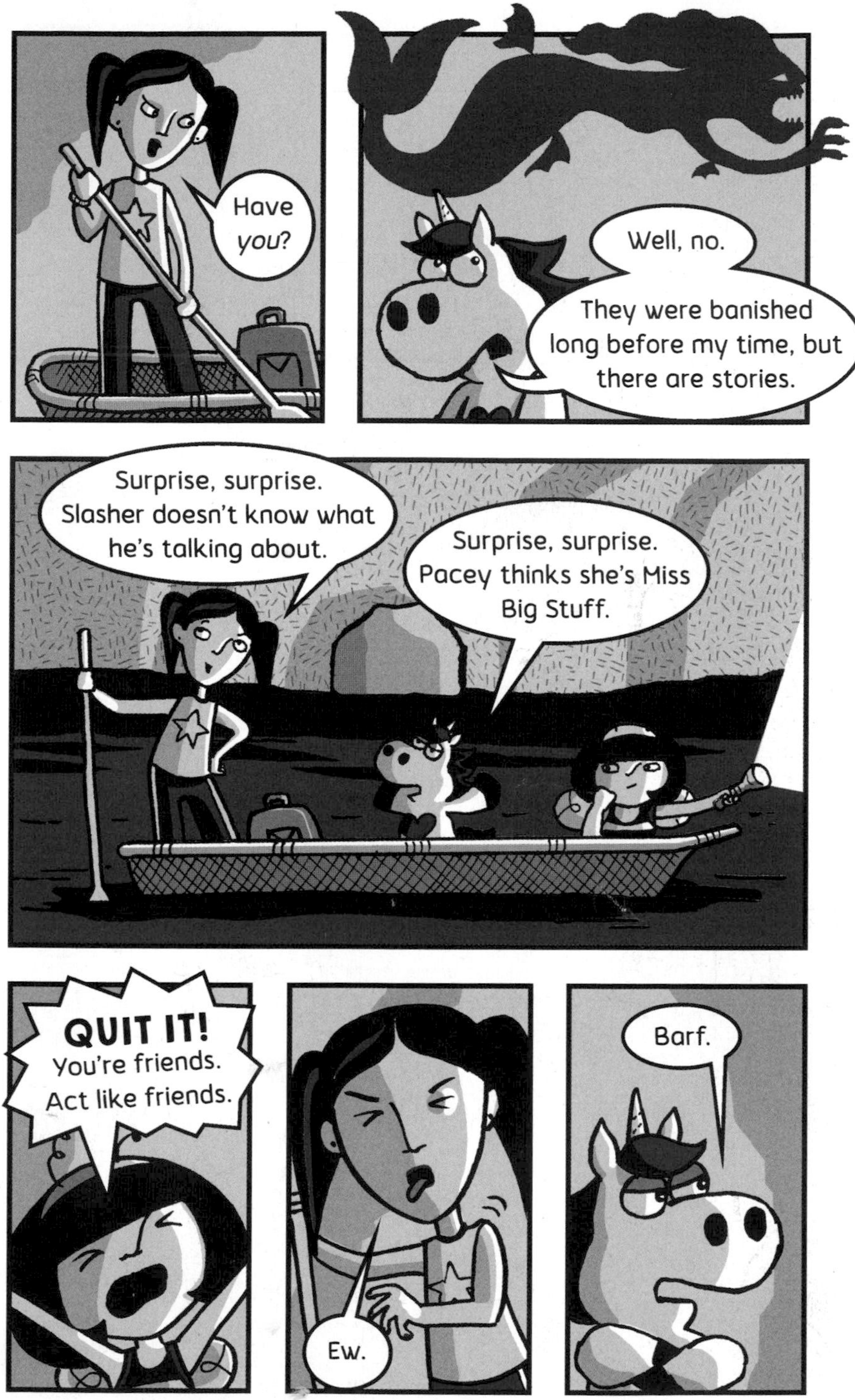
Have you?
Well, no.
They were banished long before my time, but there are stories.
Surprise, surprise. Slasher doesn't know what he's talking about.
Surprise, surprise. Pacey thinks she's Miss Big Stuff.
QUIT IT!
You're friends. Act like friends.
Ew.
Barf.

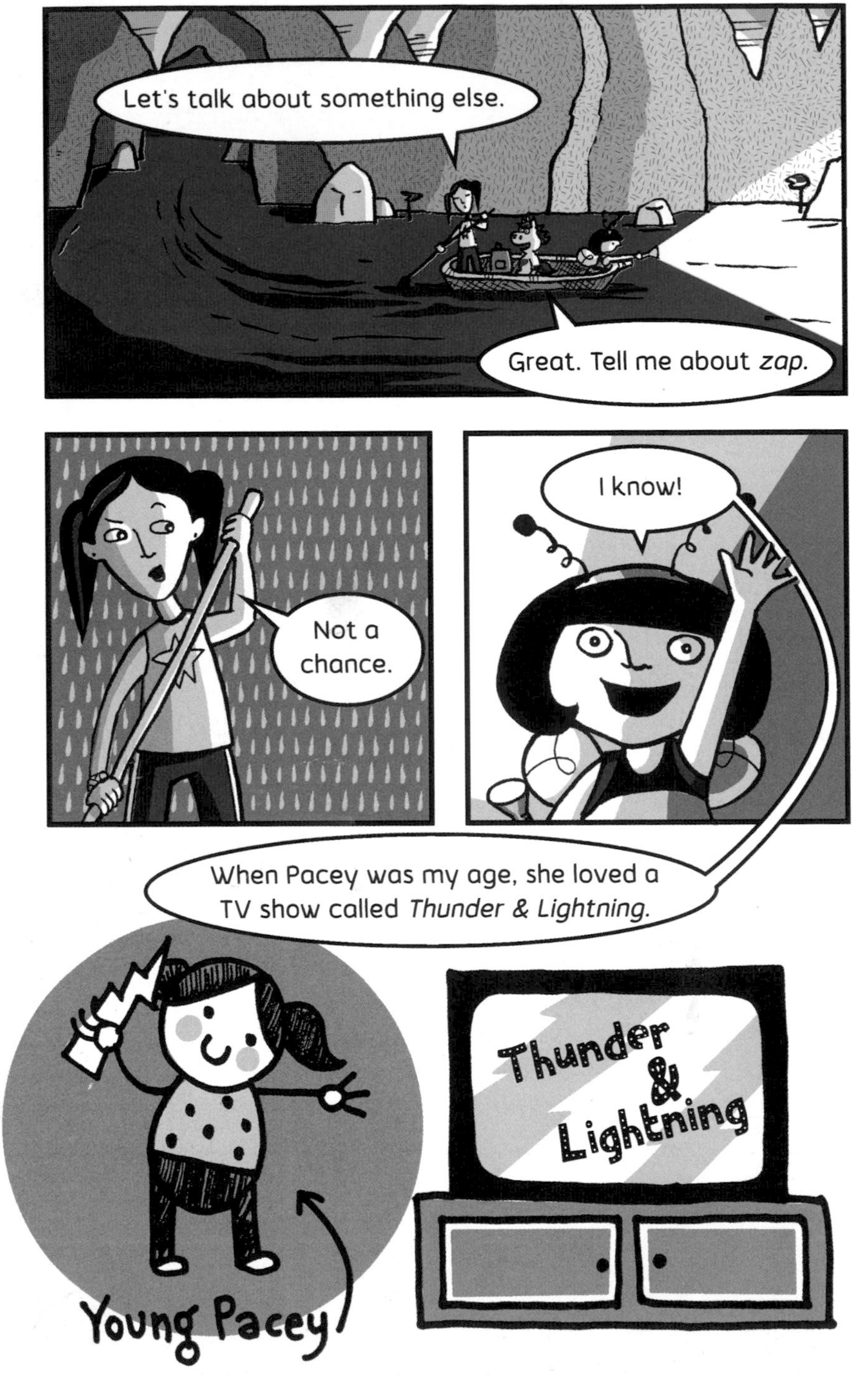
Let's talk about something else.
Great. Tell me about *zap*.
Not a chance.
I know!
When Pacey was my age, she loved a TV show called *Thunder & Lightning*.
Young Pacey
Thunder & Lightning

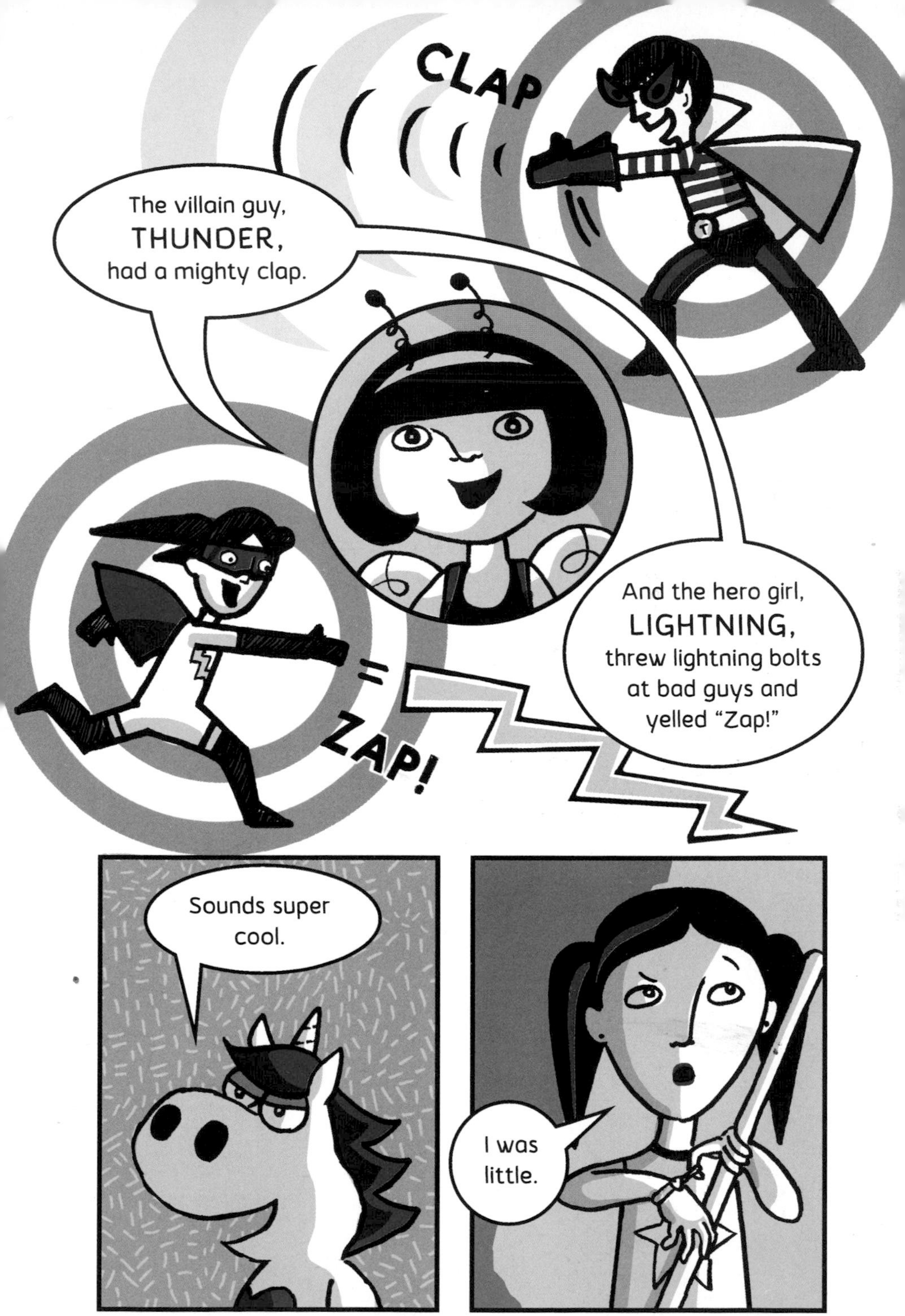
CLAP
The villain guy, THUNDER, had a mighty clap.
And the hero girl, LIGHTNING, threw lightning bolts at bad guys and yelled "Zap!"
ZAP!
Sounds super cool.
I was little.

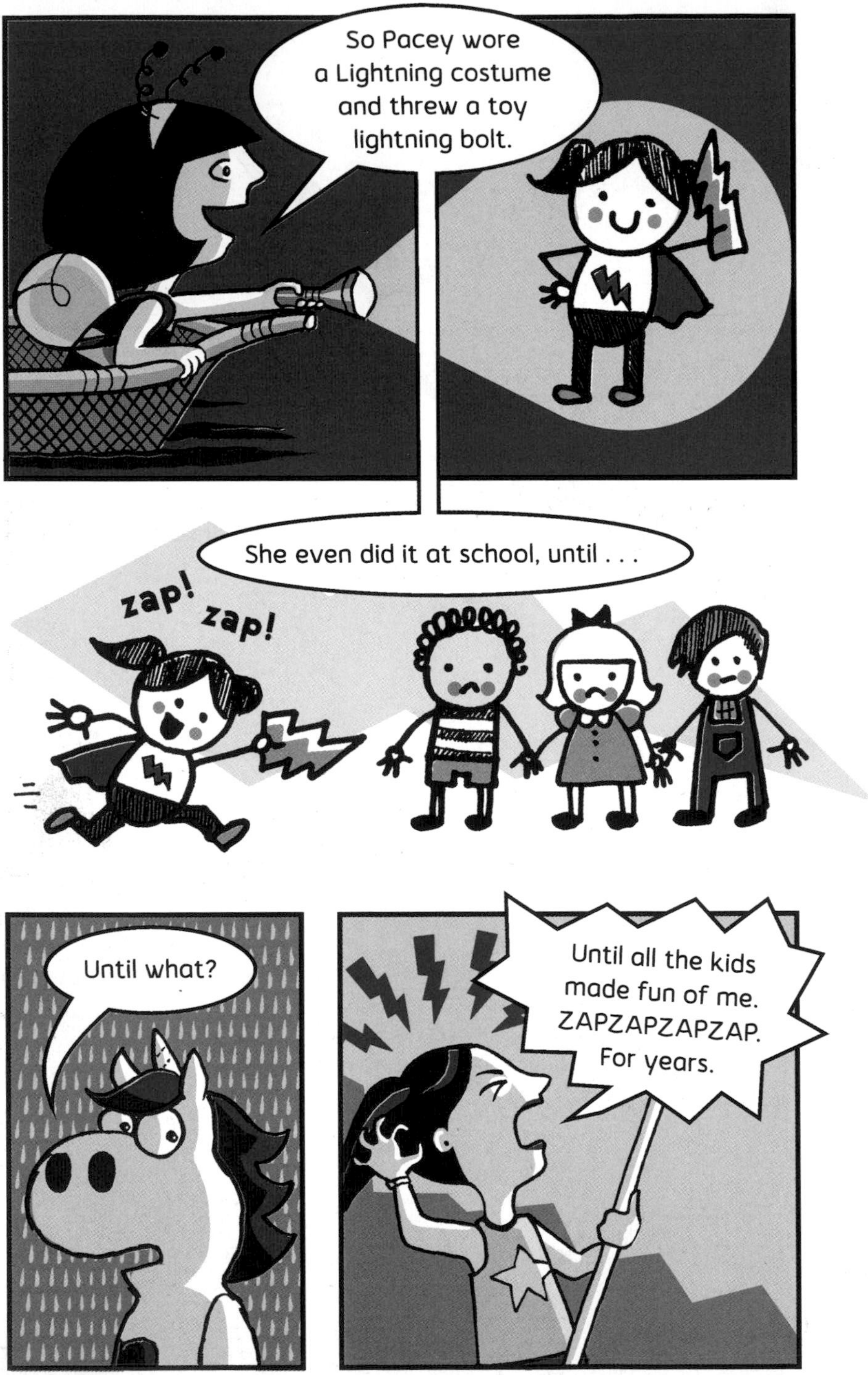
So Pacey wore a Lightning costume and threw a toy lightning bolt.
She even did it at school, until . . .
zap! zap!
Until what?
Until all the kids made fun of me. ZAPZAPZAPZAP. For years.

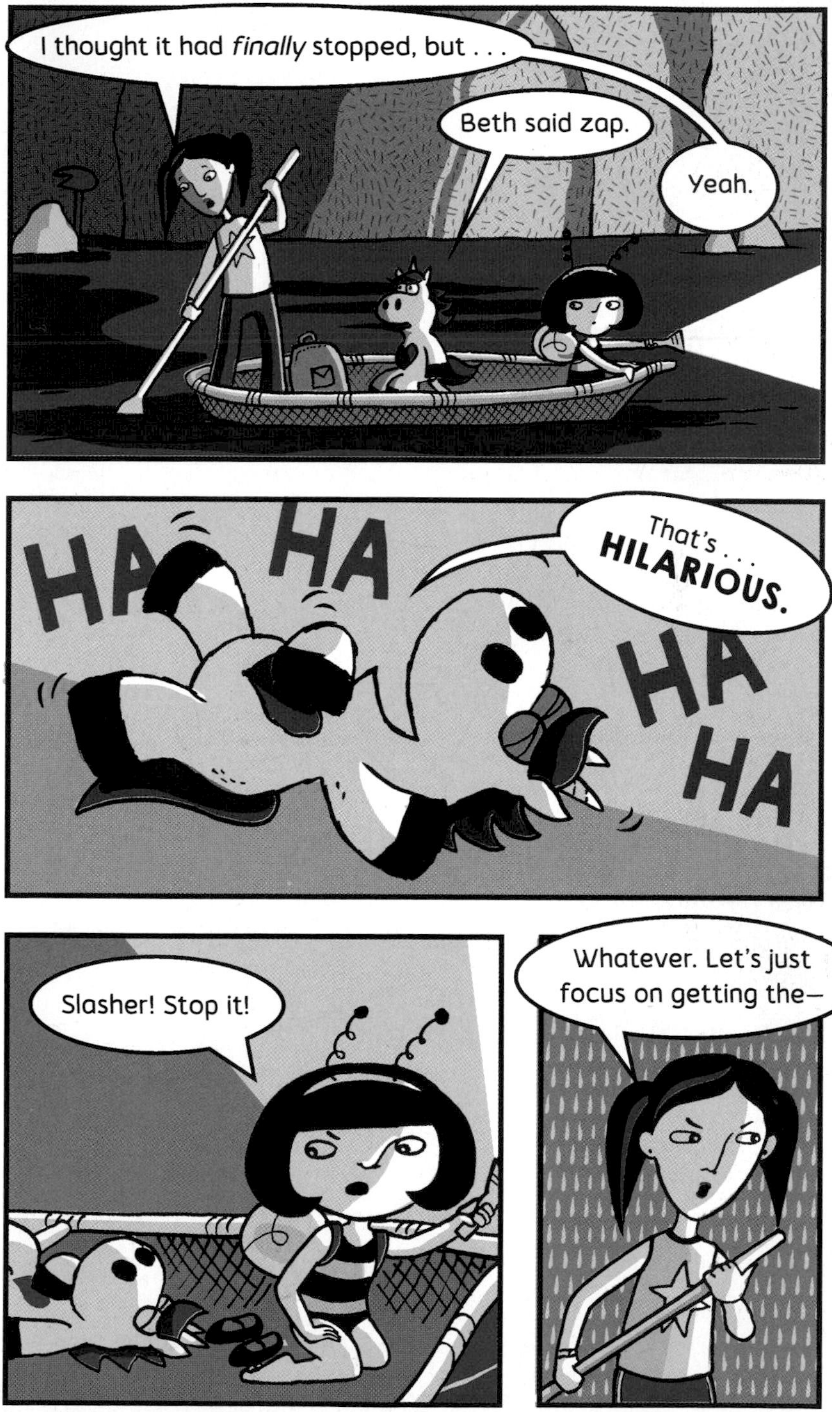
I thought it had *finally* stopped, but . . .
Beth said zap.
Yeah.
HA HA
That's . . . HILARIOUS.
HA HA
Slasher! Stop it!
Whatever. Let's just focus on getting the—

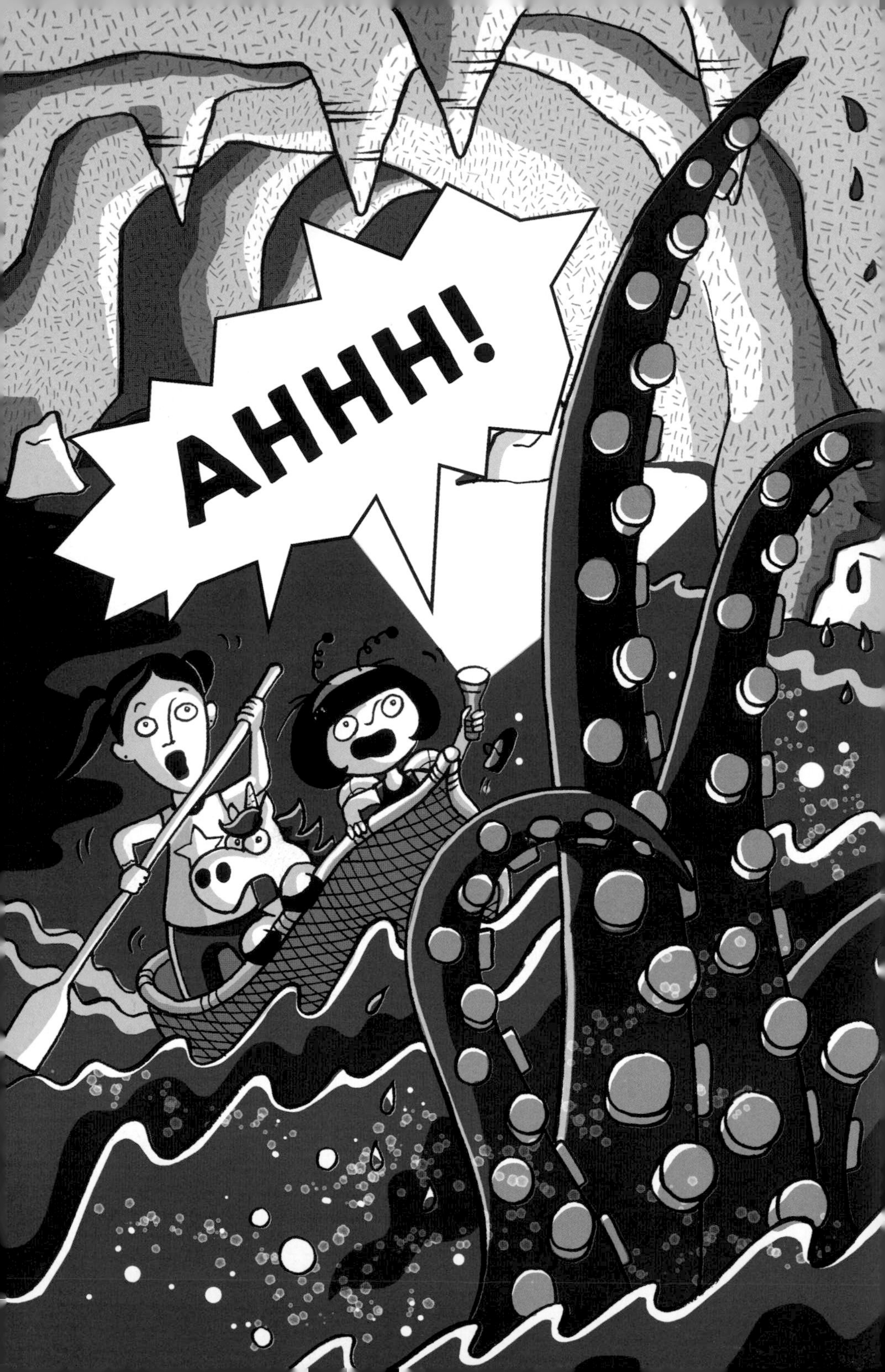
AHHH!

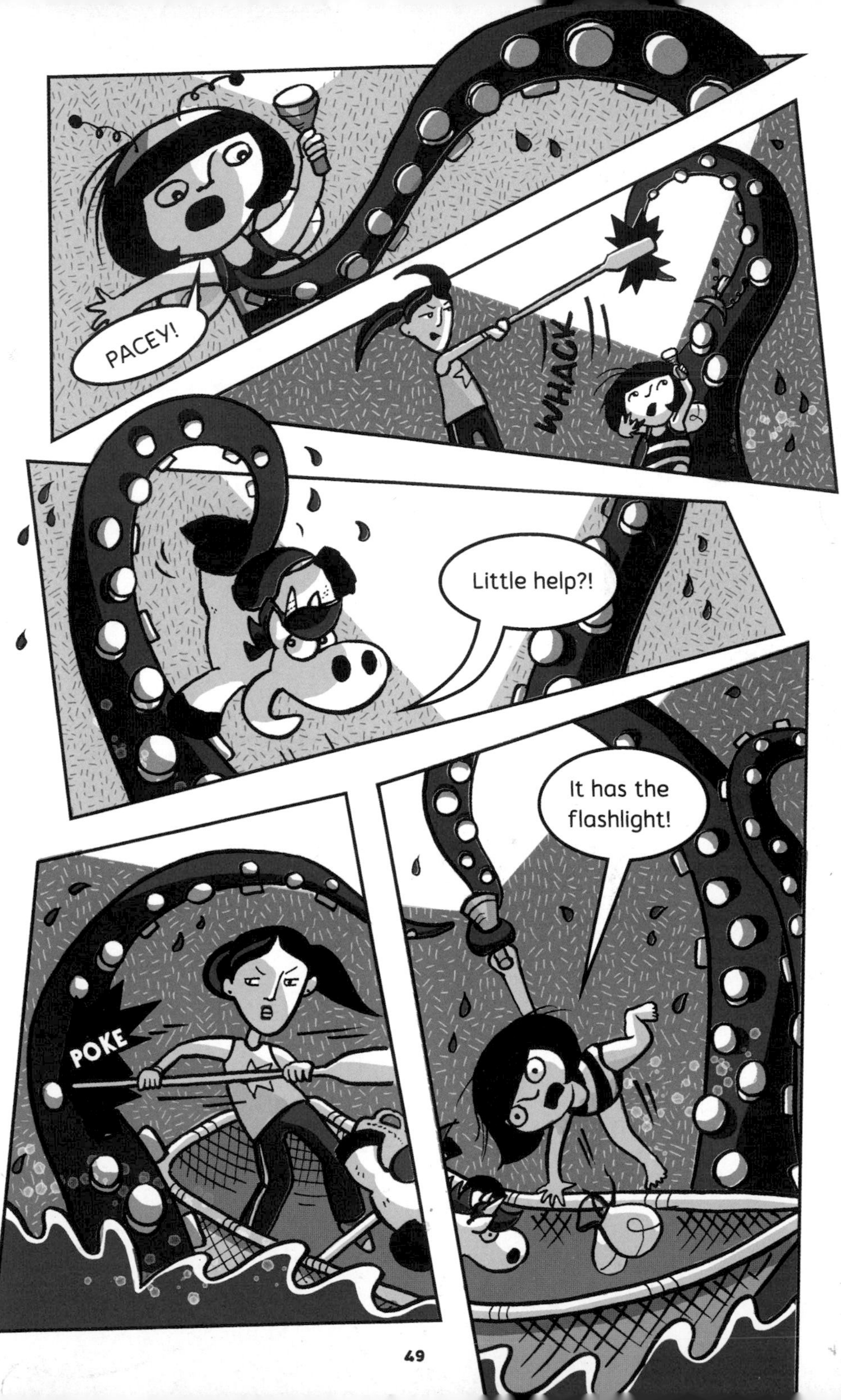
PACEY!
WHACK
Little help?!
POKE
It has the flashlight!

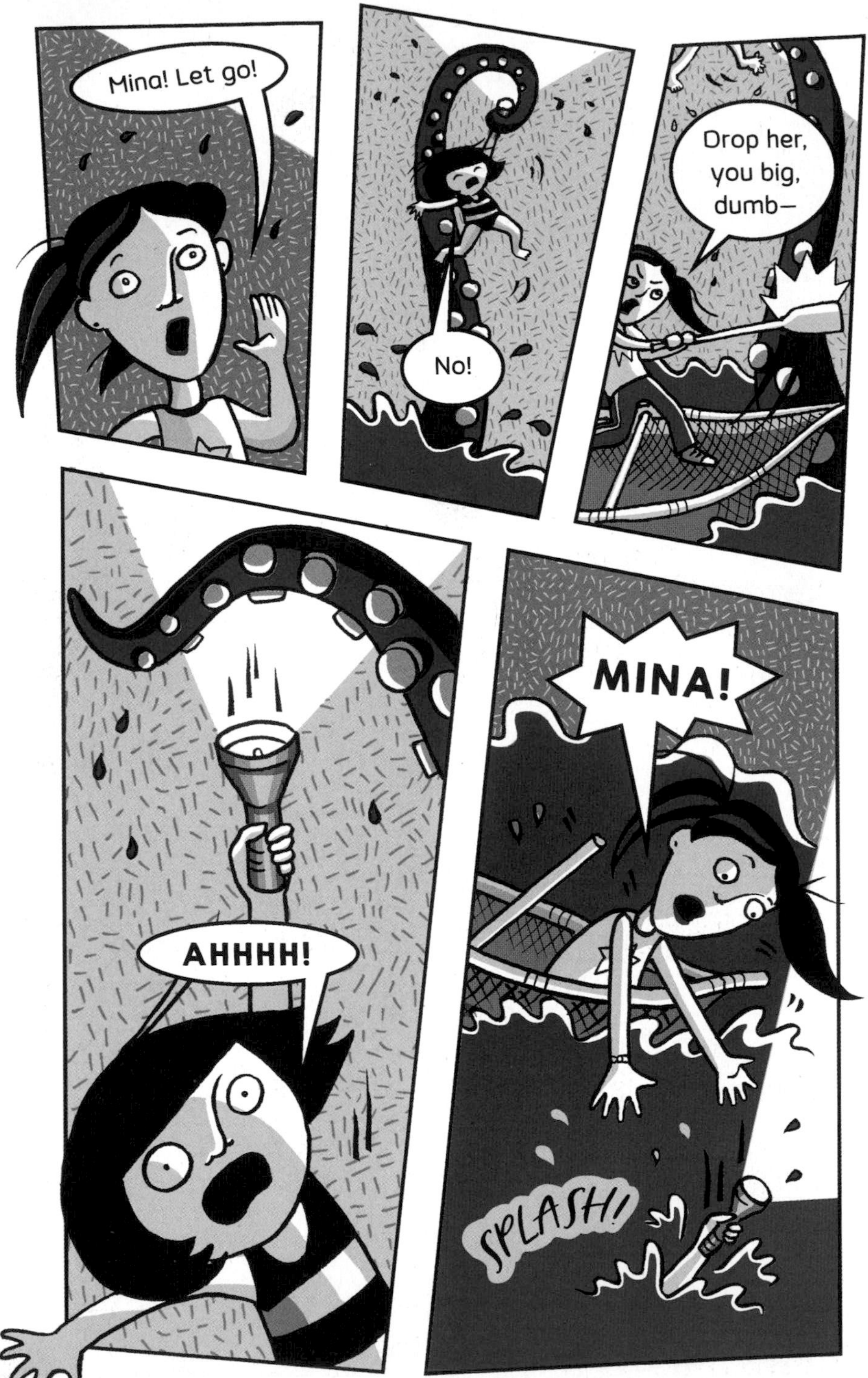
Mina! Let go!
No!
Drop her, you big, dumb—
AHHHH!
MINA!
SPLASH!

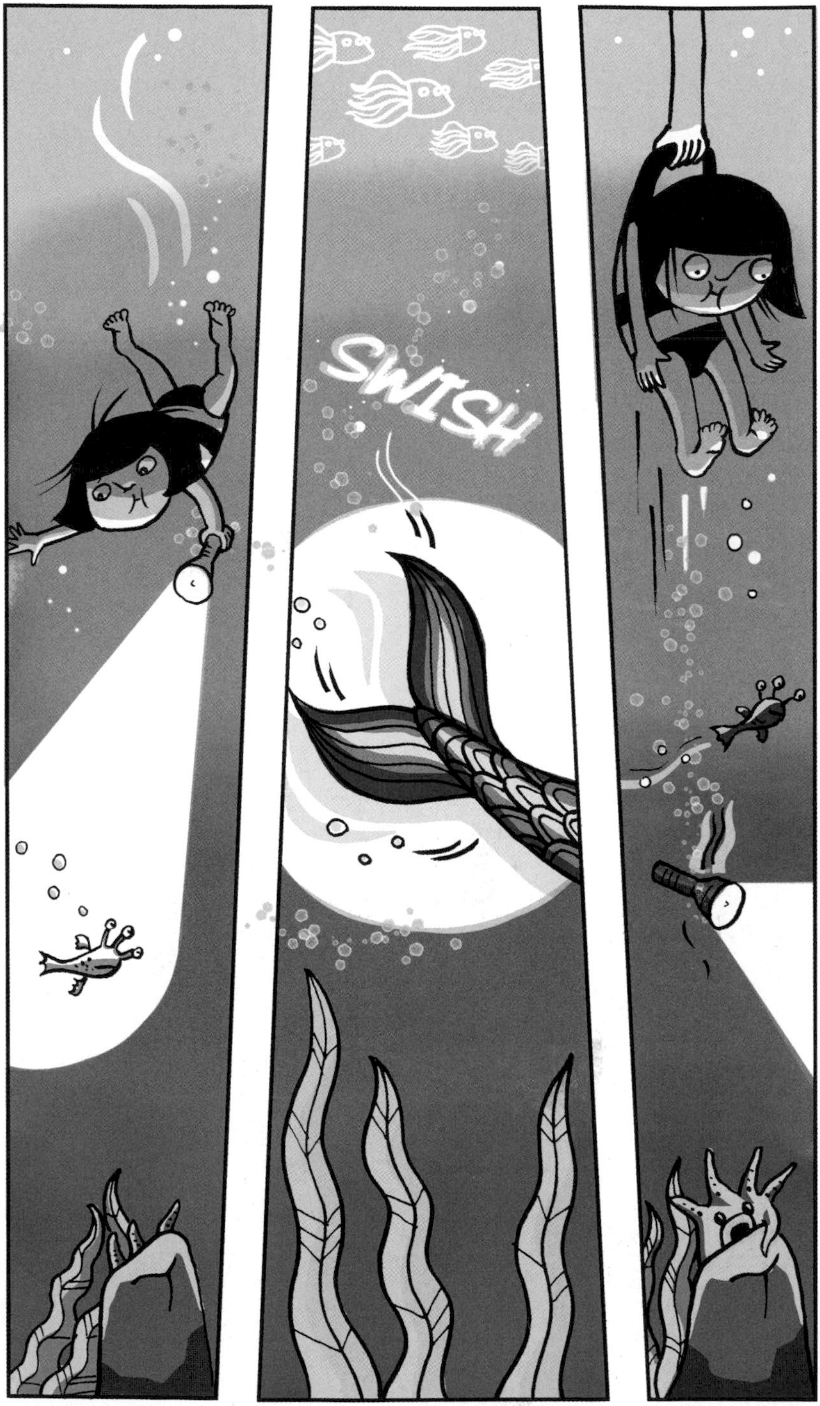
SWISH

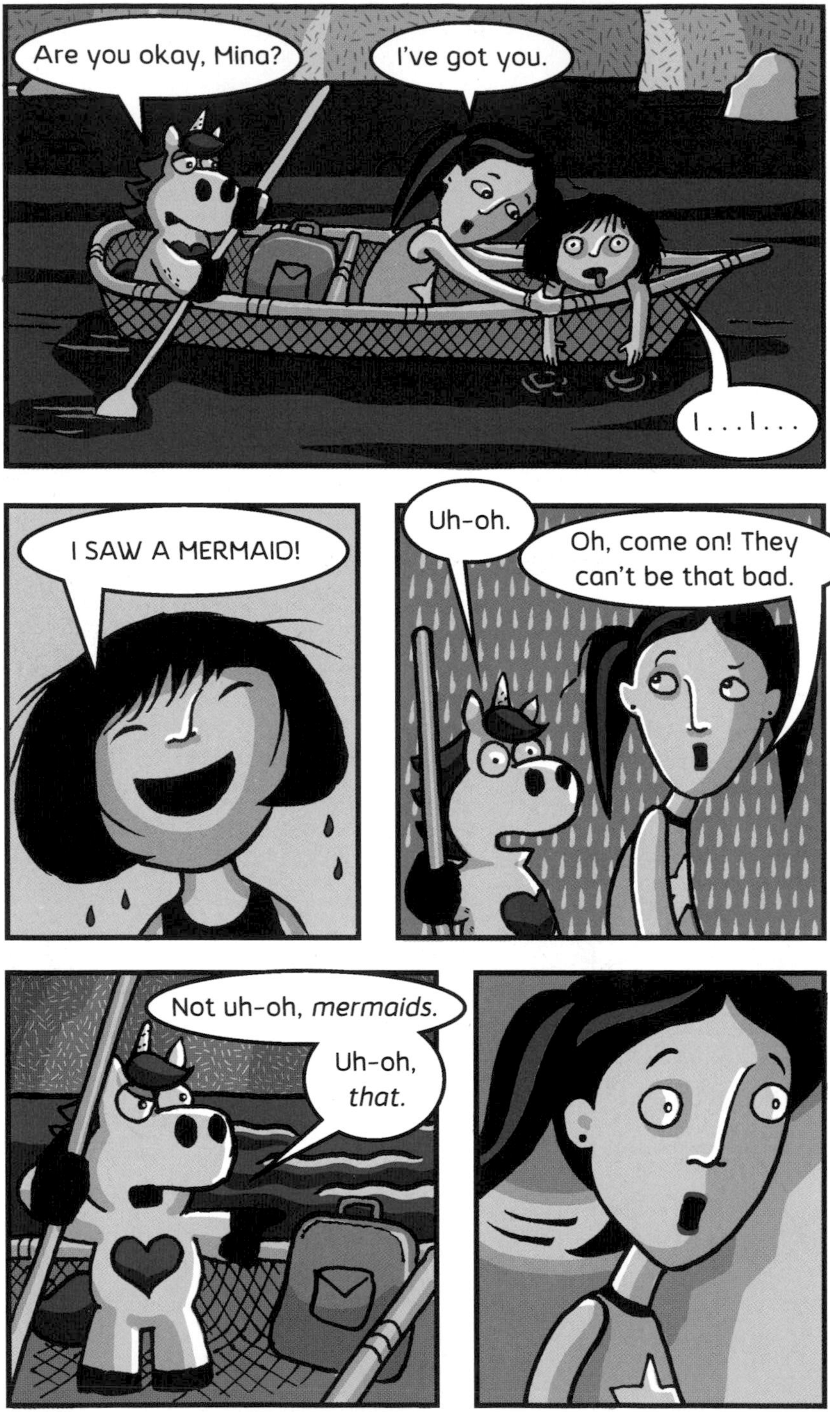
Are you okay, Mina?
I've got you.
I. . . I. . .
I SAW A MERMAID!
Uh-oh.
Oh, come on! They can't be that bad.
Not uh-oh, *mermaids.*
Uh-oh, *that.*

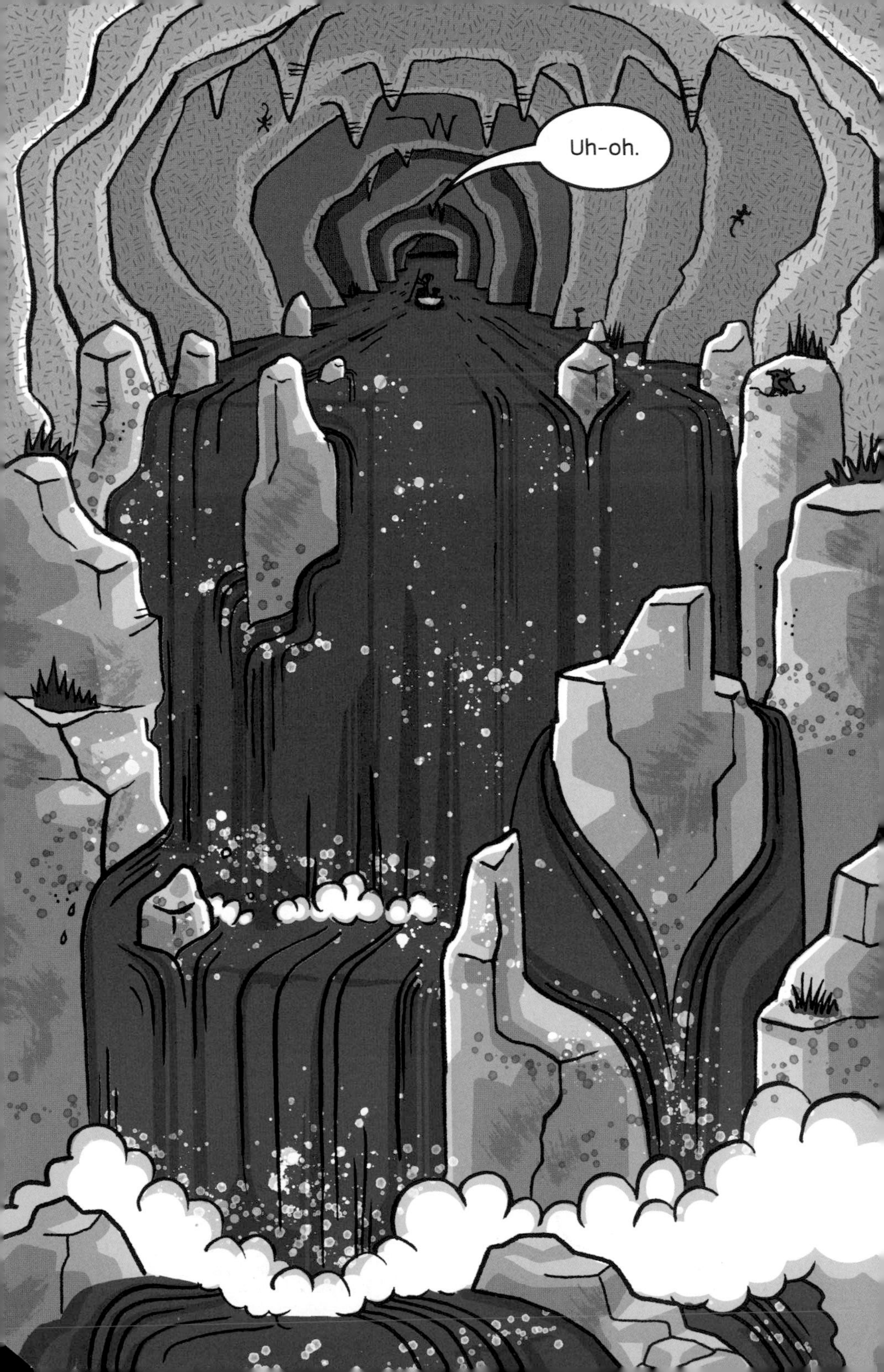
Uh-oh.

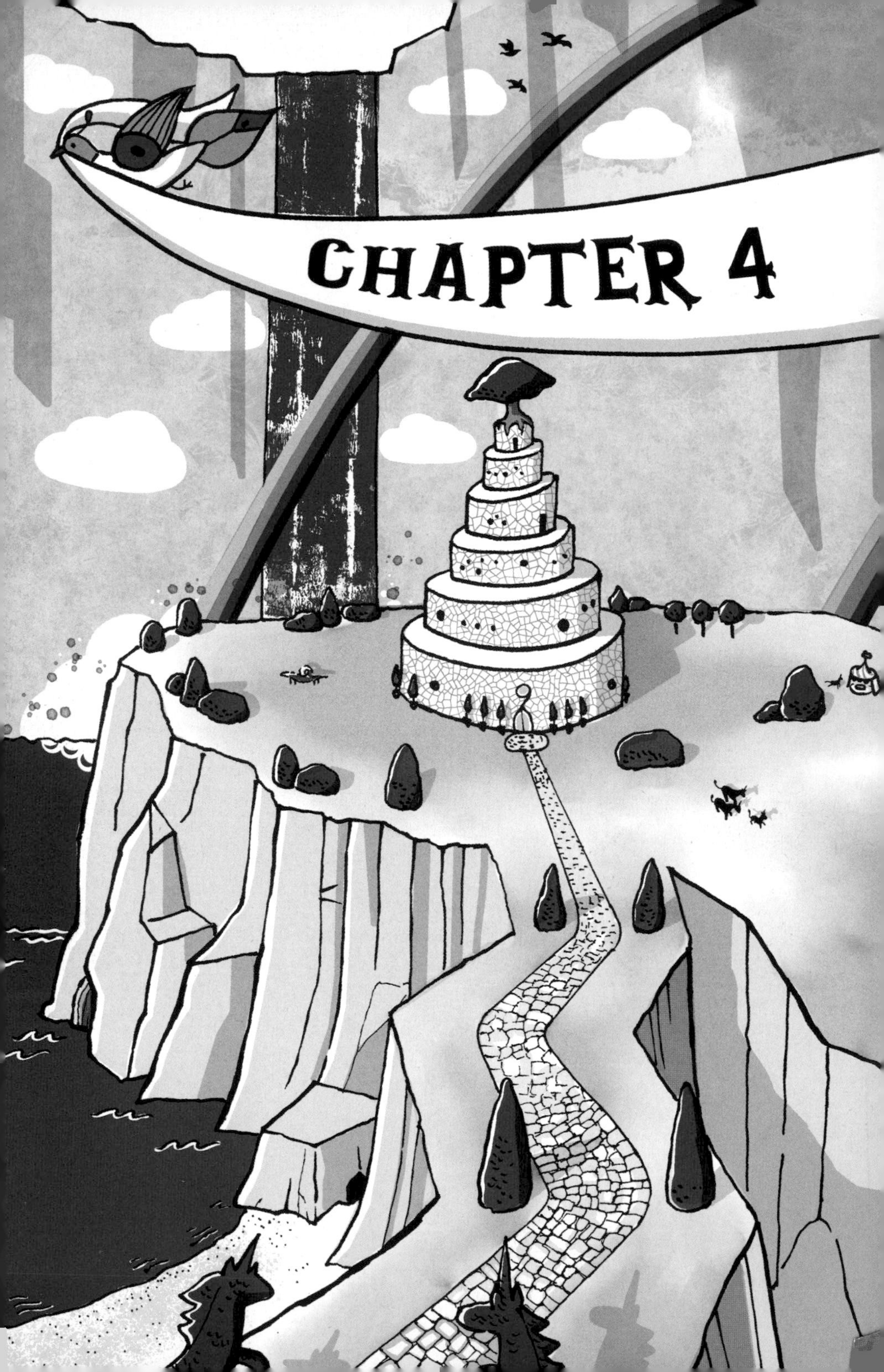
CHAPTER 4

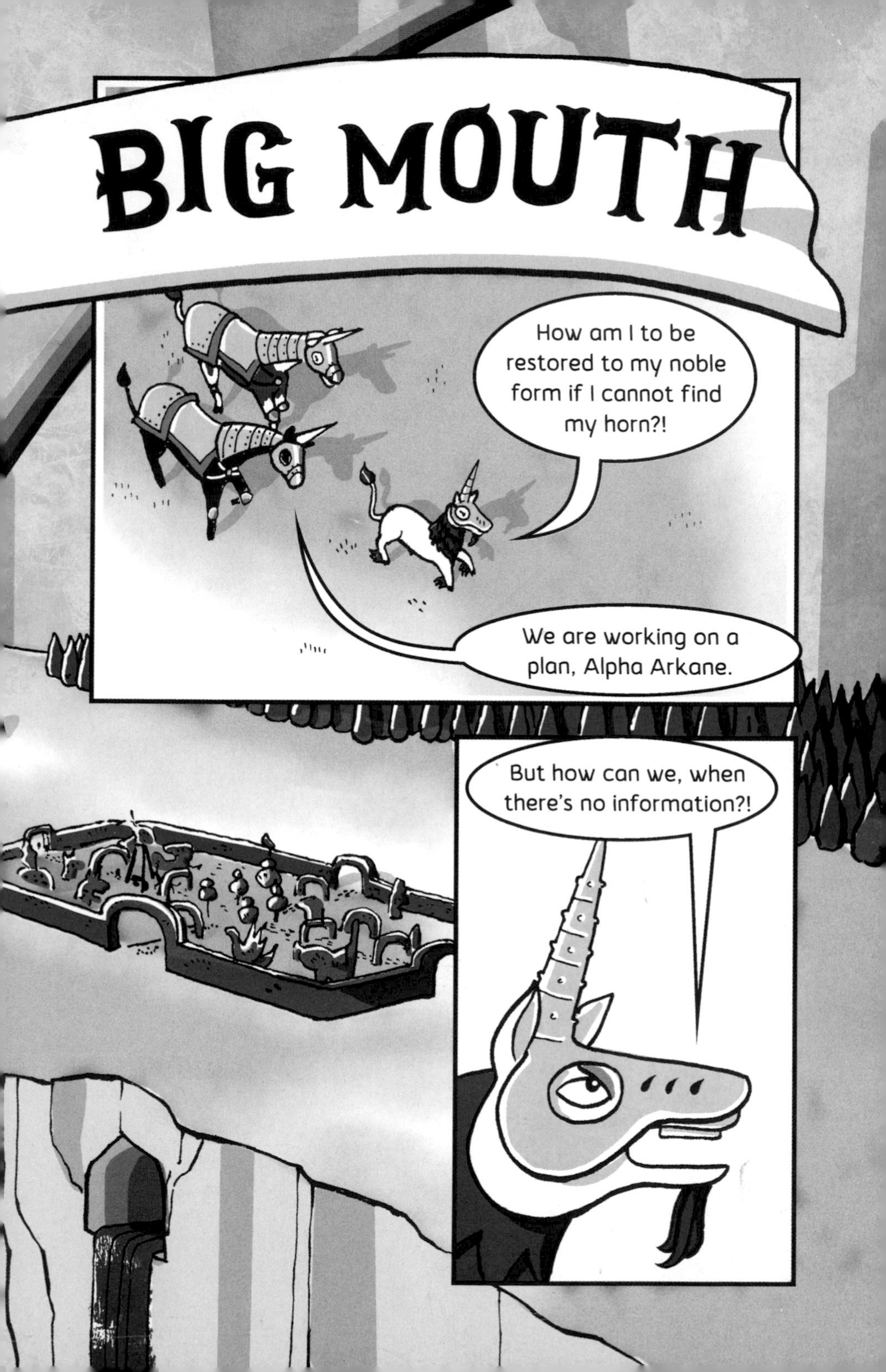
BIG MOUTH
How am I to be restored to my noble form if I cannot find my horn?!
We are working on a plan, Alpha Arkane.
But how can we, when there's no information?!

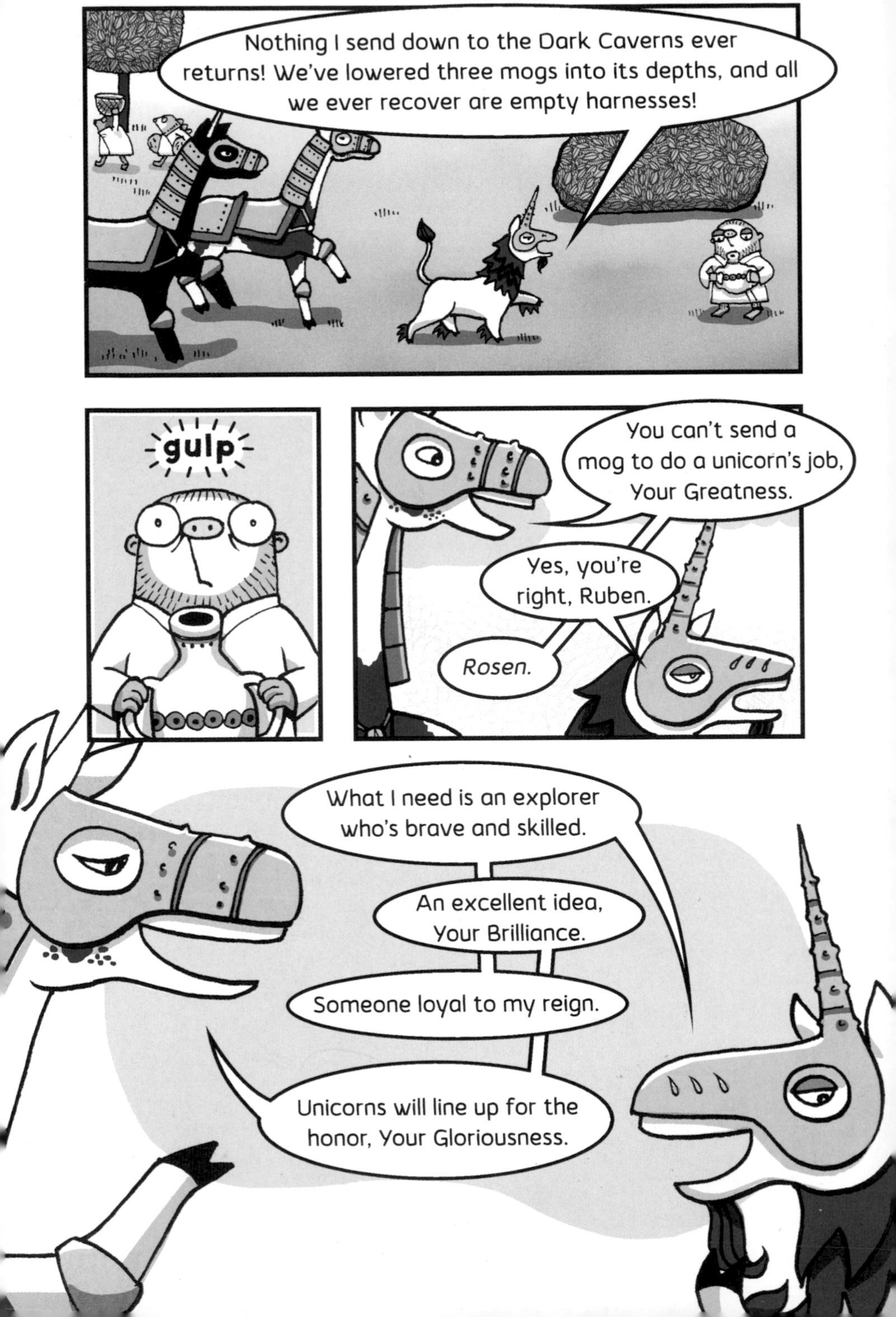

Nothing I send down to the Dark Caverns ever returns! We've lowered three mogs into its depths, and all we ever recover are empty harnesses!
gulp
You can't send a mog to do a unicorn's job, Your Greatness.
Yes, you're right, Ruben.
Rosen.
What I need is an explorer who's brave and skilled.
An excellent idea, Your Brilliance.
Someone loyal to my reign.
Unicorns will line up for the honor, Your Gloriousness.

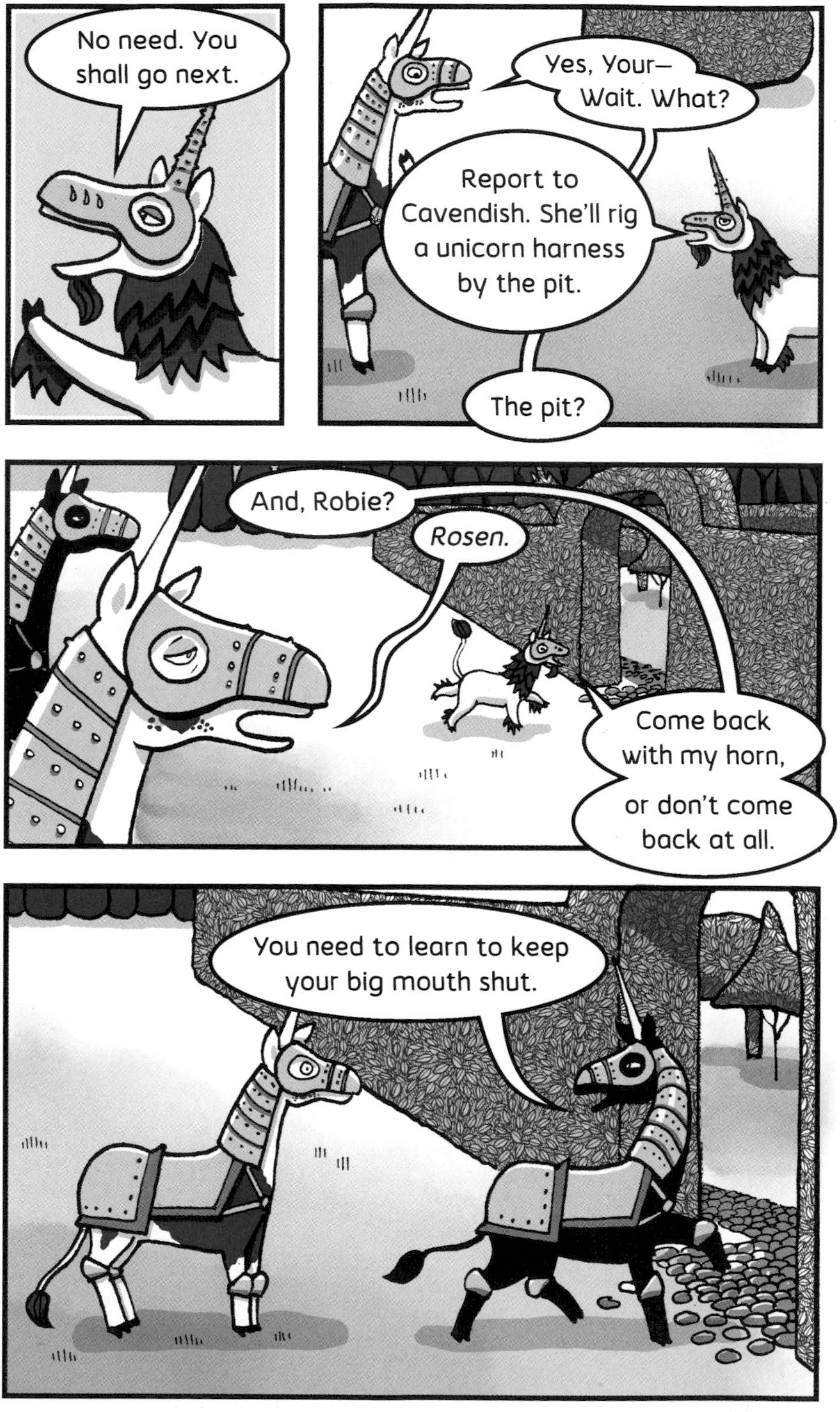
No need. You shall go next.
Yes, Your— Wait. What?
Report to Cavendish. She'll rig a unicorn harness by the pit.
The pit?
And, Robie?
Rosen.
Come back with my horn,
or don't come back at all.
You need to learn to keep your big mouth shut.

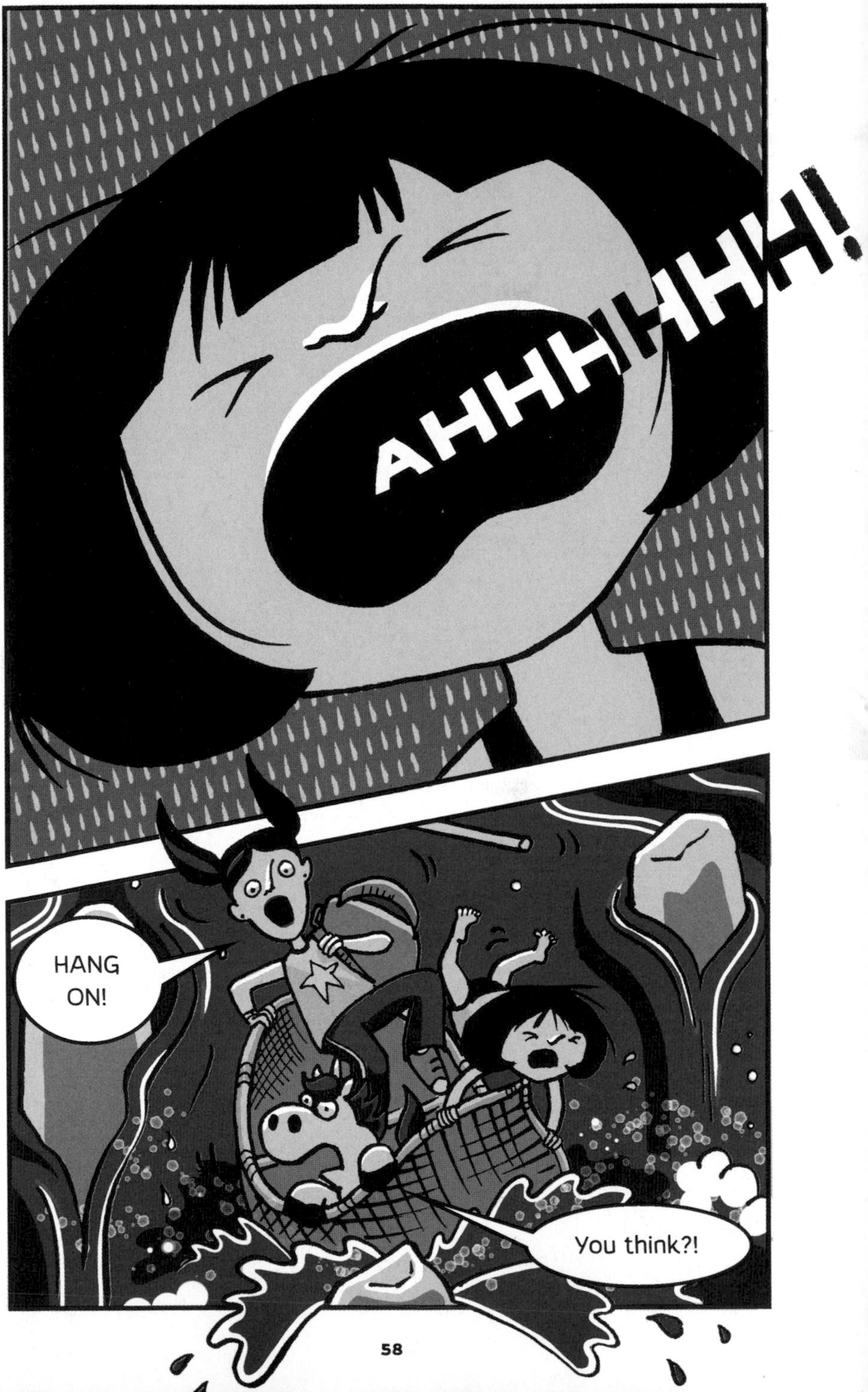
AHHHHHHHH!
HANG ON!
You think?!

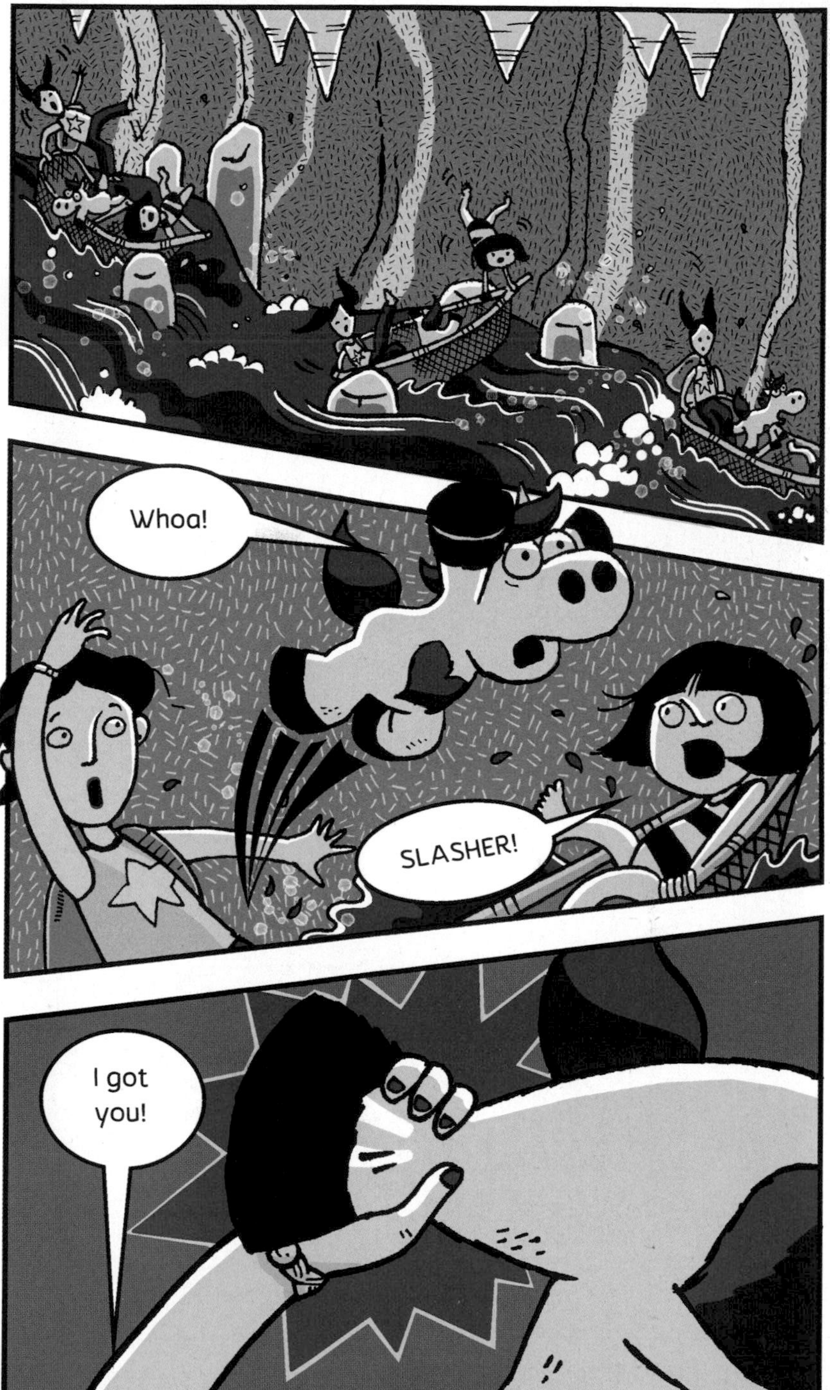
Whoa!
SLASHER!
I got you!

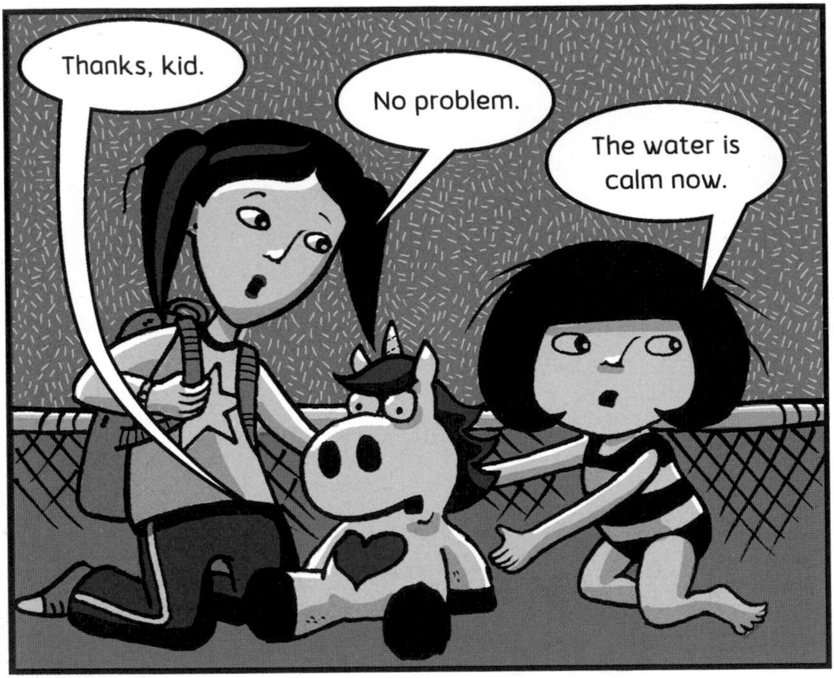
Thanks, kid.
No problem.
The water is calm now.

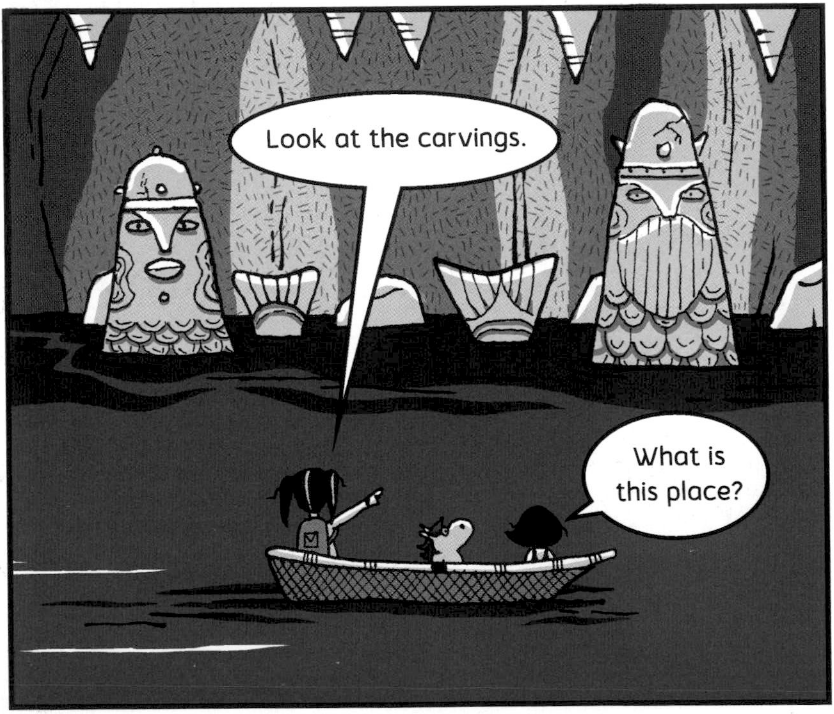
Look at the carvings.
What is this place?

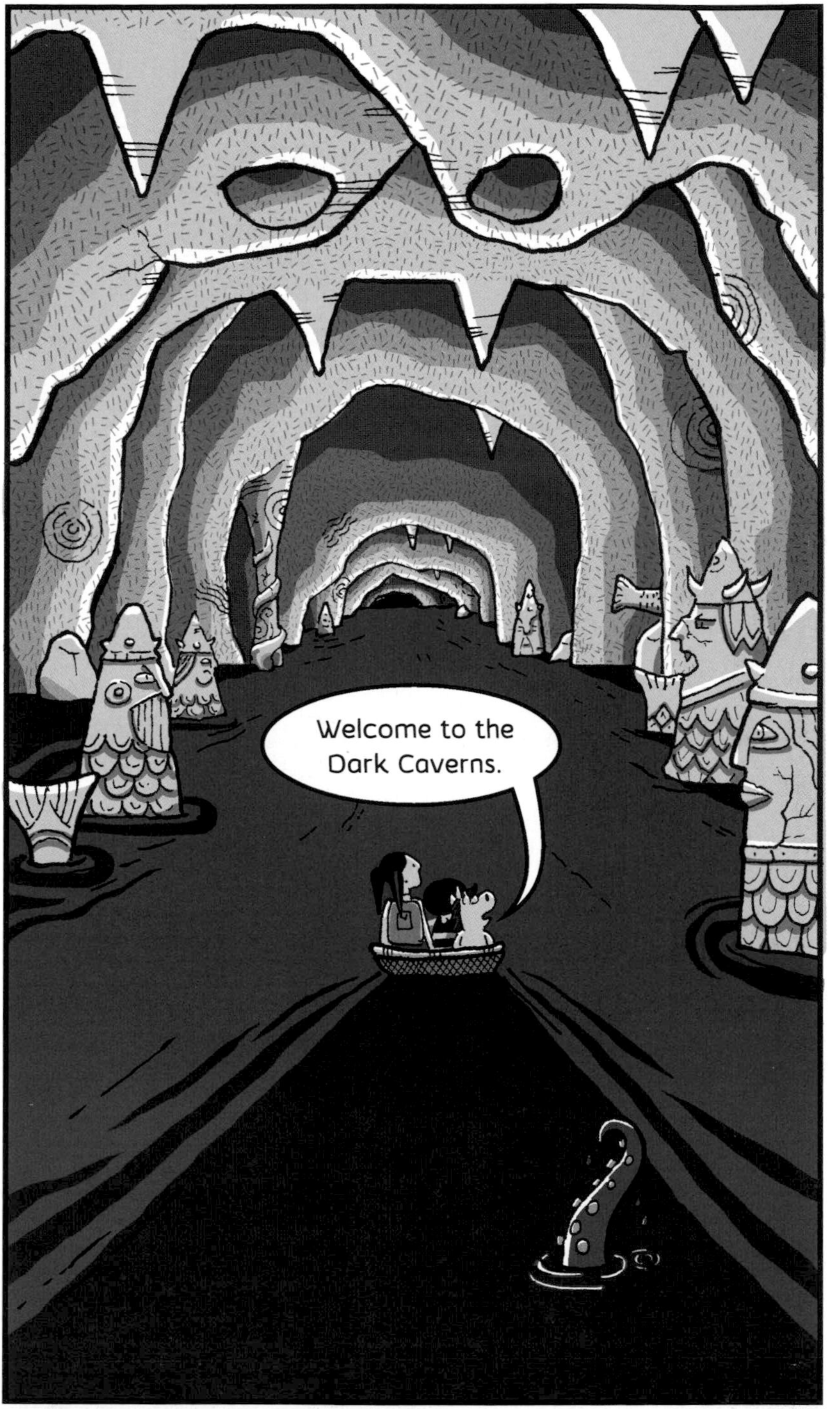
Welcome to the Dark Caverns.

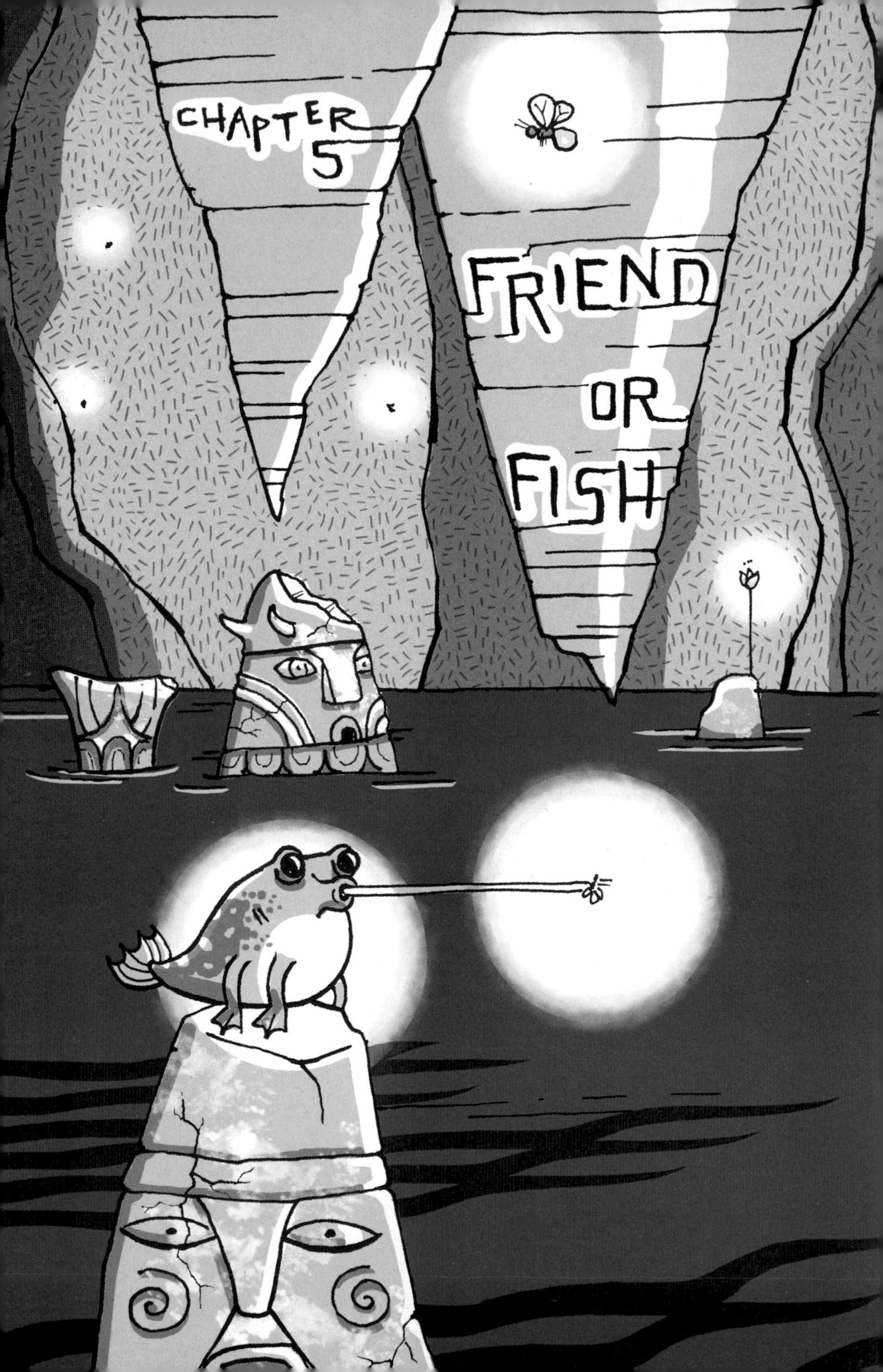
CHAPTER 5
FRIEND OR FISH

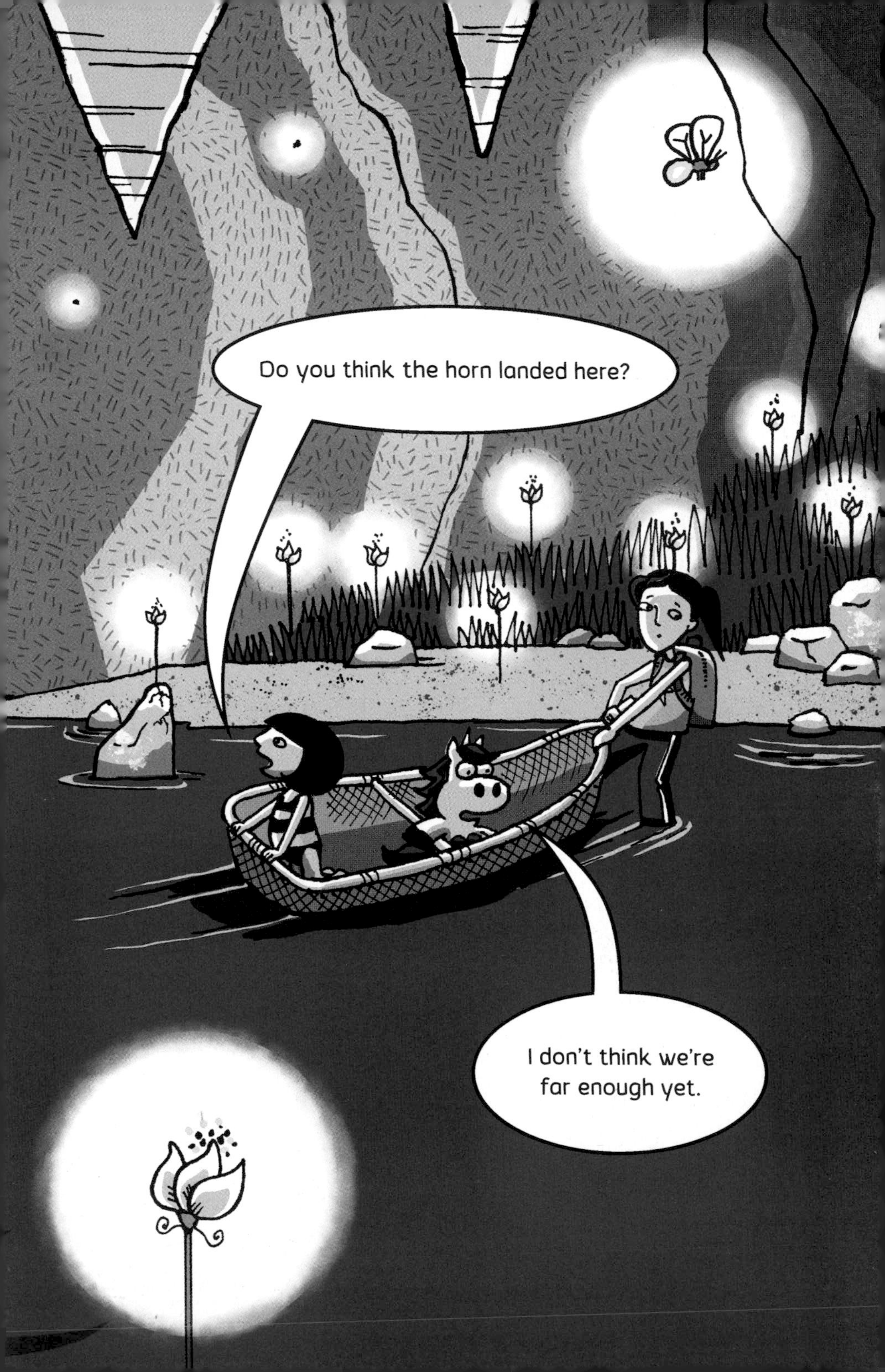
Do you think the horn landed here?
I don't think we're far enough yet.

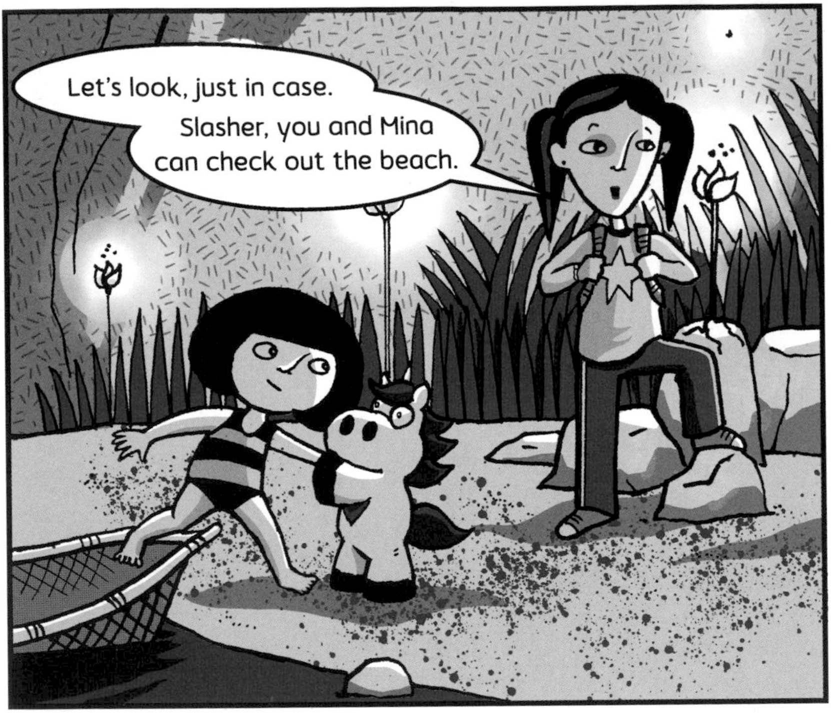
Let's look, just in case.
Slasher, you and Mina can check out the beach.

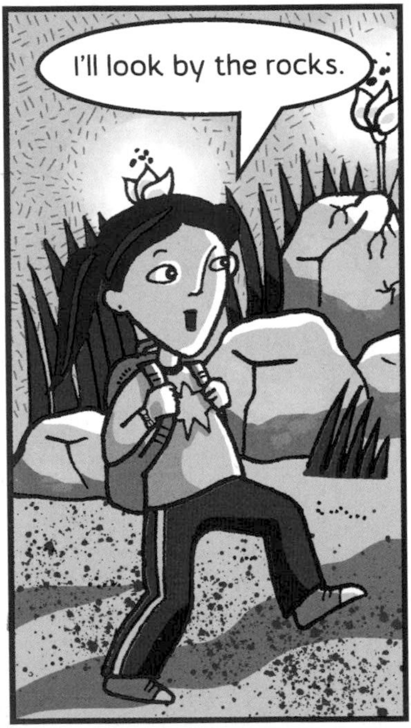
I'll look by the rocks.

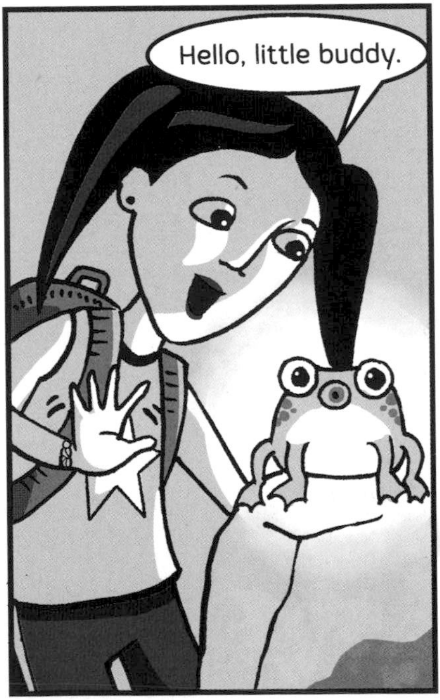
Hello, little buddy.

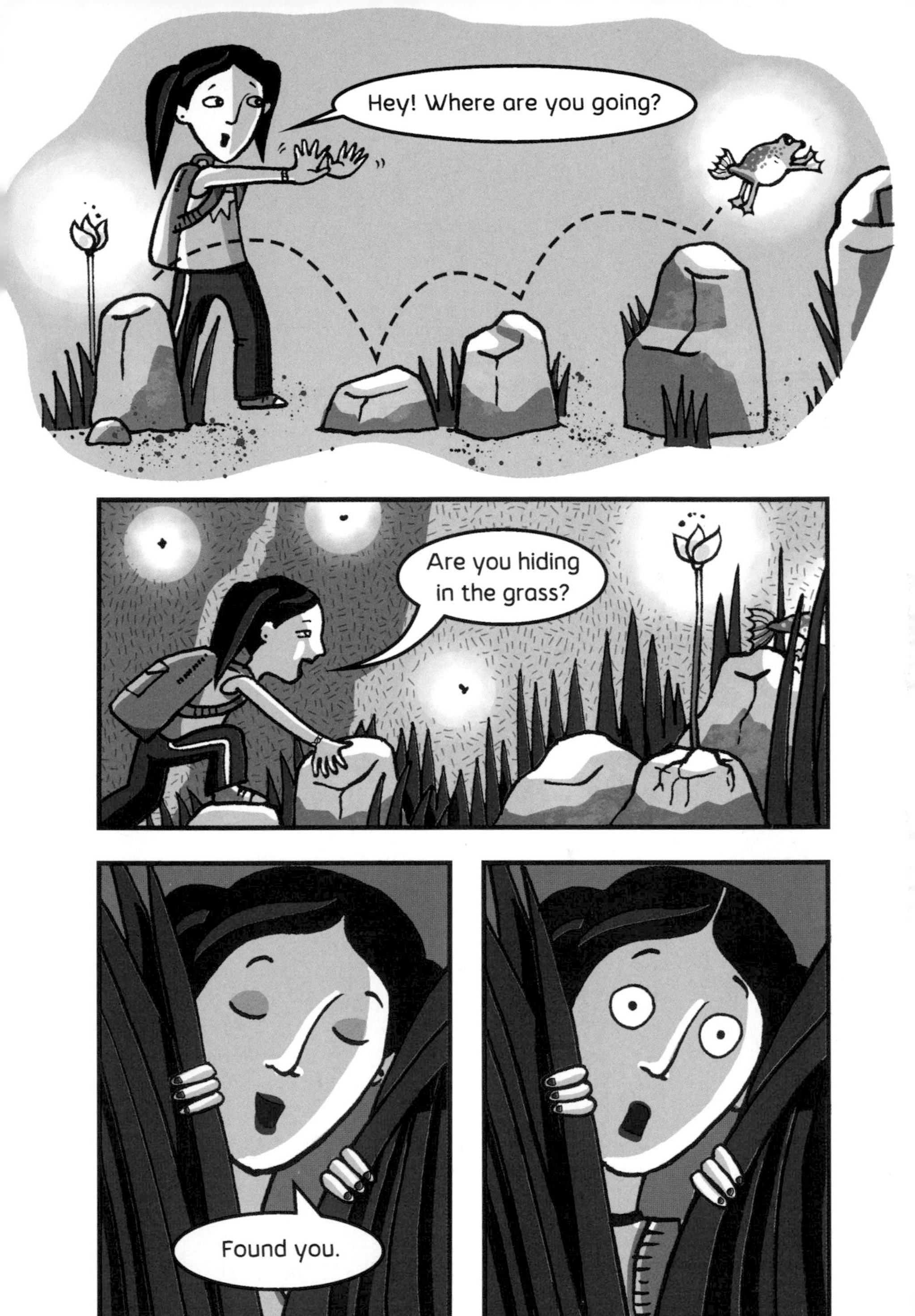
Hey! Where are you going?
Are you hiding in the grass?
Found you.

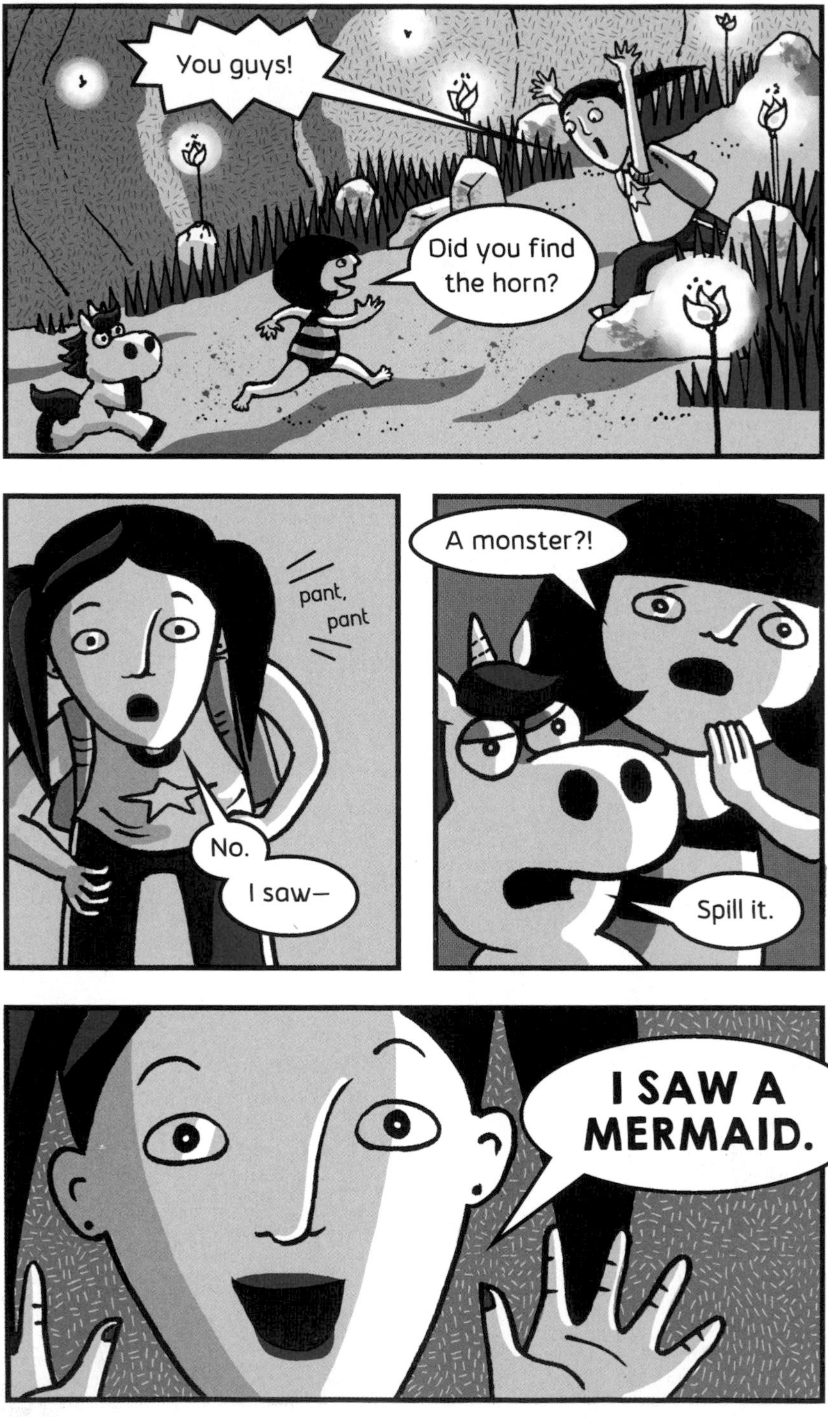
You guys!
Did you find the horn?
pant, pant
No.
I saw—
A monster?!
Spill it.
I SAW A MERMAID.

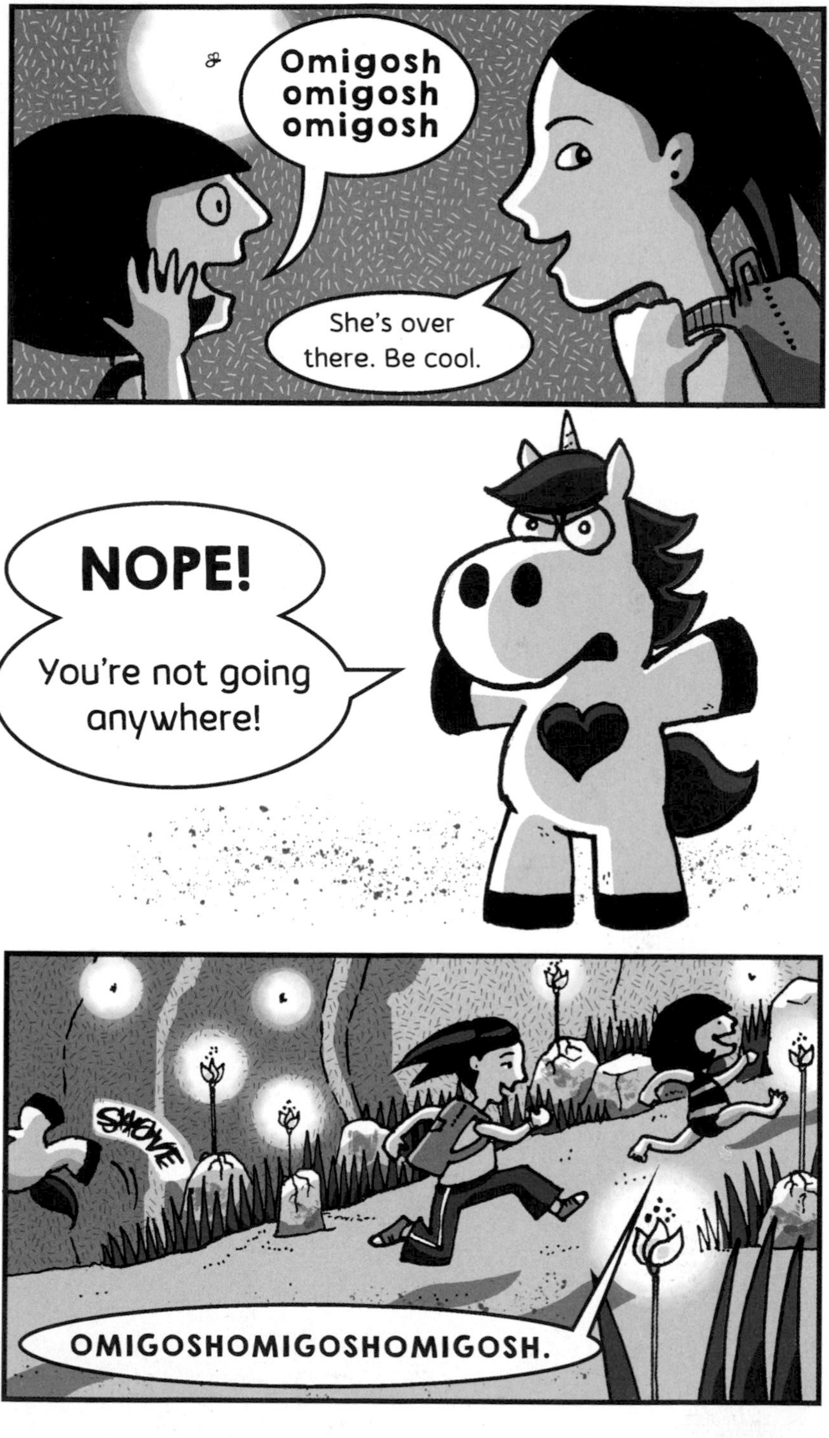
Omigosh omigosh omigosh
She's over there. Be cool.
NOPE!
You're not going anywhere!
SHOVE
OMIGOSHOMIGOSHOMIGOSH.

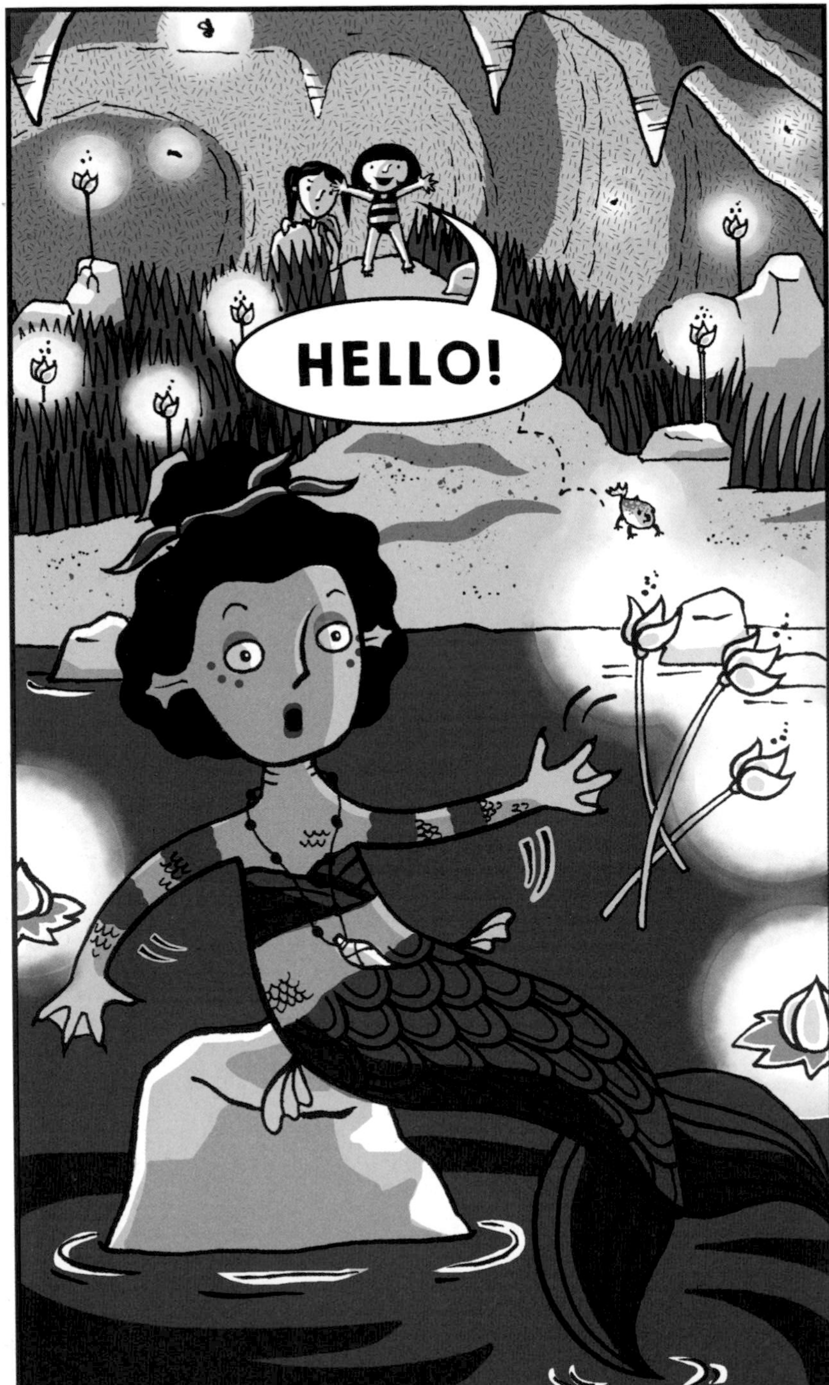
HELLO!

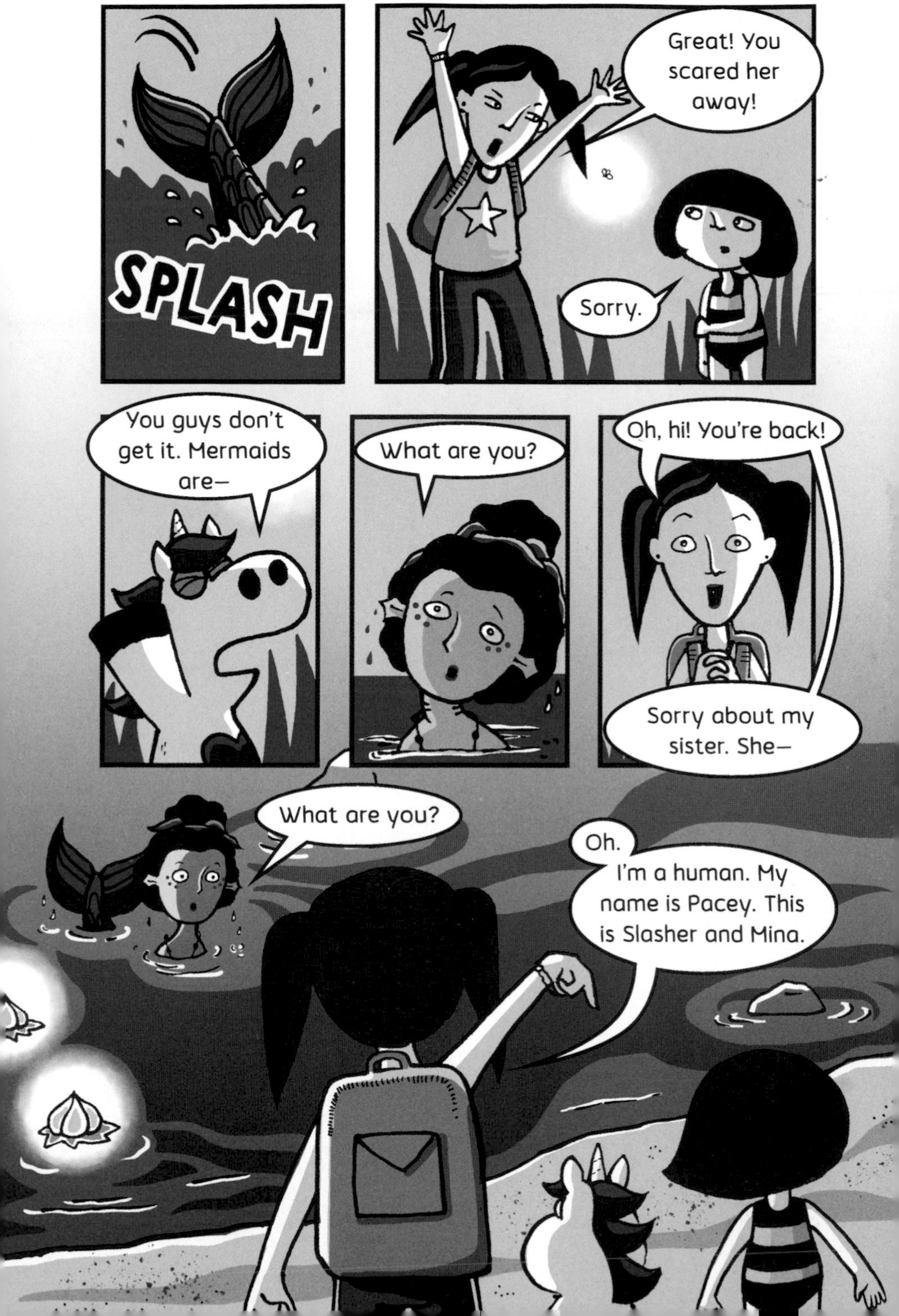
SPLASH
Great! You scared her away!
Sorry.
You guys don't get it. Mermaids are–
What are you?
Oh, hi! You're back!
Sorry about my sister. She–
What are you?
Oh.
I'm a human. My name is Pacey. This is Slasher and Mina.

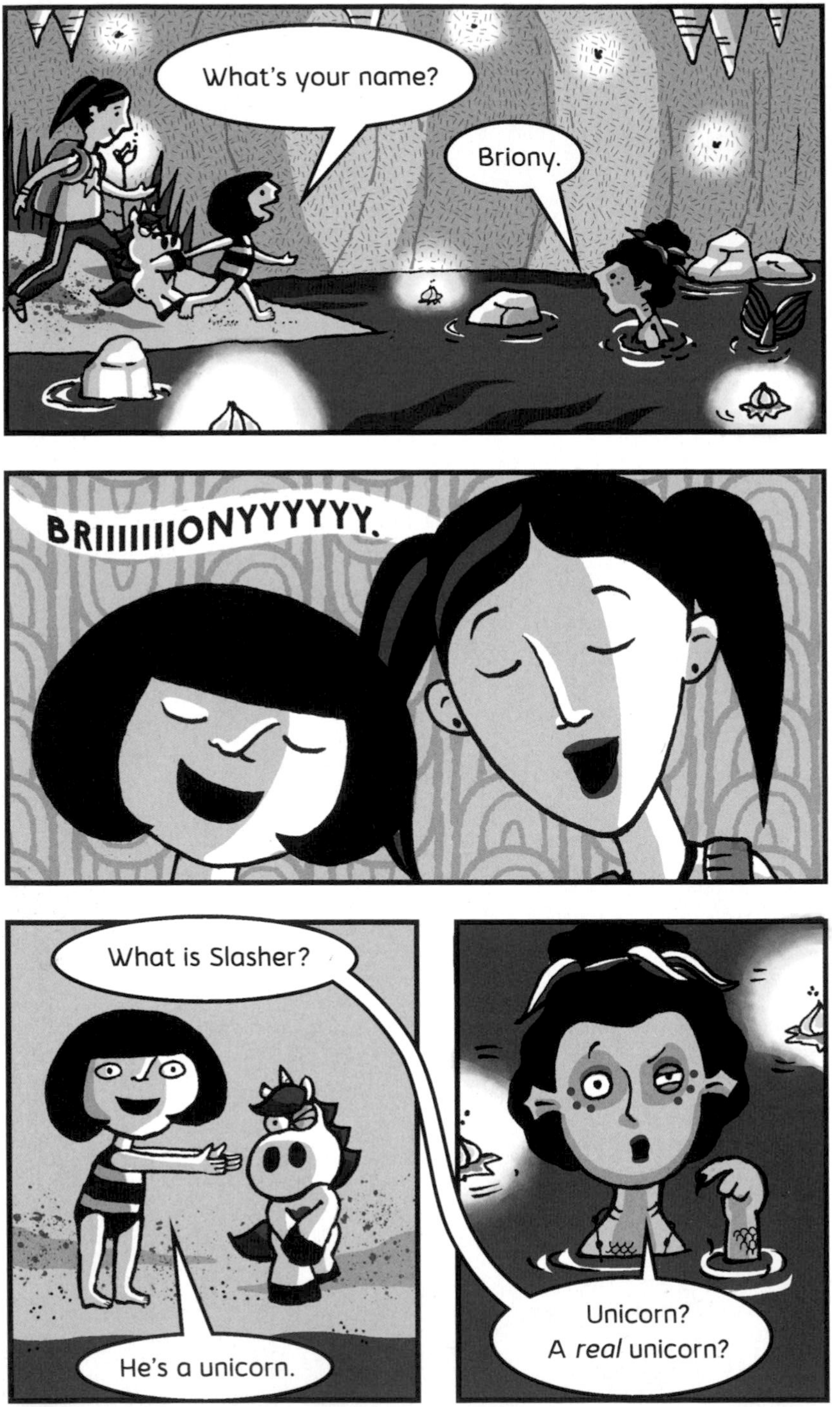
What's your name?
Briony.
BRIIIIIIIONYYYYYY.
What is Slasher?
He's a unicorn.
Unicorn?
A *real* unicorn?

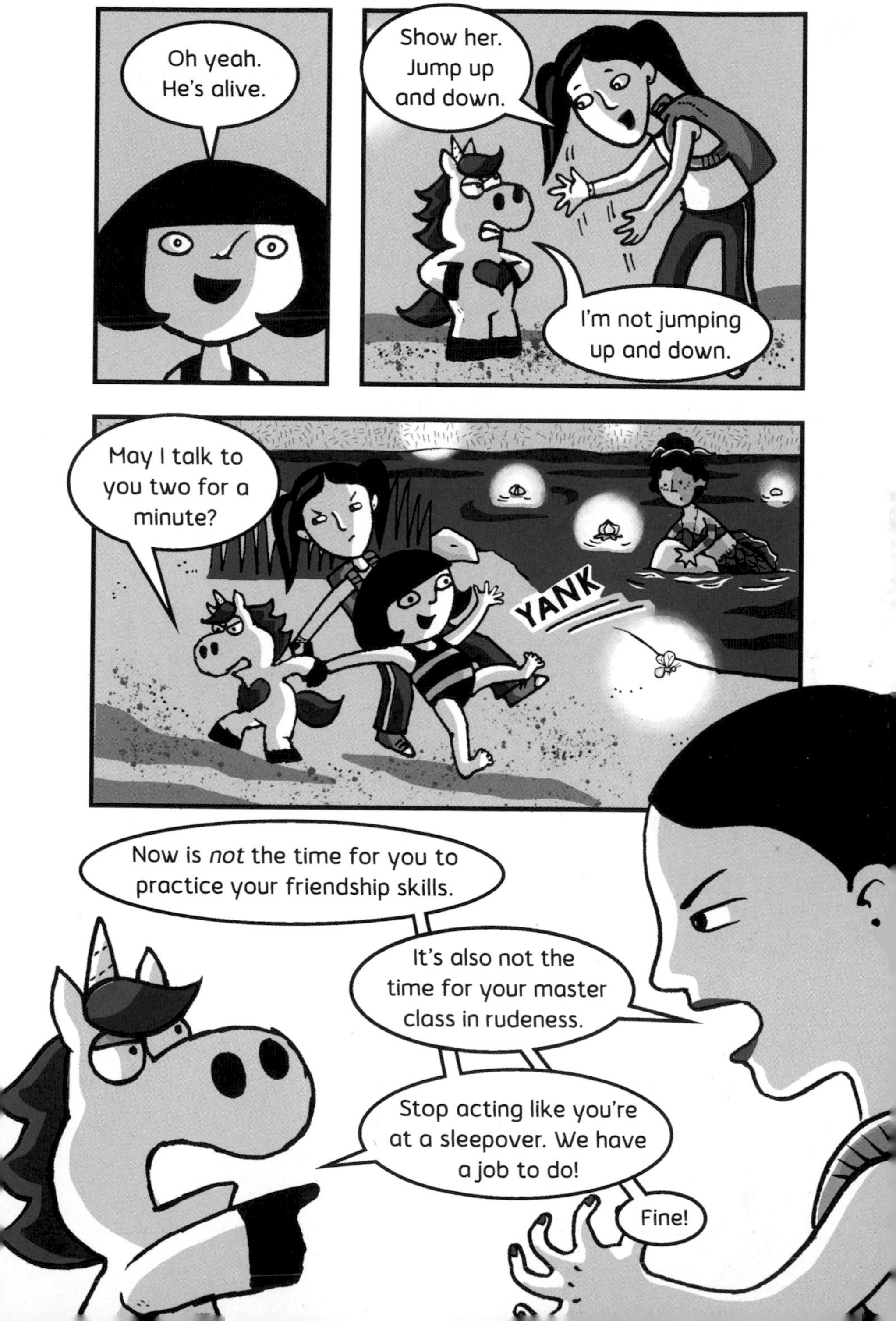
Oh yeah. He's alive.
Show her. Jump up and down.
I'm not jumping up and down.
May I talk to you two for a minute?
YANK
Now is *not* the time for you to practice your friendship skills.
It's also not the time for your master class in rudeness.
Stop acting like you're at a sleepover. We have a job to do!
Fine!

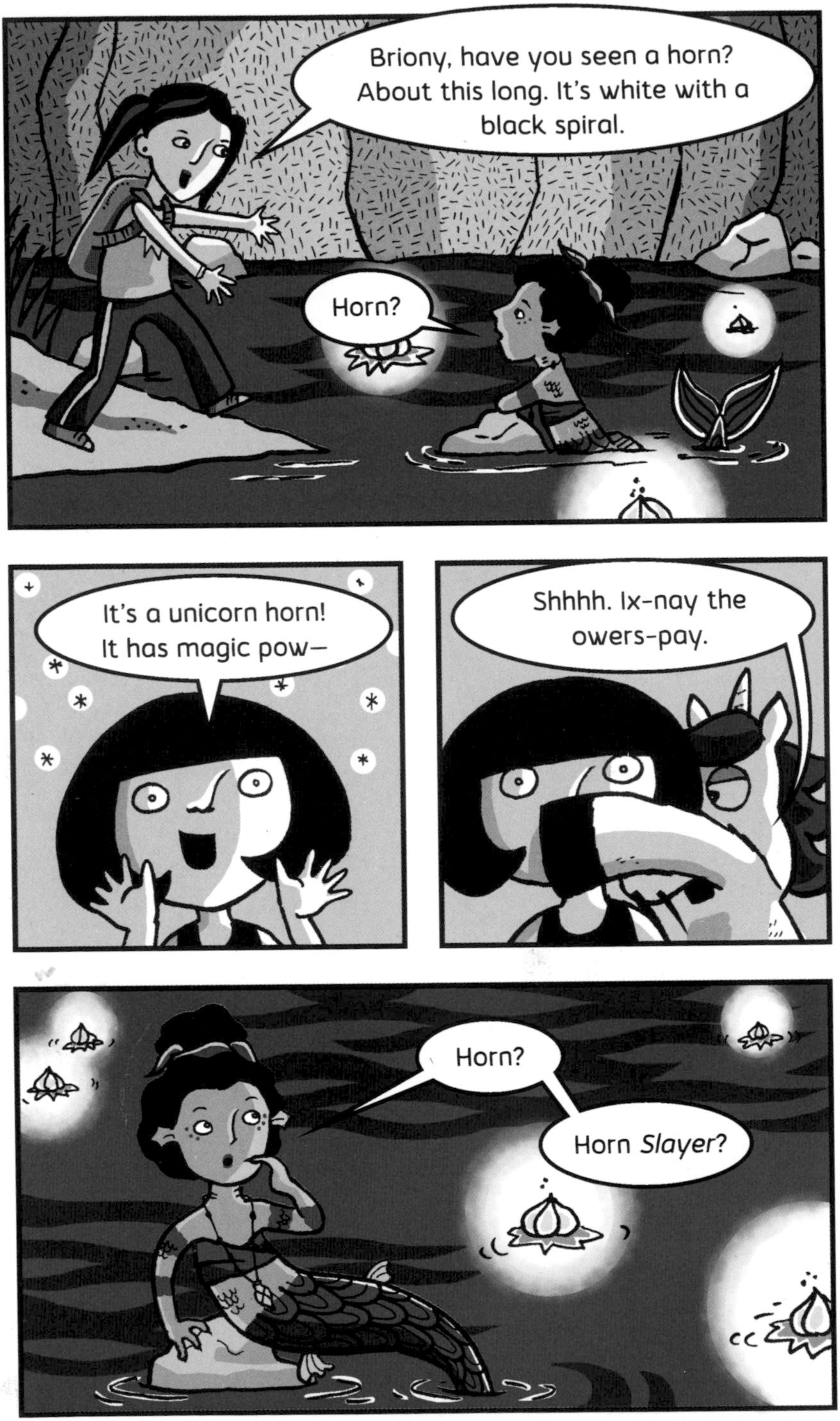
Briony, have you seen a horn? About this long. It's white with a black spiral.
Horn?
It's a unicorn horn! It has magic pow—
Shhhh. Ix-nay the owers-pay.
Horn?
Horn *Slayer*?

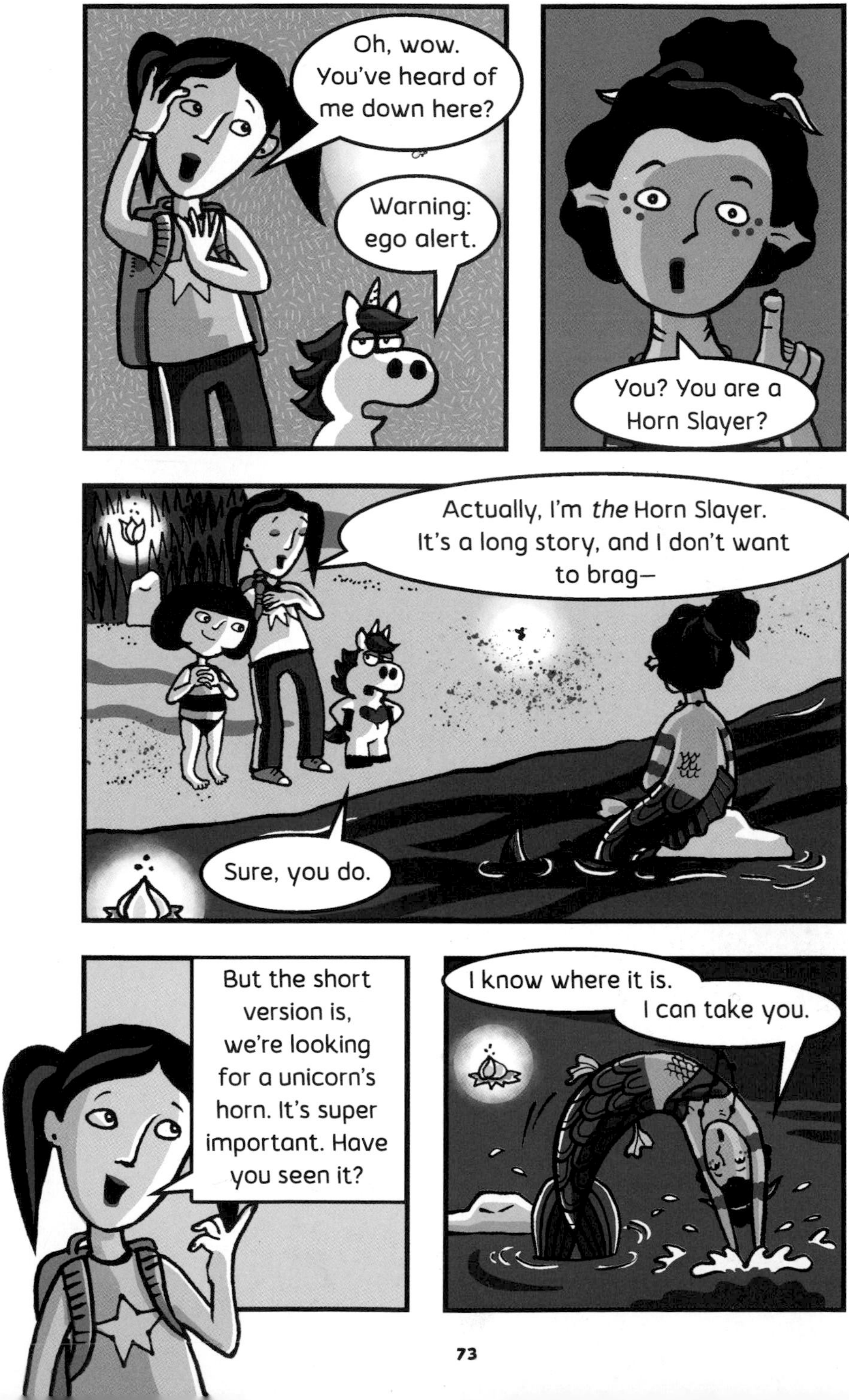
Oh, wow. You've heard of me down here?
Warning: ego alert.
You? You are a Horn Slayer?
Actually, I'm *the* Horn Slayer. It's a long story, and I don't want to brag—
Sure, you do.
But the short version is, we're looking for a unicorn's horn. It's super important. Have you seen it?
I know where it is.
I can take you.

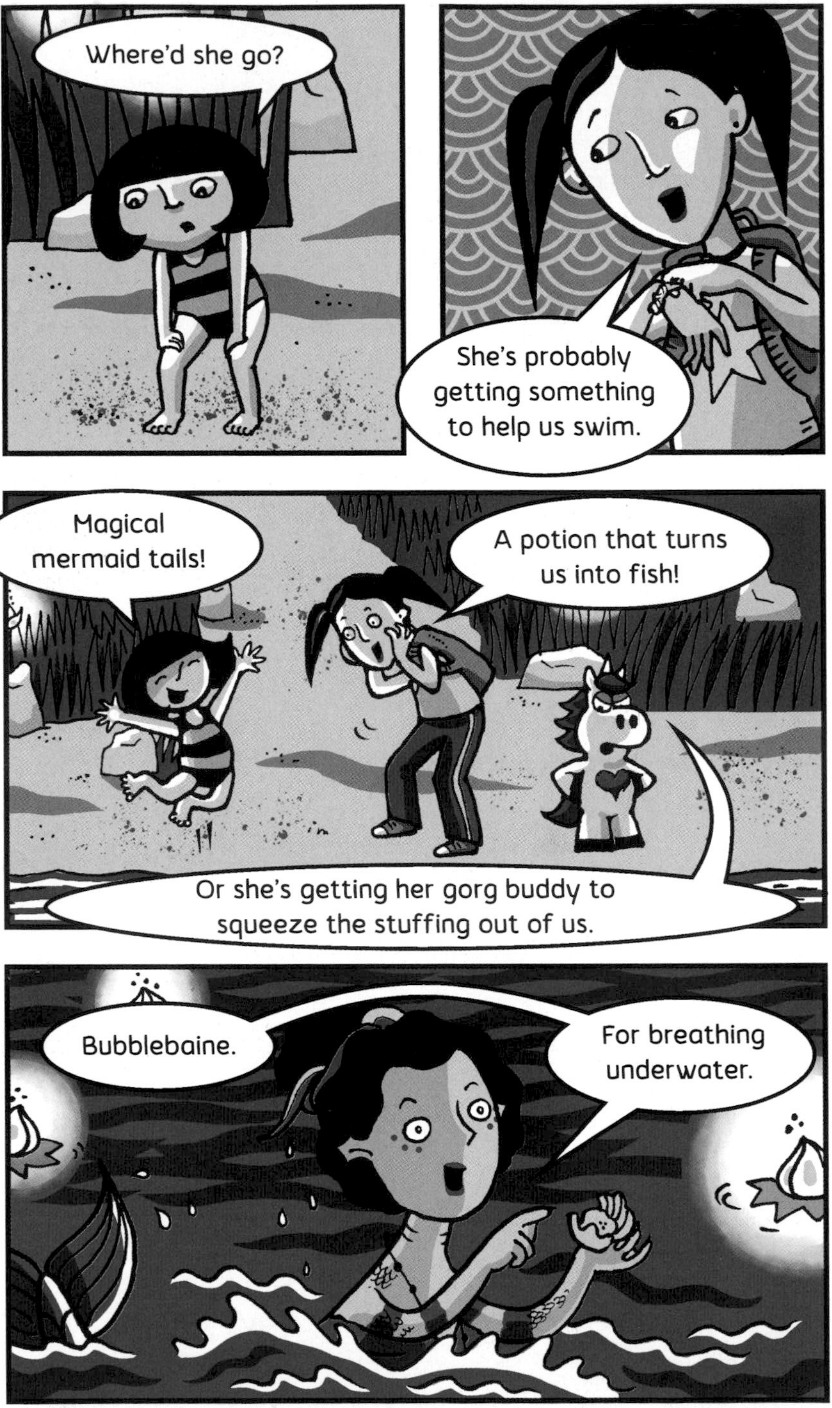
Where'd she go?
She's probably getting something to help us swim.
Magical mermaid tails!
A potion that turns us into fish!
Or she's getting her gorg buddy to squeeze the stuffing out of us.
Bubblebaine.
For breathing underwater.

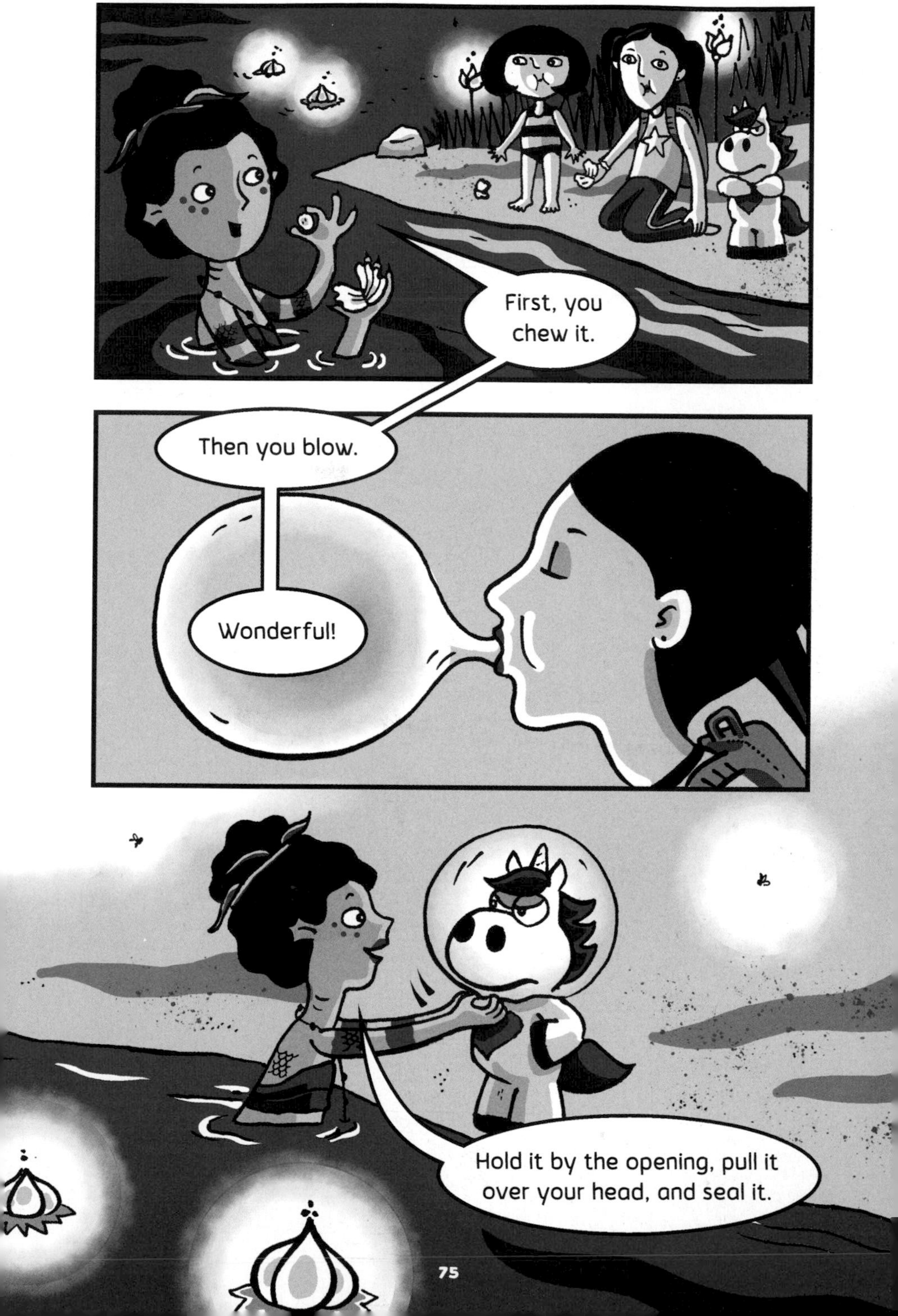
First, you chew it.
Then you blow.
Wonderful!
Hold it by the opening, pull it over your head, and seal it.

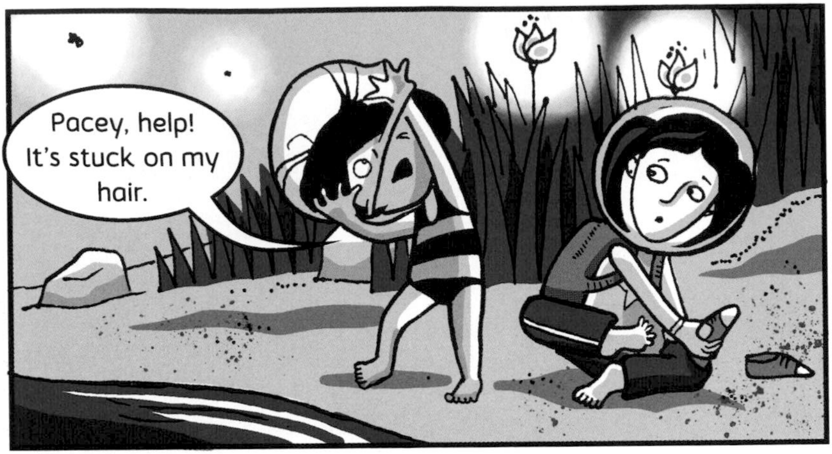
Pacey, help! It's stuck on my hair.

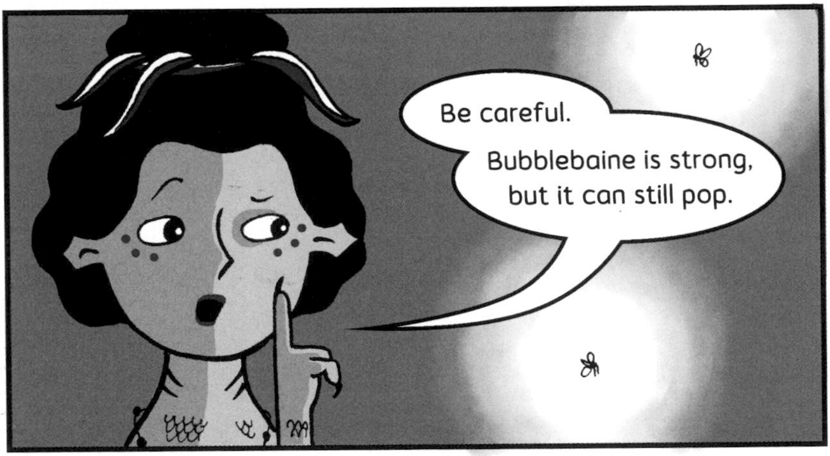
Be careful.
Bubblebaine is strong, but it can still pop.

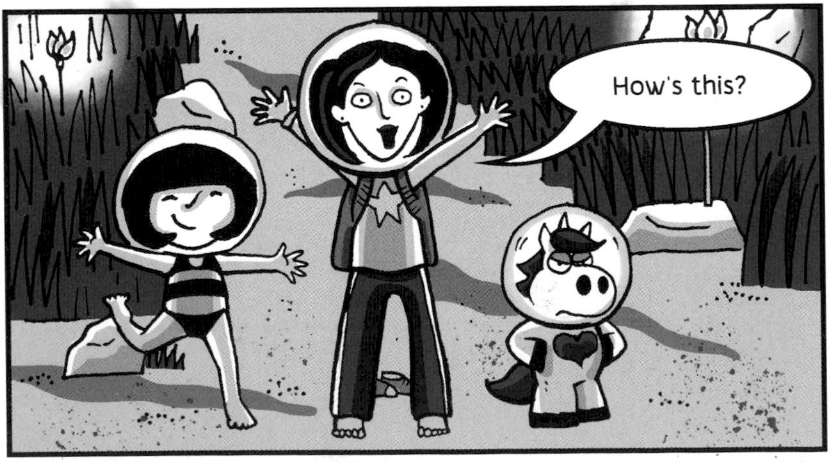
How's this?

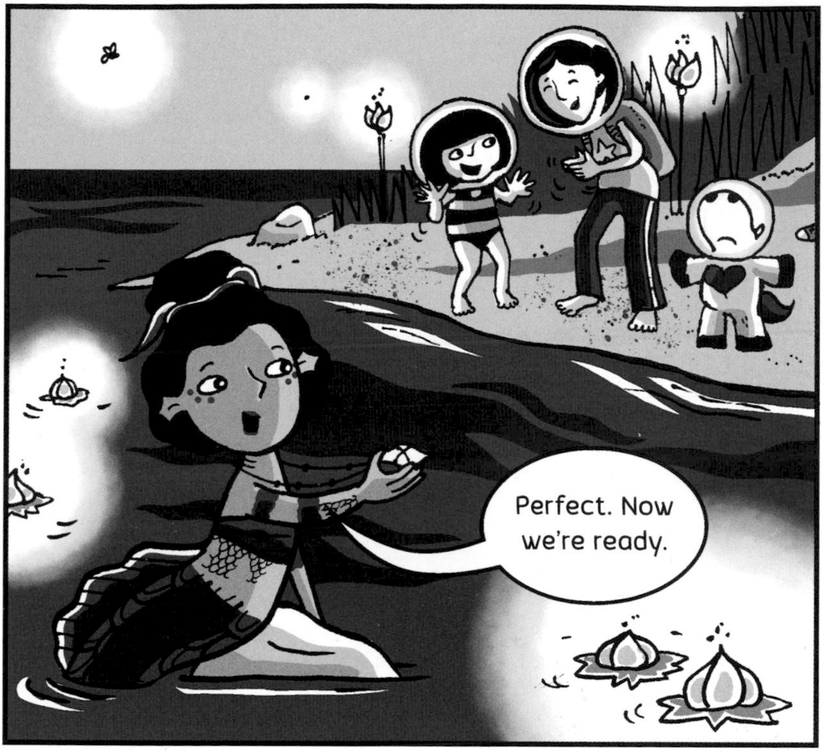
Perfect. Now we're ready.

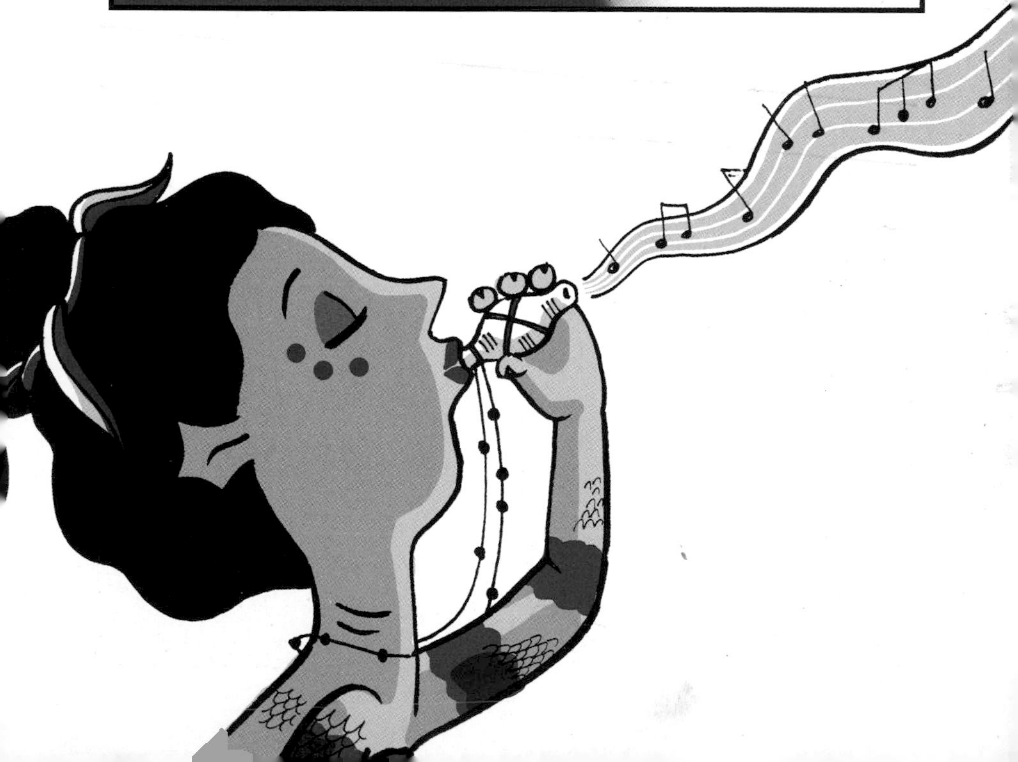

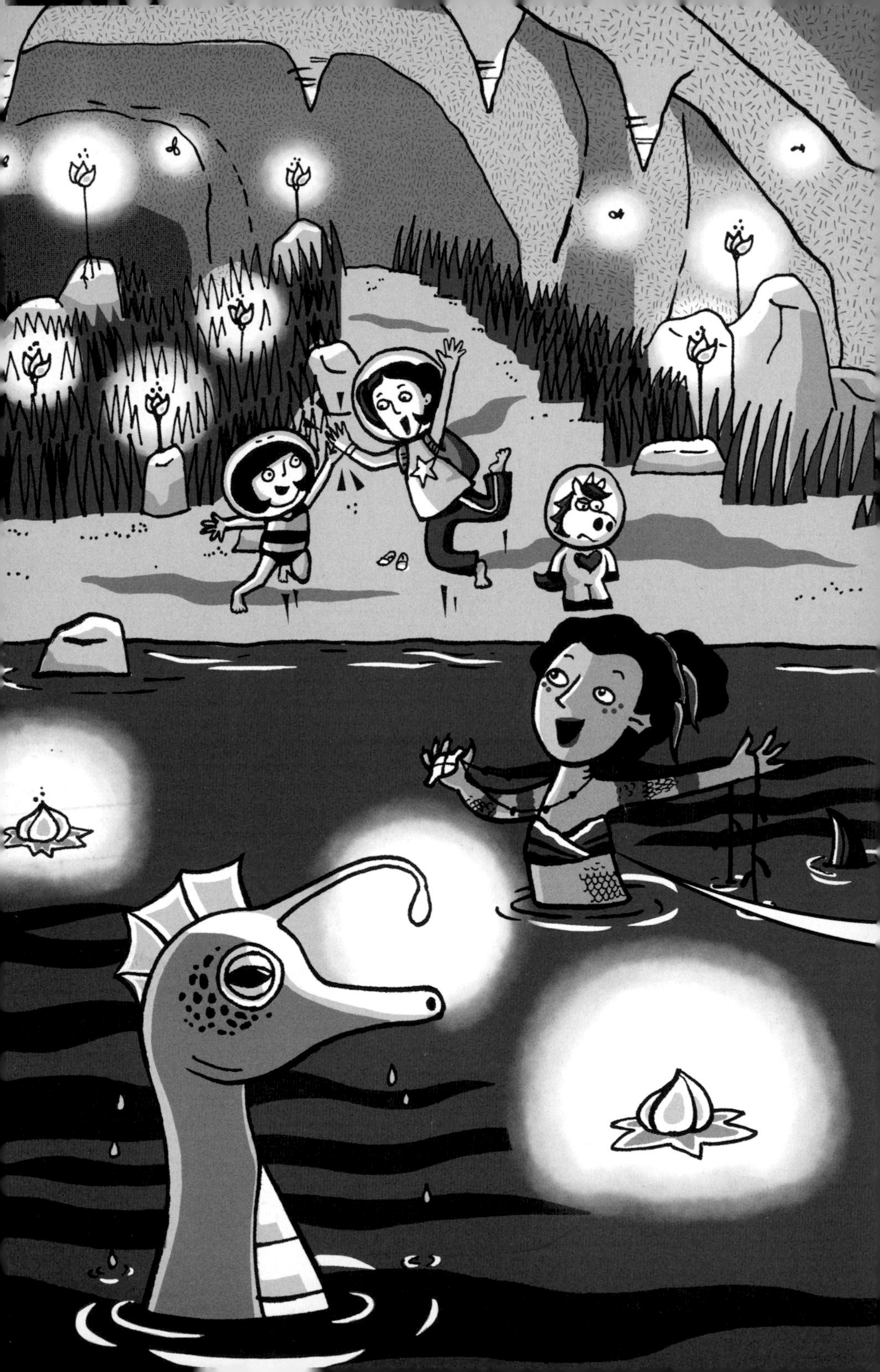

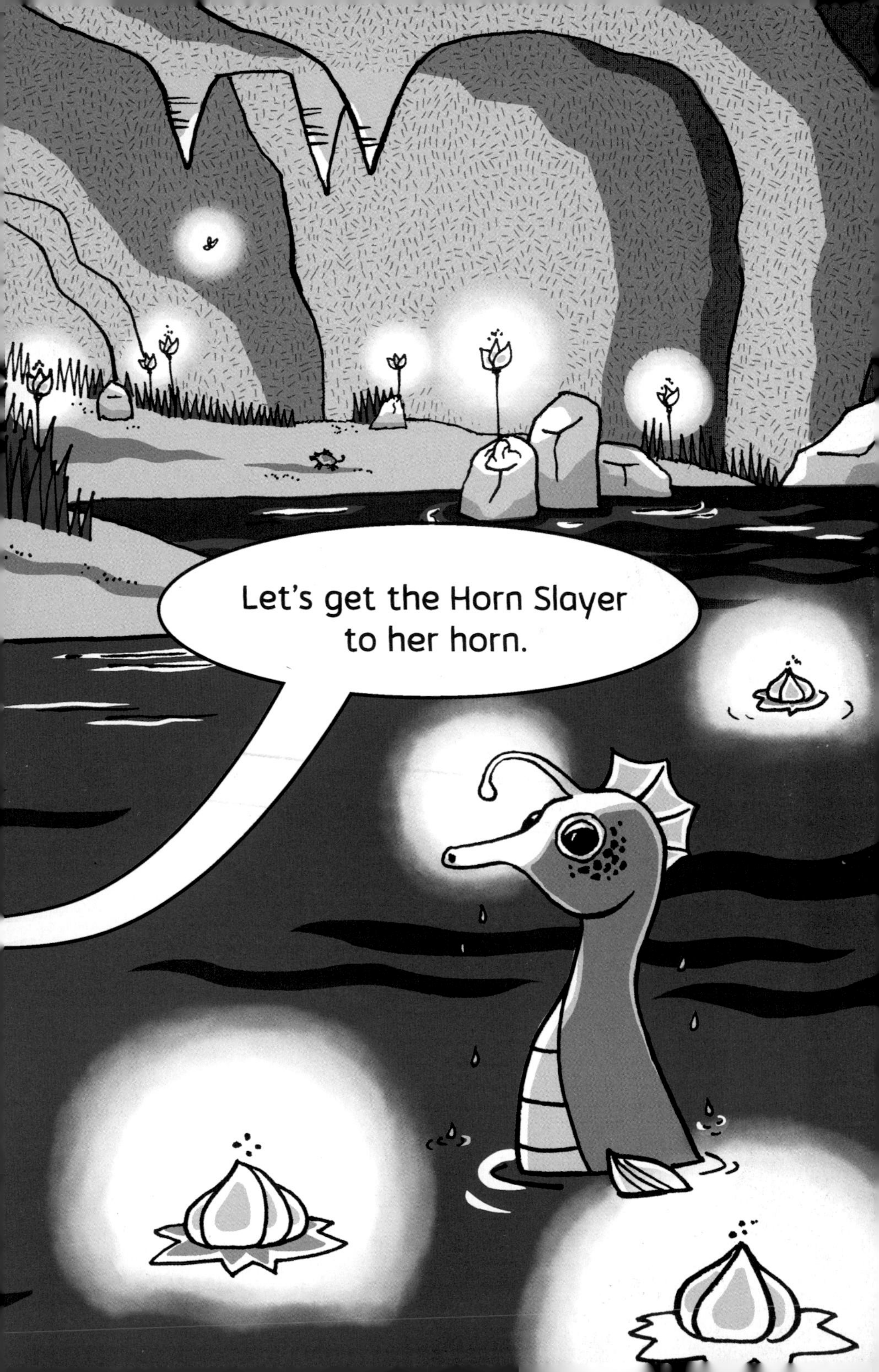
Let's get the Horn Slayer to her horn.

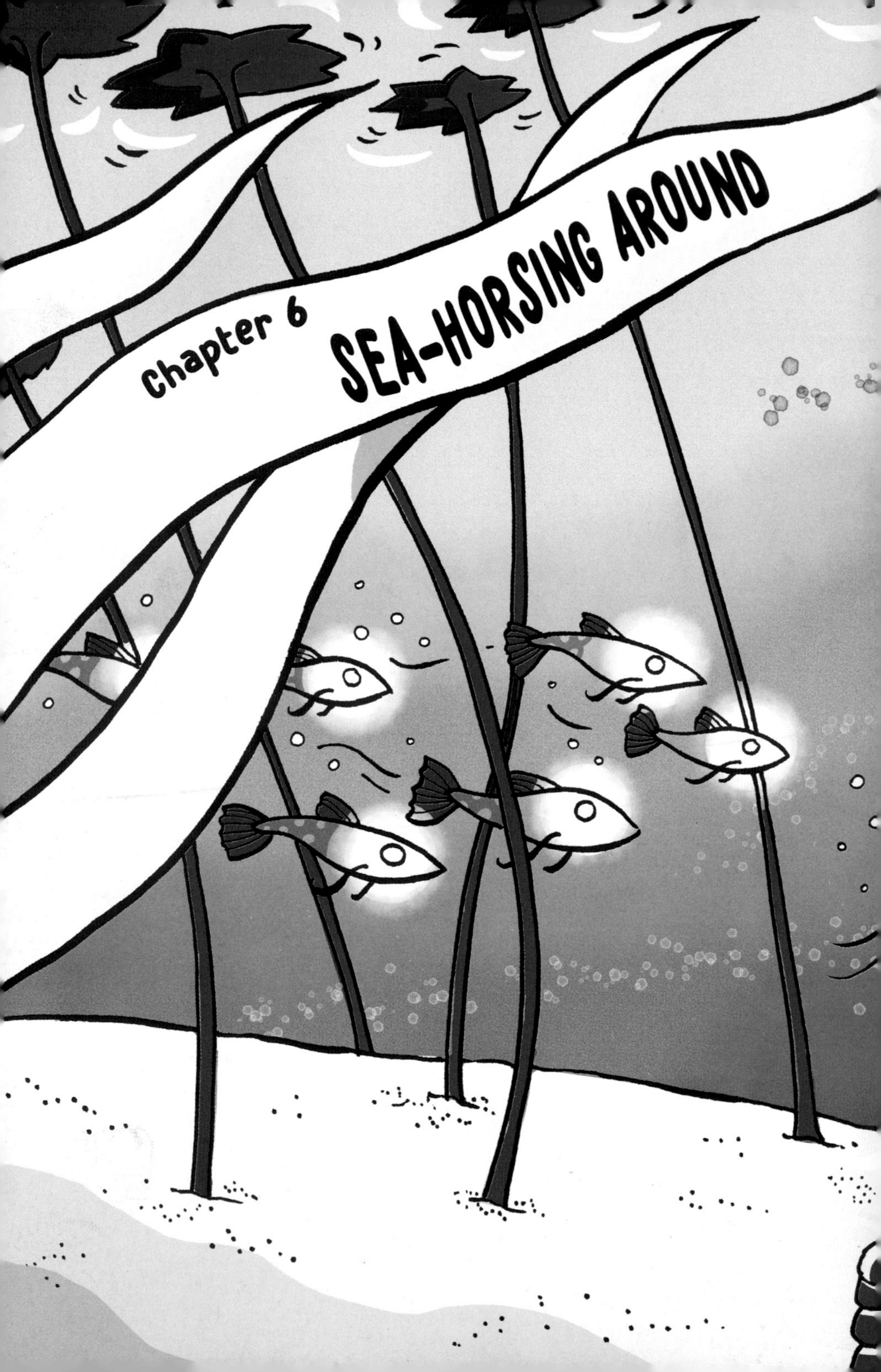
Chapter 6
SEA-HORSING AROUND

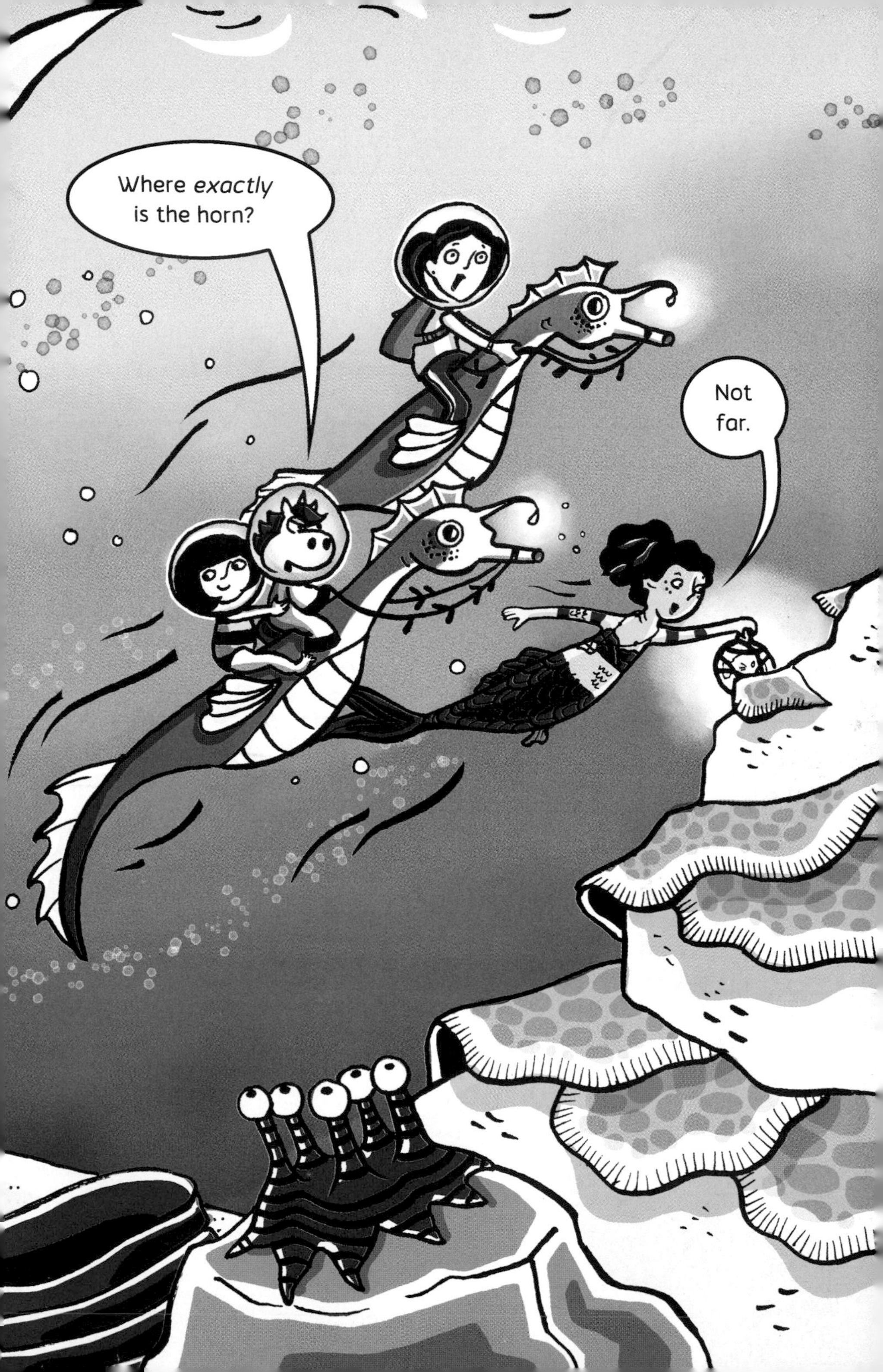
Where *exactly* is the horn?
Not far.

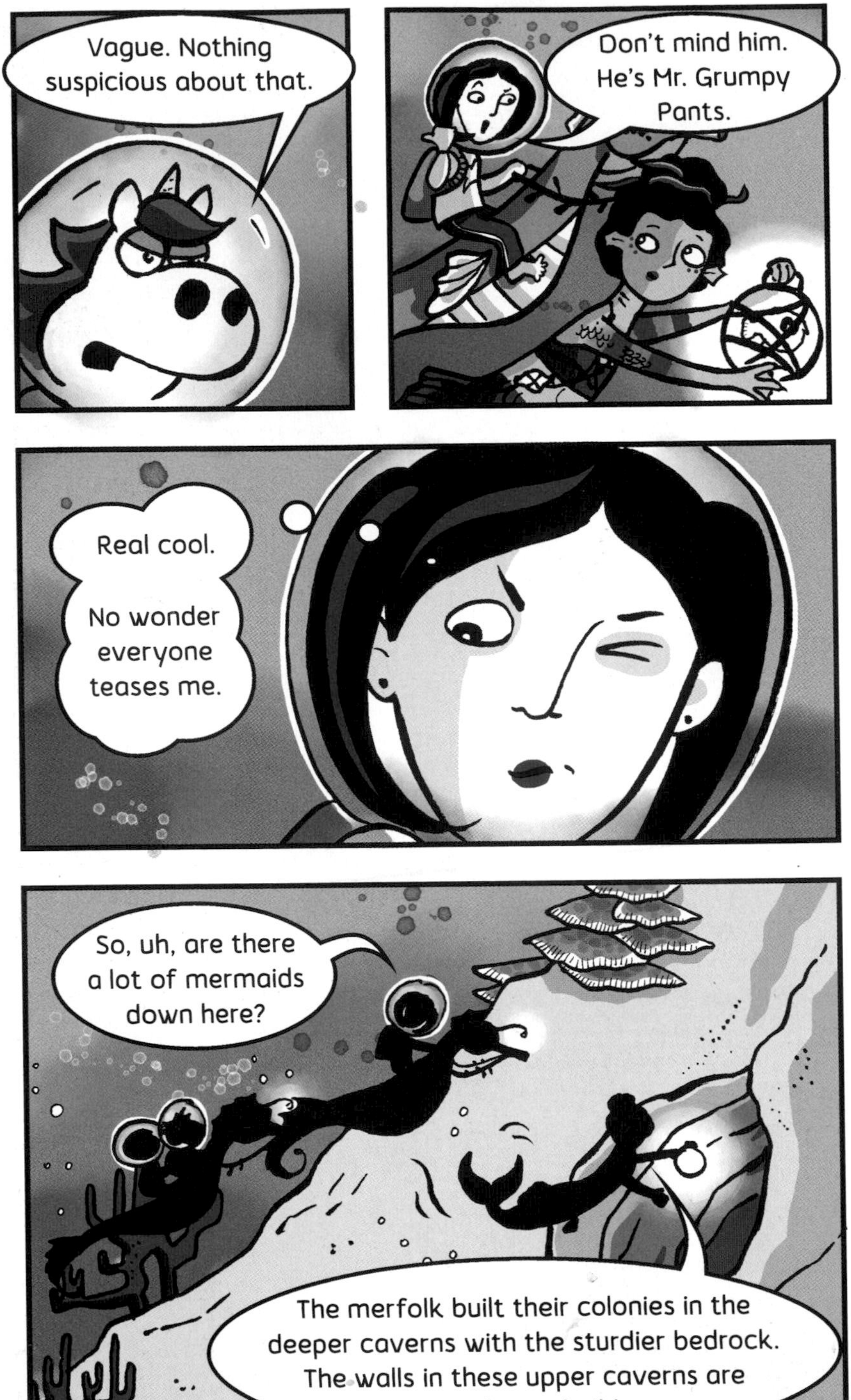
Vague. Nothing suspicious about that.
Don't mind him. He's Mr. Grumpy Pants.
Real cool.
No wonder everyone teases me.
So, uh, are there a lot of mermaids down here?
The merfolk built their colonies in the deeper caverns with the sturdier bedrock. The walls in these upper caverns are too thin to build.

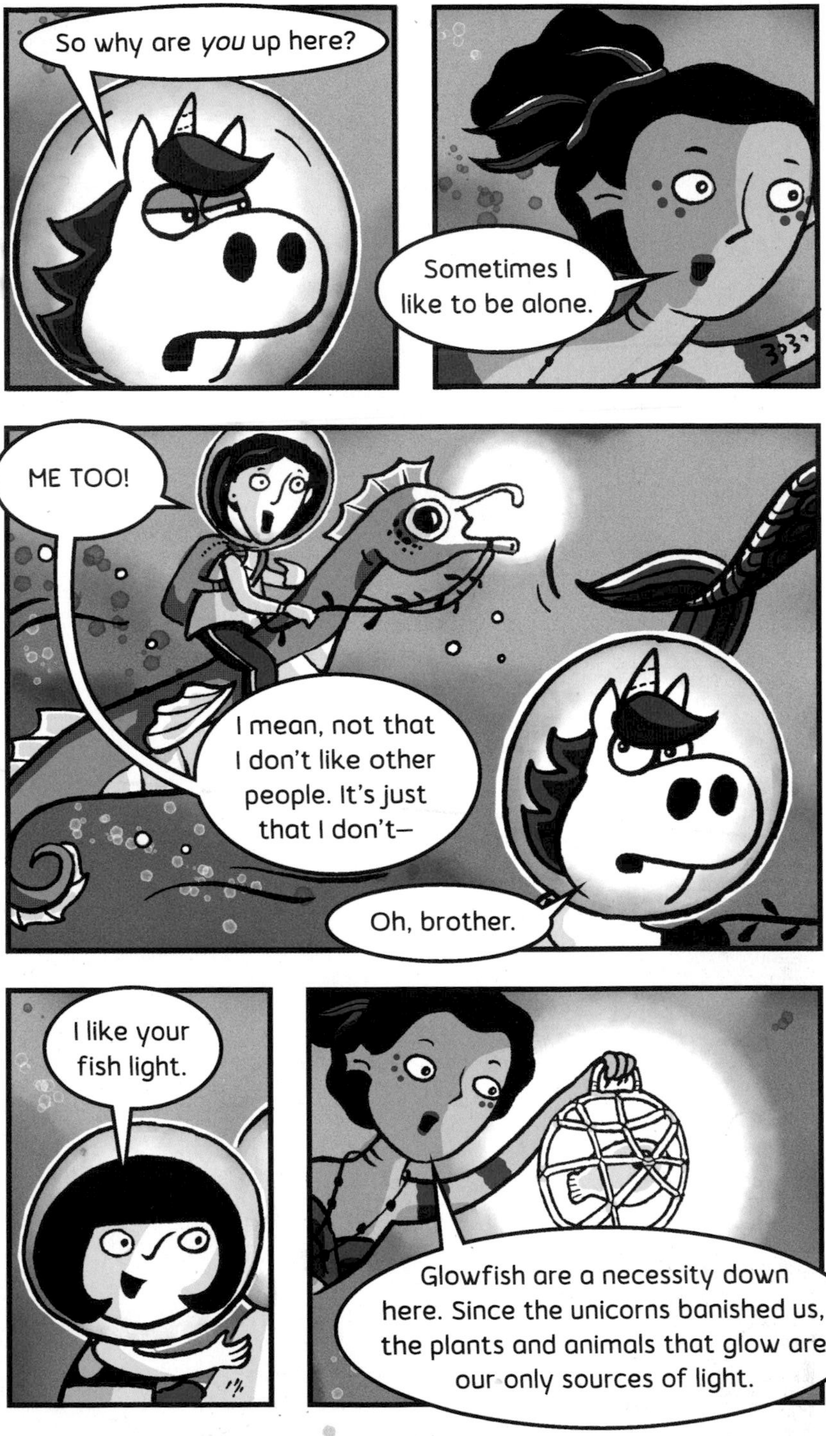
So why are *you* up here?
Sometimes I like to be alone.
ME TOO!
I mean, not that I don't like other people. It's just that I don't–
Oh, brother.
I like your fish light.
Glowfish are a necessity down here. Since the unicorns banished us, the plants and animals that glow are our only sources of light.

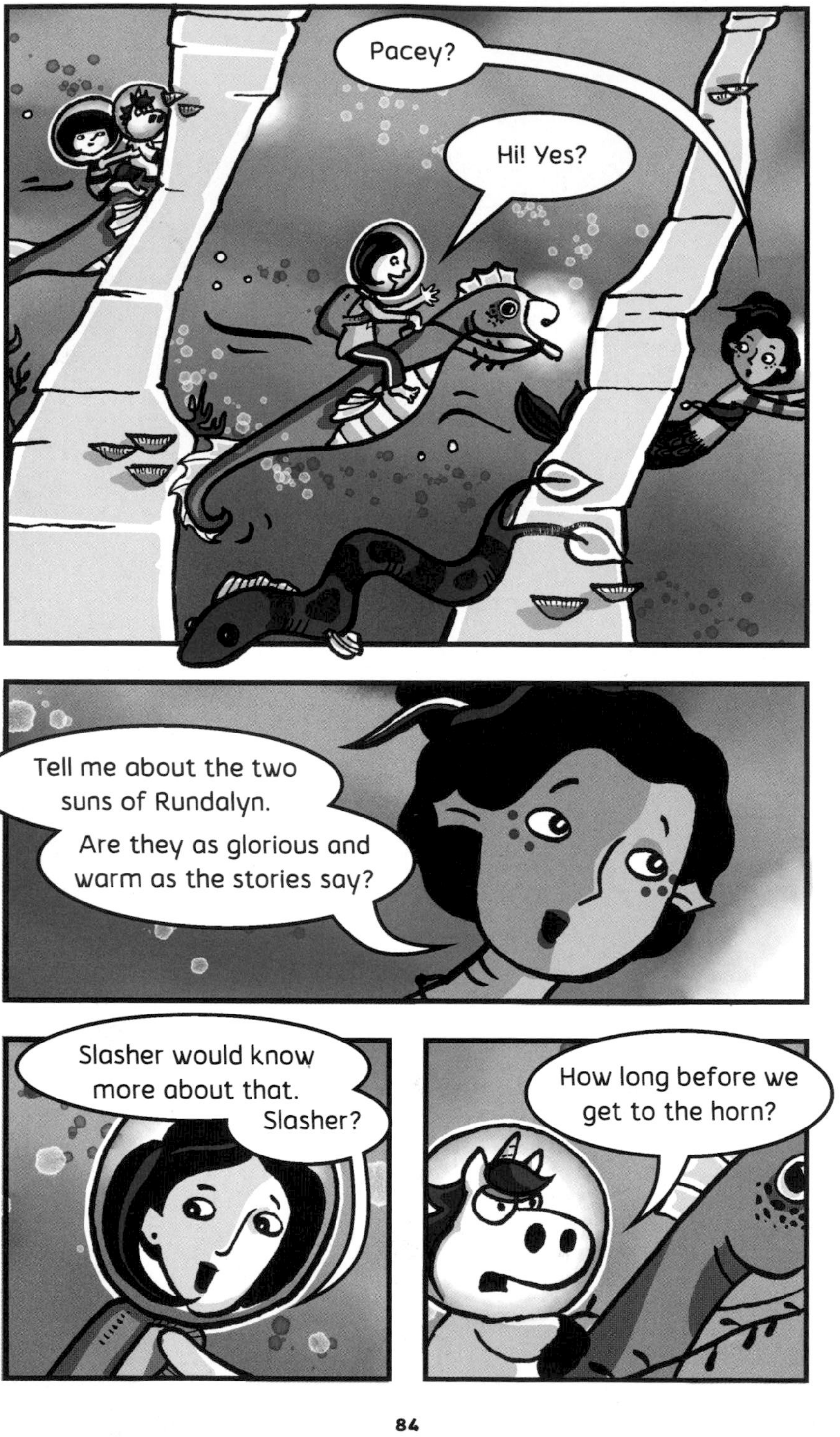
Pacey?
Hi! Yes?
Tell me about the two suns of Rundalyn.
Are they as glorious and warm as the stories say?
Slasher would know more about that.
Slasher?
How long before we get to the horn?

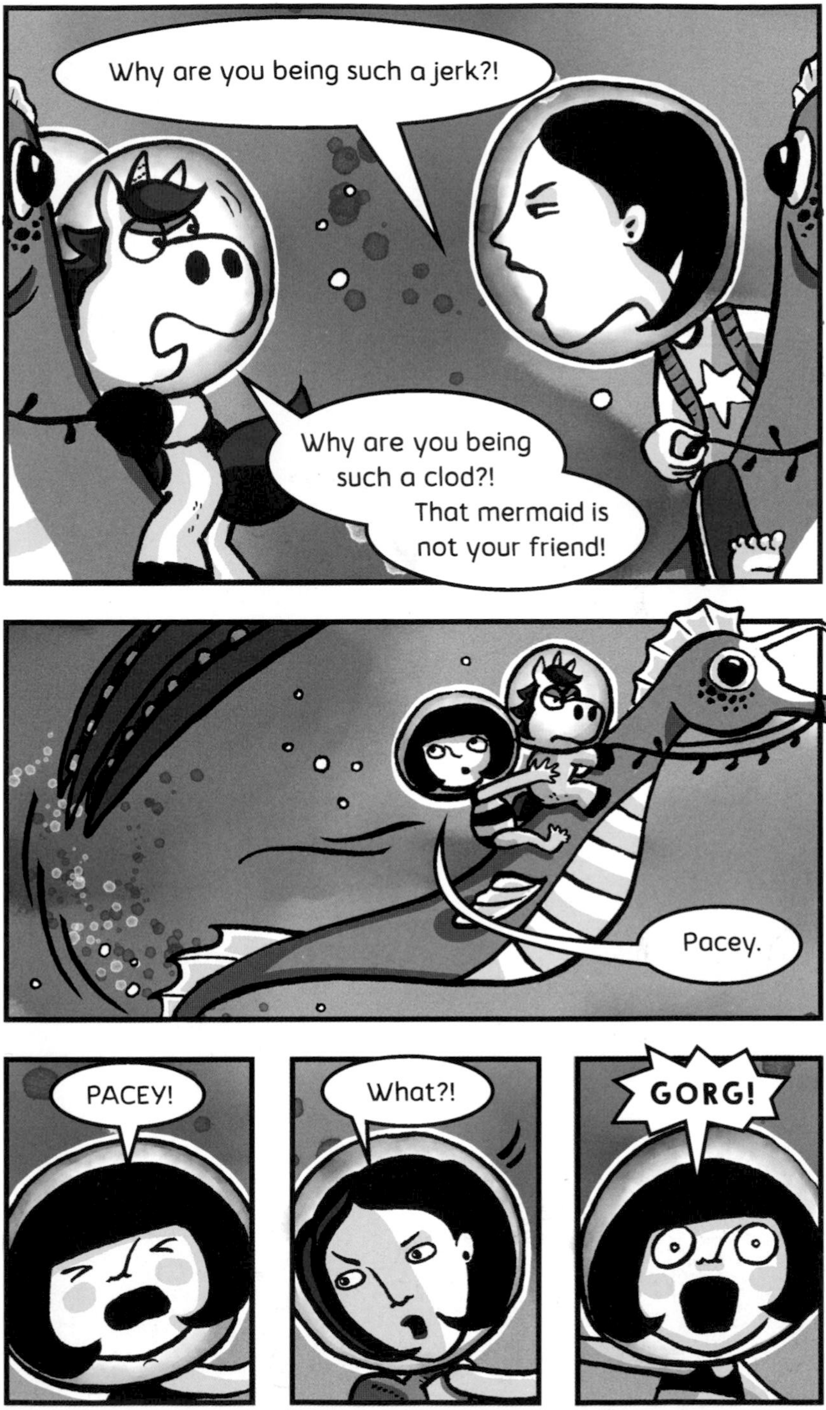
Why are you being such a jerk?!
Why are you being such a clod?! That mermaid is not your friend!
Pacey.
PACEY!
What?!
GORG!

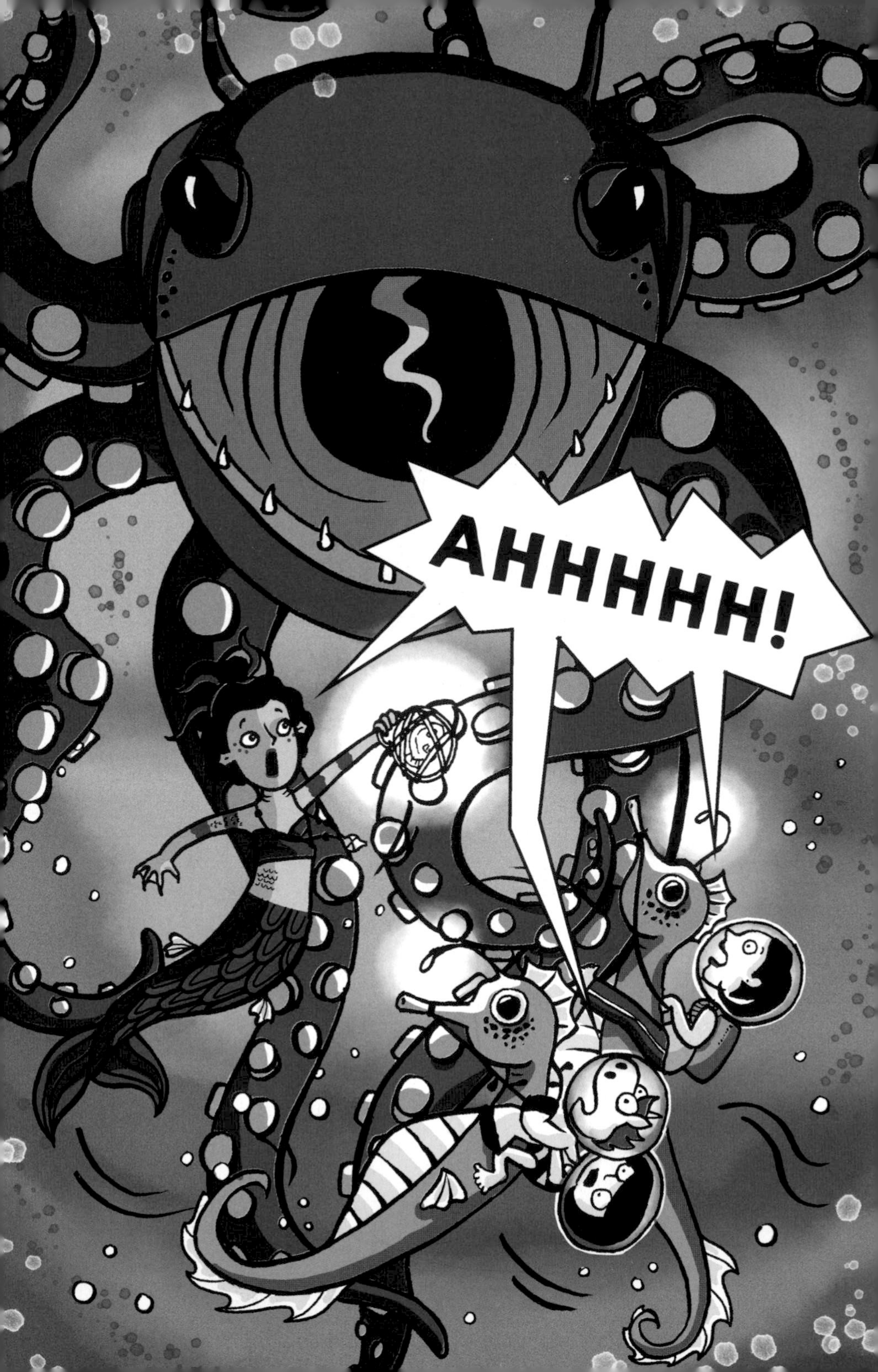
AHHHHH!

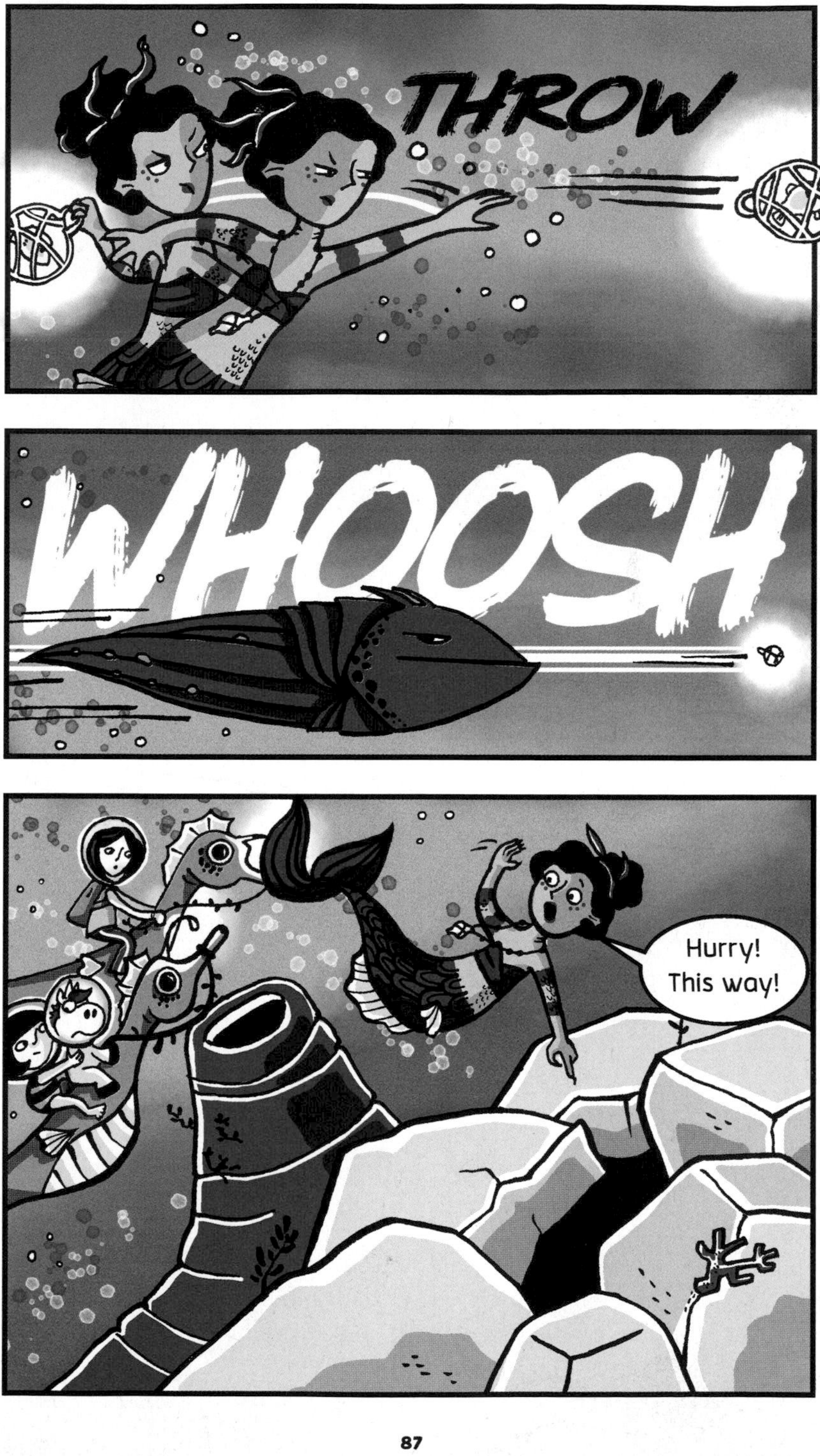
THROW
WHOOSH
Hurry! This way!

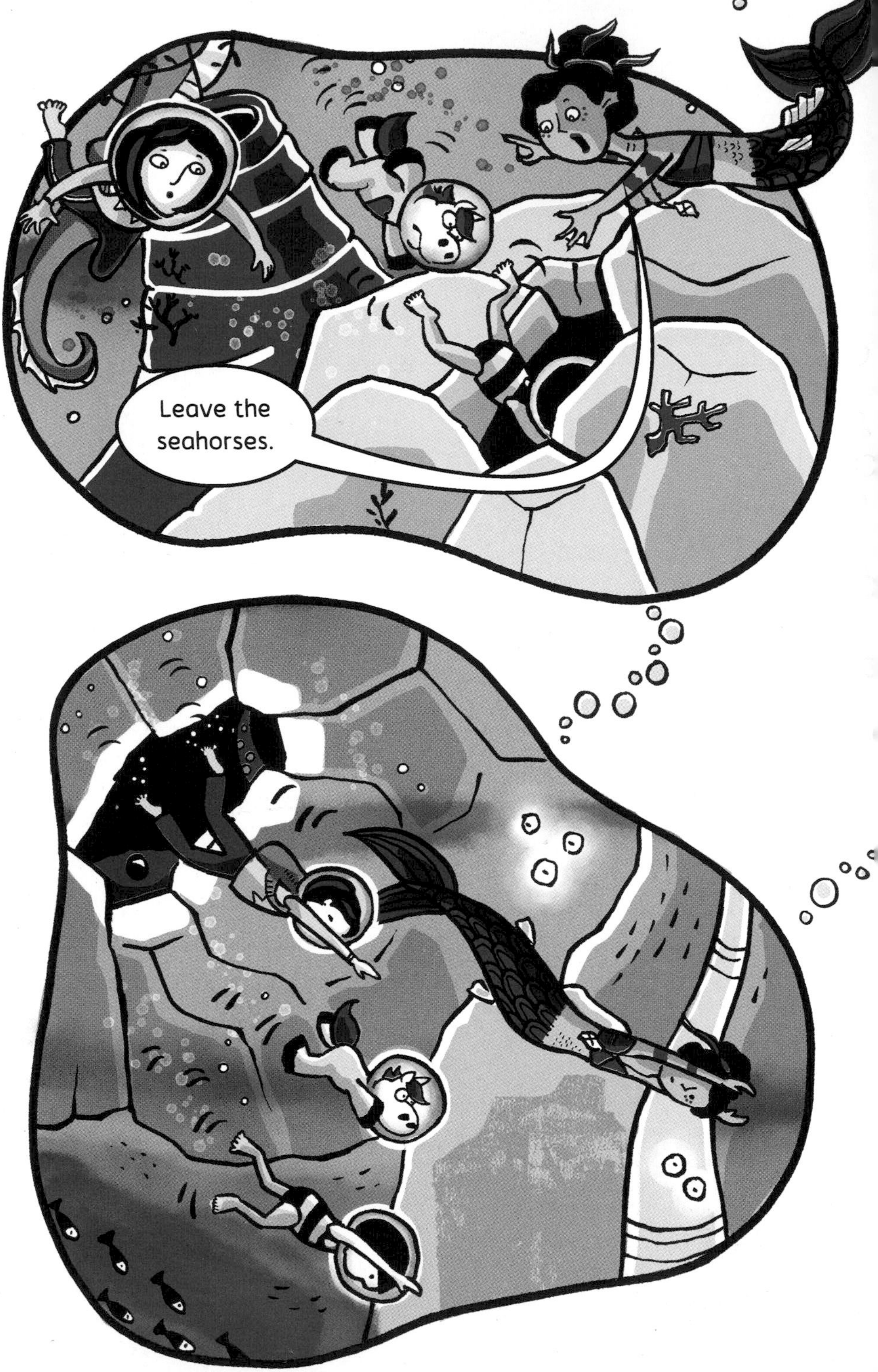
Leave the
seahorses.

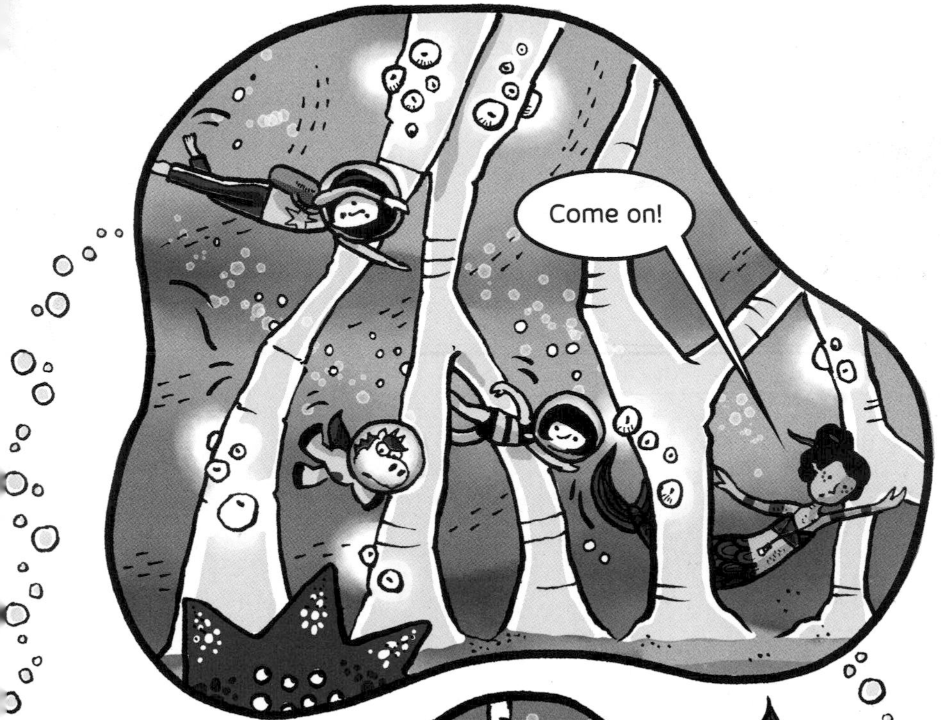
Come on!

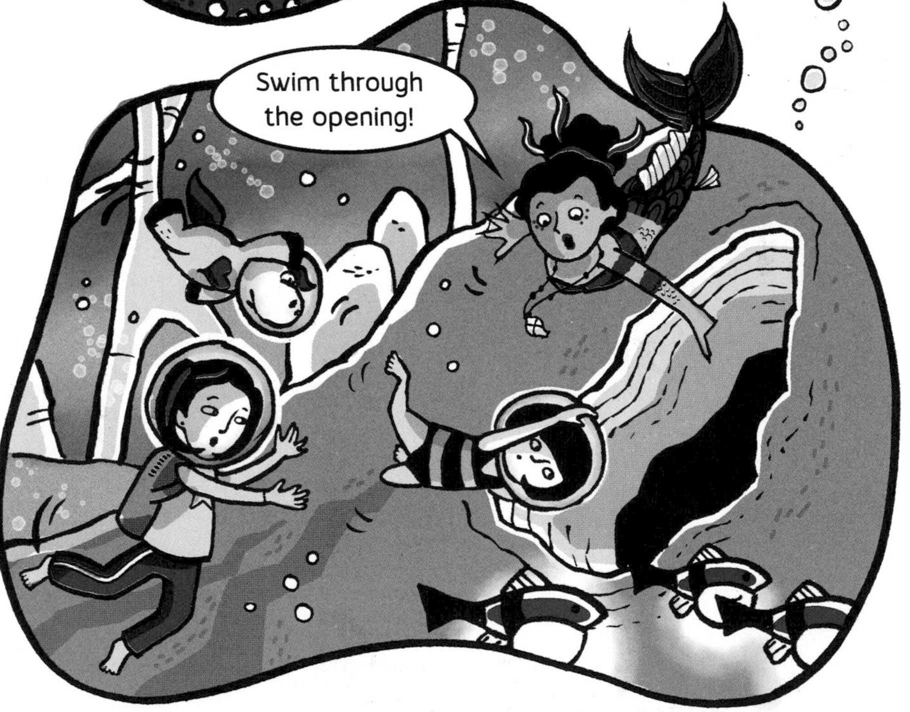
Swim through the opening!

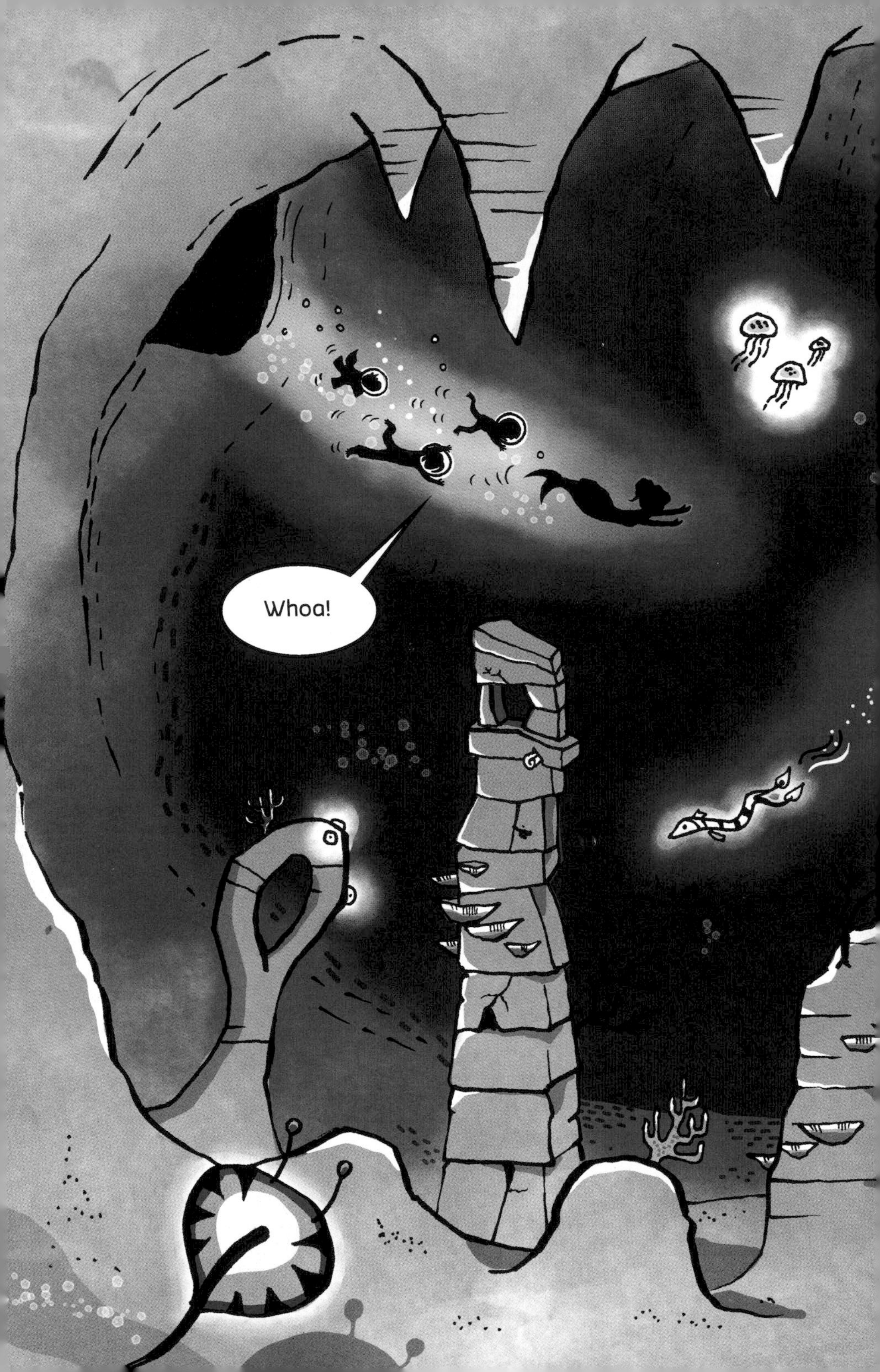
Whoa!

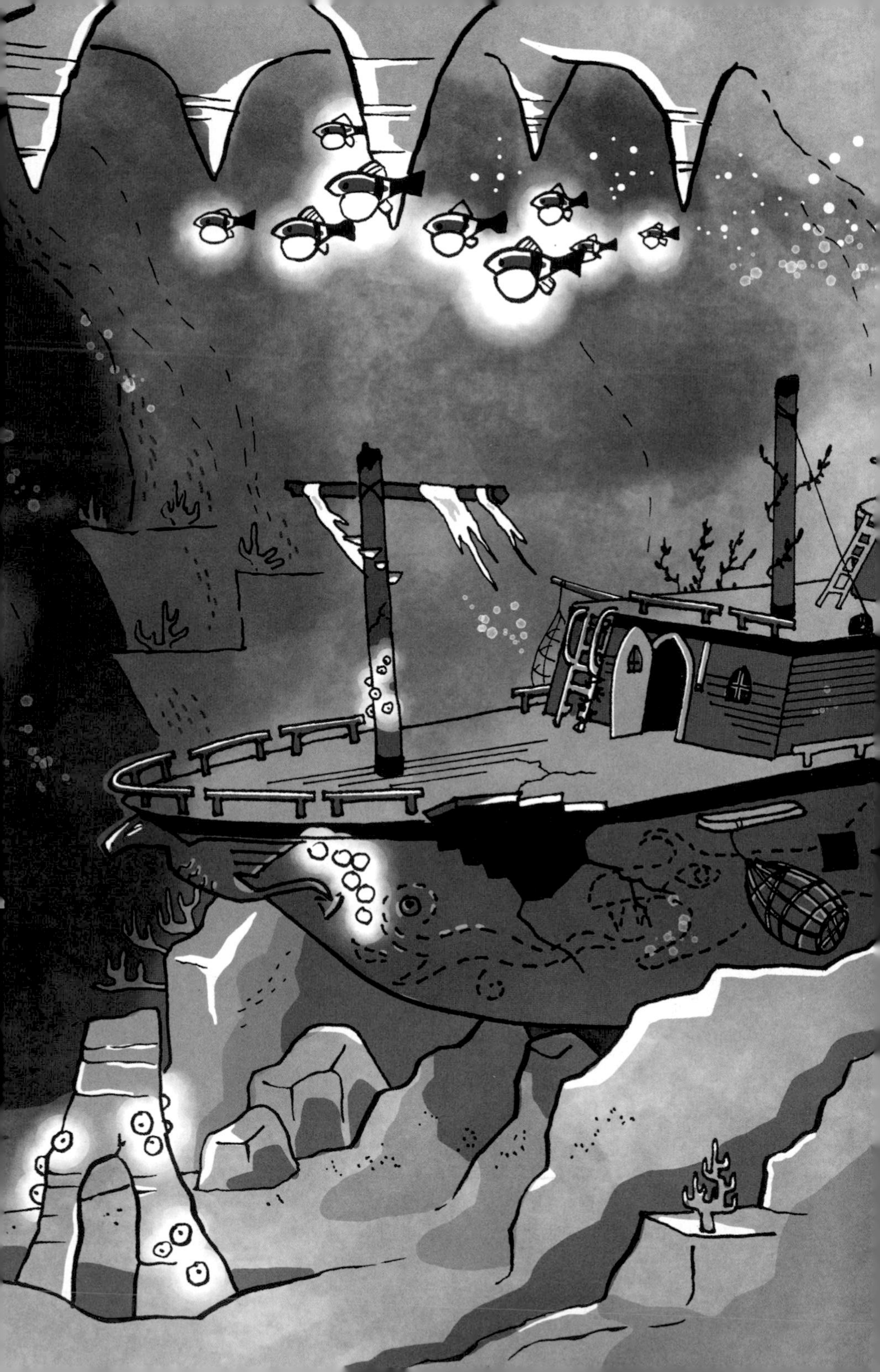

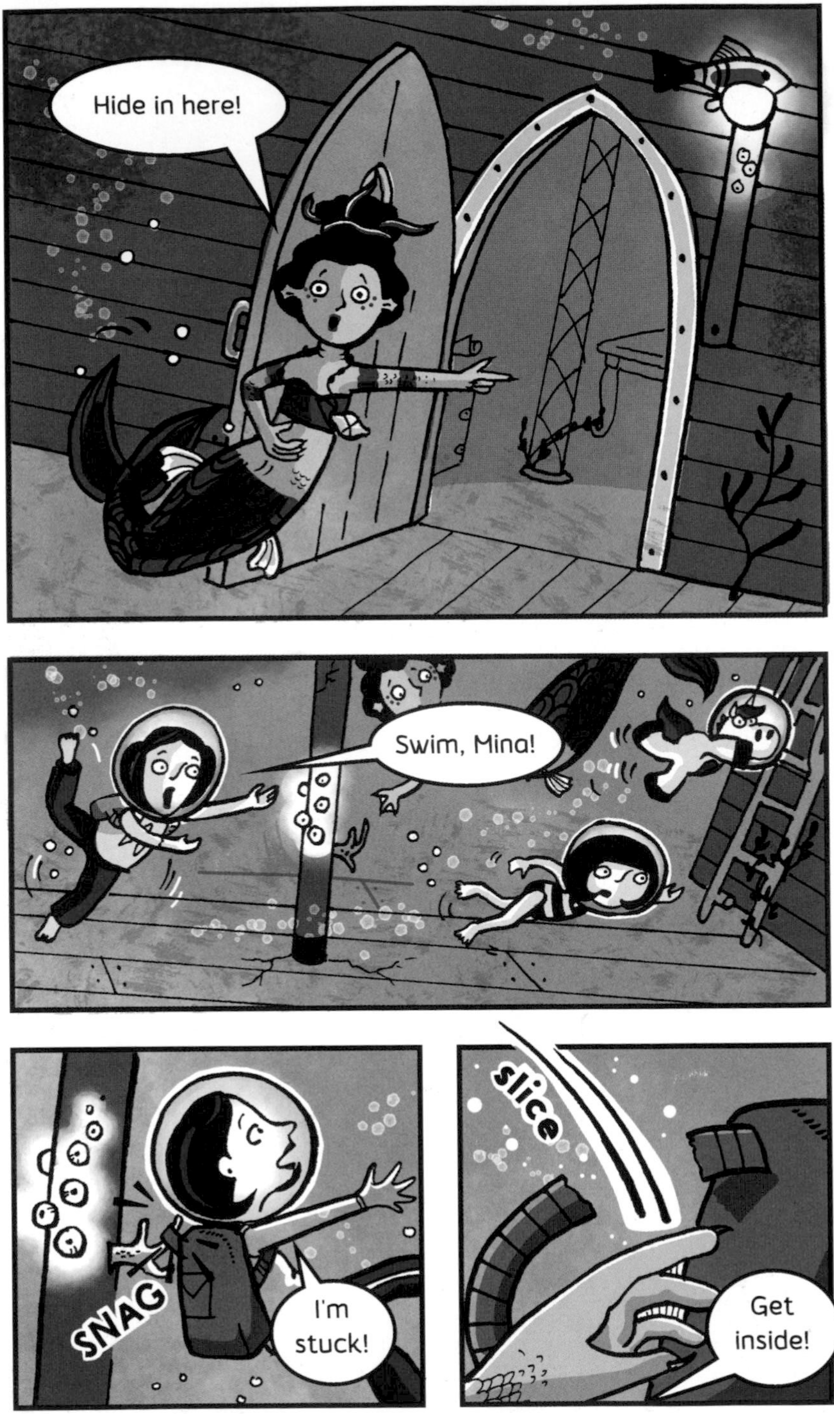
Hide in here!
Swim, Mina!
SNAG
I'm stuck!
slice
Get inside!

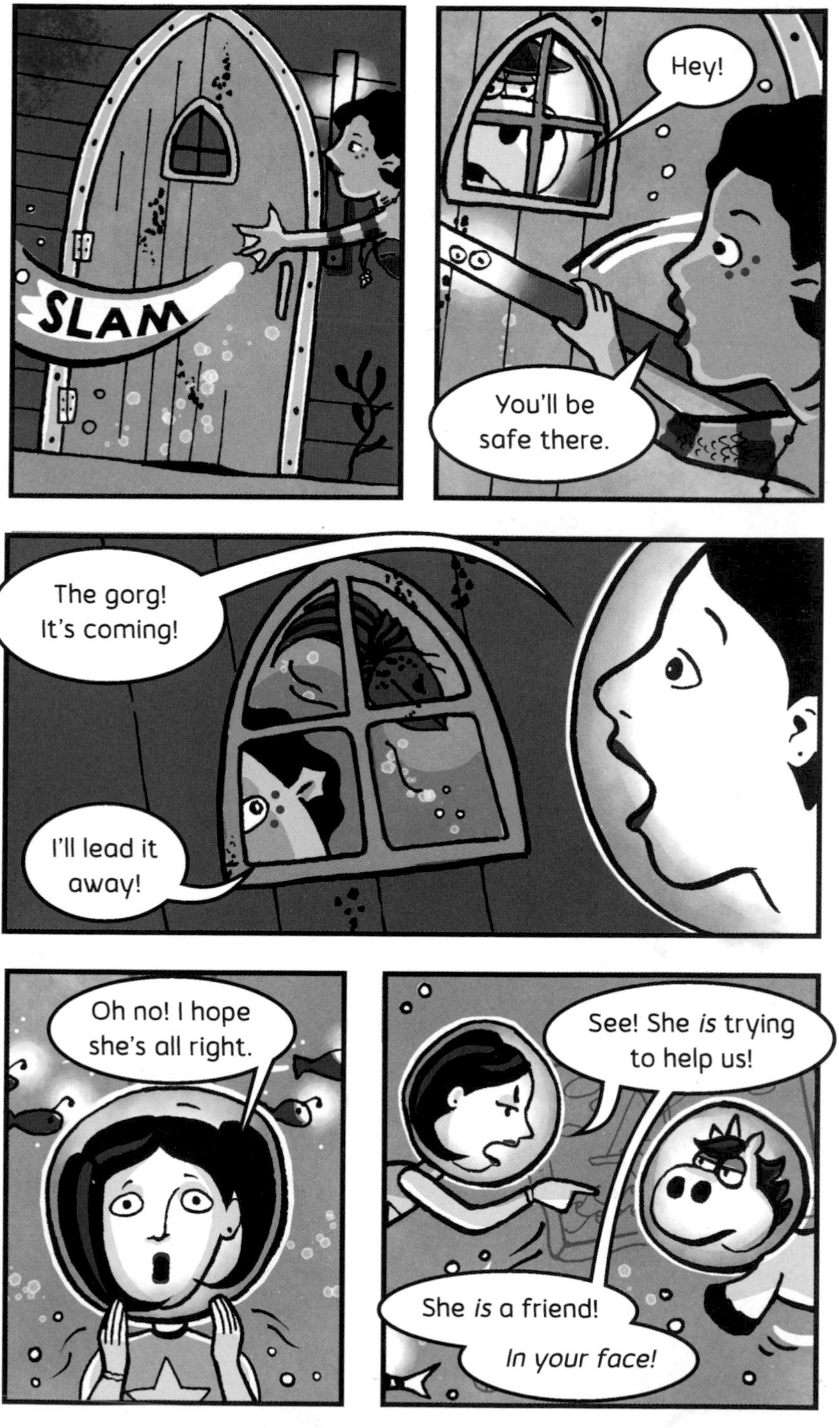
SLAM
Hey!
You'll be safe there.
The gorg! It's coming!
I'll lead it away!
Oh no! I hope she's all right.
See! She *is* trying to help us!
She *is* a friend!
In your face!

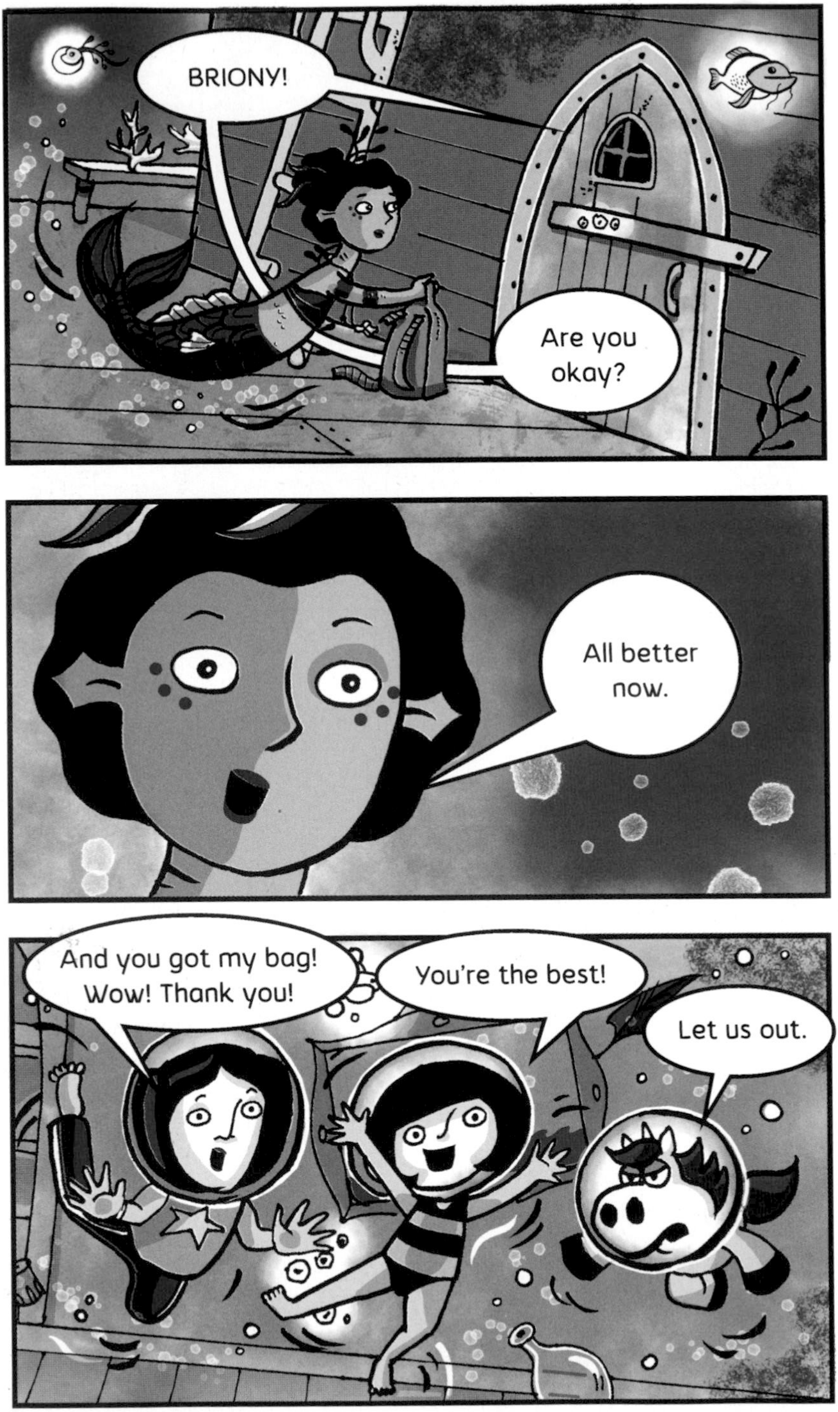

BRIONY!
Are you okay?
All better now.
And you got my bag! Wow! Thank you!
You're the best!
Let us out.

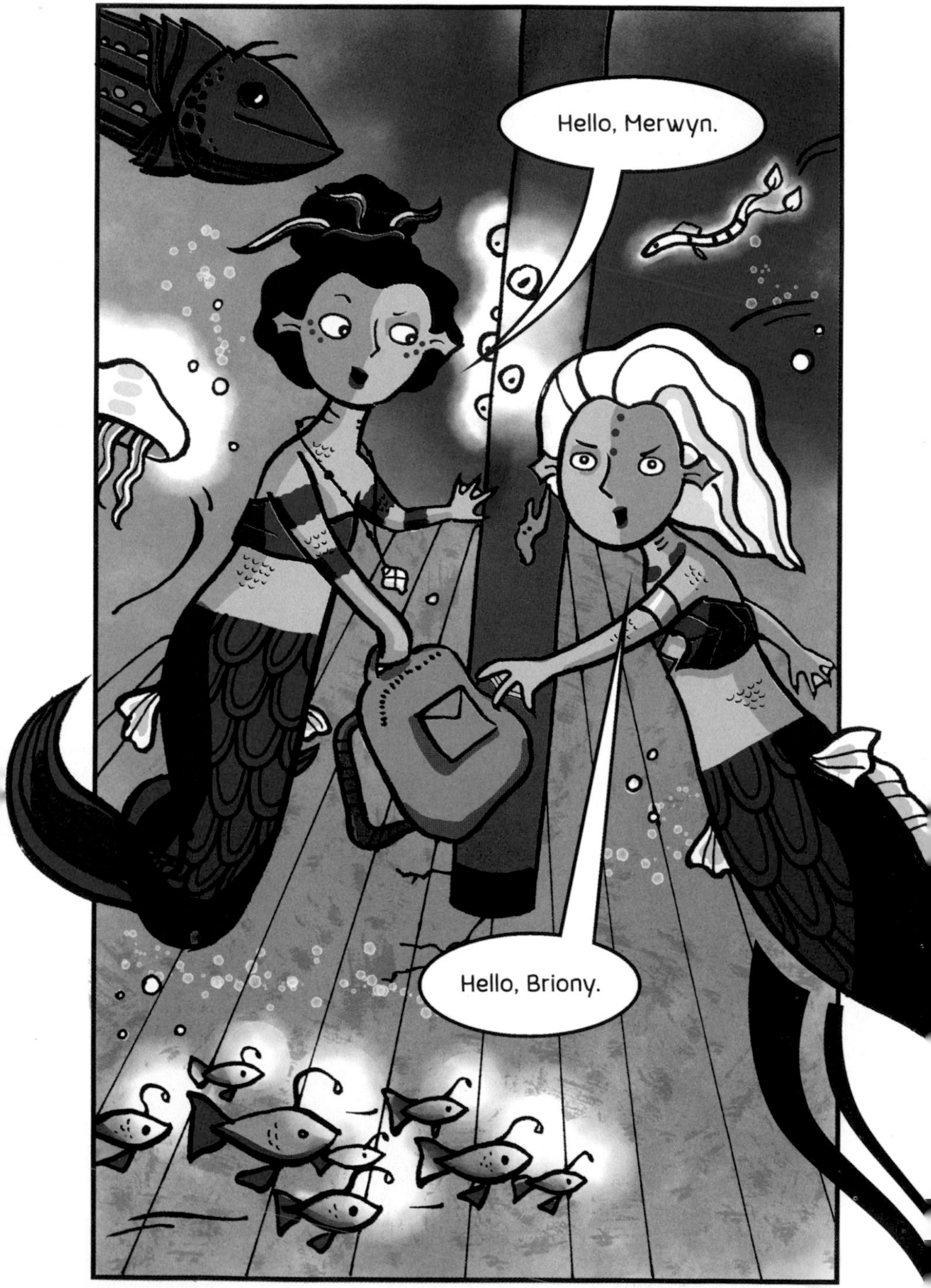
Hello, Merwyn.
Hello, Briony.

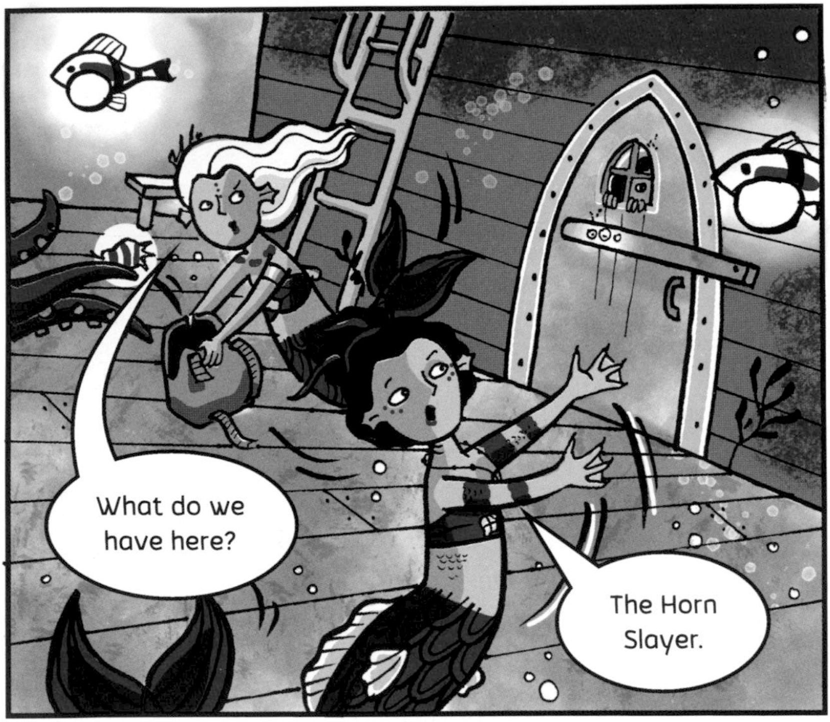
What do we have here?
The Horn Slayer.

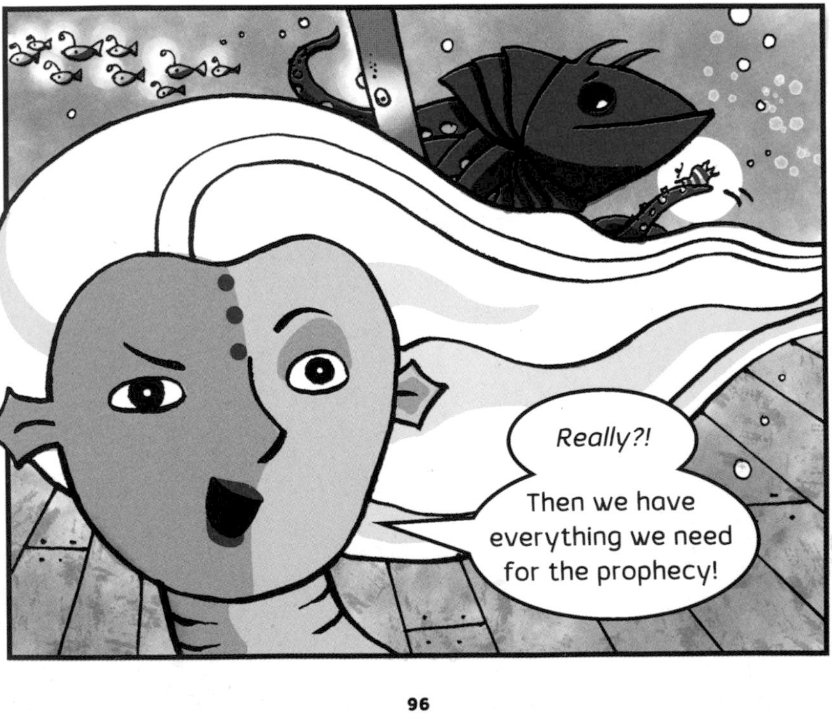
Really?!
Then we have everything we need for the prophecy!

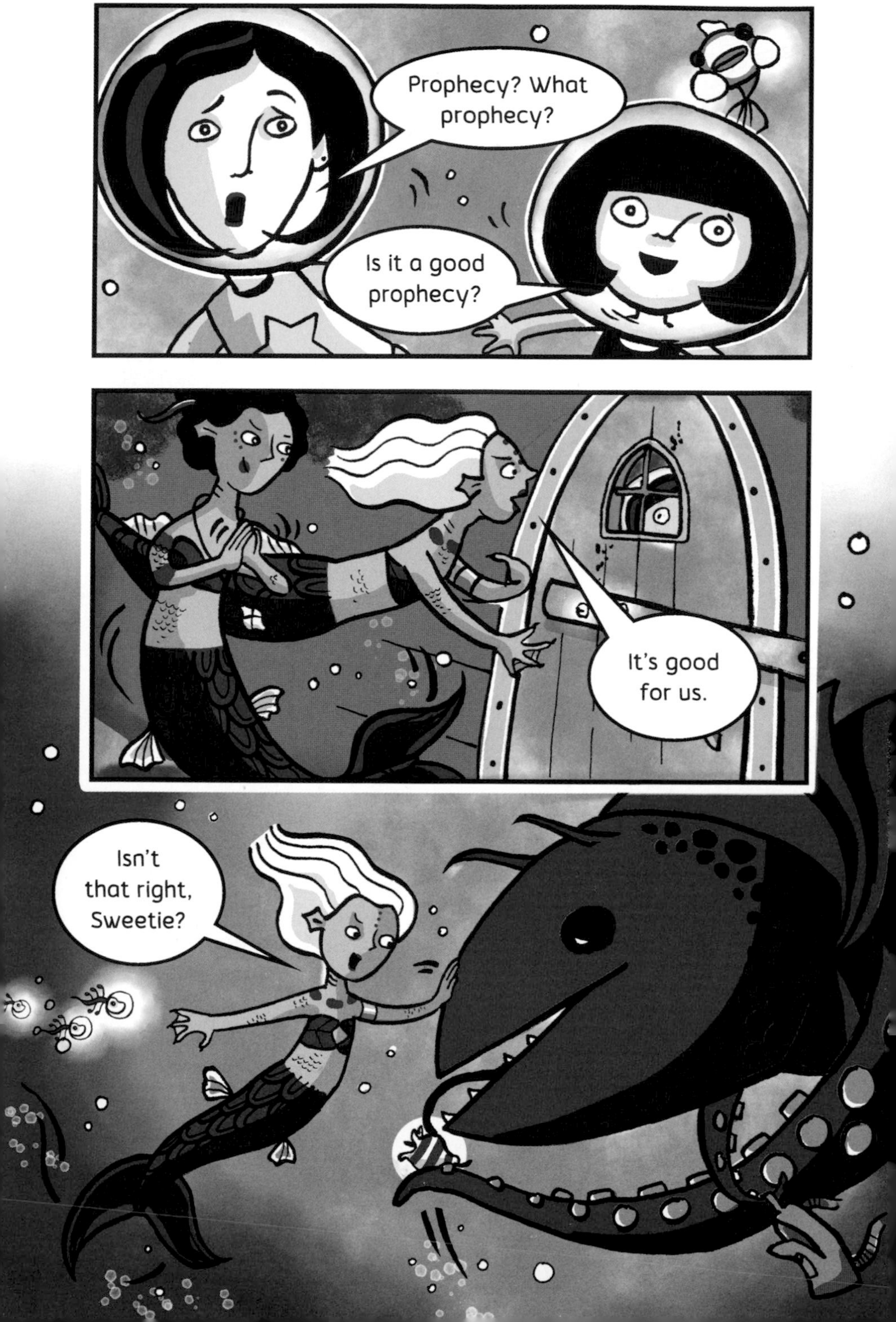
Prophecy? What prophecy?
Is it a good prophecy?
It's good for us.
Isn't that right, Sweetie?

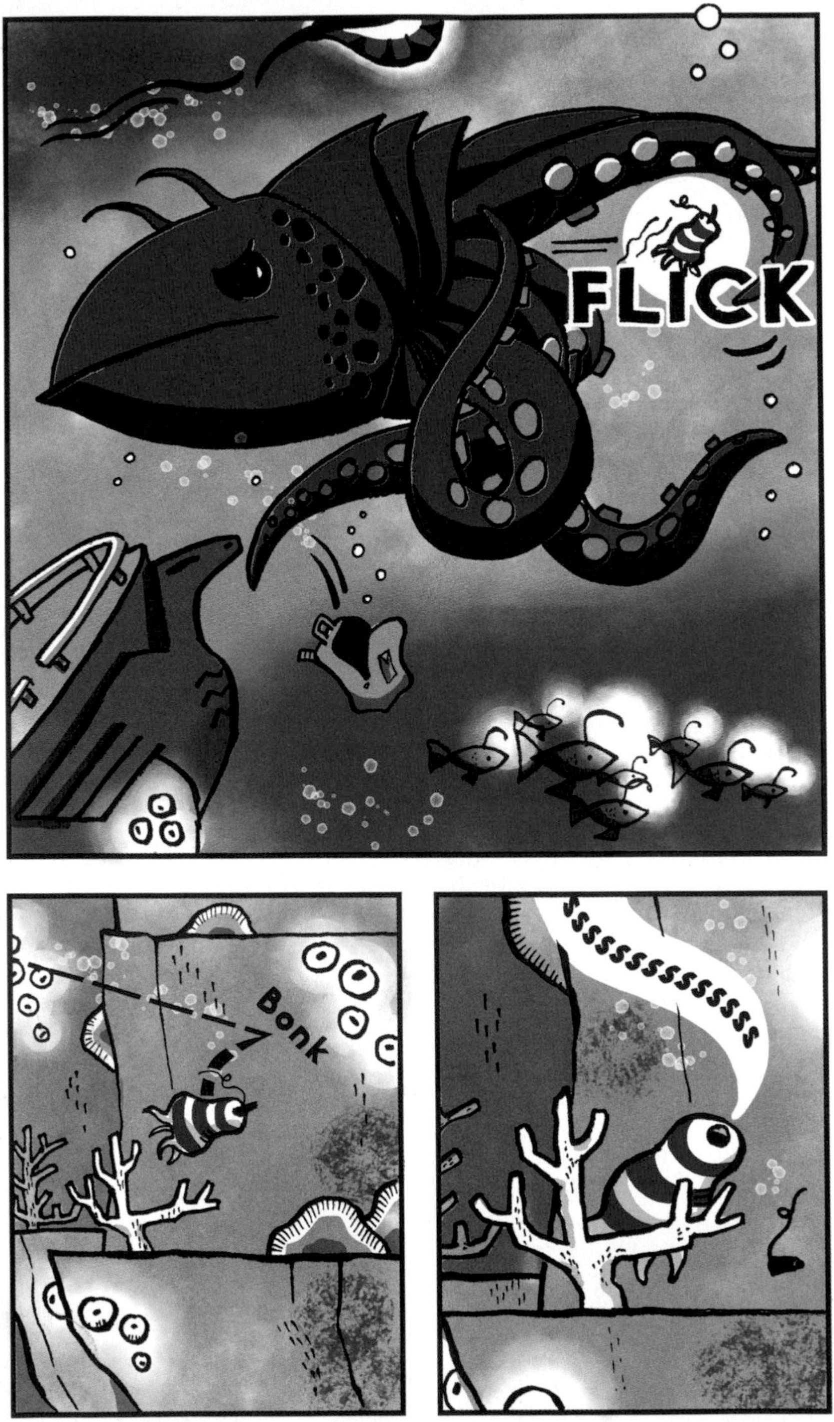
FLICK
Bonk
SSSSSSSSSSSSSSS

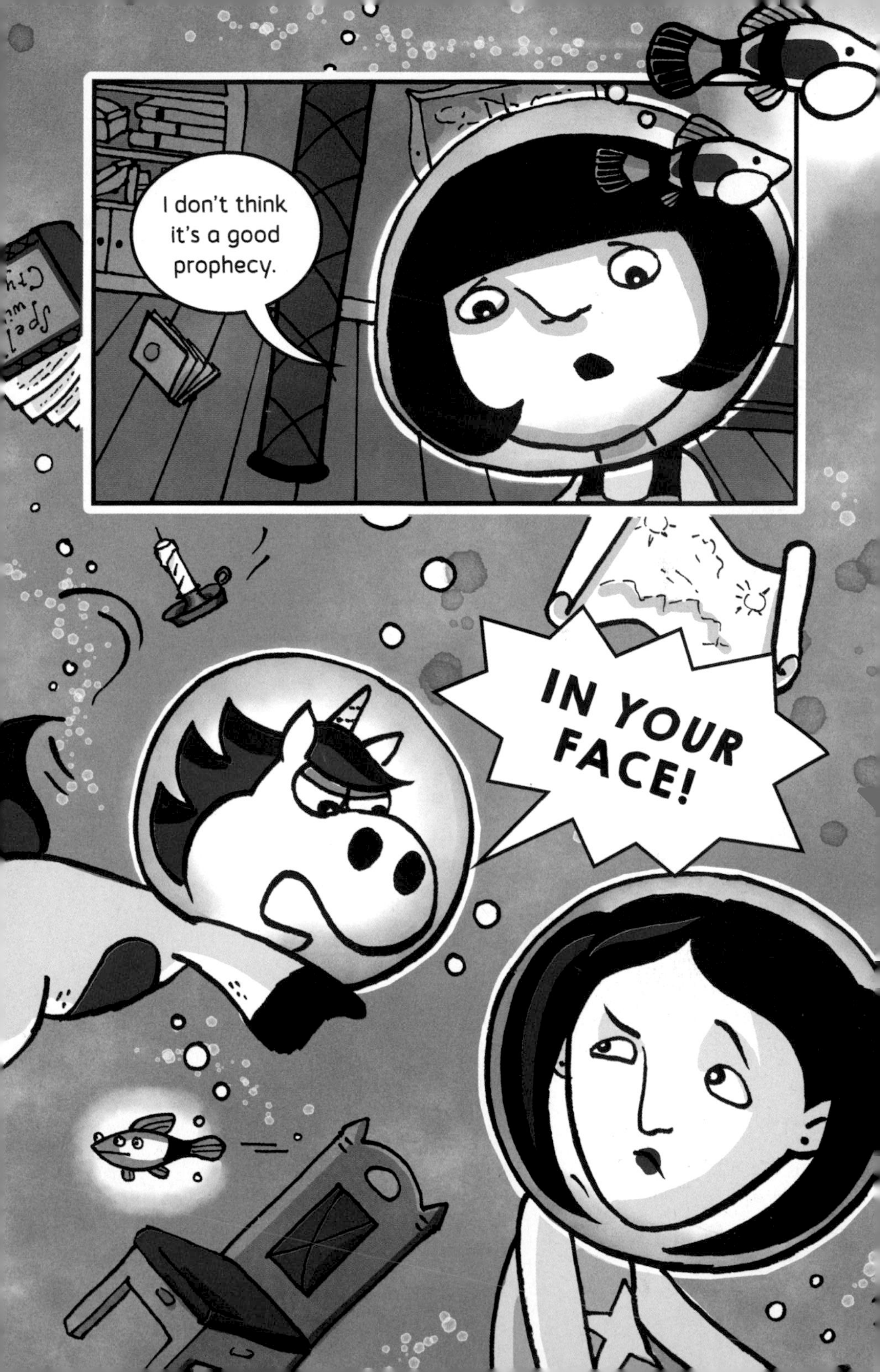
I don't think it's a good prophecy.
IN YOUR FACE!

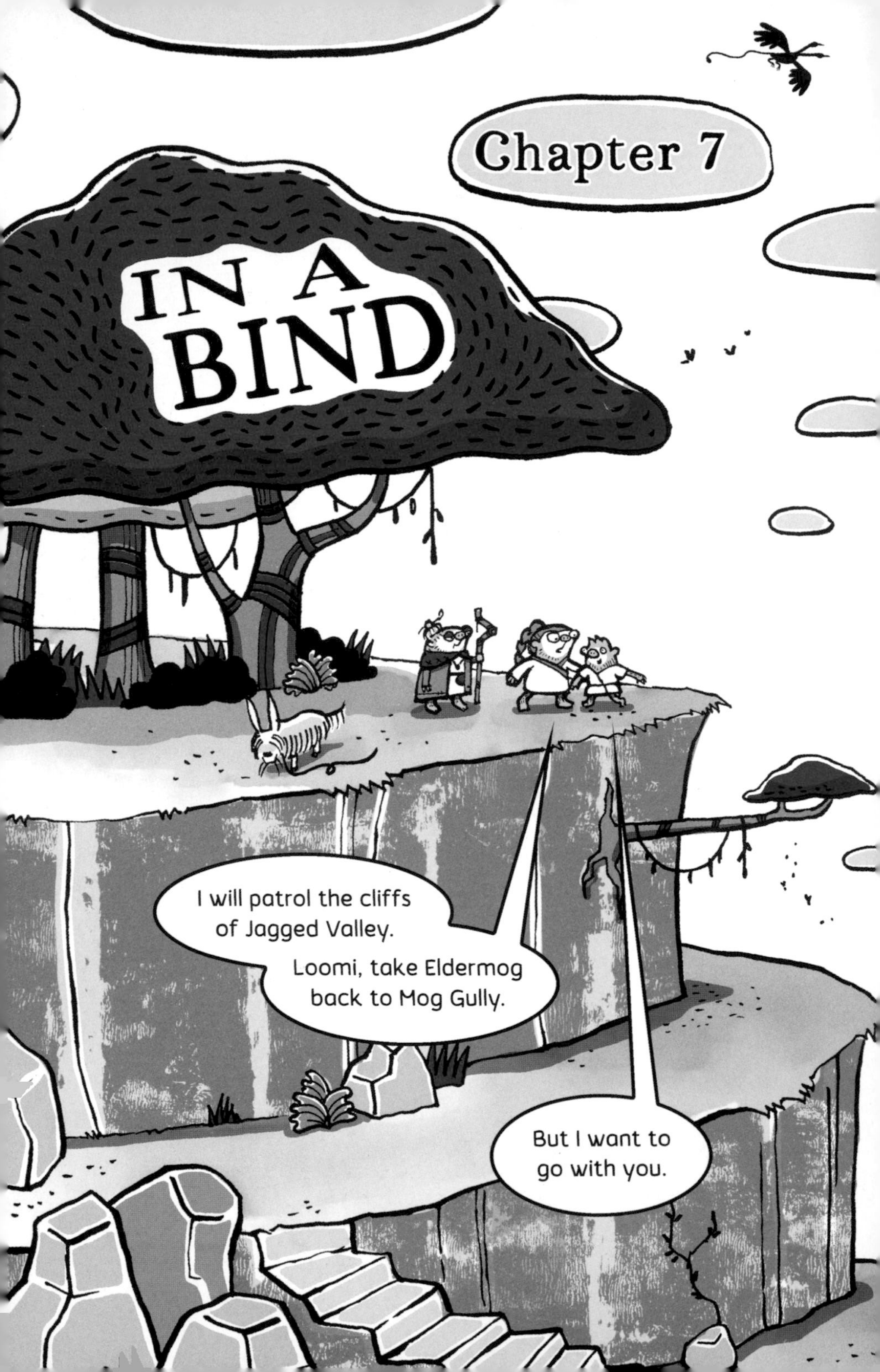
Chapter 7
IN A BIND
I will patrol the cliffs of Jagged Valley.
Loomi, take Eldermog back to Mog Gully.
But I want to go with you.

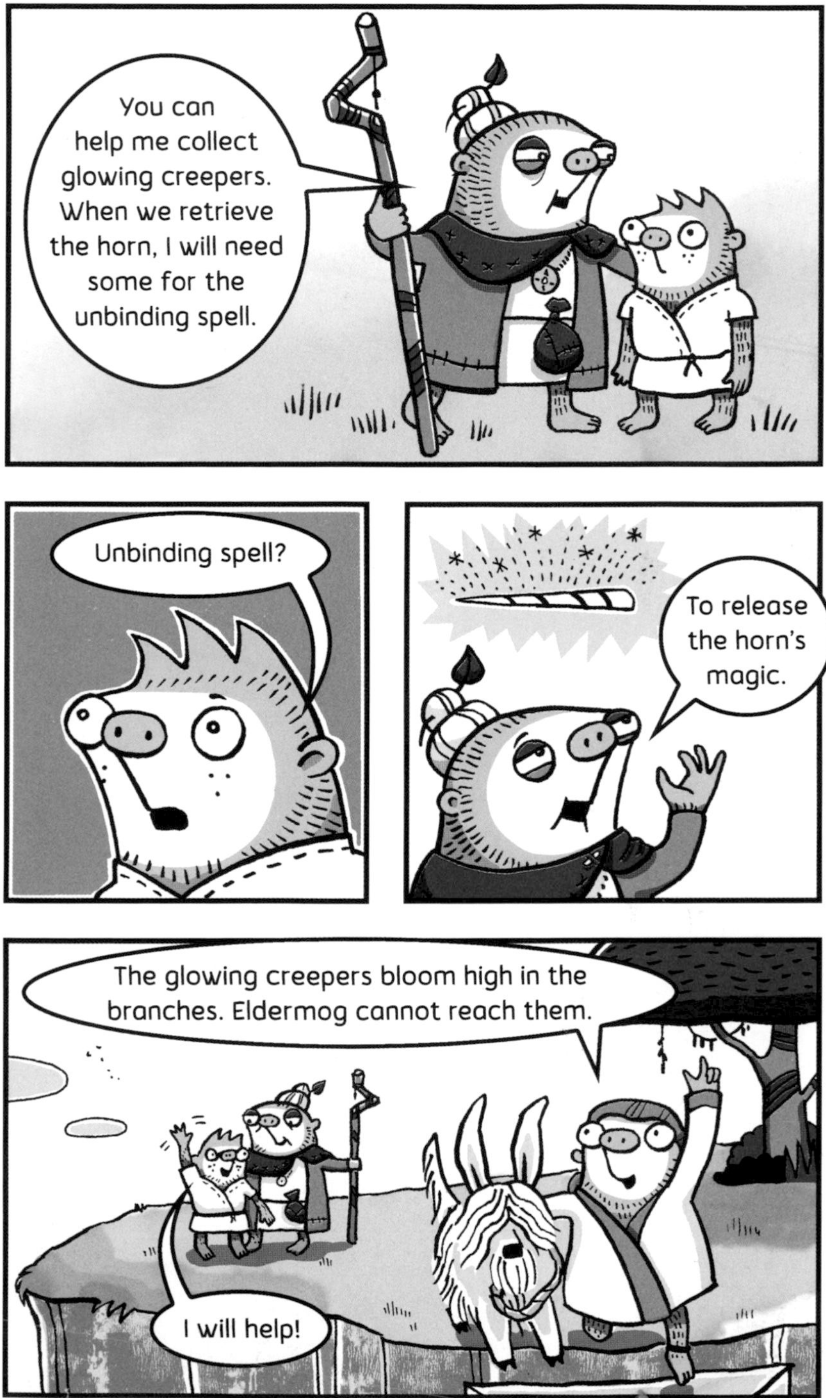
You can help me collect glowing creepers. When we retrieve the horn, I will need some for the unbinding spell.
Unbinding spell?
To release the horn's magic.
The glowing creepers bloom high in the branches. Eldermog cannot reach them.
I will help!

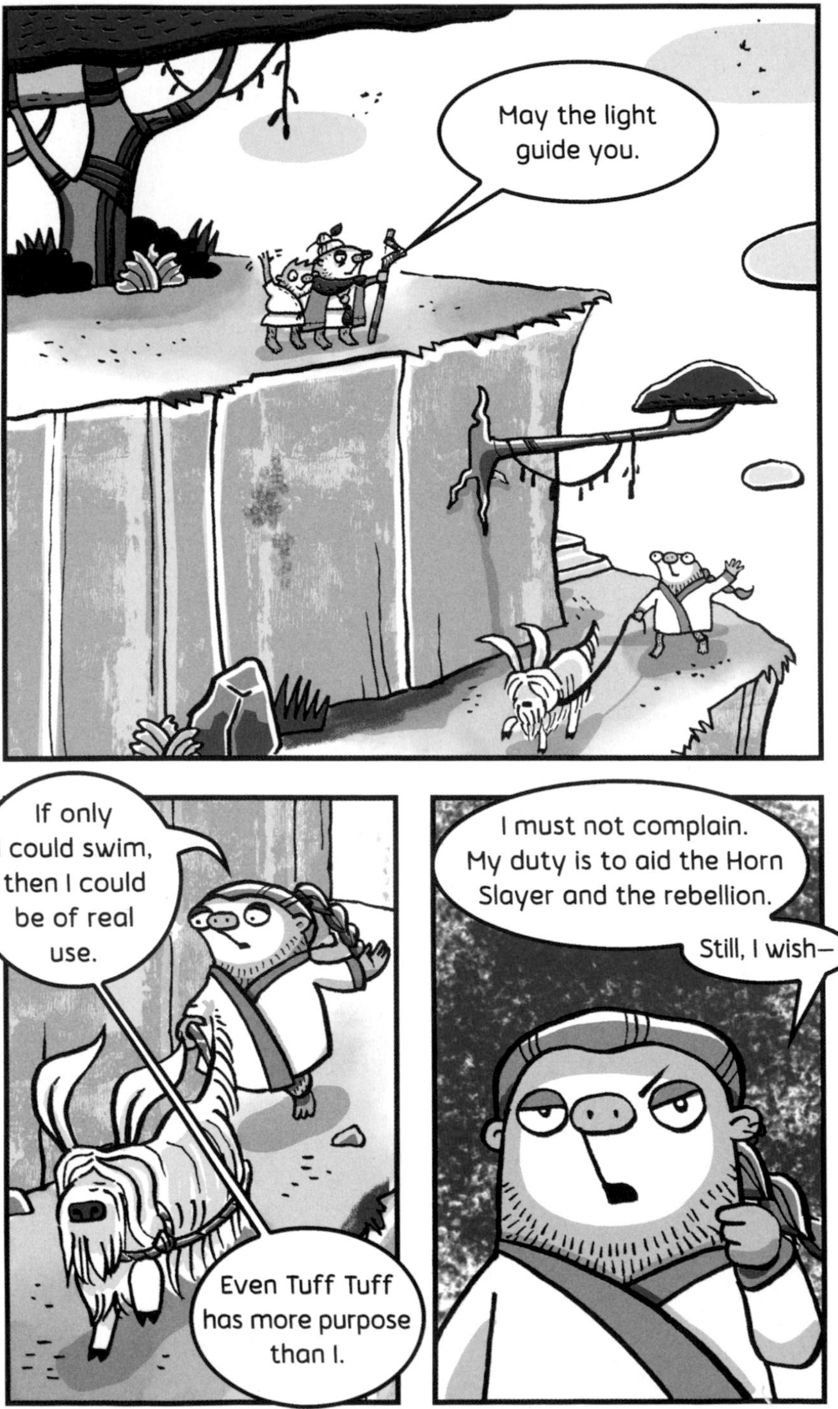
May the light guide you.
If only I could swim, then I could be of real use.
Even Tuff Tuff has more purpose than I.
I must not complain. My duty is to aid the Horn Slayer and the rebellion.
Still, I wish—

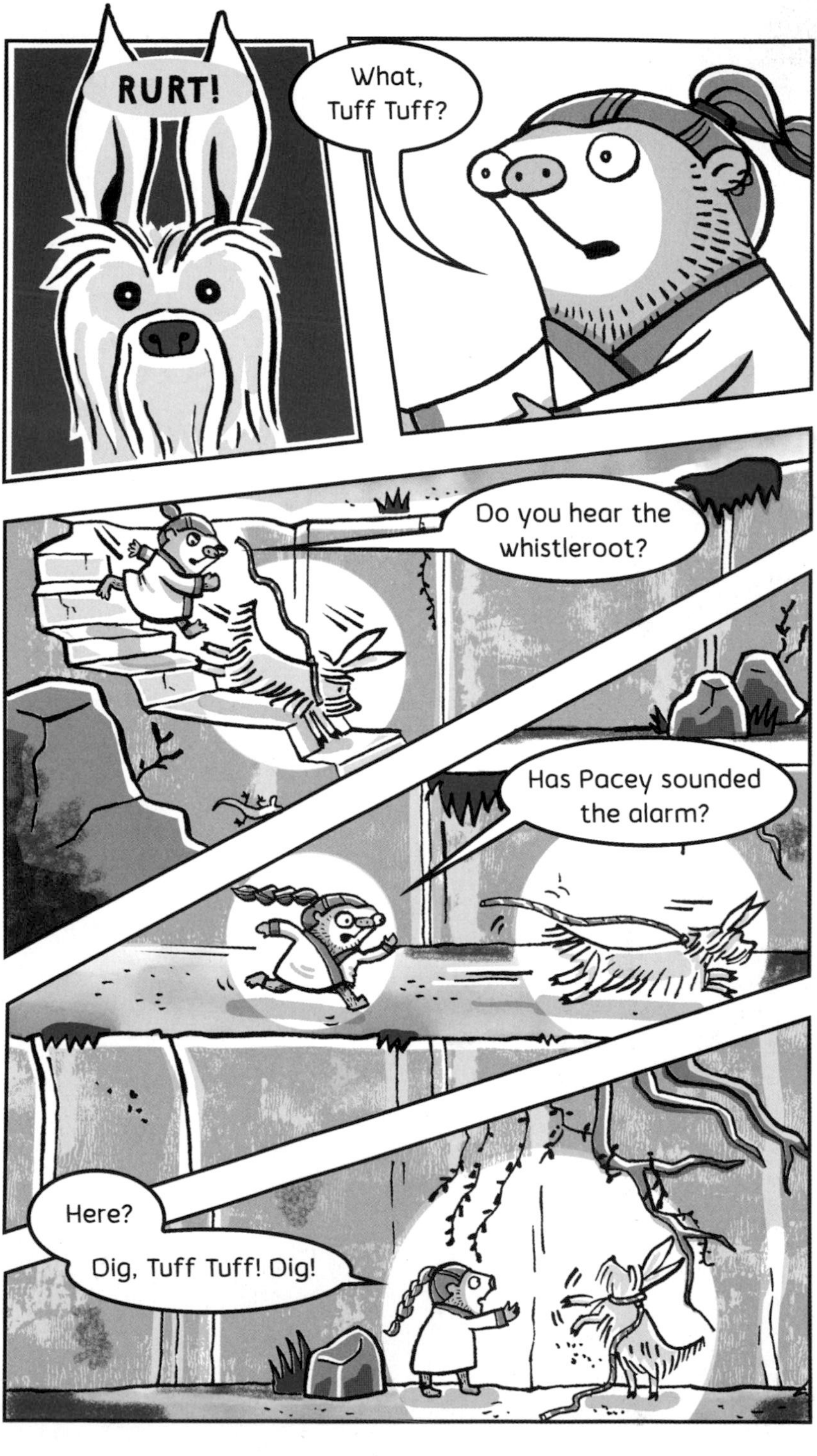
RURT!
What, Tuff Tuff?
Do you hear the whistleroot?
Has Pacey sounded the alarm?
Here?
Dig, Tuff Tuff! Dig!

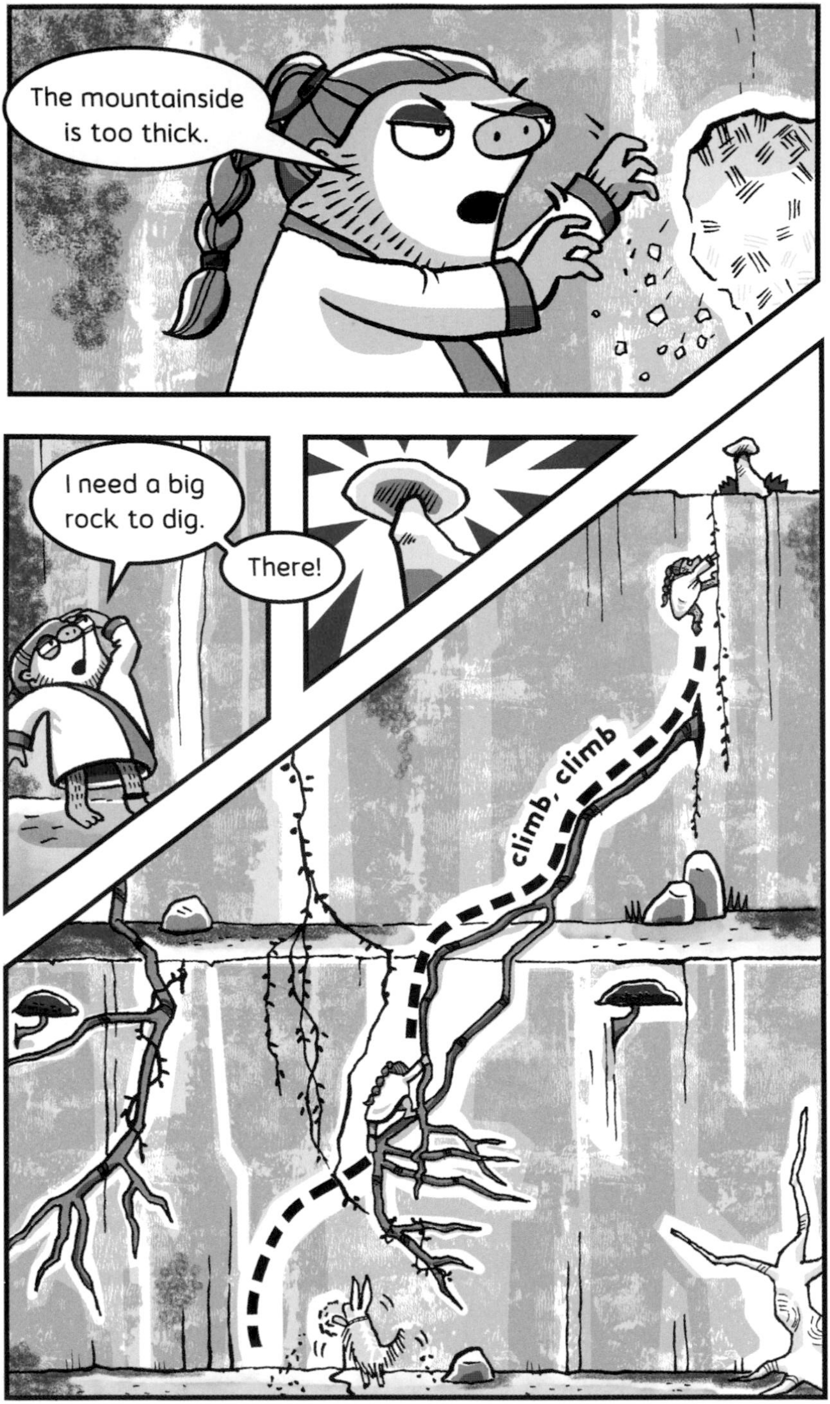
The mountainside is too thick.
I need a big rock to dig.
There!
climb, climb

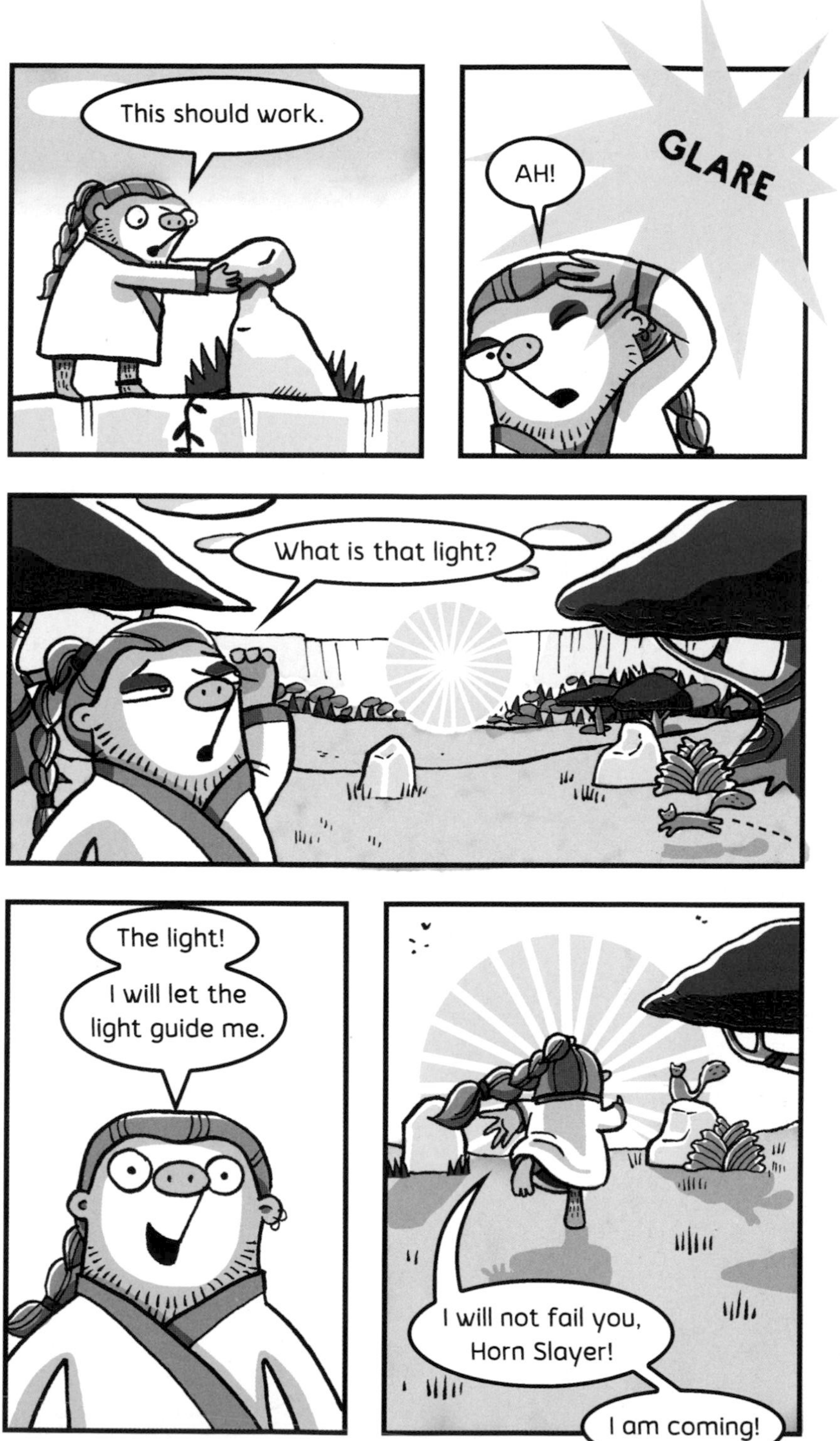
This should work.
AH!
GLARE
What is that light?
The light!
I will let the light guide me.
I will not fail you, Horn Slayer!
I am coming!

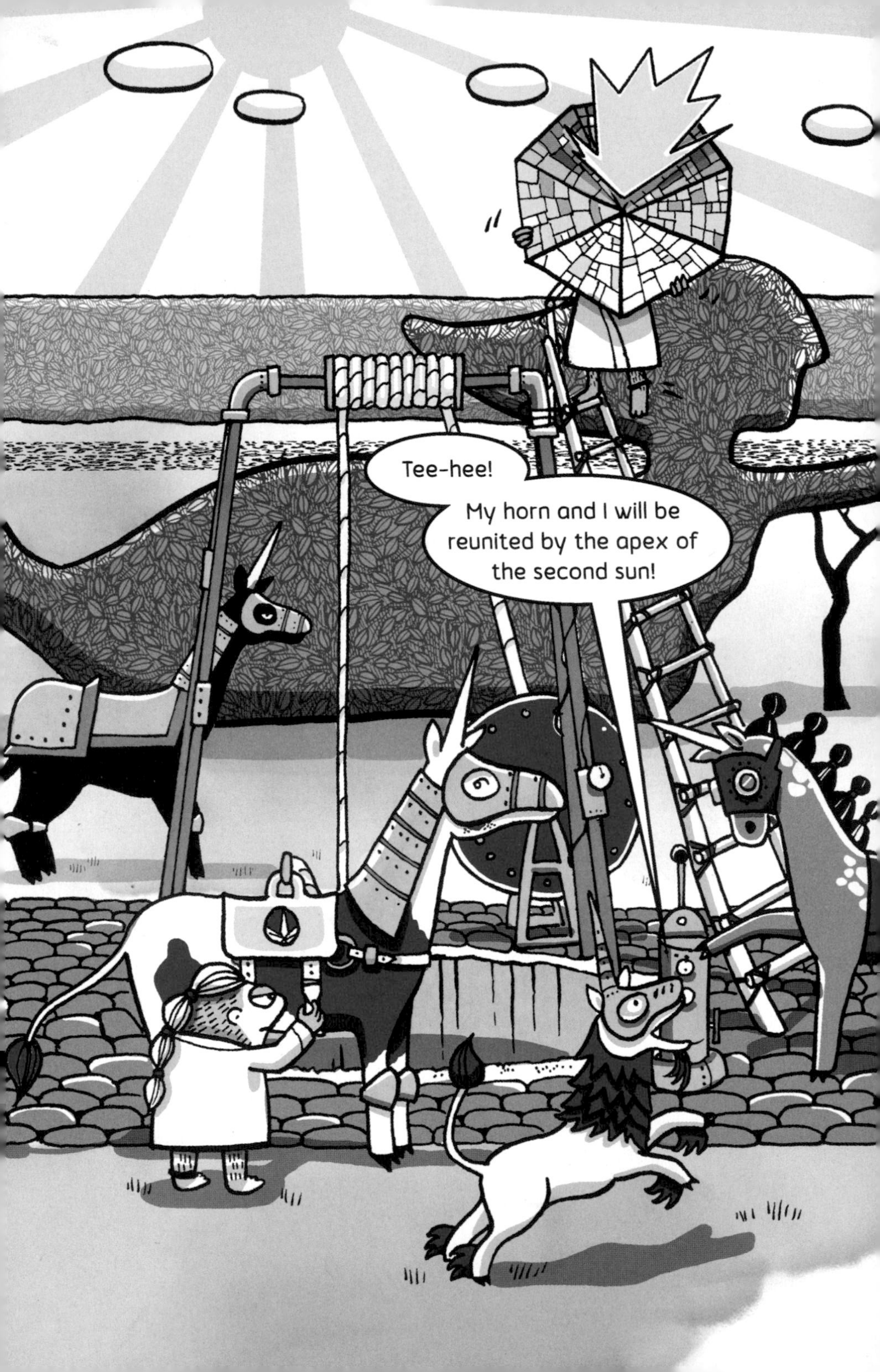
Tee-hee!
My horn and I will be reunited by the apex of the second sun!

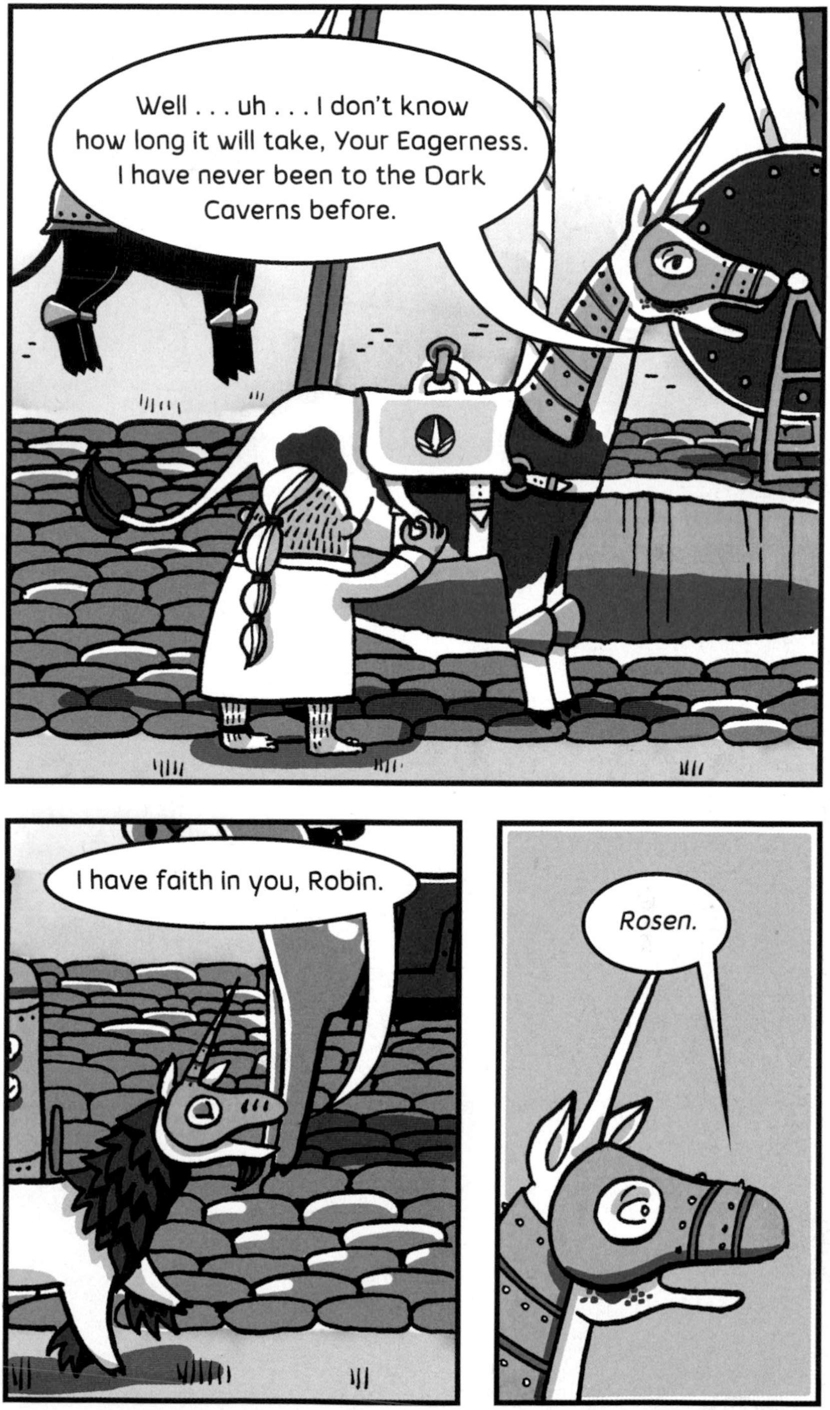
Well . . . uh . . . I don't know how long it will take, Your Eagerness. I have never been to the Dark Caverns before.
I have faith in you, Robin.
Rosen.

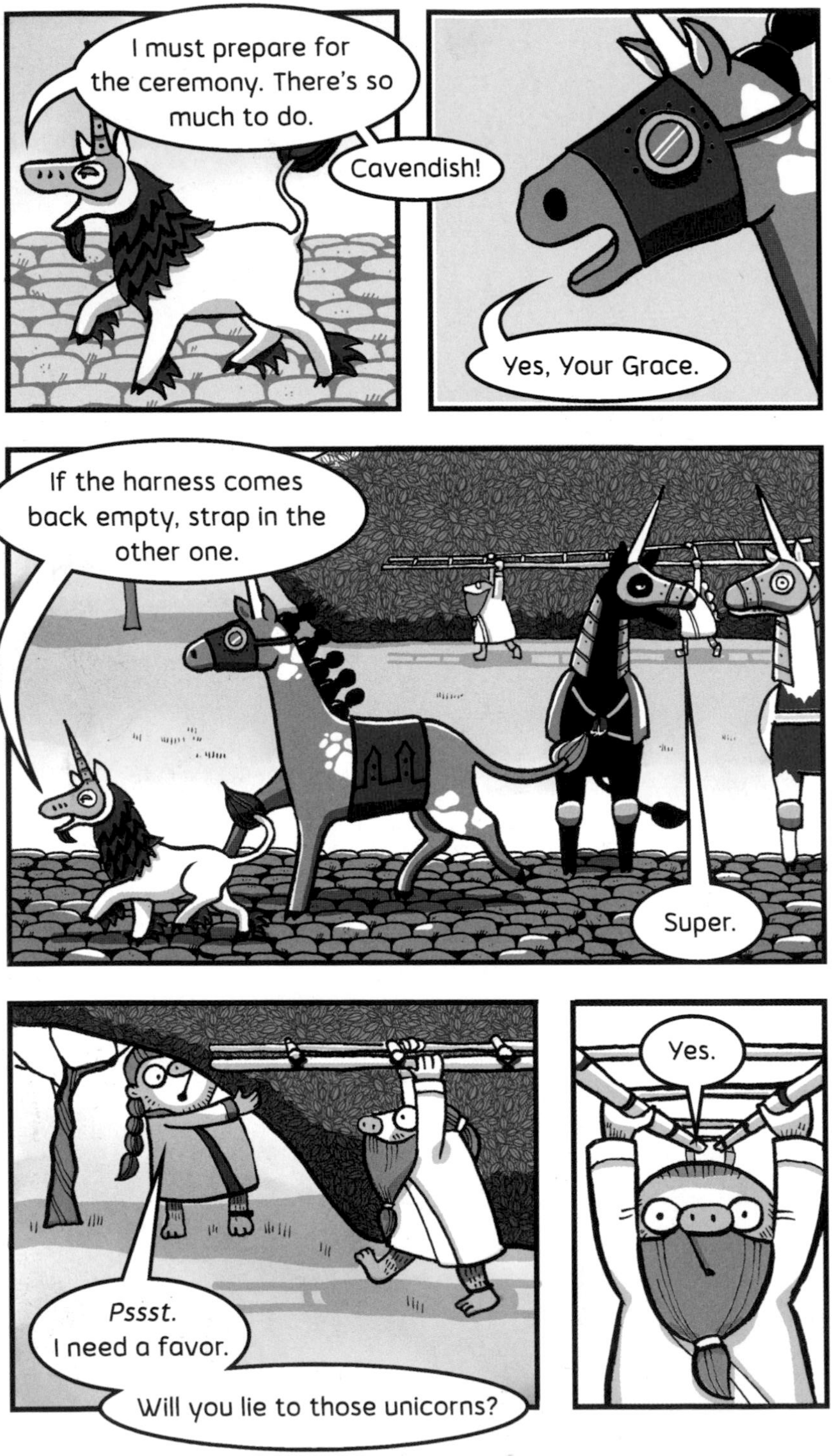
I must prepare for the ceremony. There's so much to do.
Cavendish!
Yes, Your Grace.
If the harness comes back empty, strap in the other one.
Super.
Pssst. I need a favor.
Will you lie to those unicorns?
Yes.

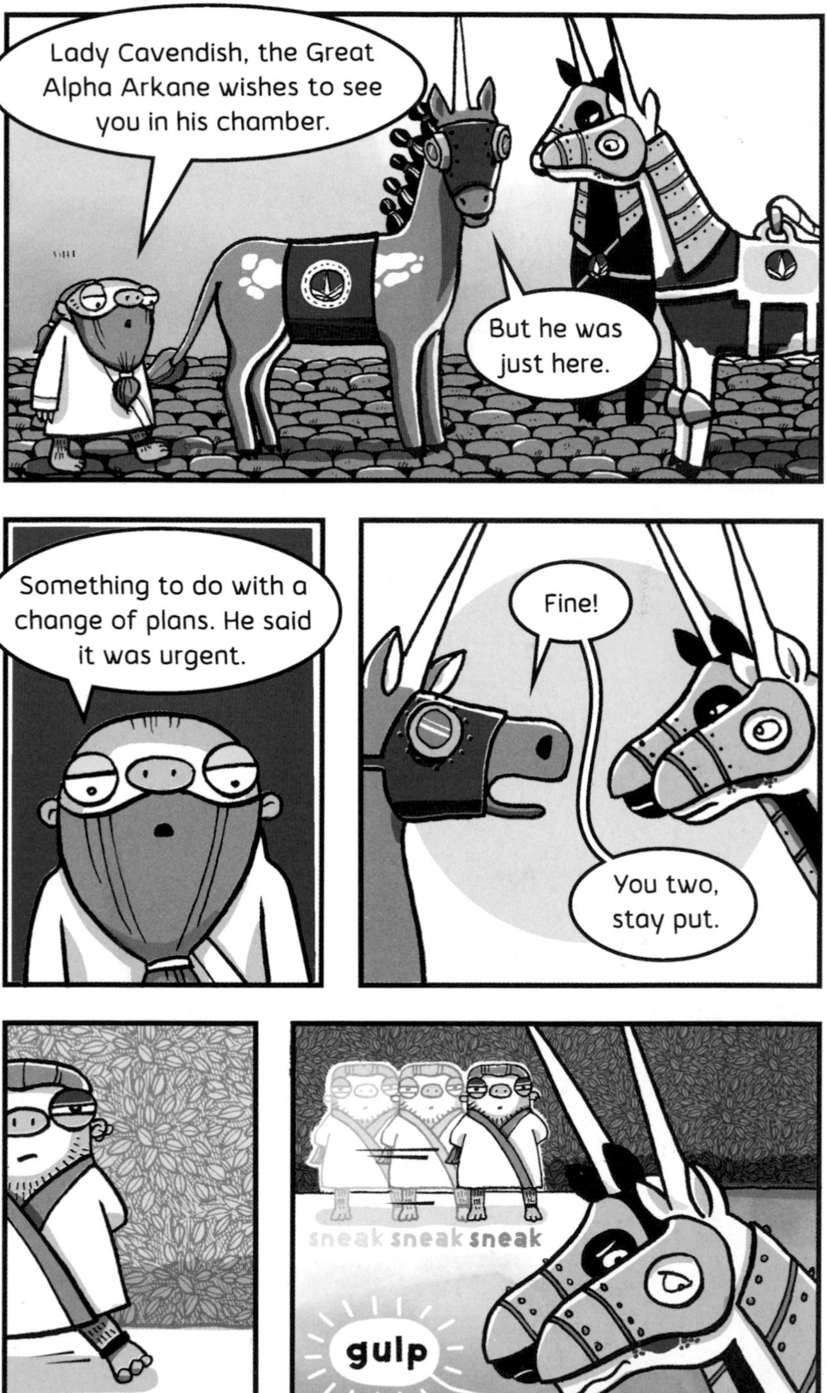
Lady Cavendish, the Great Alpha Arkane wishes to see you in his chamber.
But he was just here.
Something to do with a change of plans. He said it was urgent.
Fine!
You two, stay put.
sneak sneak sneak
gulp

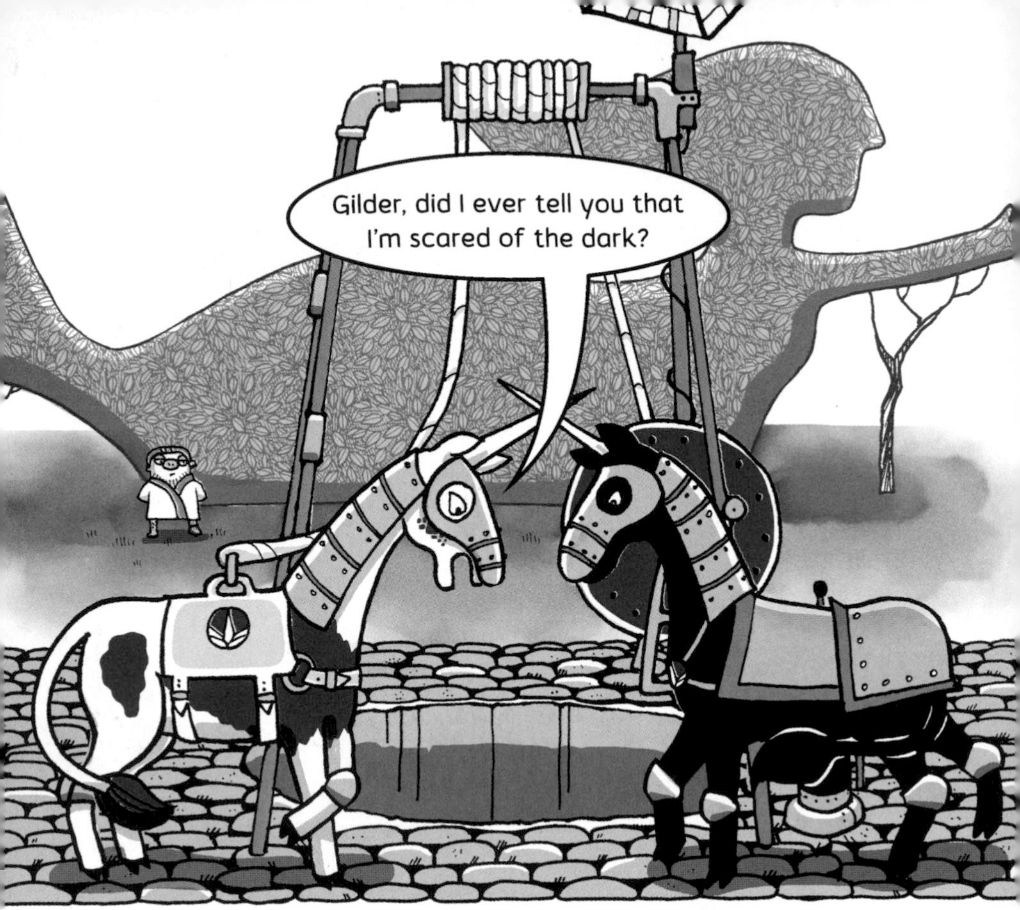
Gilder, did I ever tell you that
I'm scared of the dark?

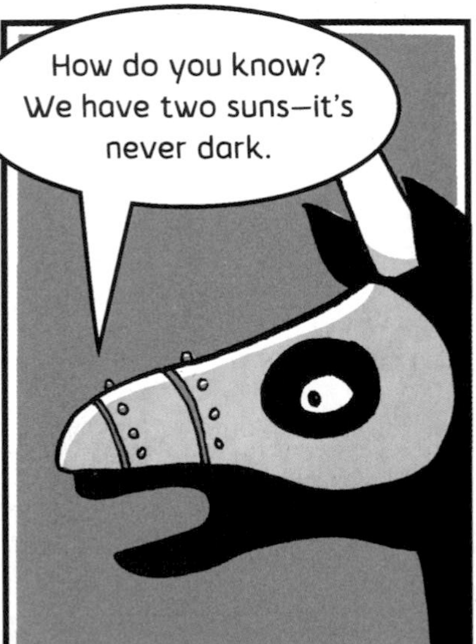
How do you know?
We have two suns—it's
never dark.

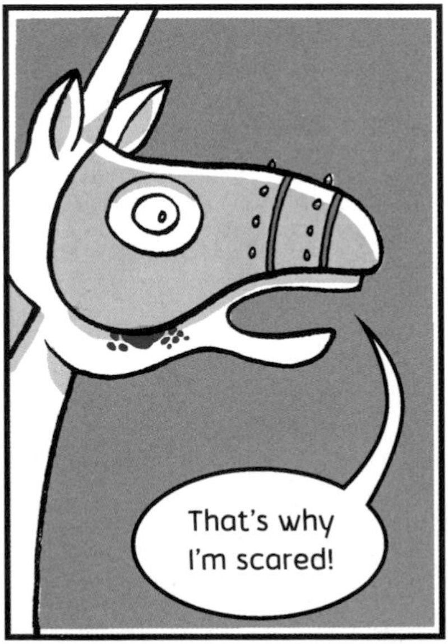
That's why
I'm scared!

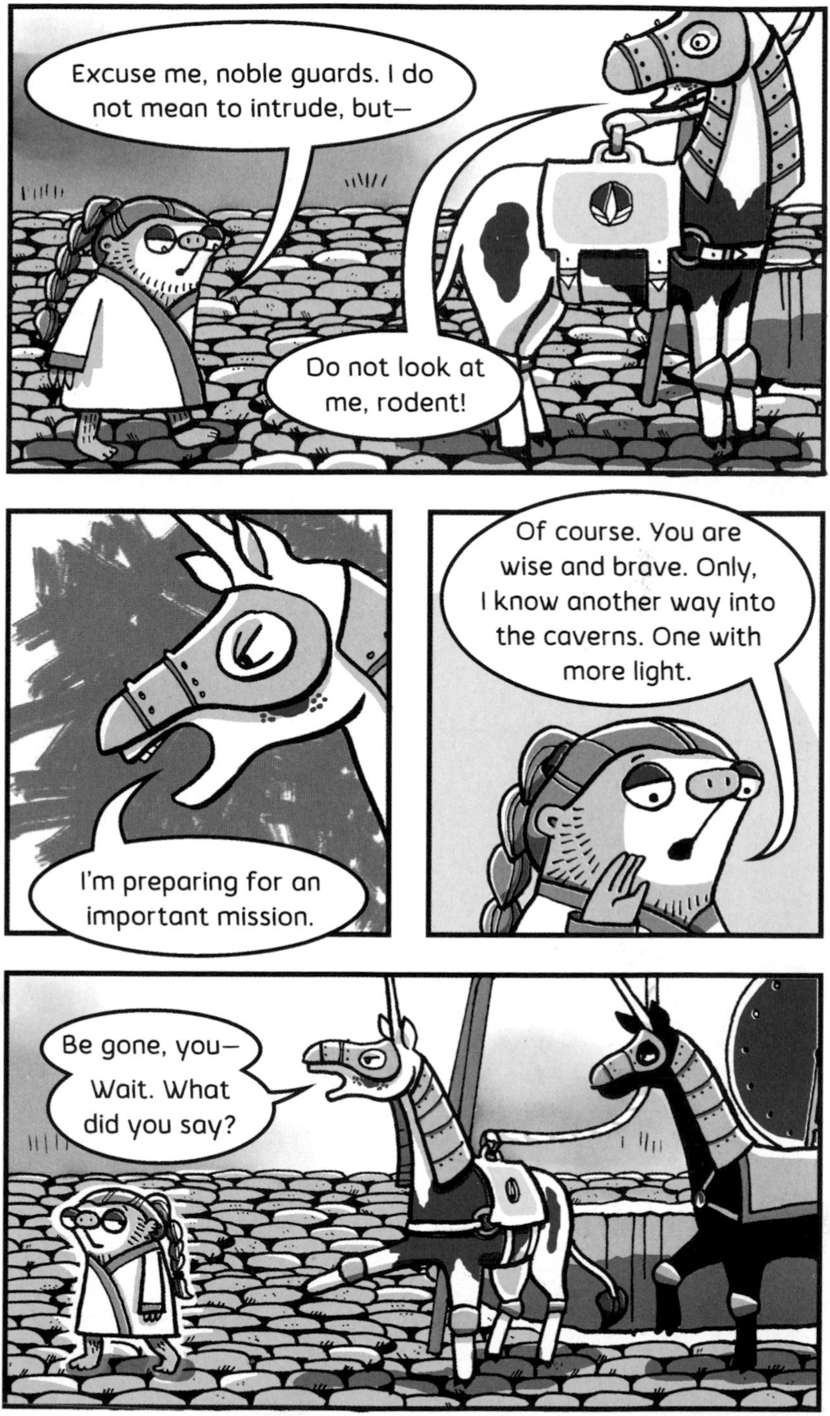

Excuse me, noble guards. I do not mean to intrude, but—
Do not look at me, rodent!
I'm preparing for an important mission.
Of course. You are wise and brave. Only, I know another way into the caverns. One with more light.
Be gone, you—
Wait. What did you say?

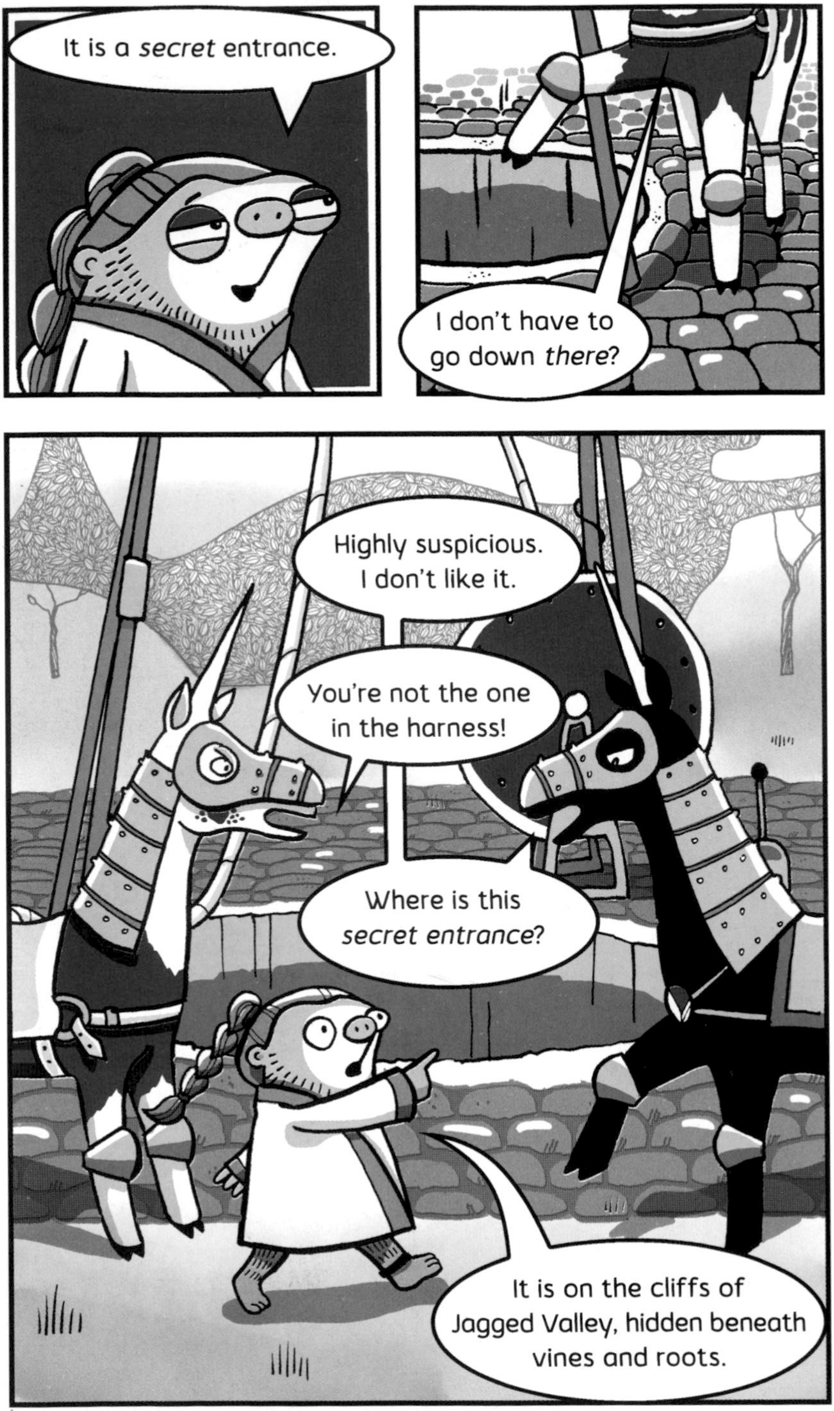
It is a *secret* entrance.
I don't have to go down *there*?
Highly suspicious. I don't like it.
You're not the one in the harness!
Where is this *secret entrance*?
It is on the cliffs of Jagged Valley, hidden beneath vines and roots.

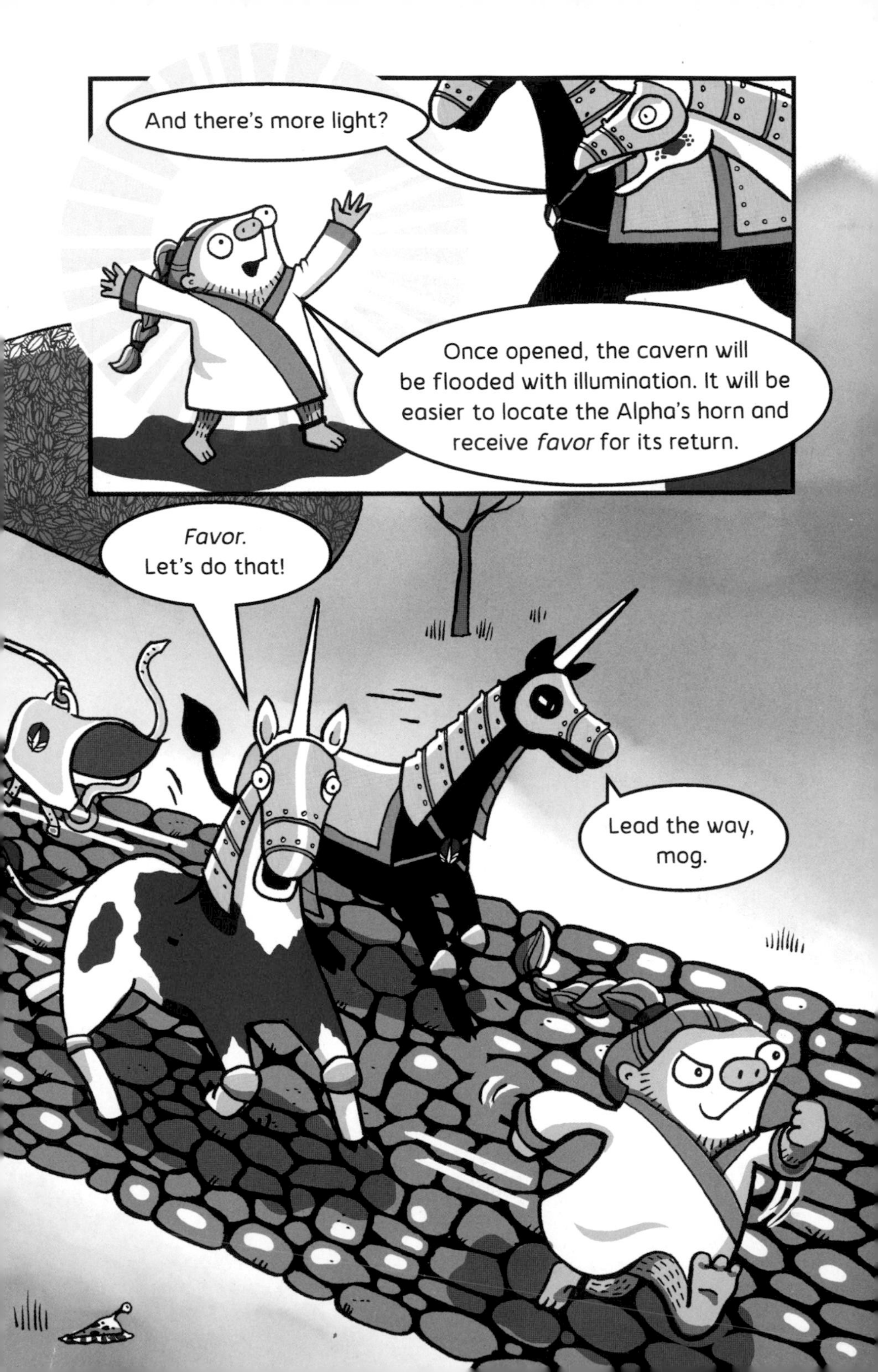
And there's more light?
Once opened, the cavern will be flooded with illumination. It will be easier to locate the Alpha's horn and receive *favor* for its return.
Favor. Let's do that!
Lead the way, mog.

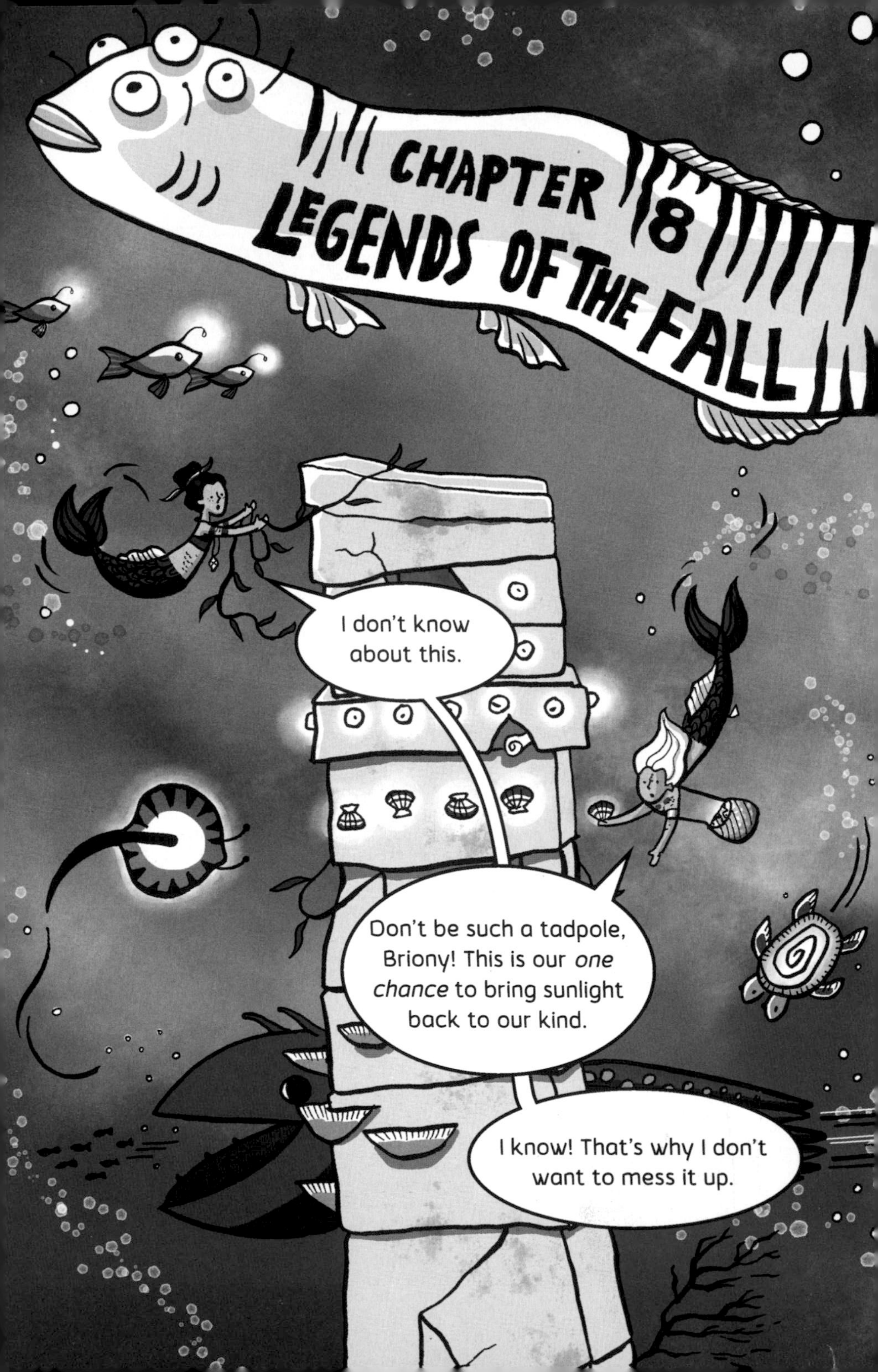
CHAPTER 8
LEGENDS OF THE FALL
I don't know about this.
Don't be such a tadpole, Briony! This is our *one chance* to bring sunlight back to our kind.
I know! That's why I don't want to mess it up.

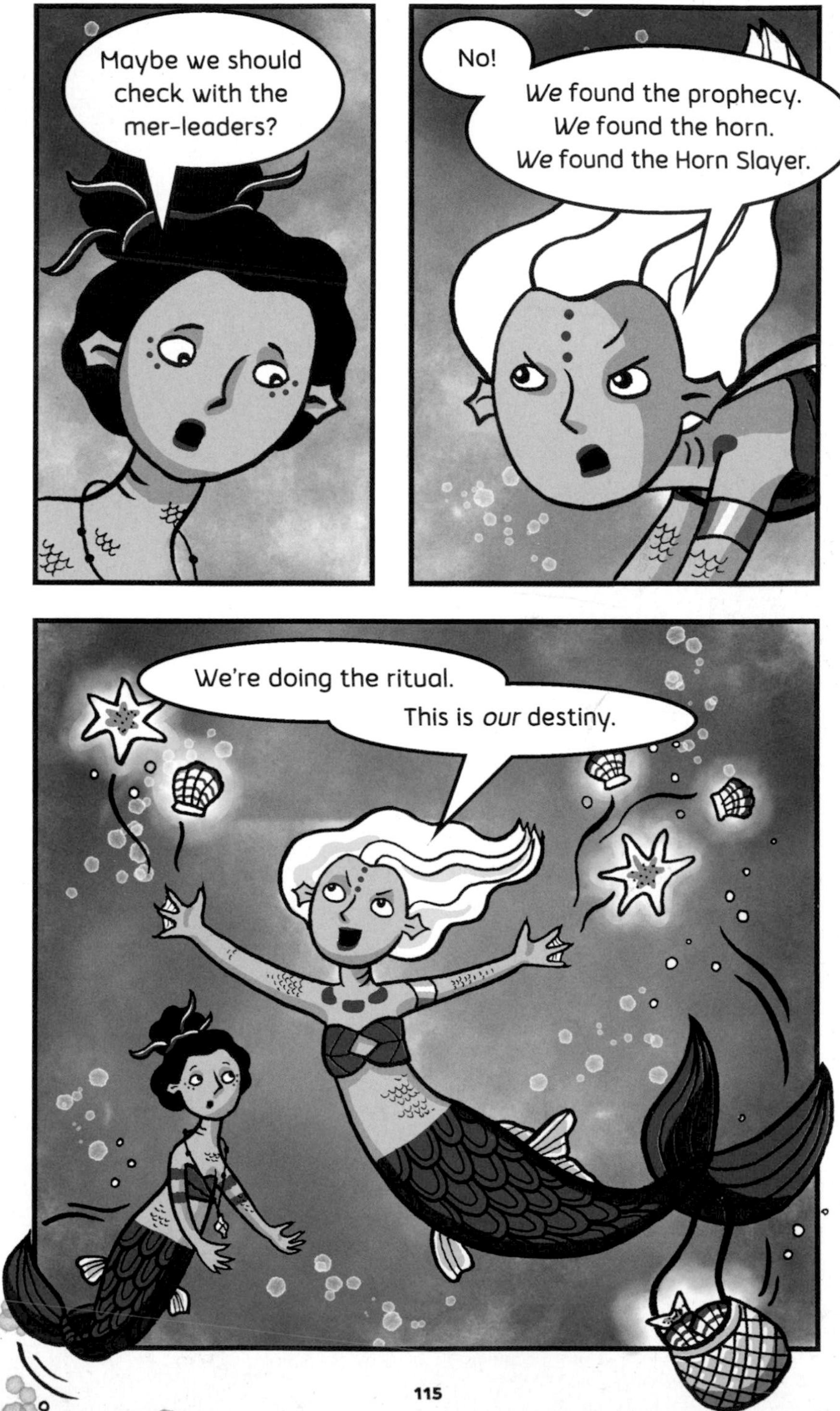
Maybe we should check with the mer-leaders?
No!
We found the prophecy. *We* found the horn. *We* found the Horn Slayer.
We're doing the ritual.
This is *our* destiny.

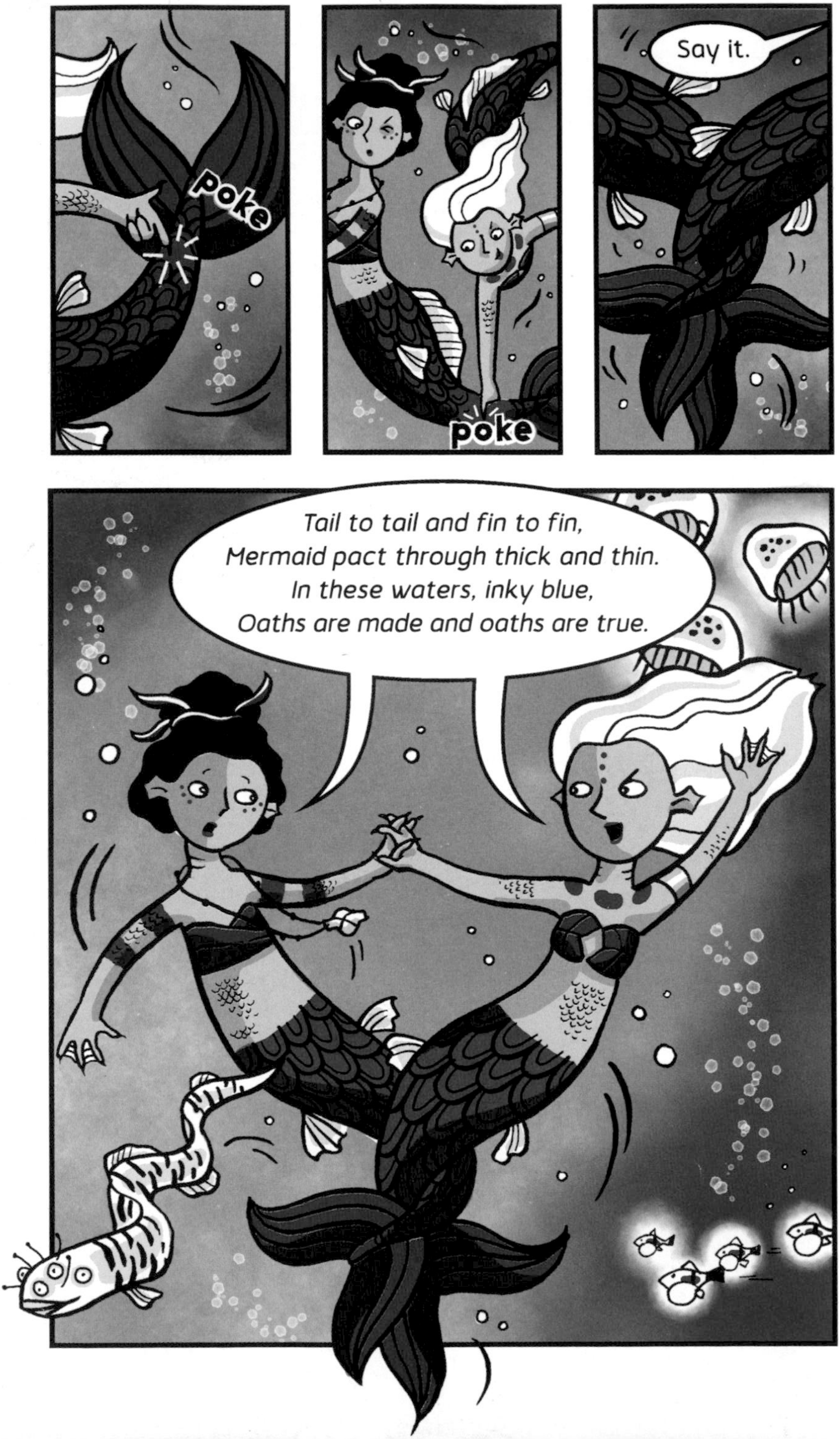
poke
poke
Say it.
Tail to tail and fin to fin,
Mermaid pact through thick and thin.
In these waters, inky blue,
Oaths are made and oaths are true.

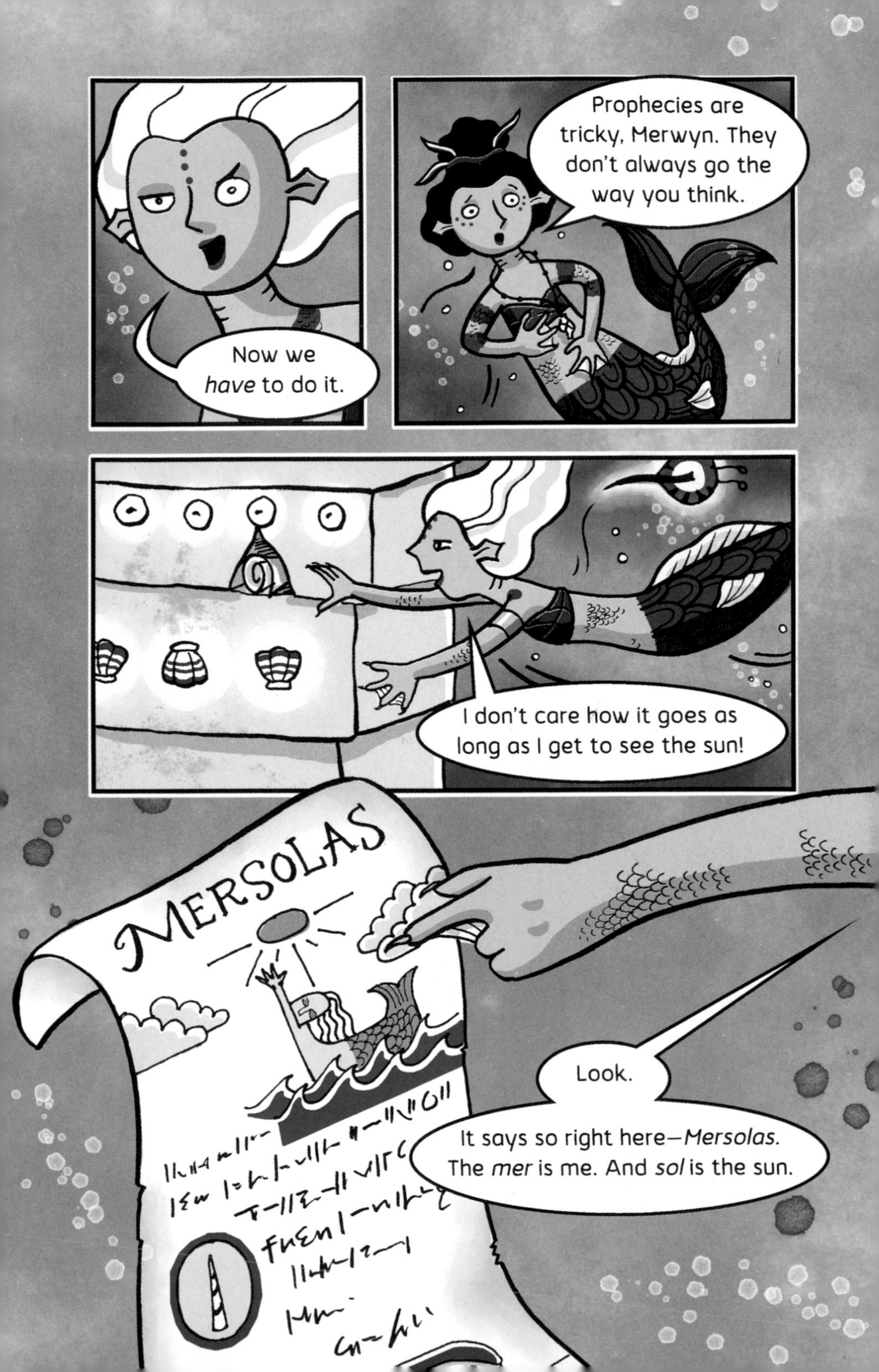
Now we *have* to do it.
Prophecies are tricky, Merwyn. They don't always go the way you think.
I don't care how it goes as long as I get to see the sun!
MERSOLAS
Look.
It says so right here—*Mersolas.* The *mer* is me. And *sol* is the sun.

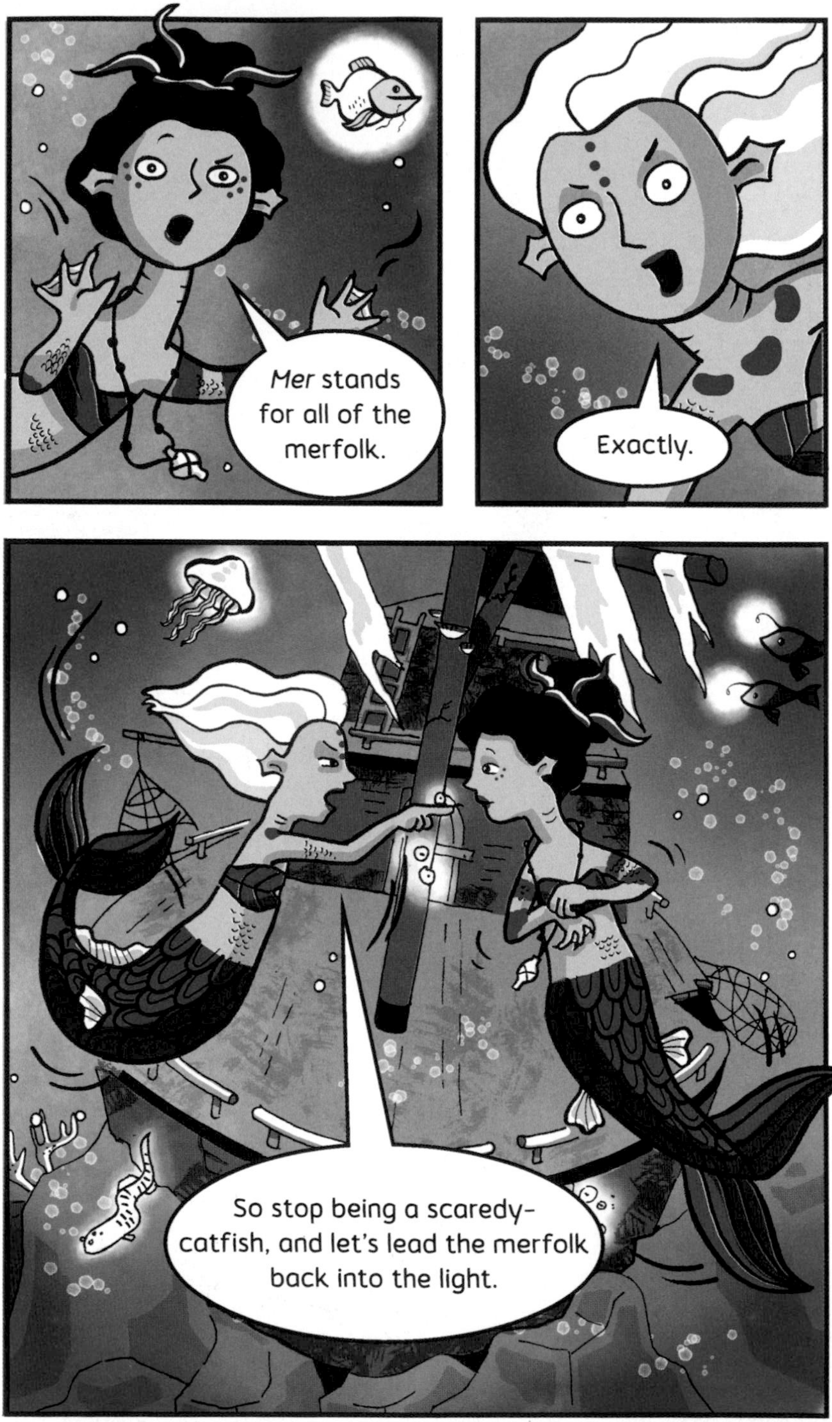

Mer stands for all of the merfolk.
Exactly.
So stop being a scaredy-catfish, and let's lead the merfolk back into the light.

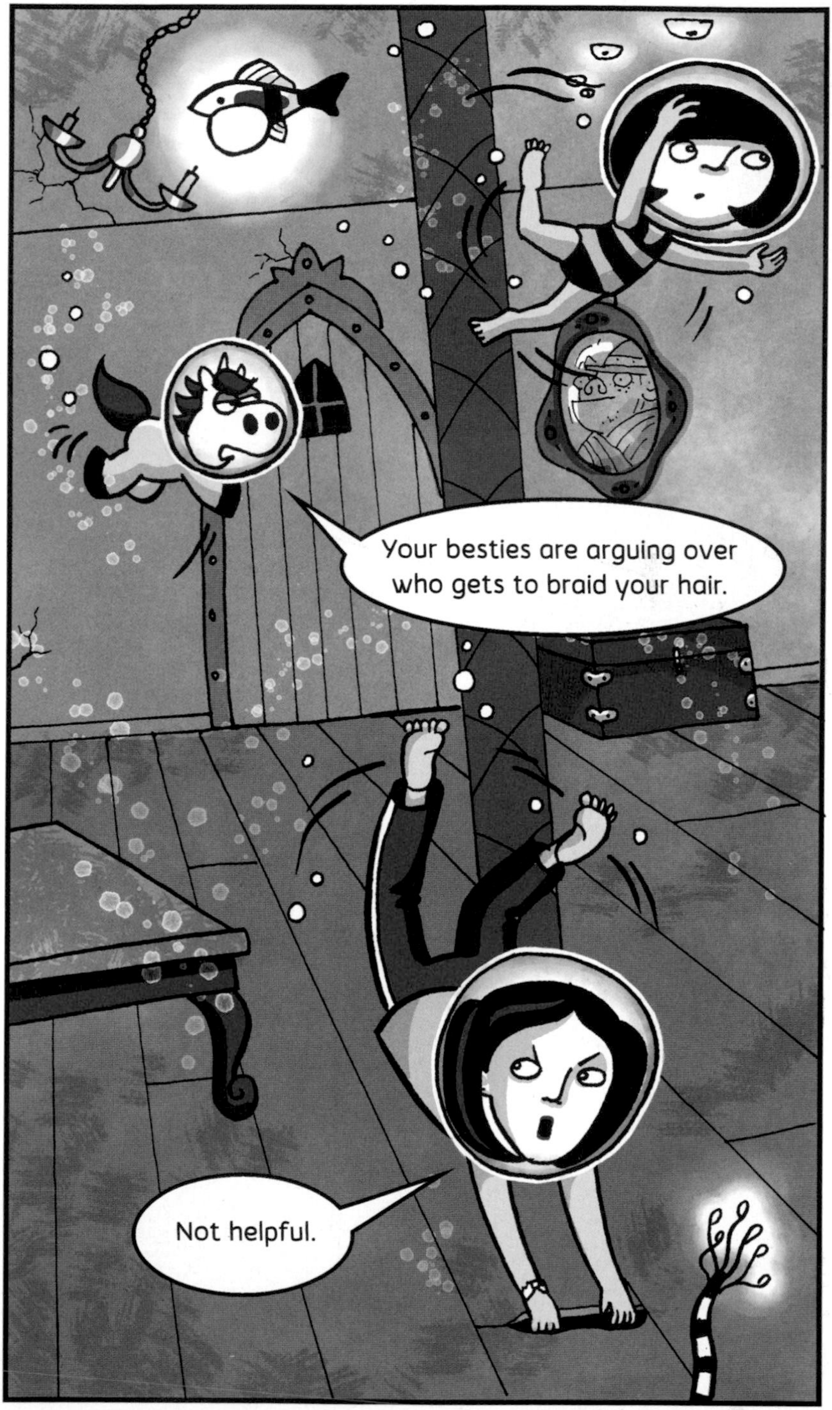
Your besties are arguing over who gets to braid your hair.
Not helpful.

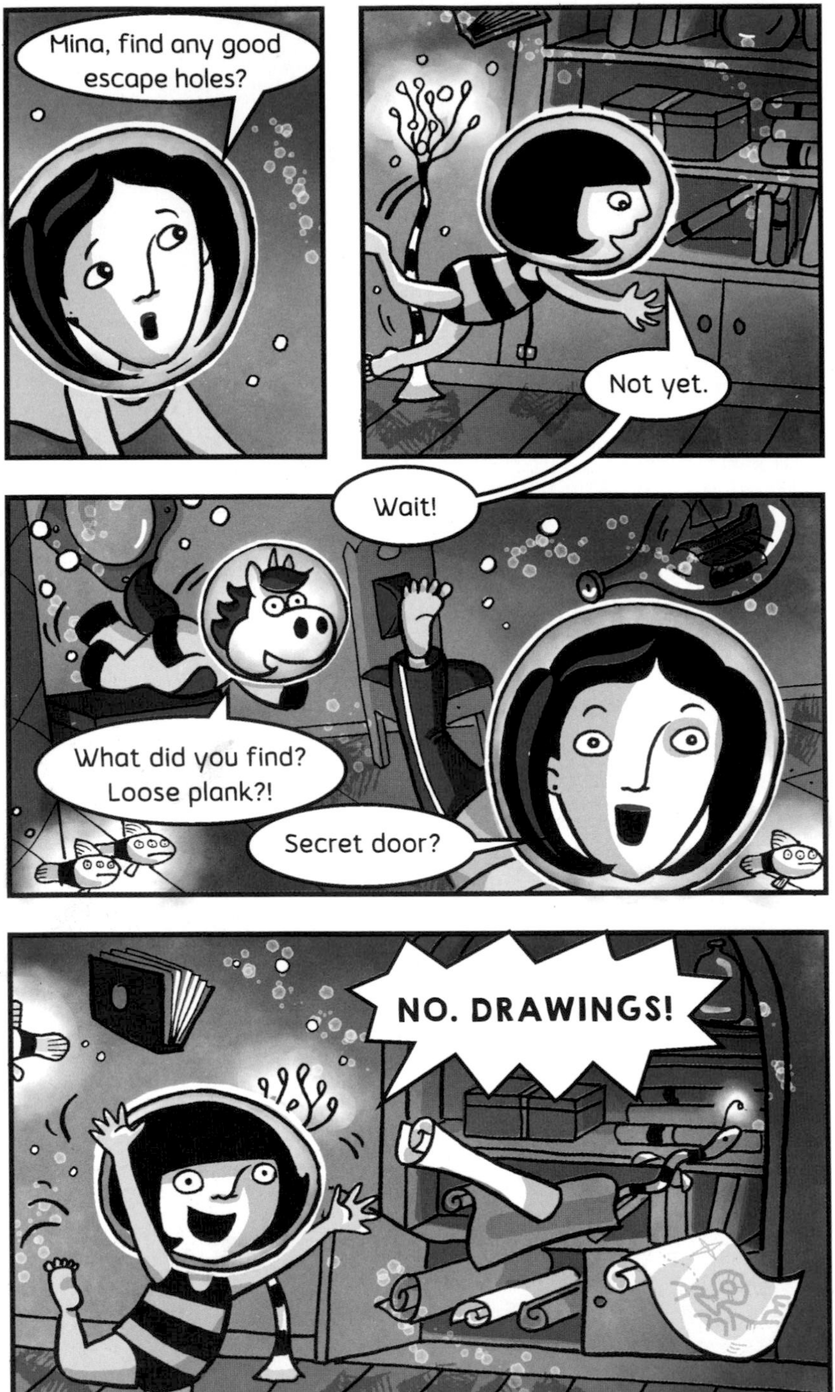
Mina, find any good escape holes?
Not yet.
Wait!
What did you find? Loose plank?!
Secret door?
NO. DRAWINGS!

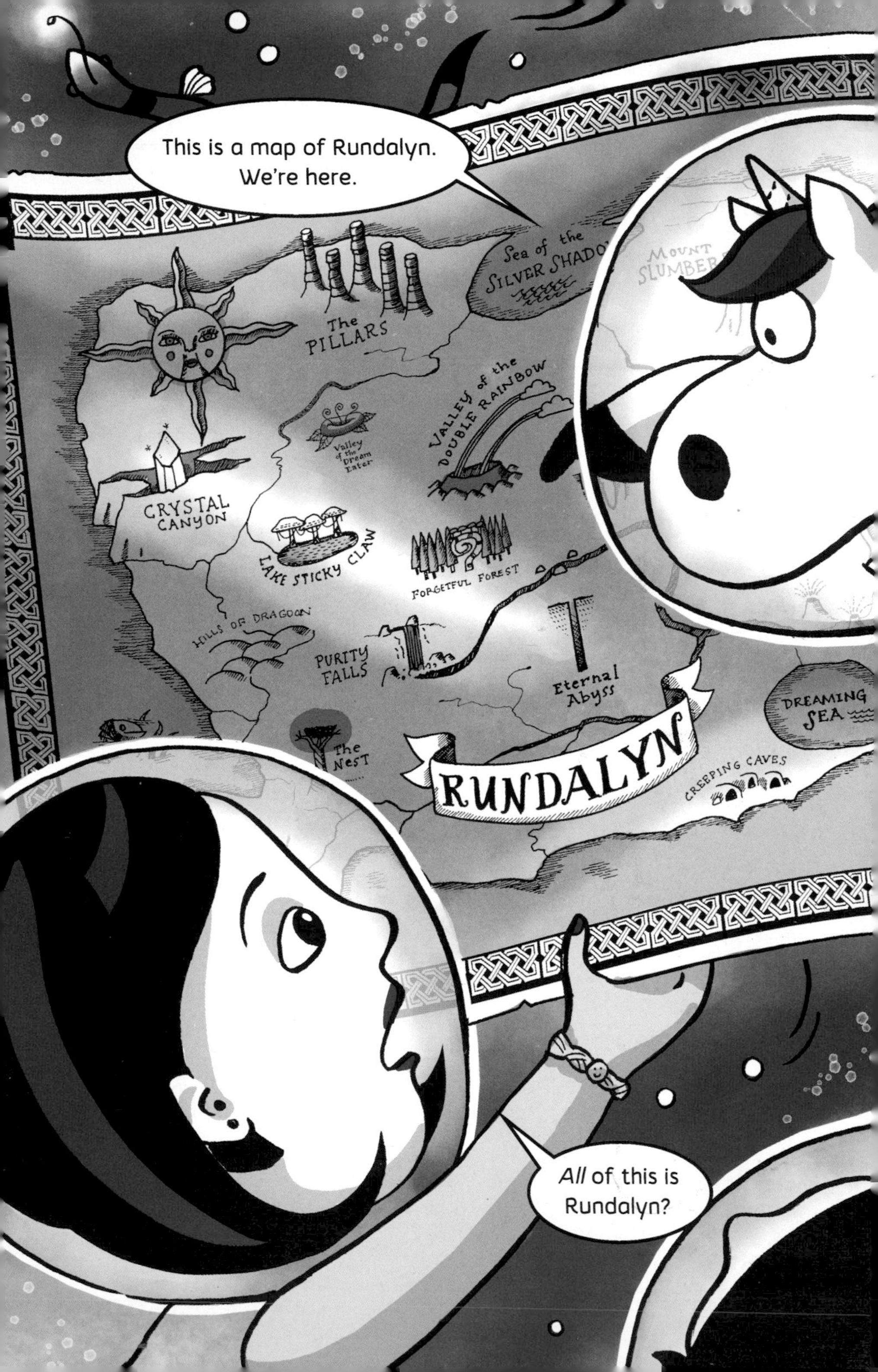
This is a map of Rundalyn. We're here.
Sea of the Silver Shado
Mount Slumber
The Pillars
Valley of the Double Rainbow
Valley of the Dream Eater
Crystal Canyon
Lake Sticky Claw
Forgetful Forest
Hills of Dragoon
Purity Falls
Eternal Abyss
Dreaming Sea
The Nest
Rundalyn
Creeping Caves
All of this is Rundalyn?

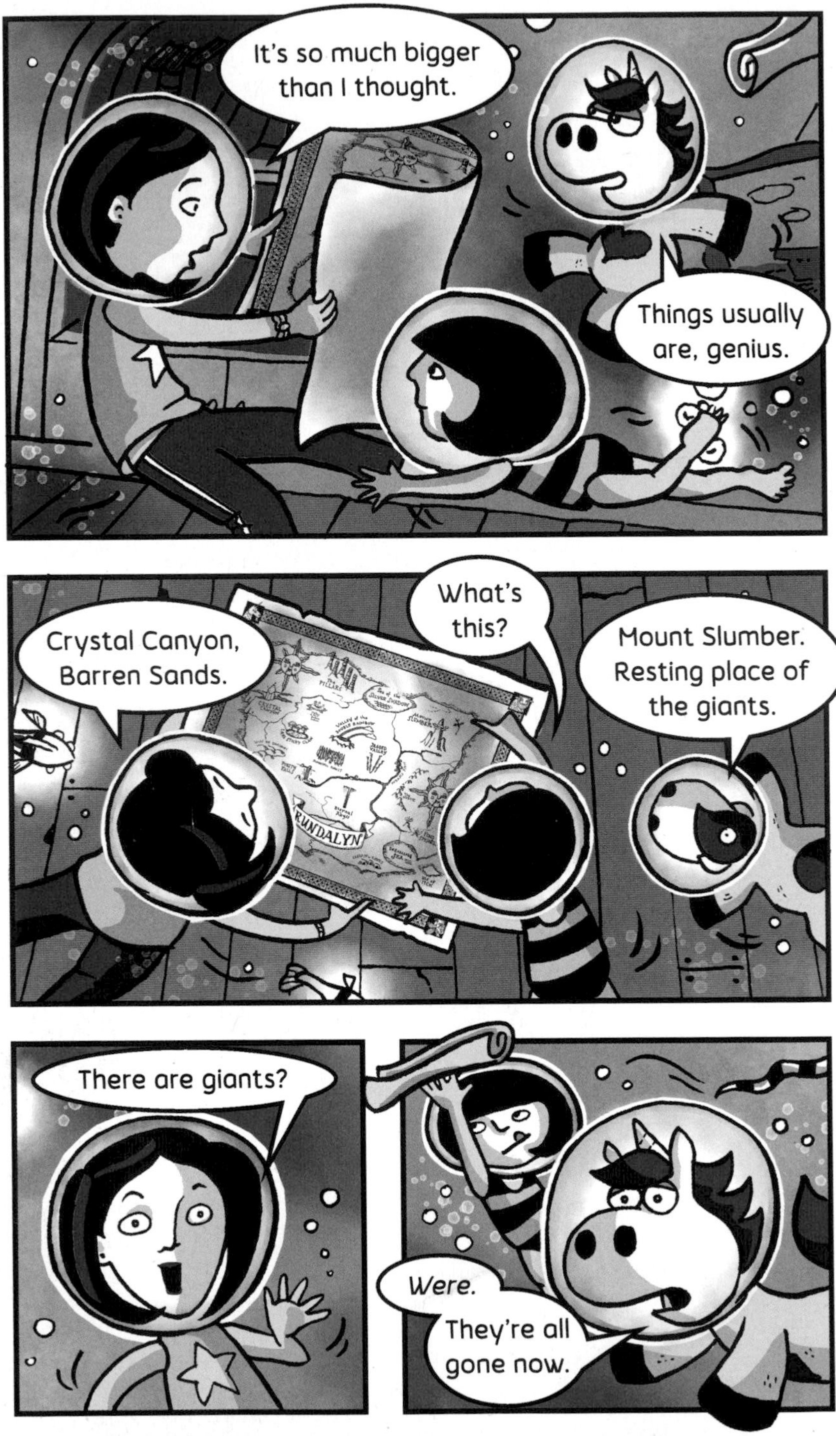

It's so much bigger than I thought.
Things usually are, genius.
Crystal Canyon, Barren Sands.
What's this?
Mount Slumber. Resting place of the giants.
There are giants?
Were.
They're all gone now.

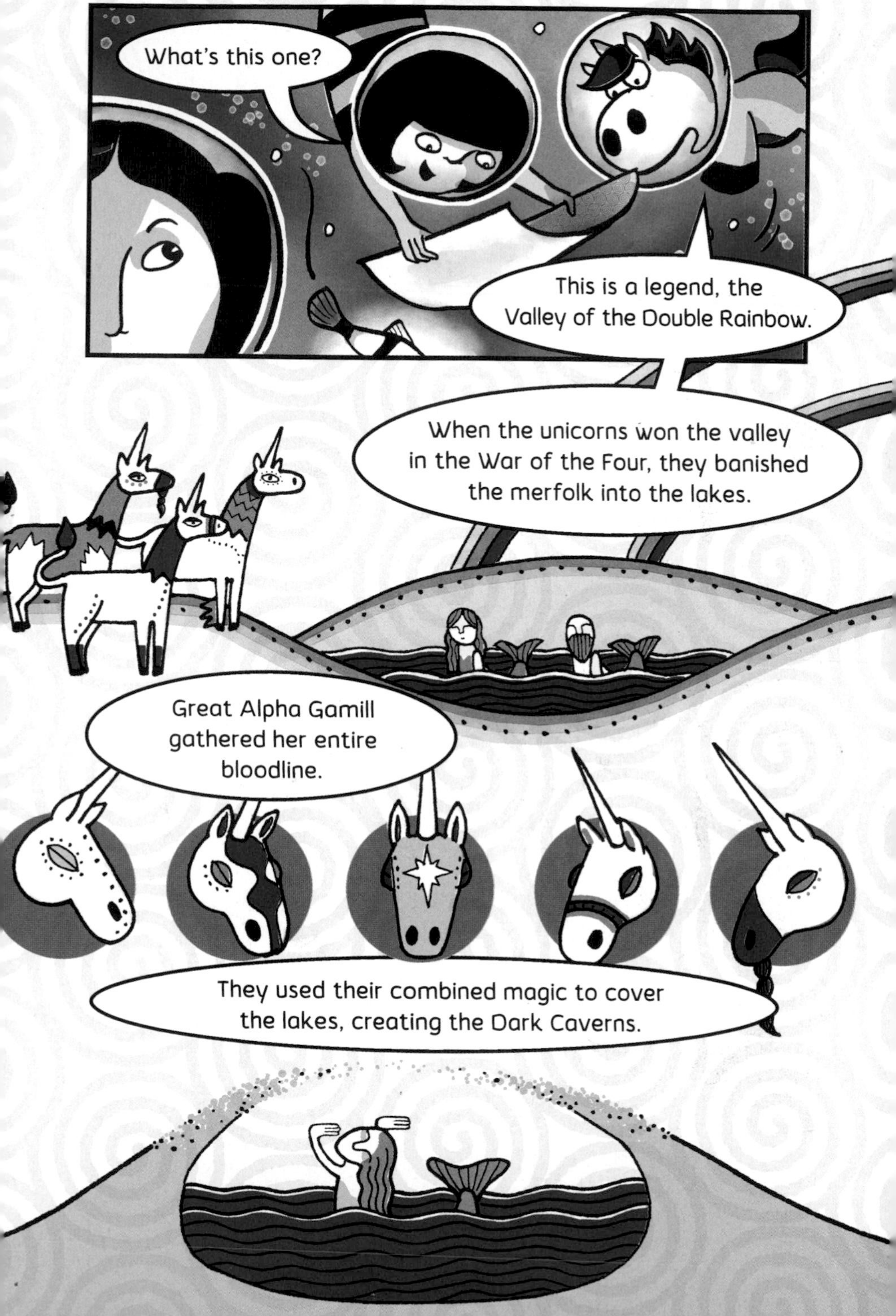
What's this one?
This is a legend, the Valley of the Double Rainbow.
When the unicorns won the valley in the War of the Four, they banished the merfolk into the lakes.
Great Alpha Gamill gathered her entire bloodline.
They used their combined magic to cover the lakes, creating the Dark Caverns.

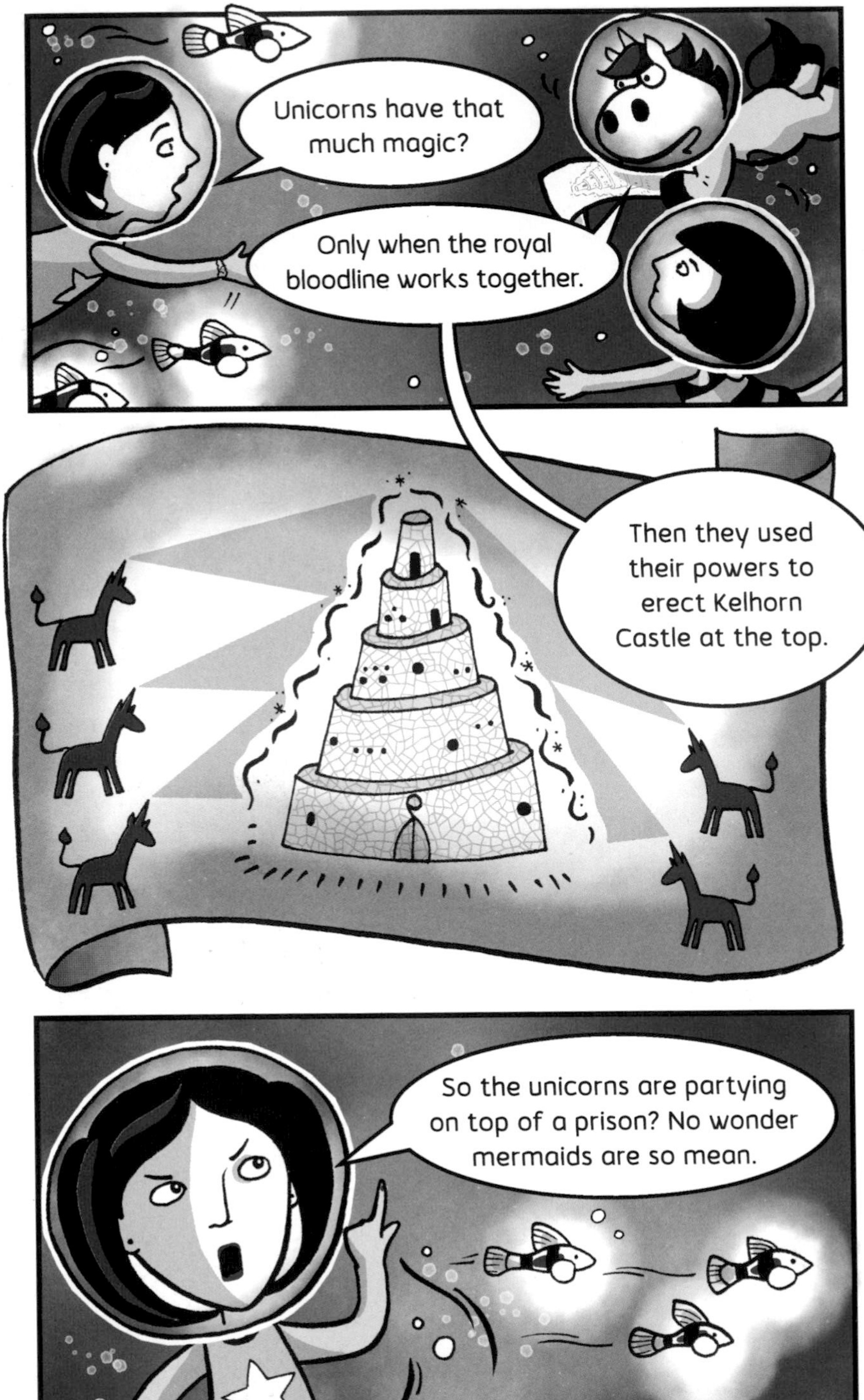
Unicorns have that much magic?
Only when the royal bloodline works together.
Then they used their powers to erect Kelhorn Castle at the top.
So the unicorns are partying on top of a prison? No wonder mermaids are so mean.

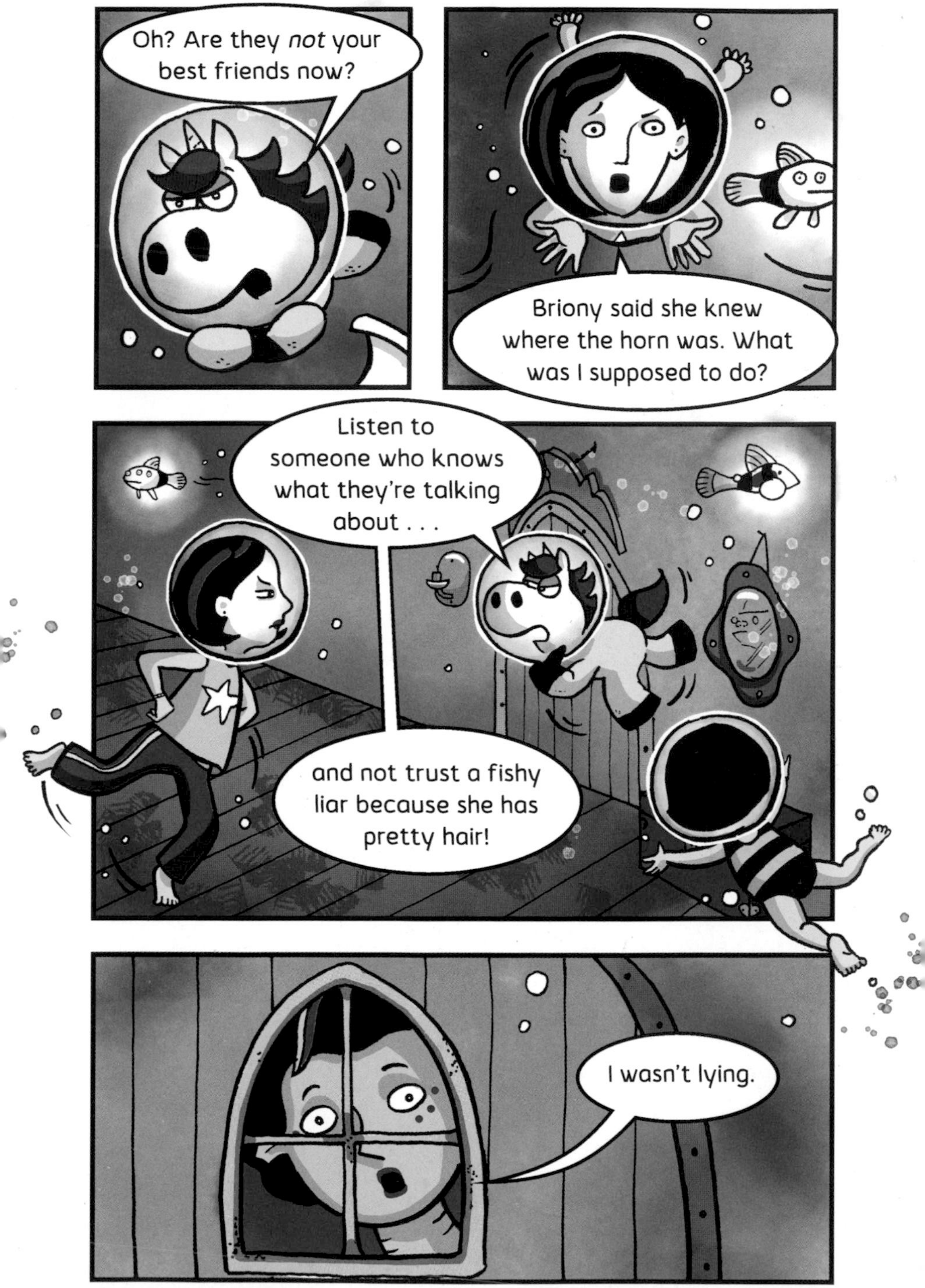
Oh? Are they *not* your best friends now?
Briony said she knew where the horn was. What was I supposed to do?
Listen to someone who knows what they're talking about . . .
and not trust a fishy liar because she has pretty hair!
I wasn't lying.

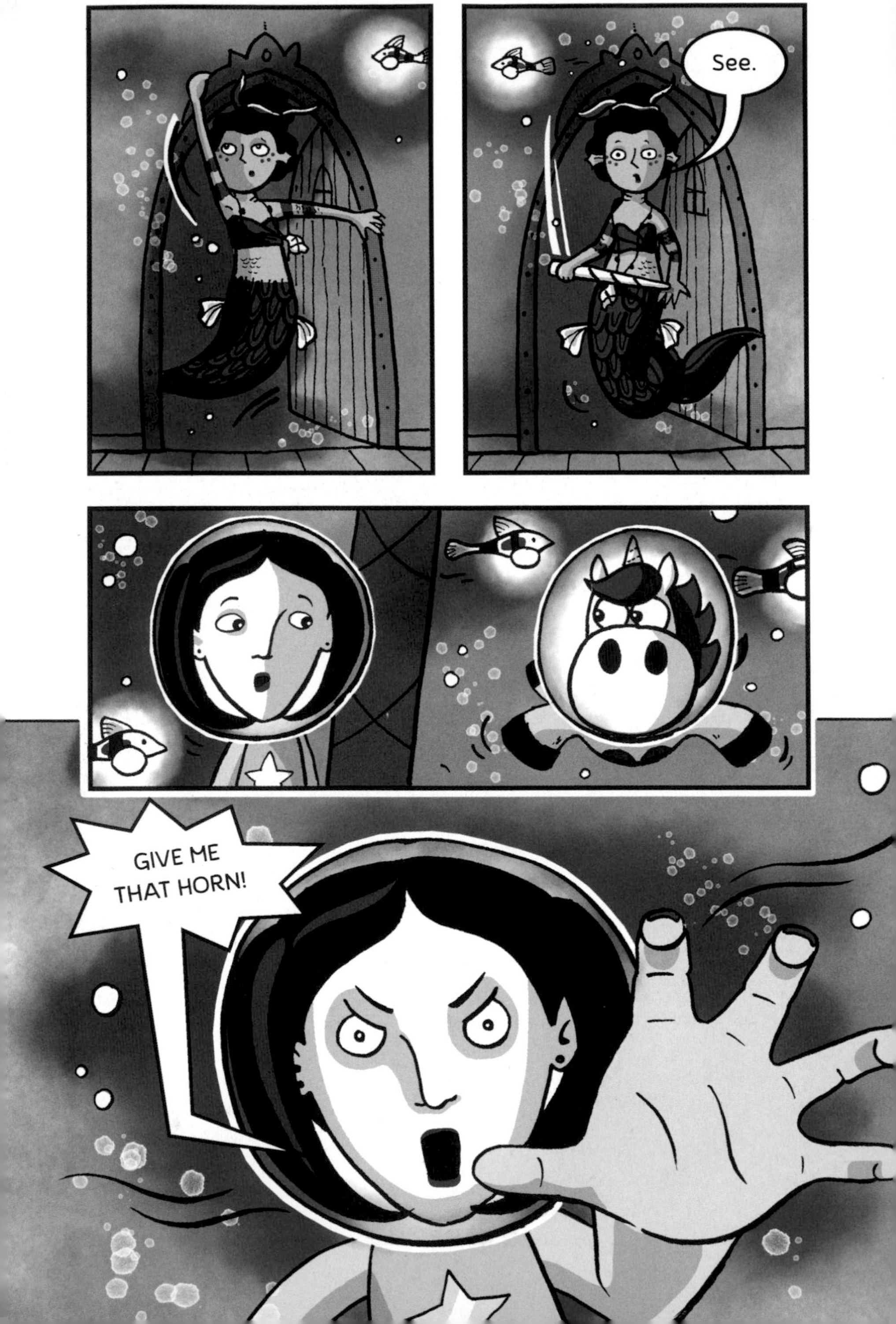
See.
GIVE ME THAT HORN!

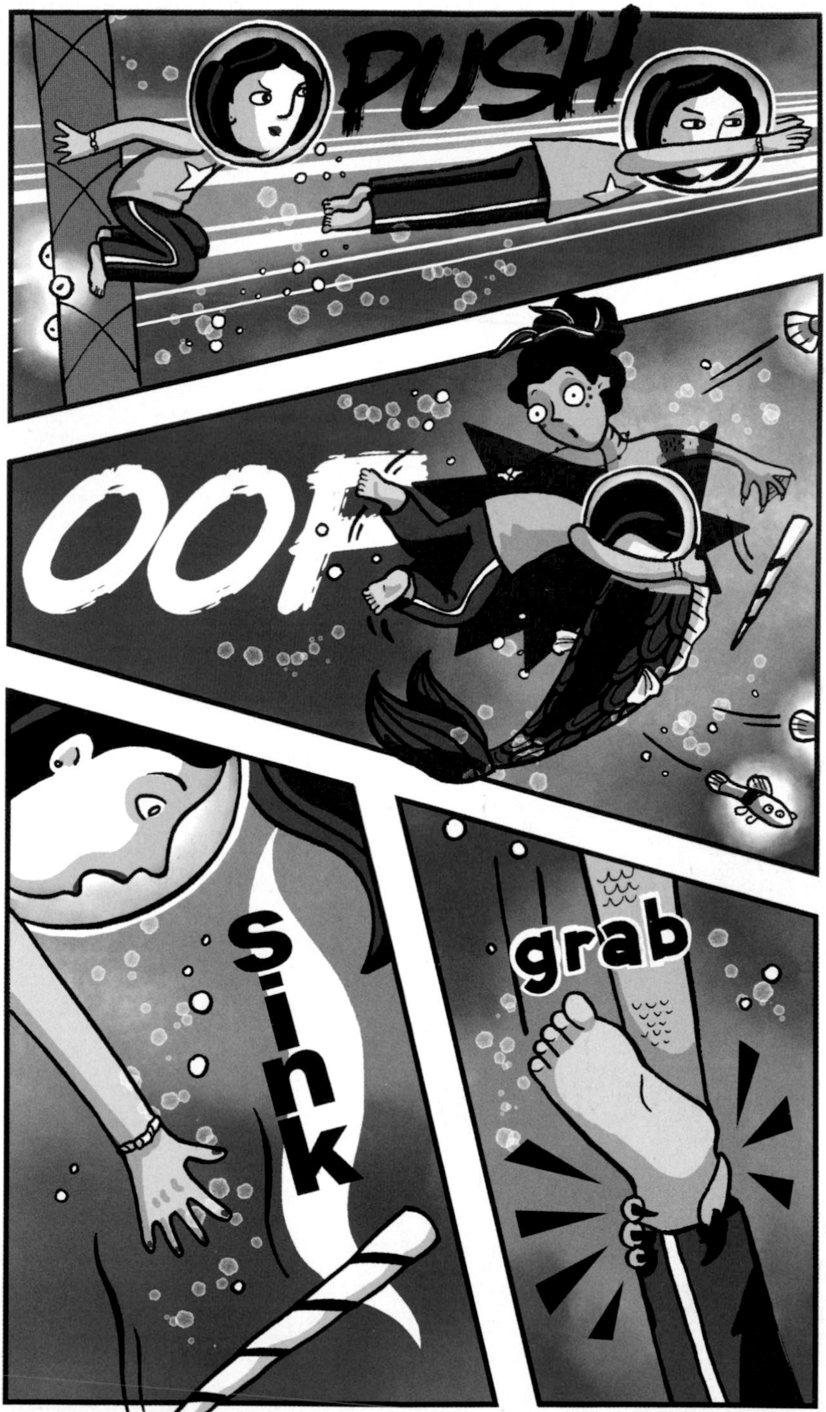
PUSH
OOF
sink
grab

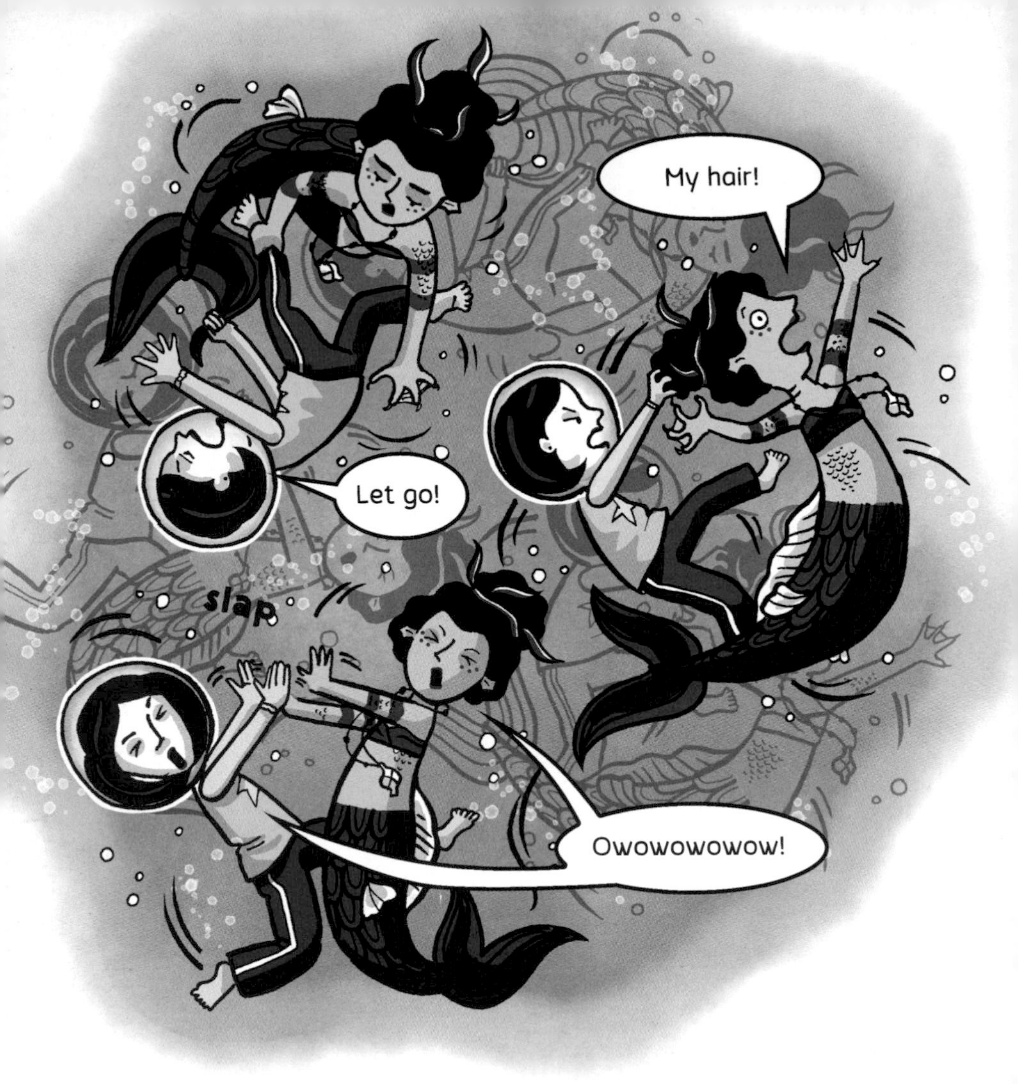
My hair!
Let go!
slap
Owowowowowow!

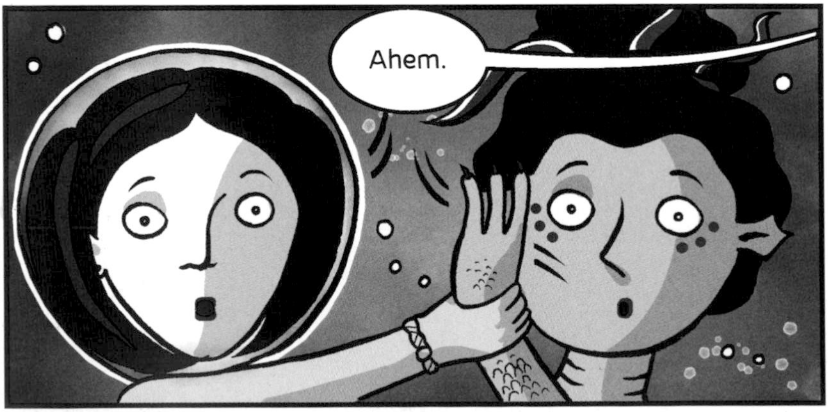
Ahem.

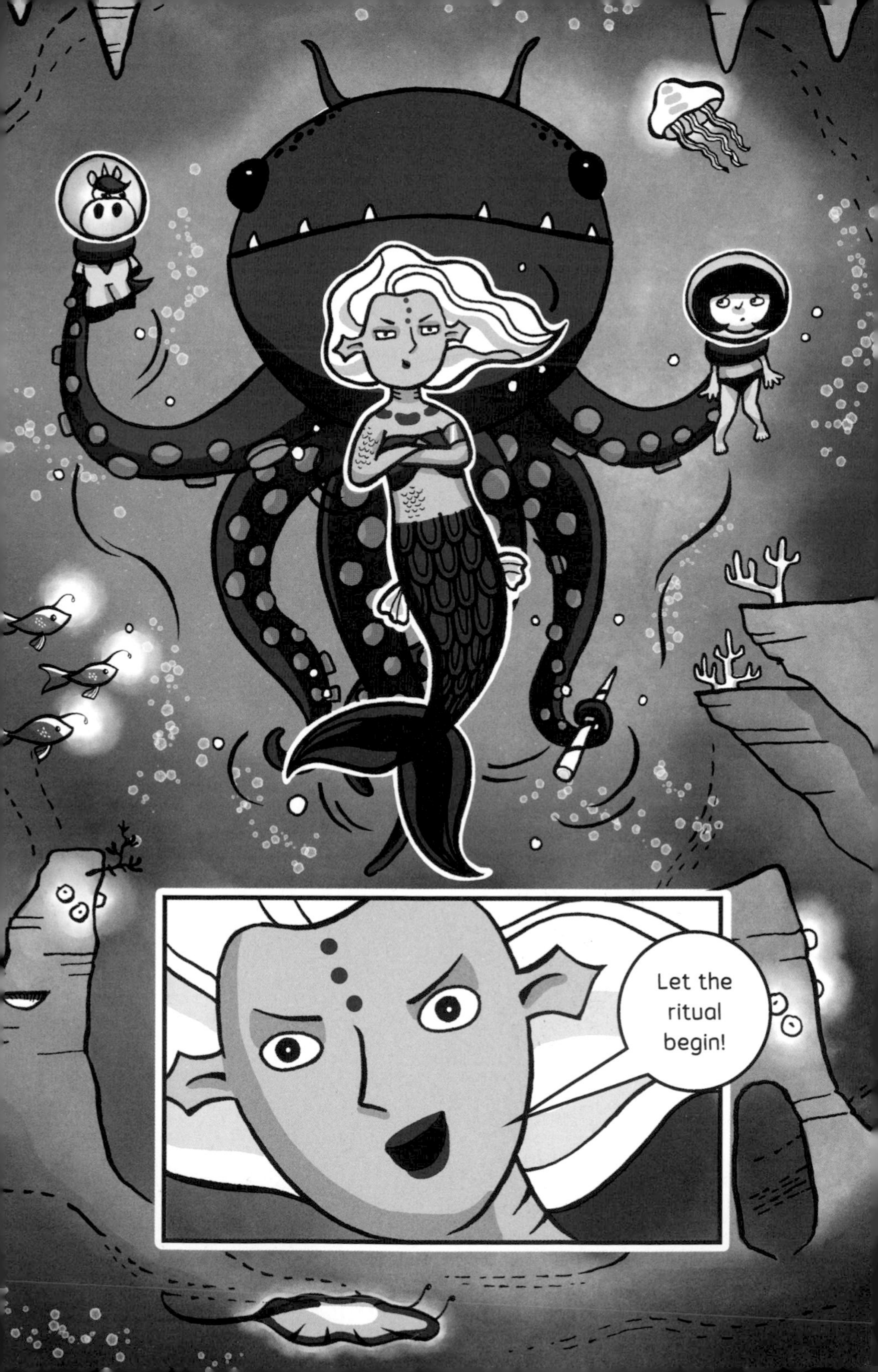
Let the ritual begin!

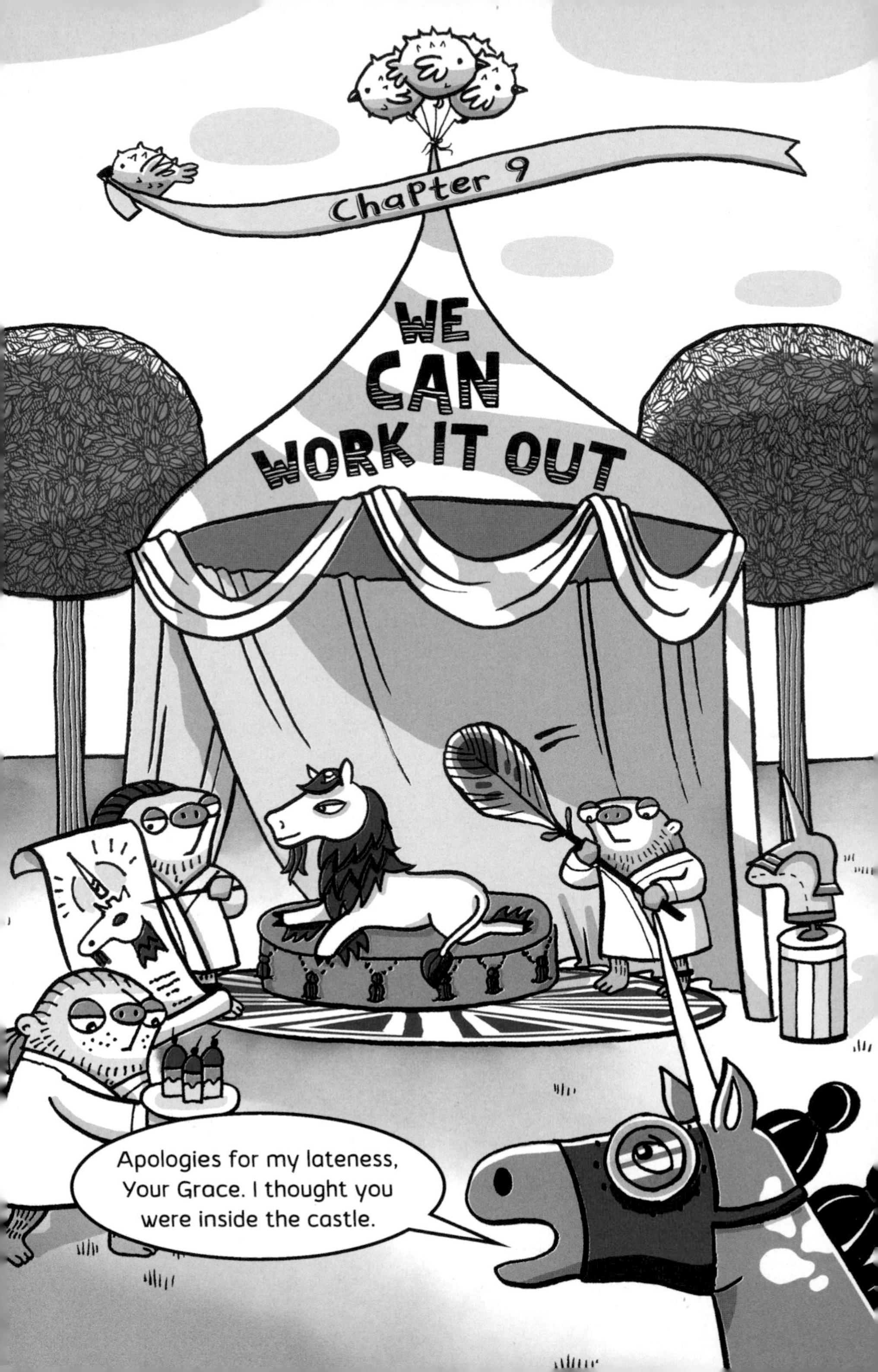
Chapter 9
WE CAN WORK IT OUT
Apologies for my lateness, Your Grace. I thought you were inside the castle.

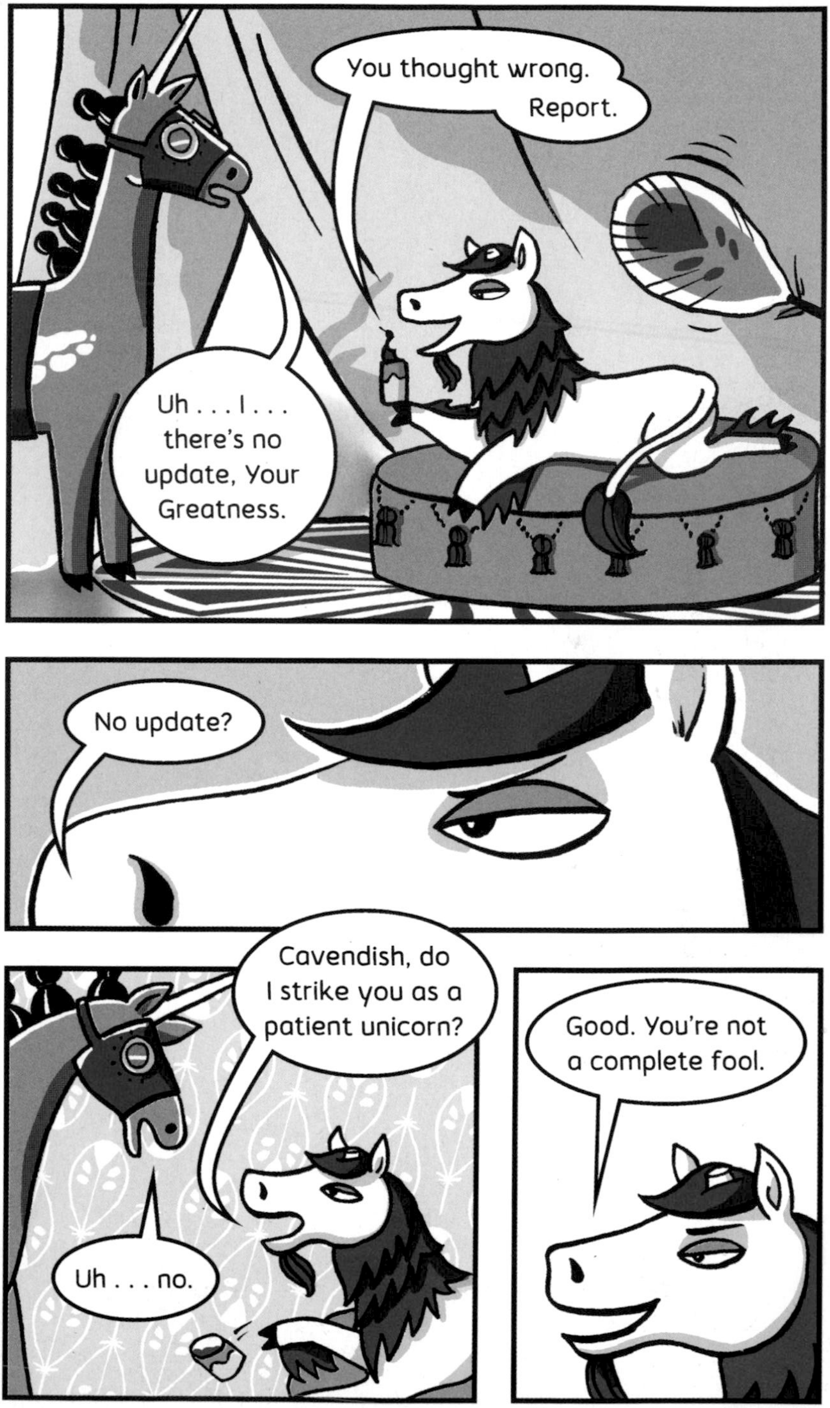
You thought wrong. Report.
Uh . . . I . . . there's no update, Your Greatness.
No update?
Cavendish, do I strike you as a patient unicorn?
Uh . . . no.
Good. You're not a complete fool.

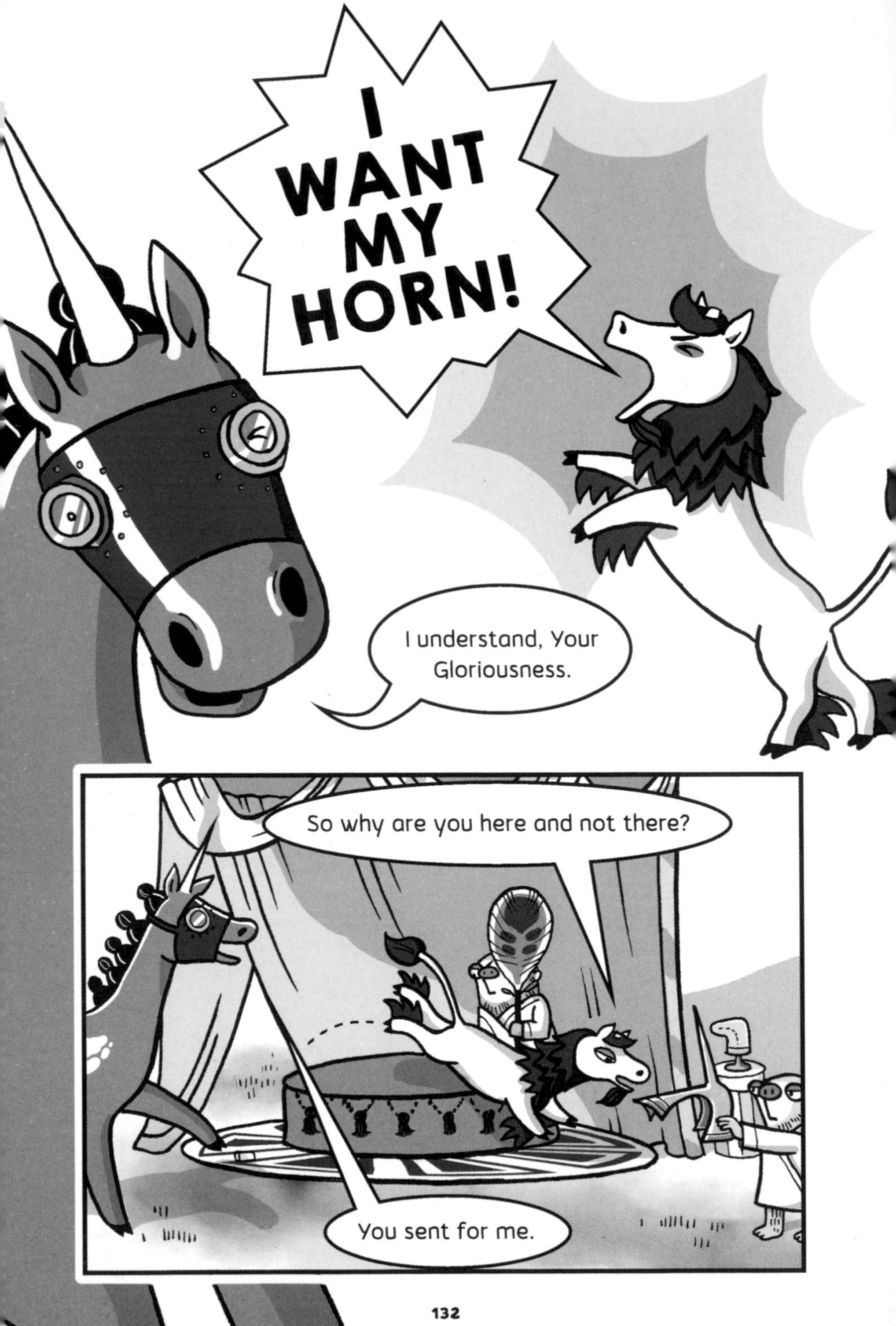
I WANT MY HORN!
I understand, Your Gloriousness.
So why are you here and not there?
You sent for me.

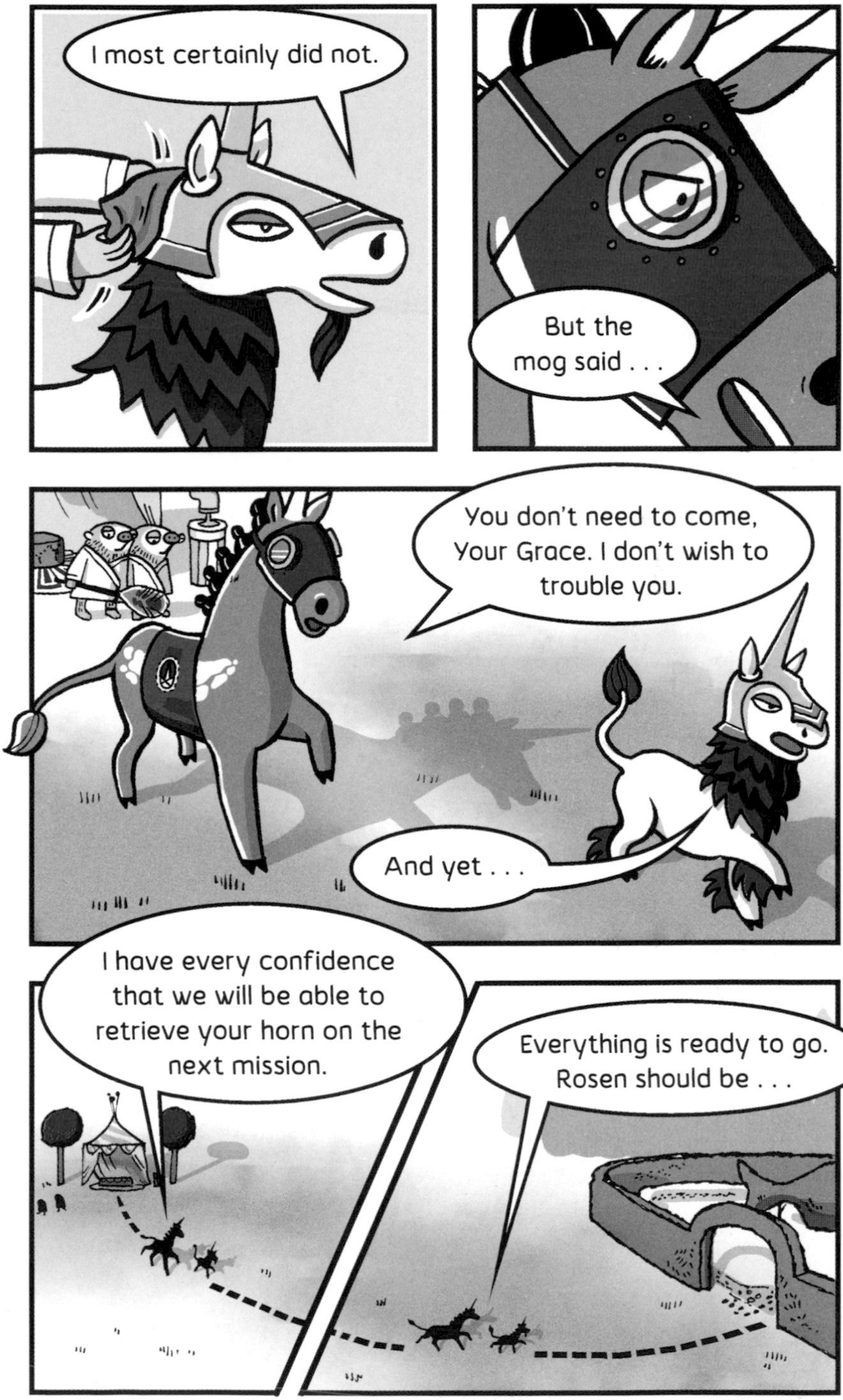
I most certainly did not.
But the mog said . . .
You don't need to come, Your Grace. I don't wish to trouble you.
And yet . . .
I have every confidence that we will be able to retrieve your horn on the next mission.
Everything is ready to go. Rosen should be . . .

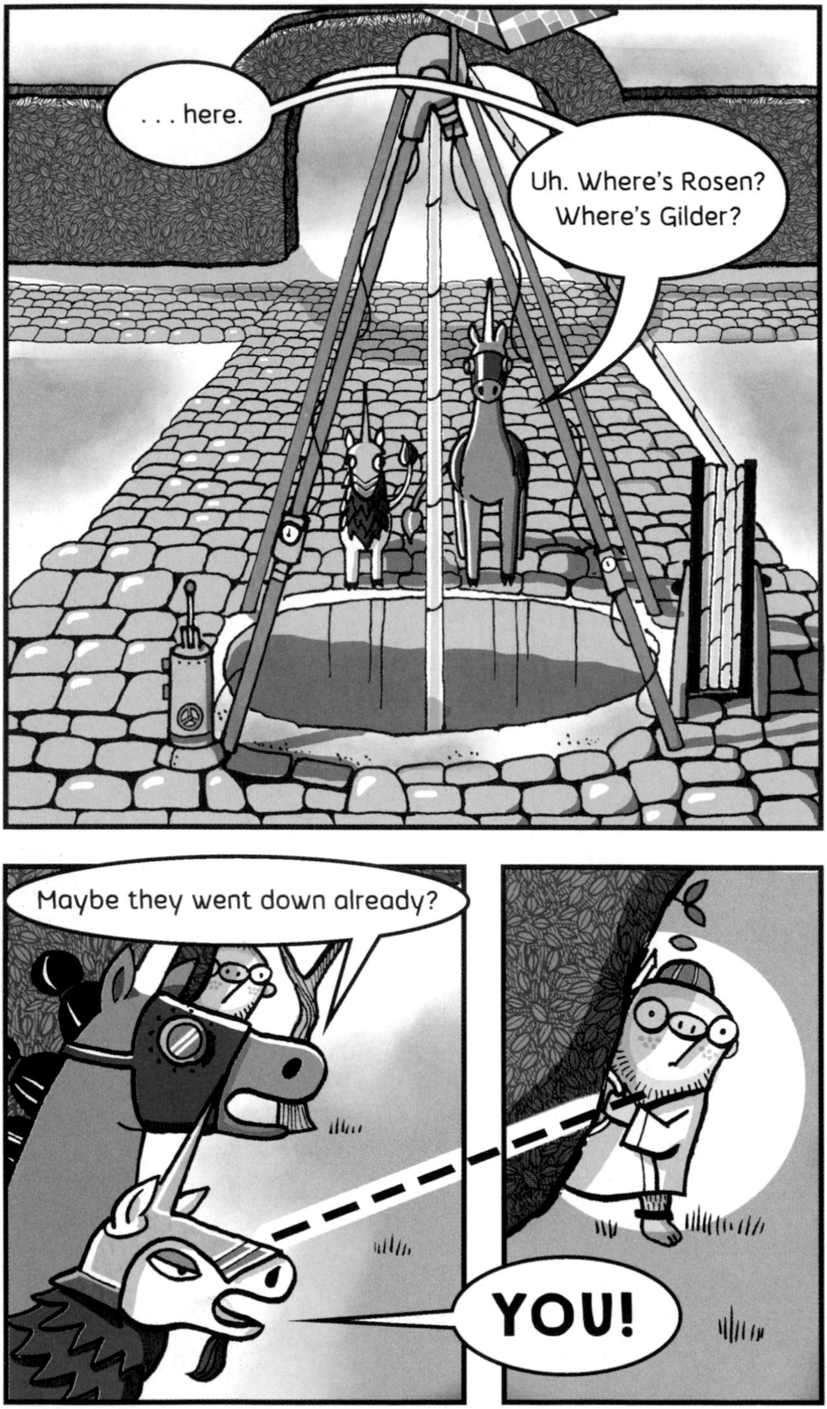
. . . here.
Uh. Where's Rosen? Where's Gilder?
Maybe they went down already?
YOU!

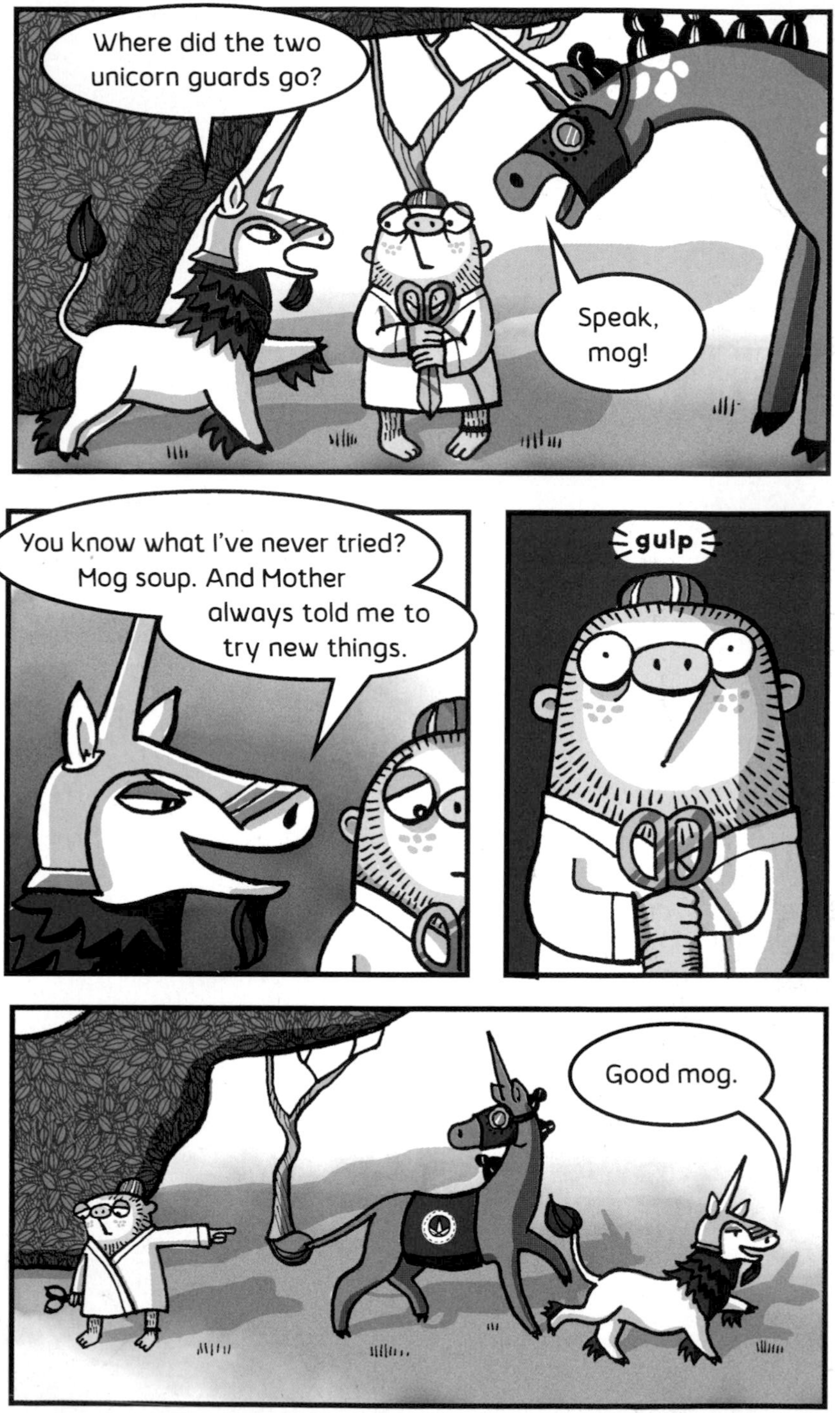
Where did the two unicorn guards go?
Speak, mog!
You know what I've never tried? Mog soup. And Mother always told me to try new things.
gulp
Good mog.

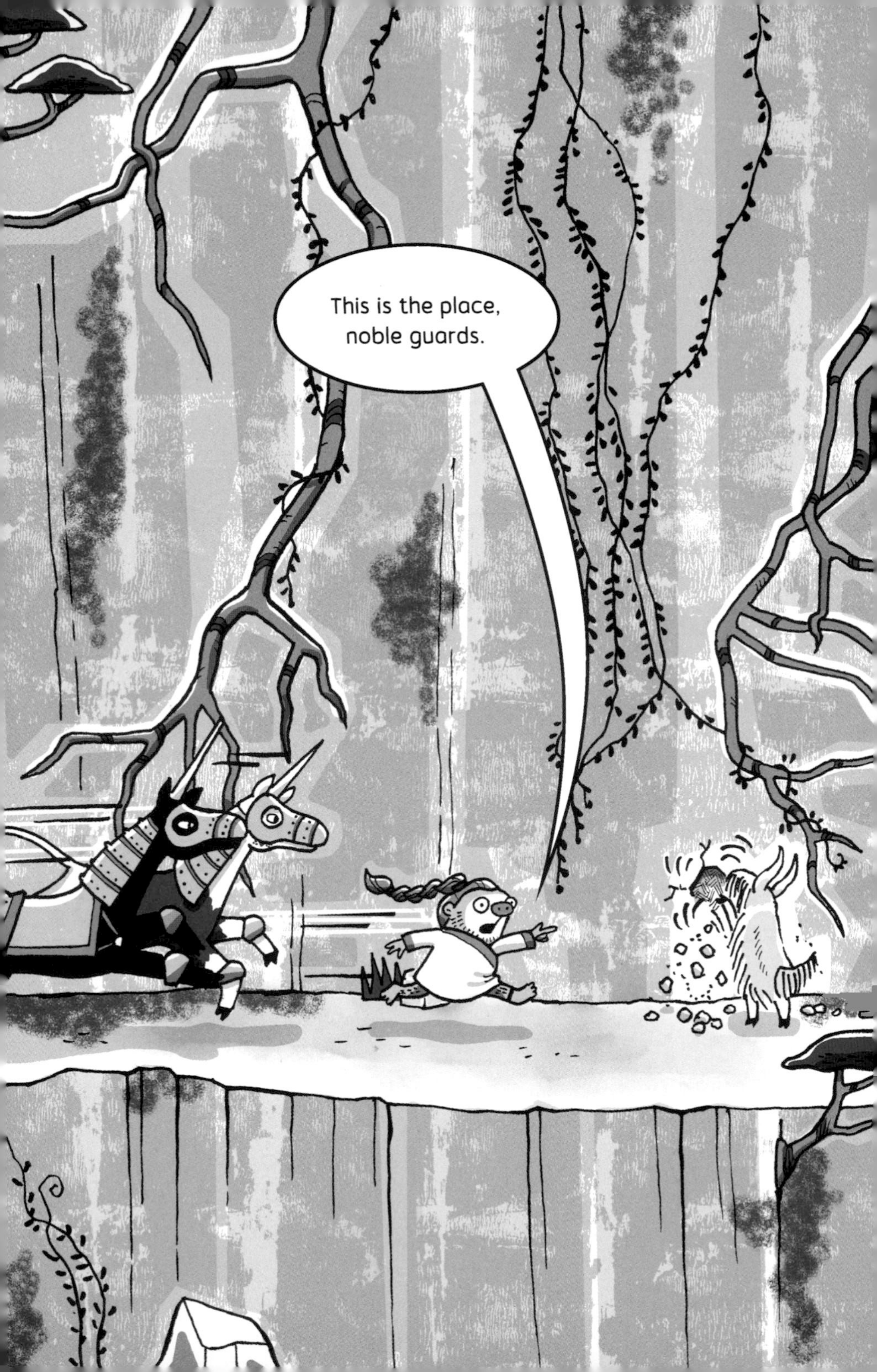
This is the place, noble guards.

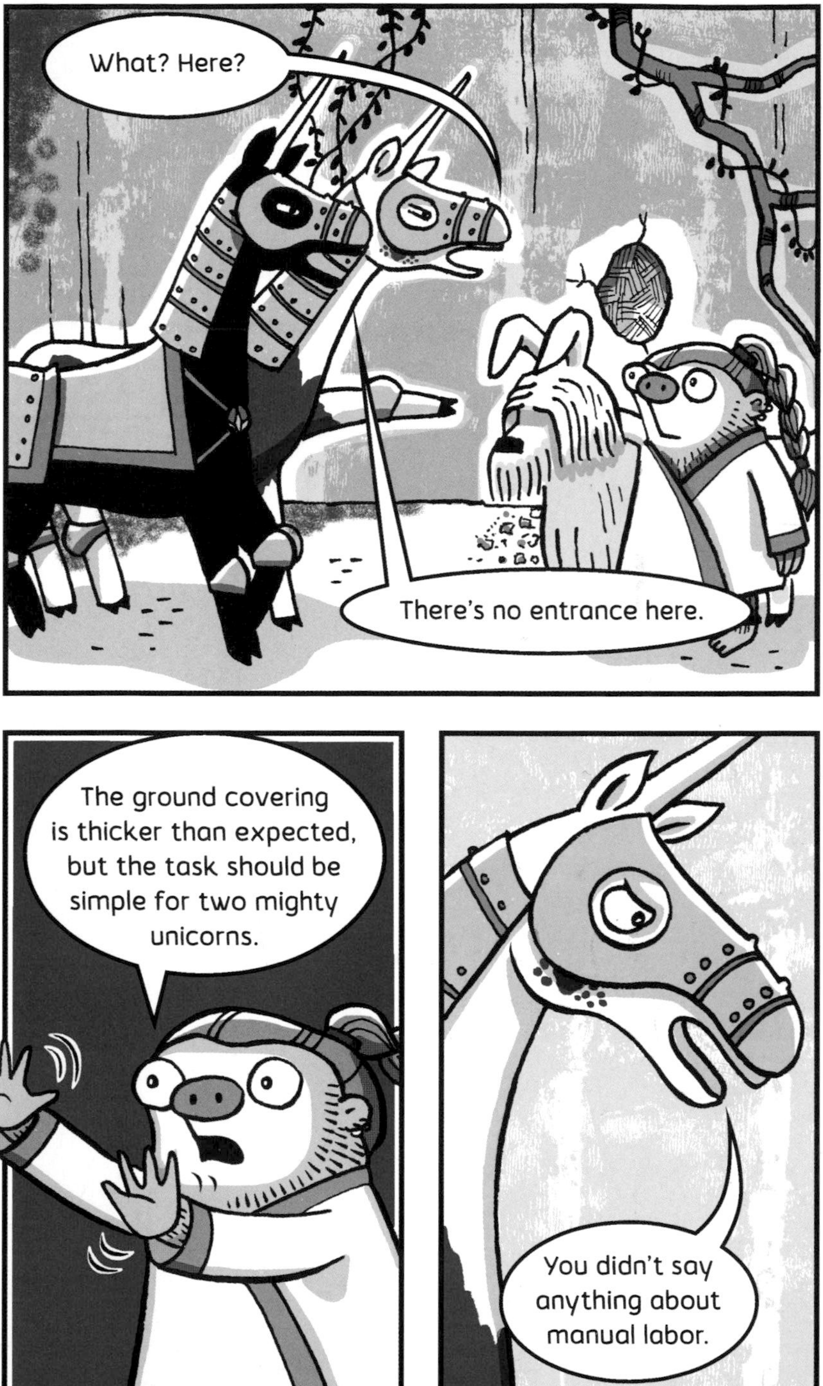
What? Here?
There's no entrance here.
The ground covering is thicker than expected, but the task should be simple for two mighty unicorns.
You didn't say anything about manual labor.

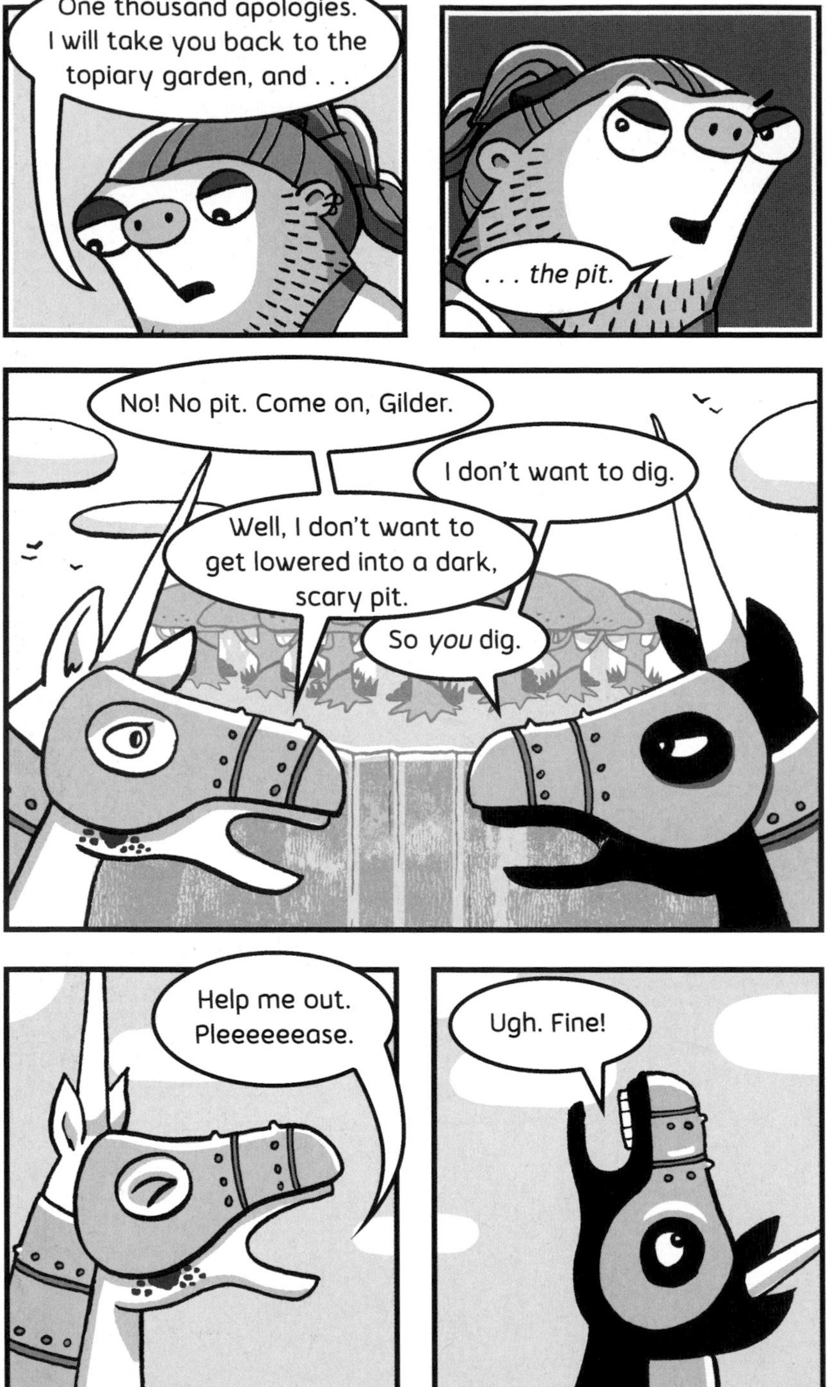
One thousand apologies. I will take you back to the topiary garden, and . . .
. . . *the pit.*
No! No pit. Come on, Gilder.
I don't want to dig.
Well, I don't want to get lowered into a dark, scary pit.
So *you* dig.
Help me out. Pleeeeeease.
Ugh. Fine!

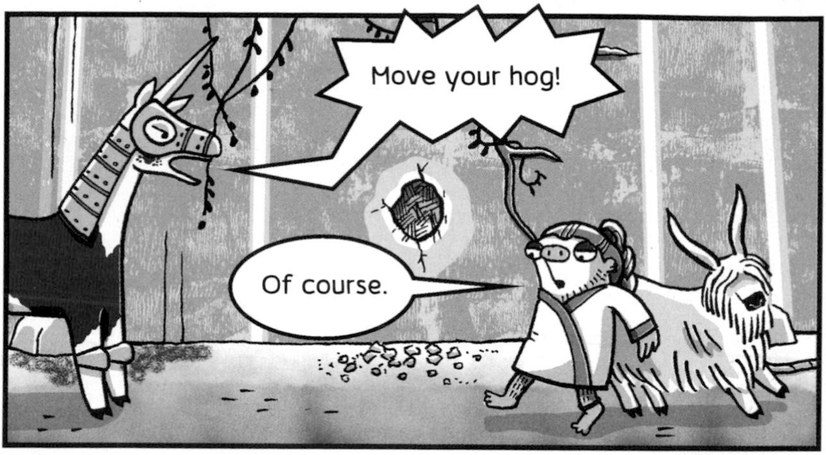
Move your hog!
Of course.

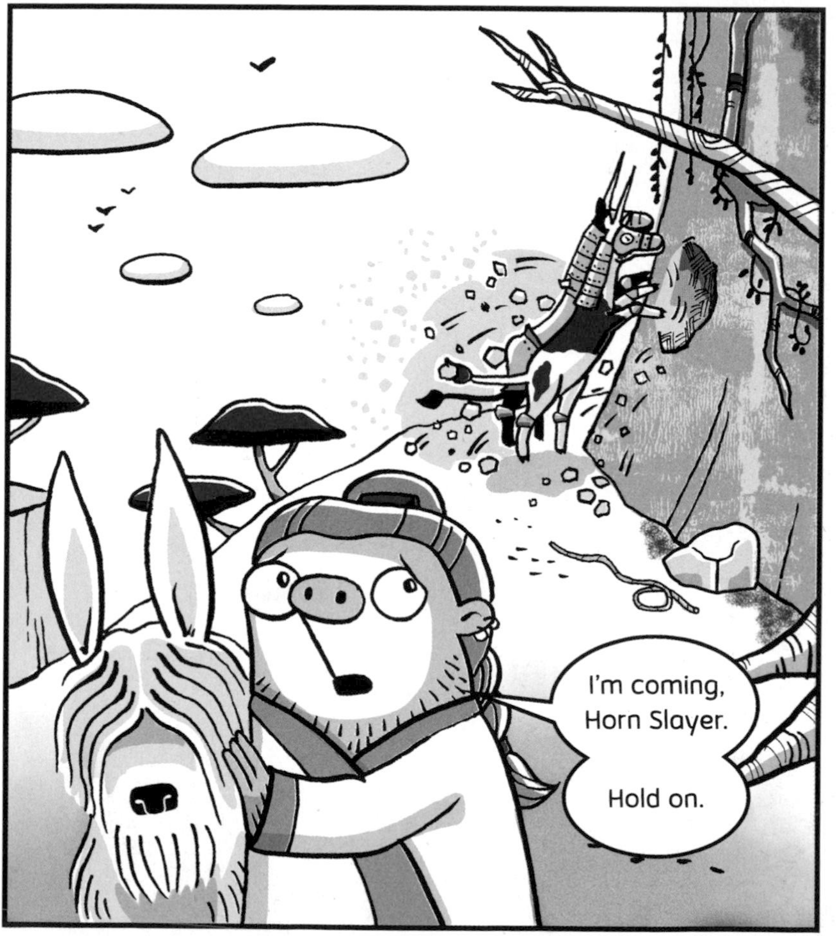
I'm coming, Horn Slayer.
Hold on.

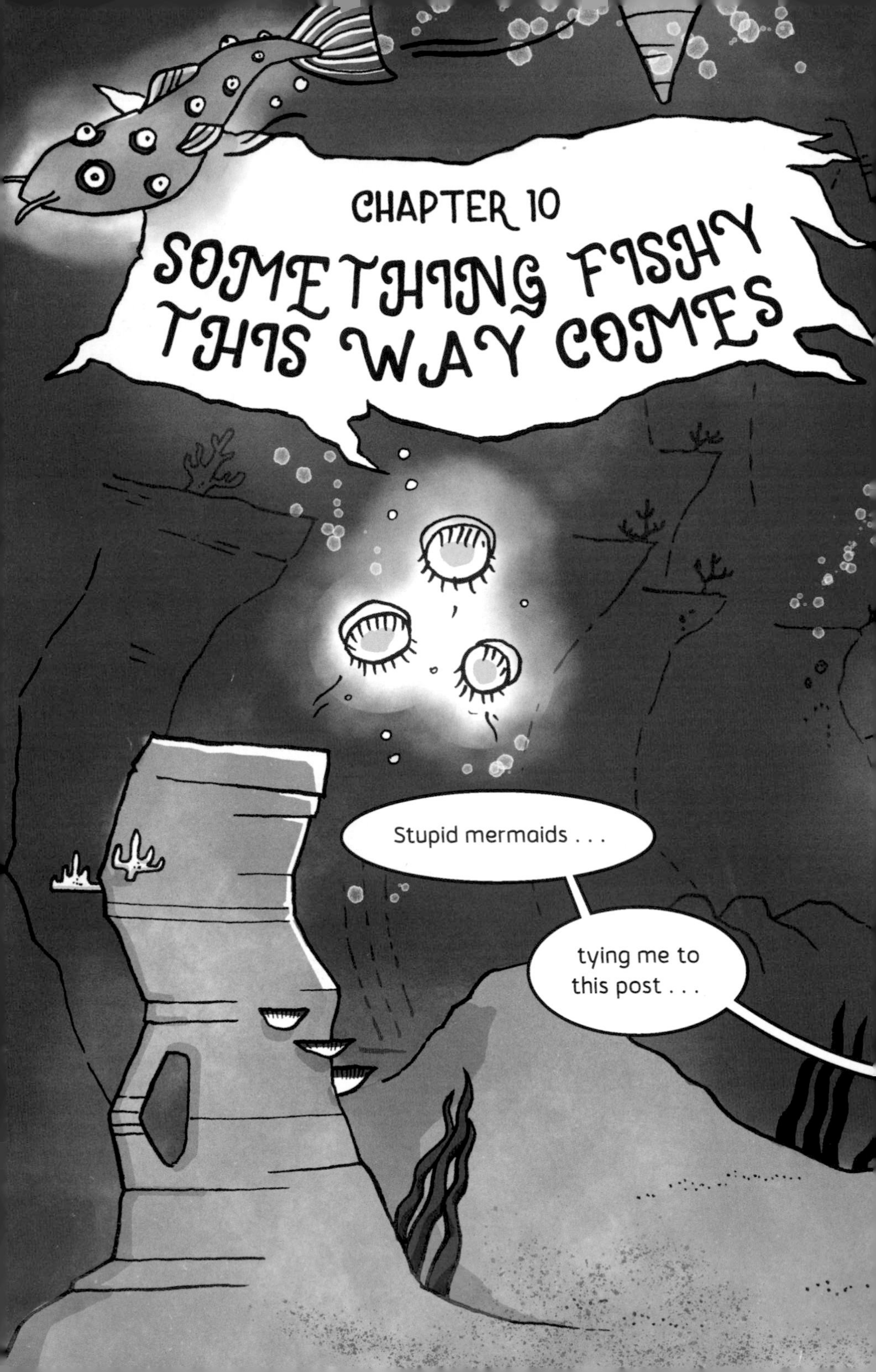
CHAPTER 10
SOMETHING FISHY THIS WAY COMES
Stupid mermaids . . .
tying me to this post . . .

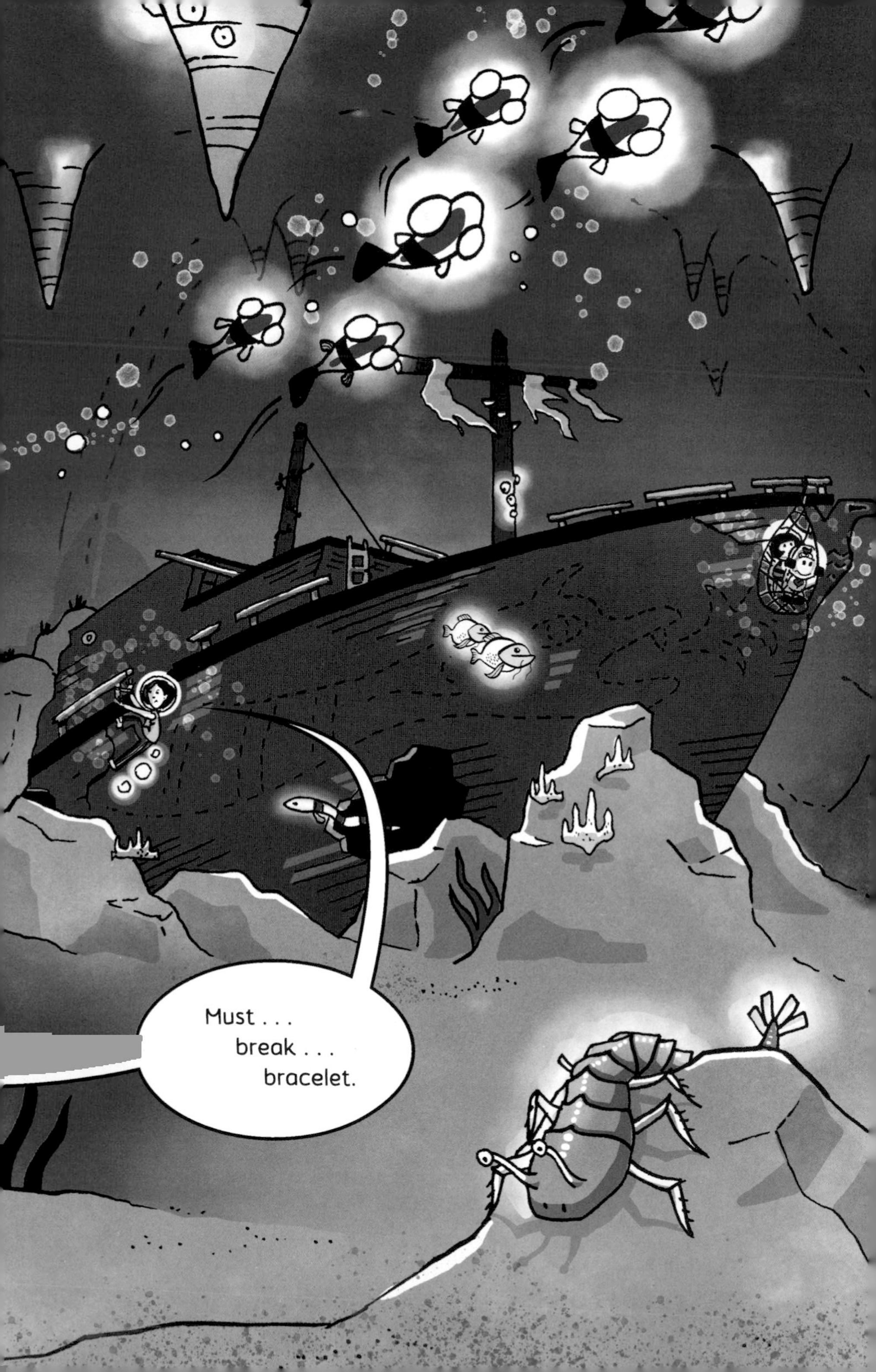
Must . . . break . . . bracelet.

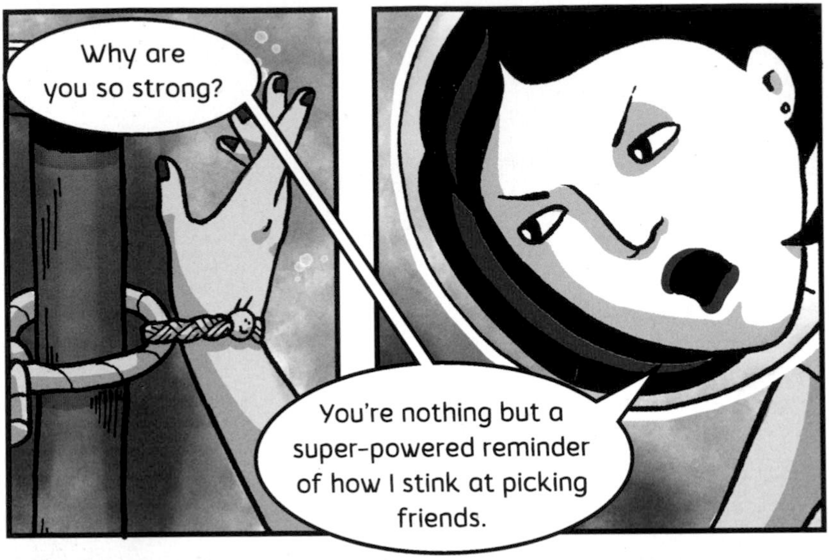
Why are you so strong?
You're nothing but a super-powered reminder of how I stink at picking friends.

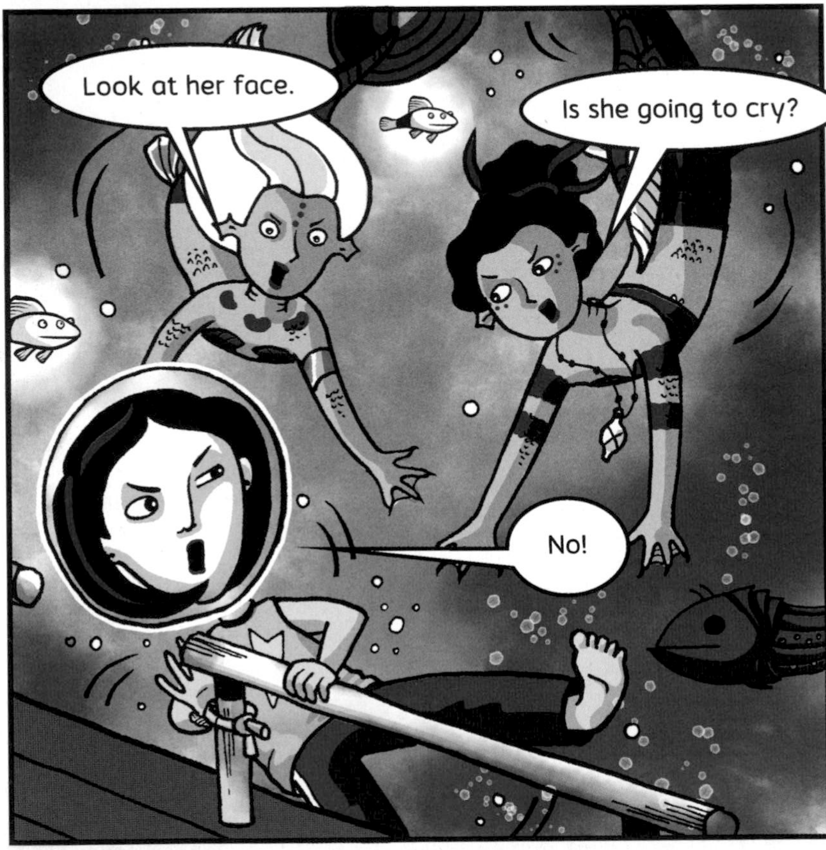
Look at her face.
Is she going to cry?
No!

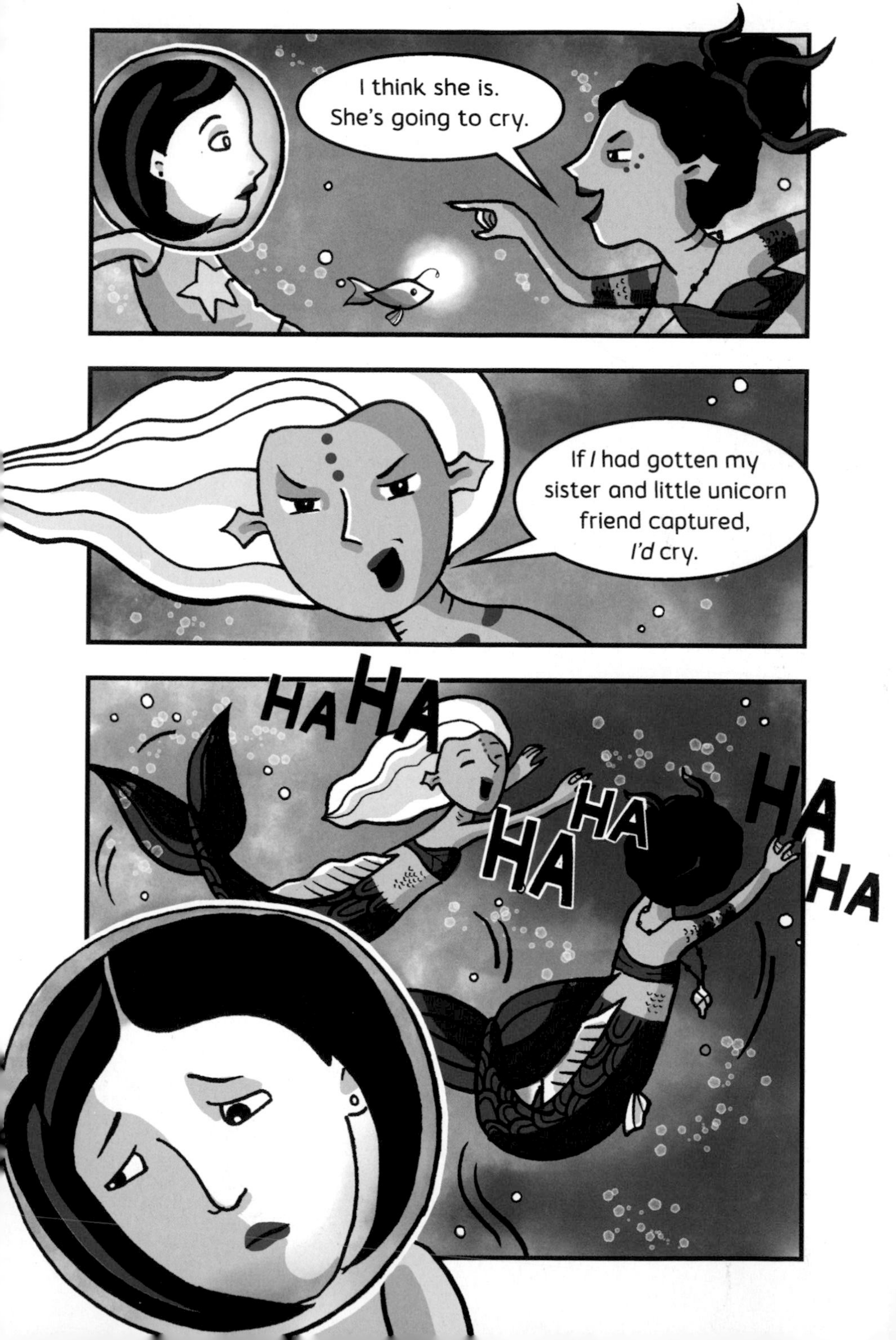
I think she is. She's going to cry.
If *I* had gotten my sister and little unicorn friend captured, *I'd* cry.
HAHA
HAHA
HA HA
HA

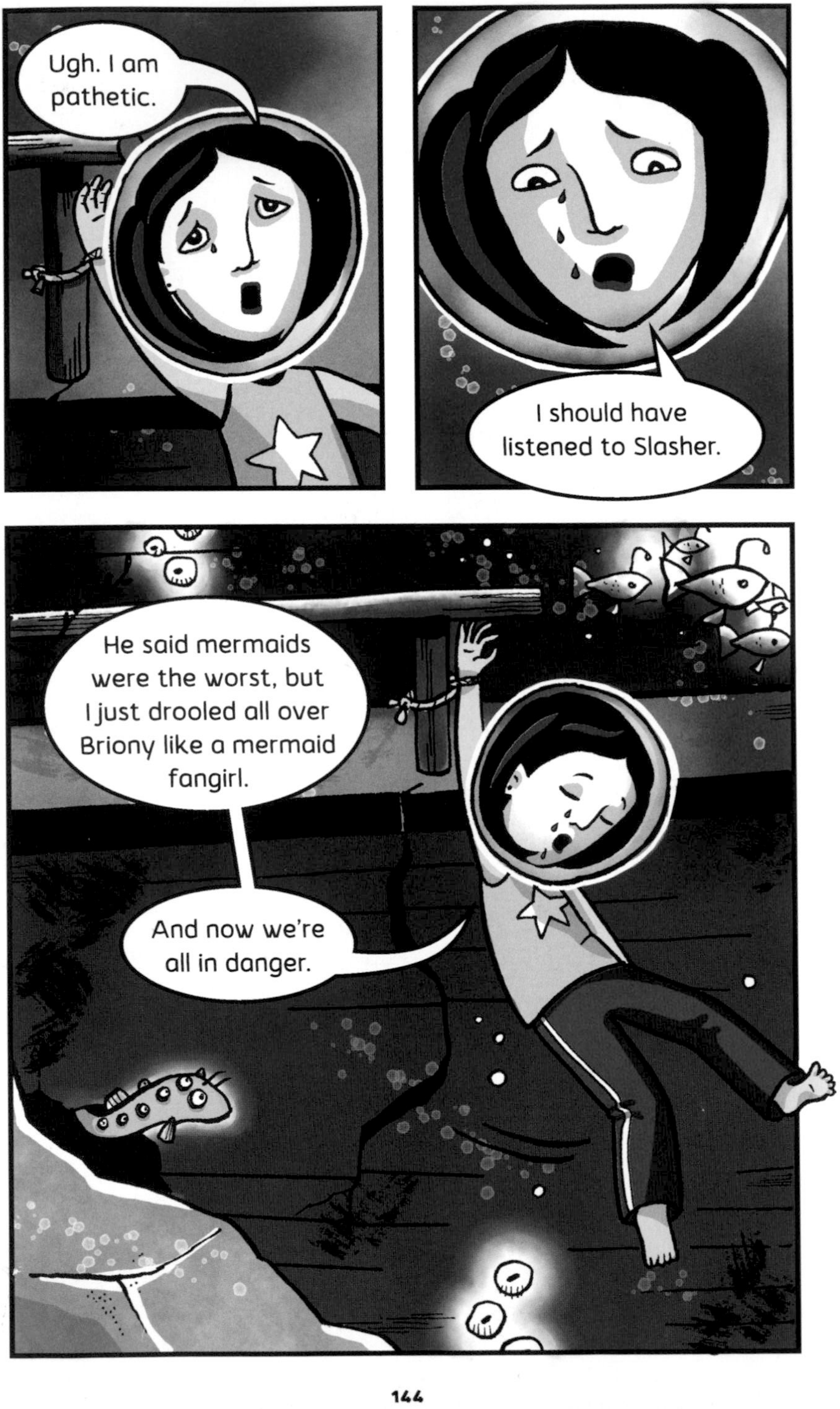
Ugh. I am pathetic.
I should have listened to Slasher.
He said mermaids were the worst, but I just drooled all over Briony like a mermaid fangirl.
And now we're all in danger.

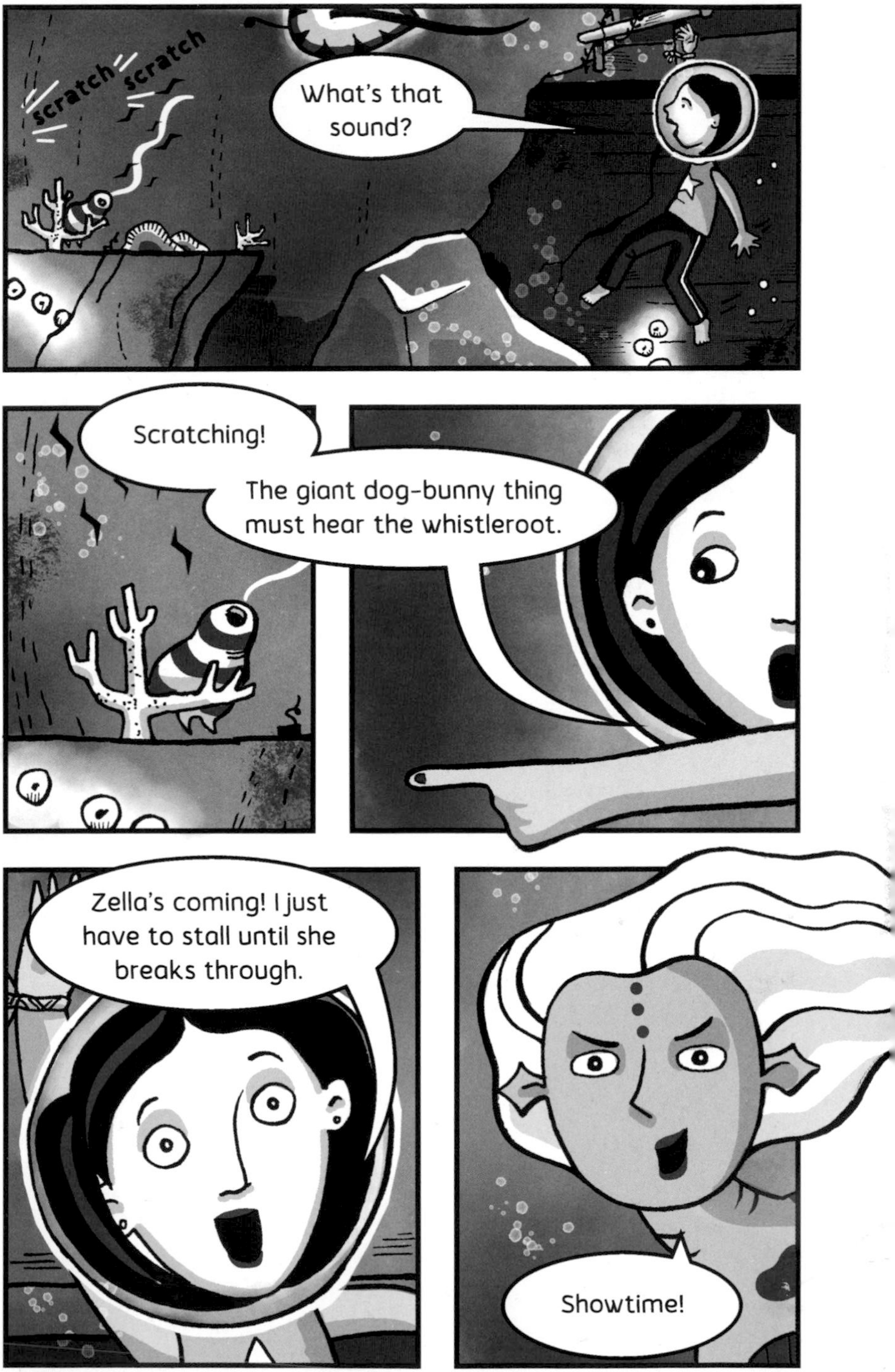
scratch scratch
What's that sound?
Scratching!
The giant dog-bunny thing must hear the whistleroot.
Zella's coming! I just have to stall until she breaks through.
Showtime!

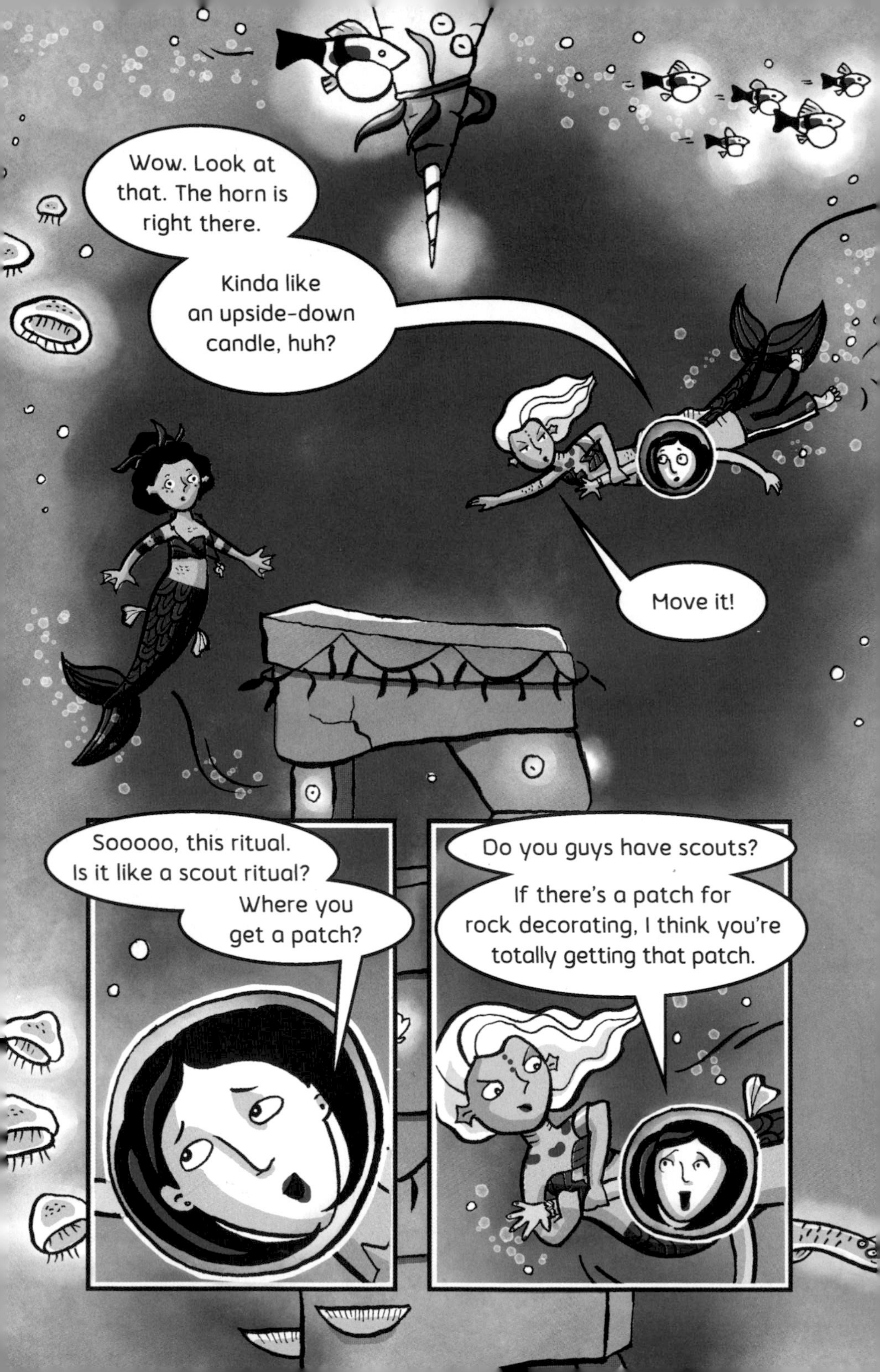
Wow. Look at that. The horn is right there.
Kinda like an upside-down candle, huh?
Move it!
Sooooo, this ritual. Is it like a scout ritual?
Where you get a patch?
Do you guys have scouts?
If there's a patch for rock decorating, I think you're totally getting that patch.

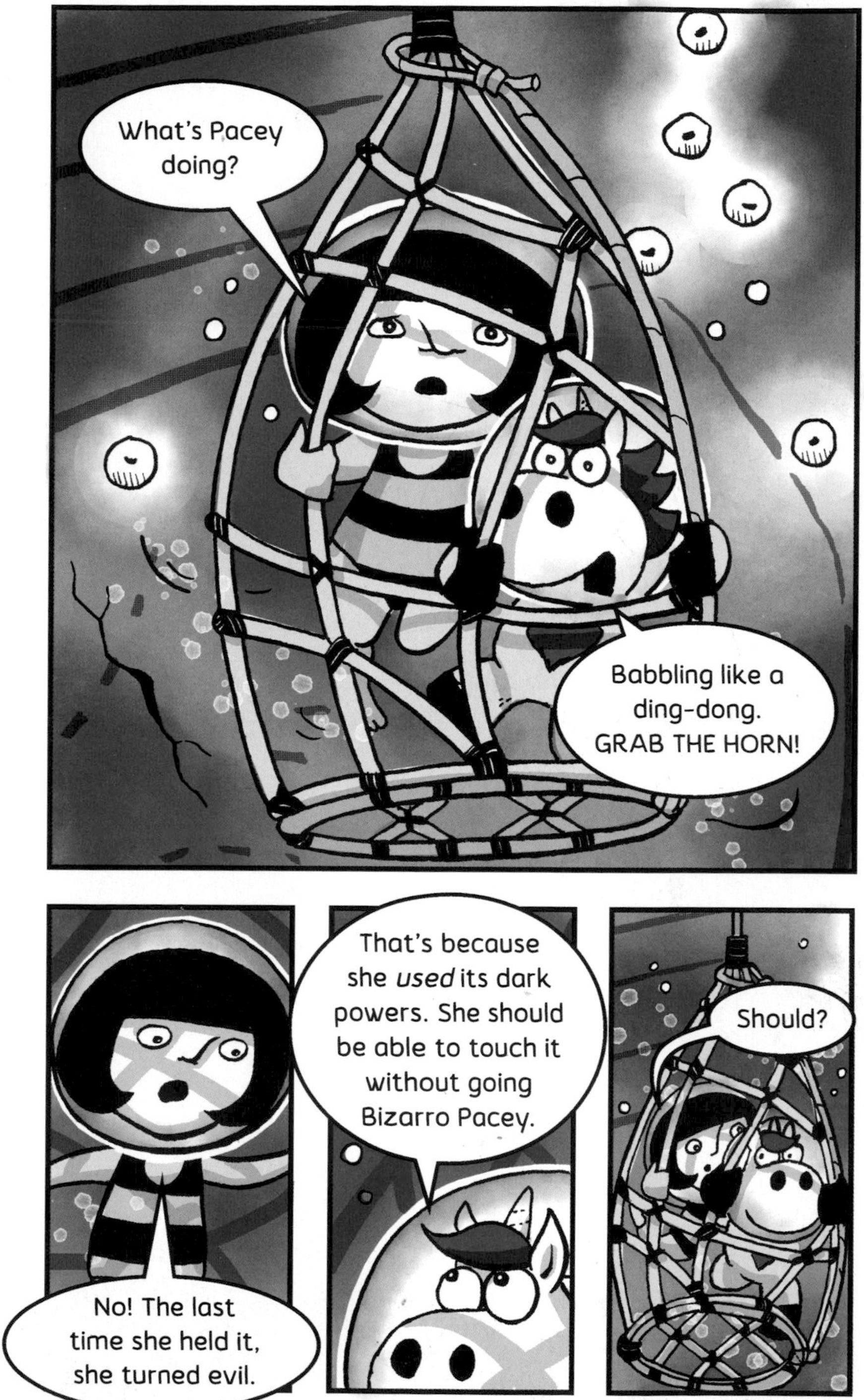
What's Pacey doing?
Babbling like a ding-dong. GRAB THE HORN!
No! The last time she held it, she turned evil.
That's because she *used* its dark powers. She should be able to touch it without going Bizarro Pacey.
Should?

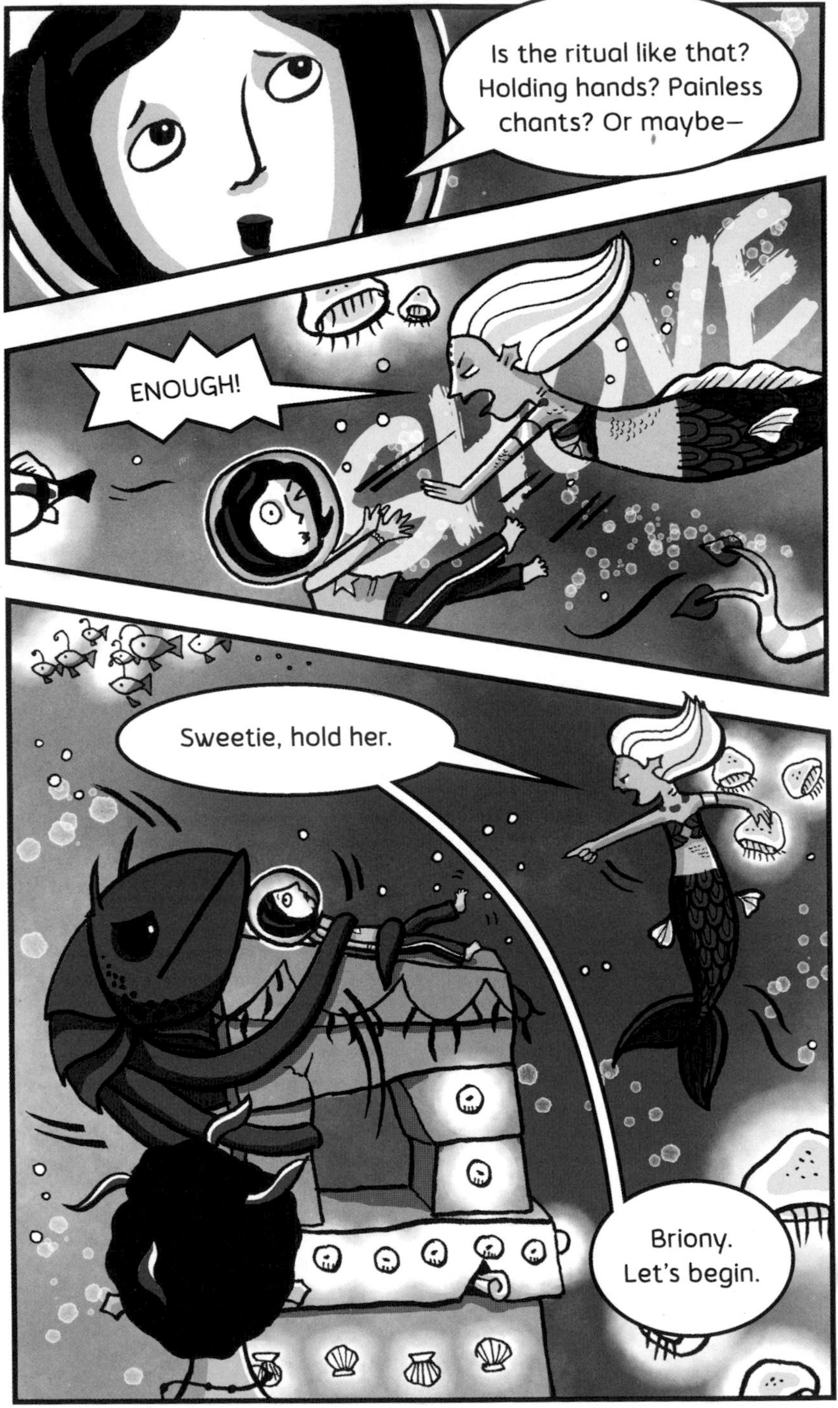
Is the ritual like that? Holding hands? Painless chants? Or maybe—
SHOVE
ENOUGH!
Sweetie, hold her.
Briony. Let's begin.

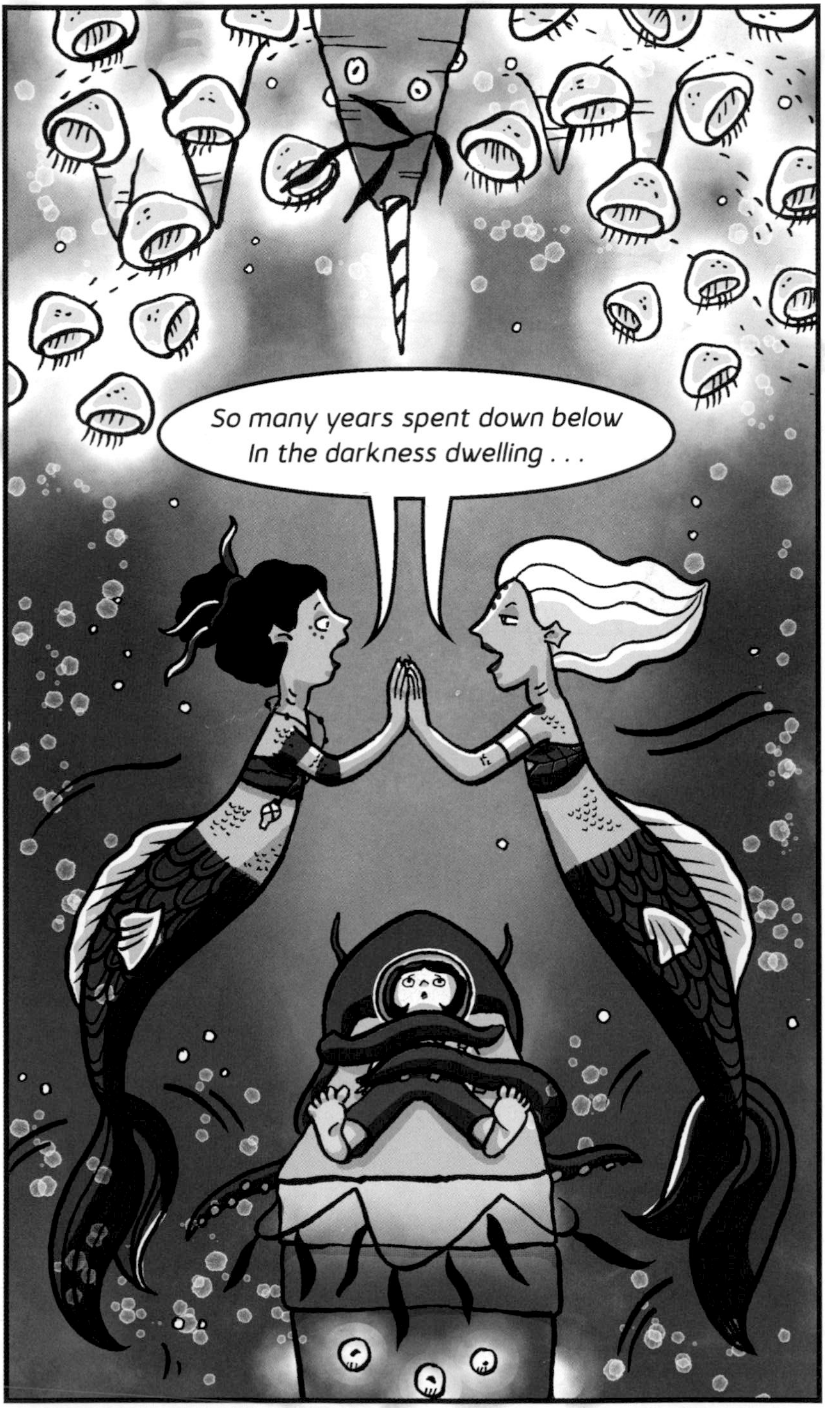
So many years spent down below
In the darkness dwelling . . .

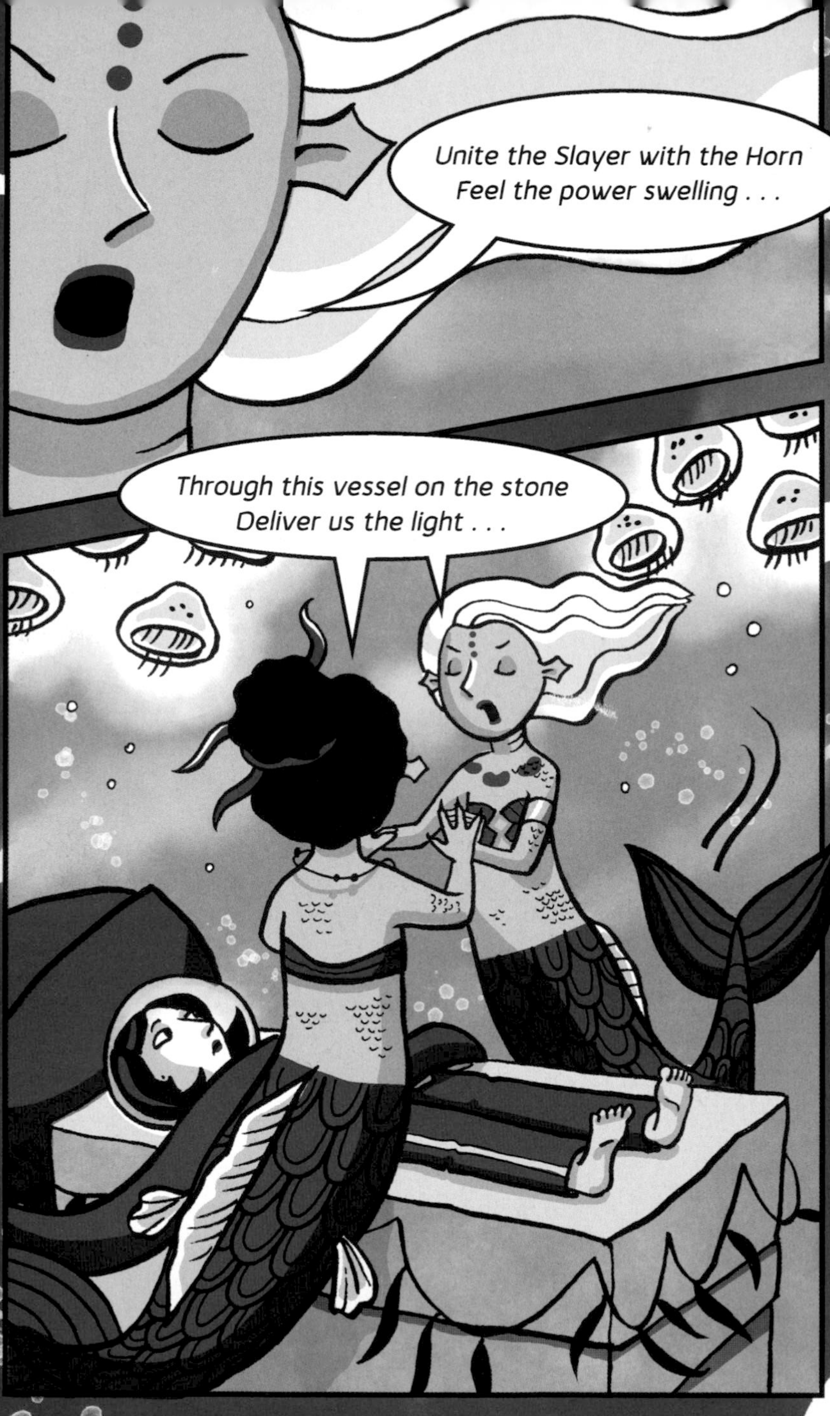
Unite the Slayer with the Horn
Feel the power swelling . . .
Through this vessel on the stone
Deliver us the light . . .

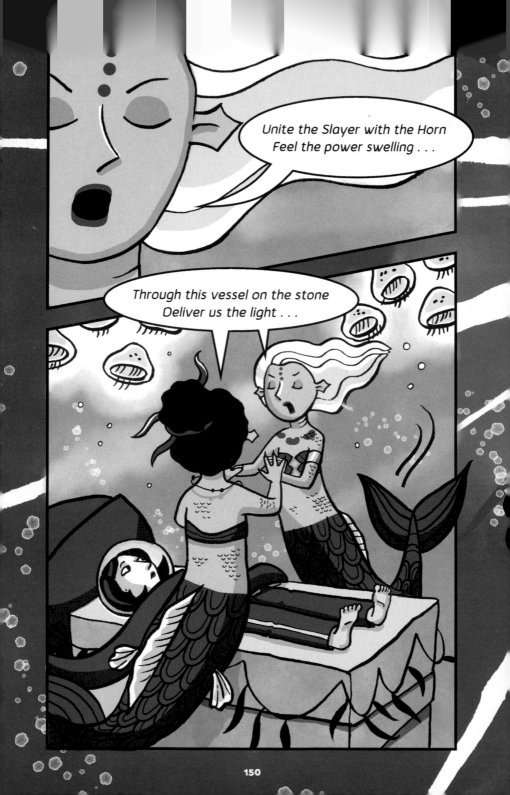

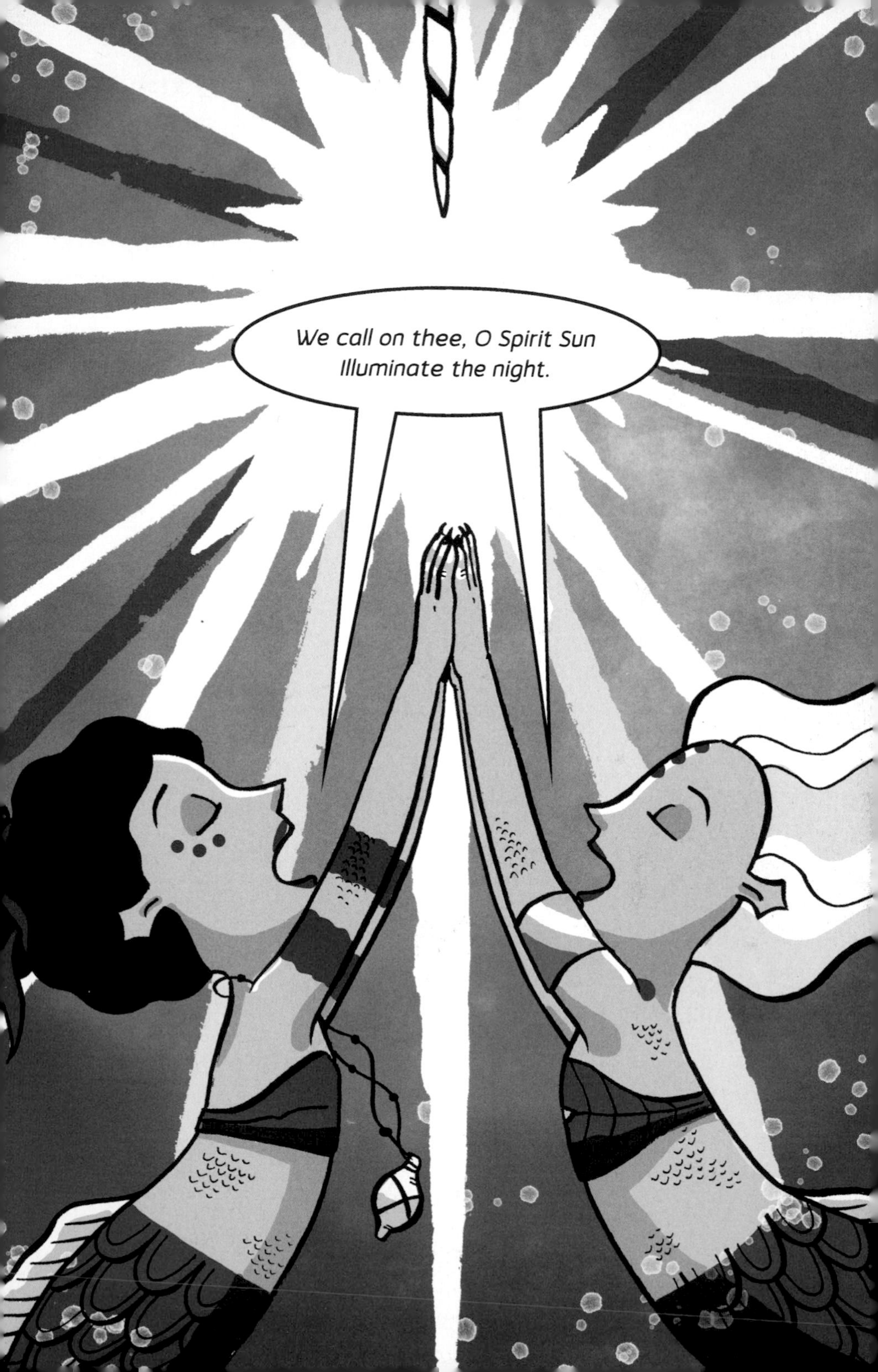
We call on thee, O Spirit Sun
Illuminate the night.

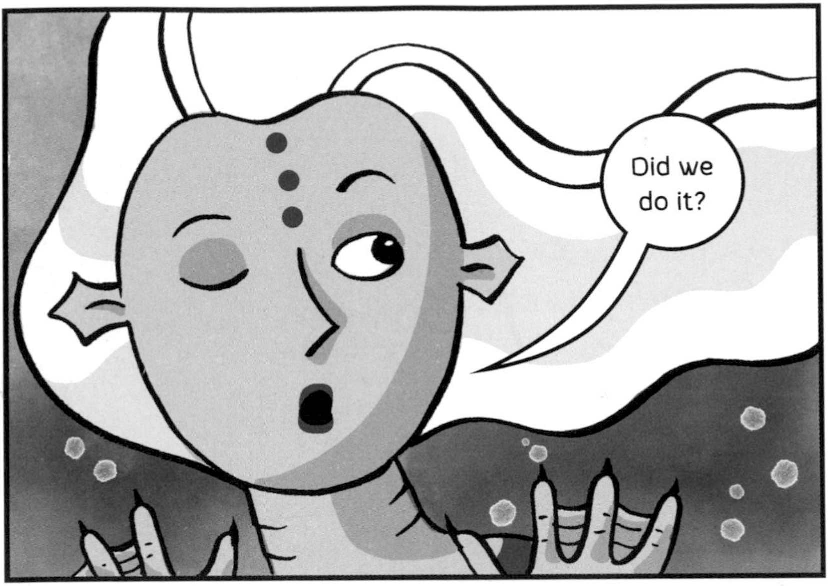
Did we do it?

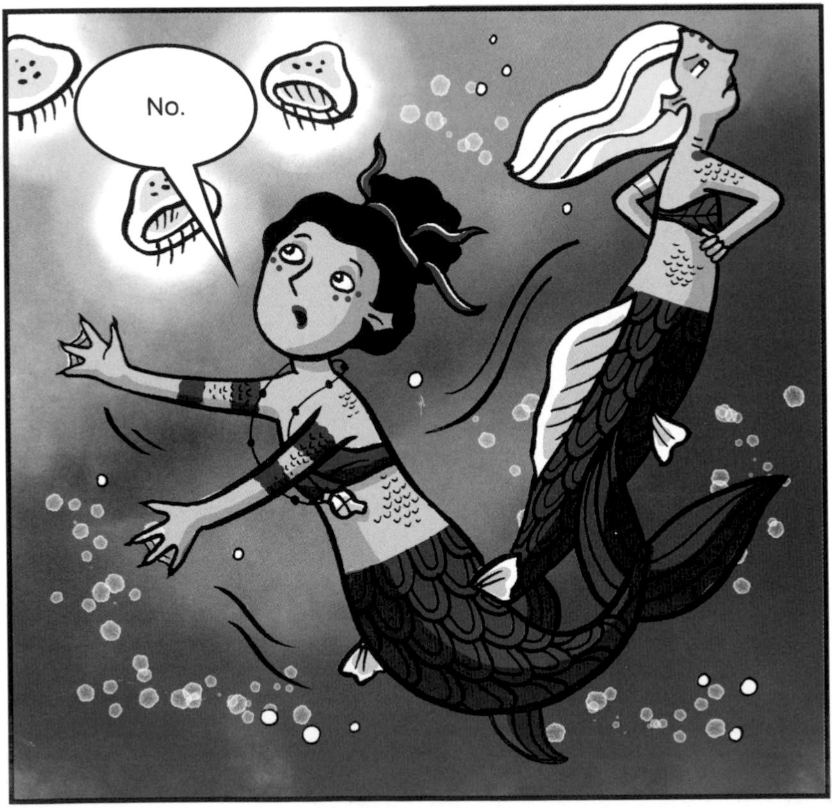
No.

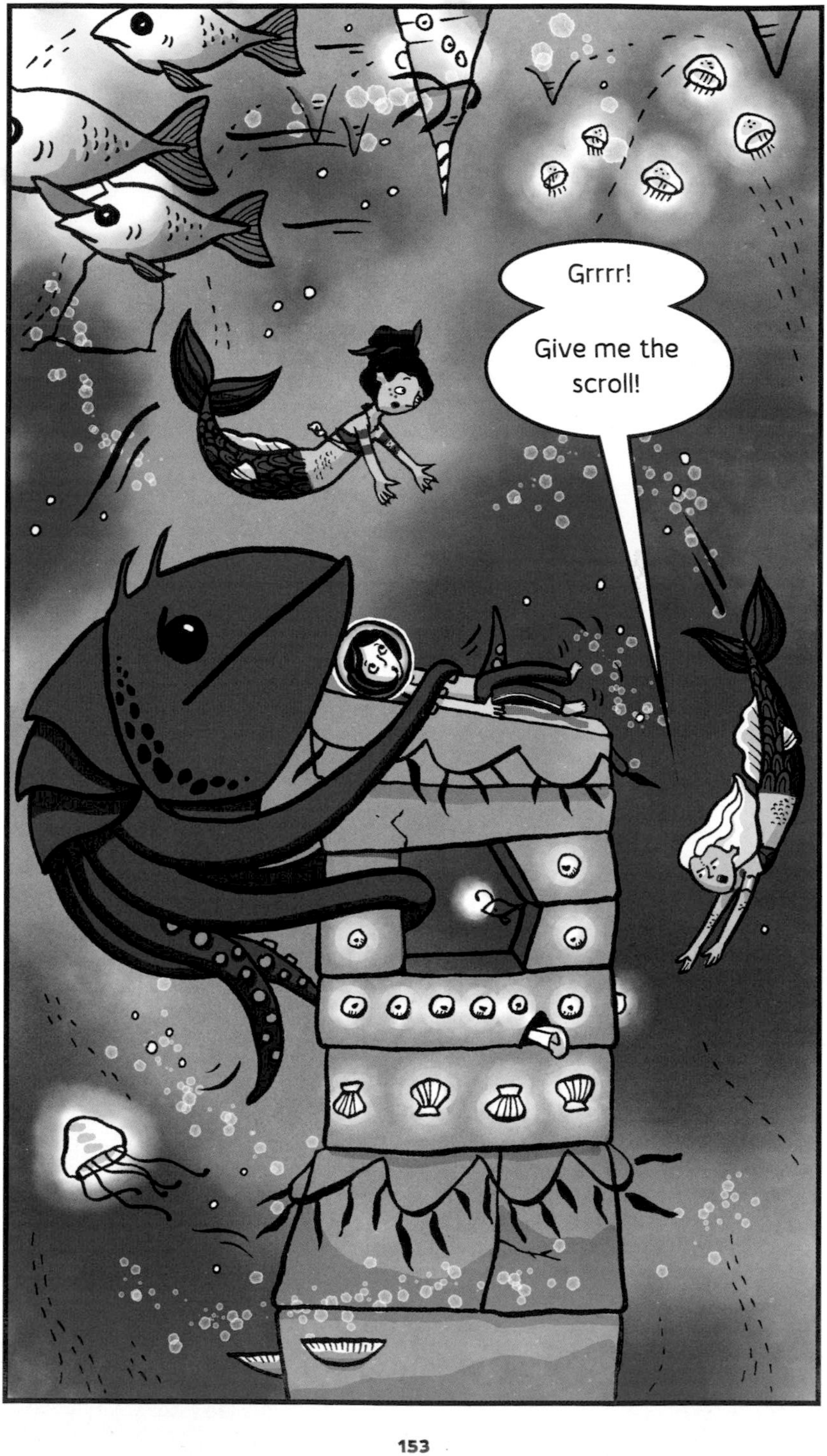
Grrrr!
Give me the scroll!

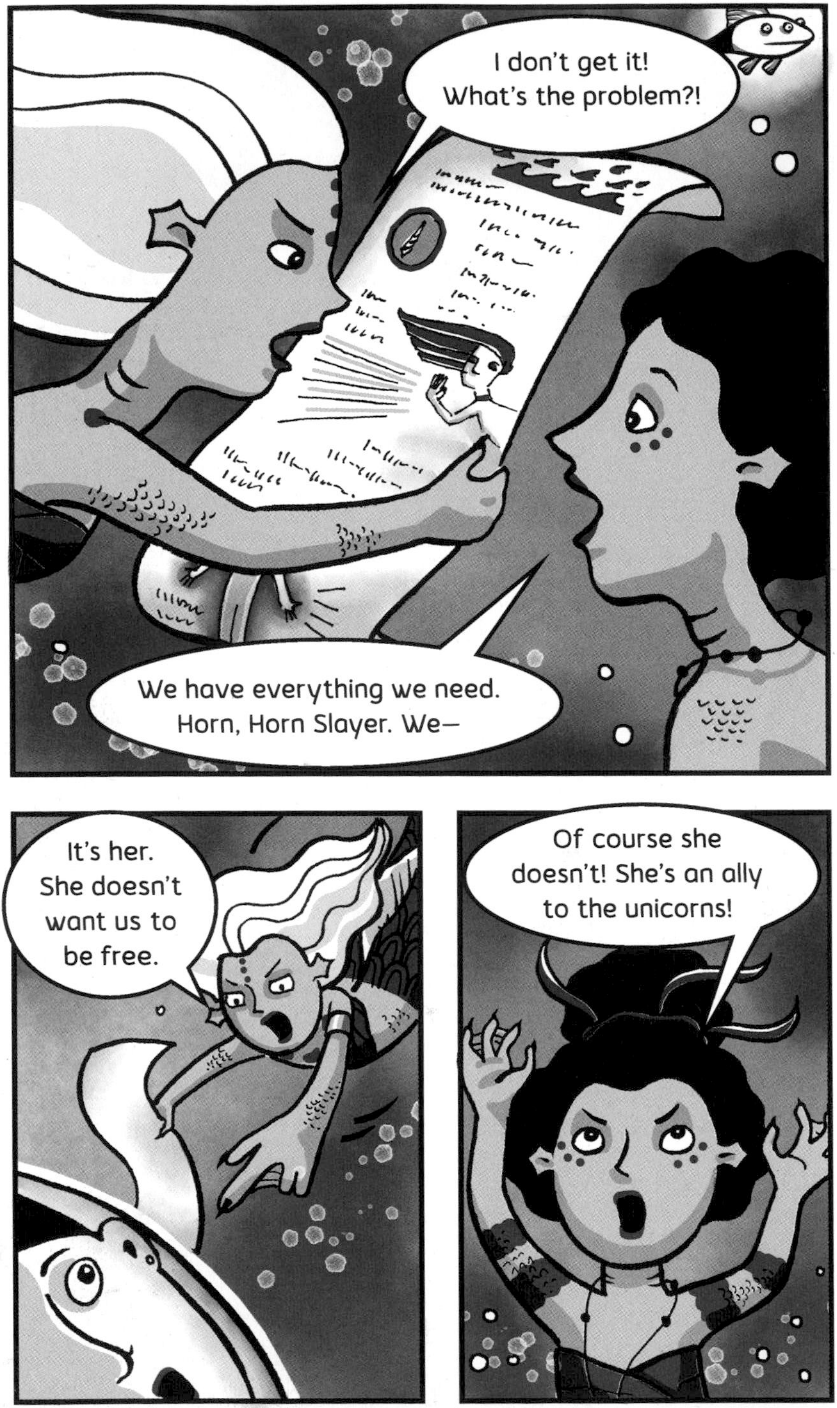
I don't get it! What's the problem?!
We have everything we need. Horn, Horn Slayer. We—
It's her. She doesn't want us to be free.
Of course she doesn't! She's an ally to the unicorns!

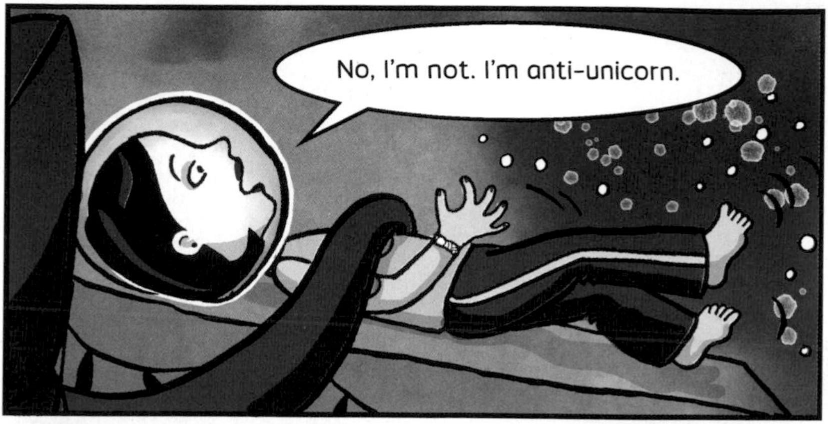
No, I'm not. I'm anti-unicorn.

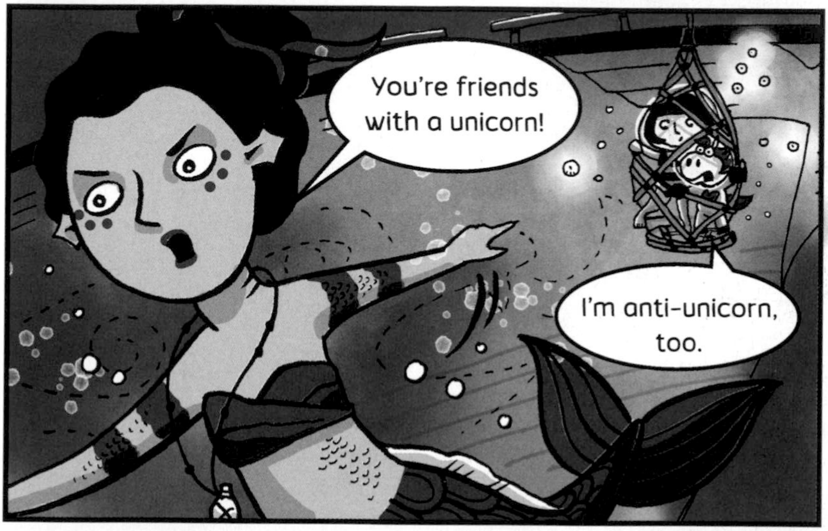
You're friends with a unicorn!
I'm anti-unicorn, too.

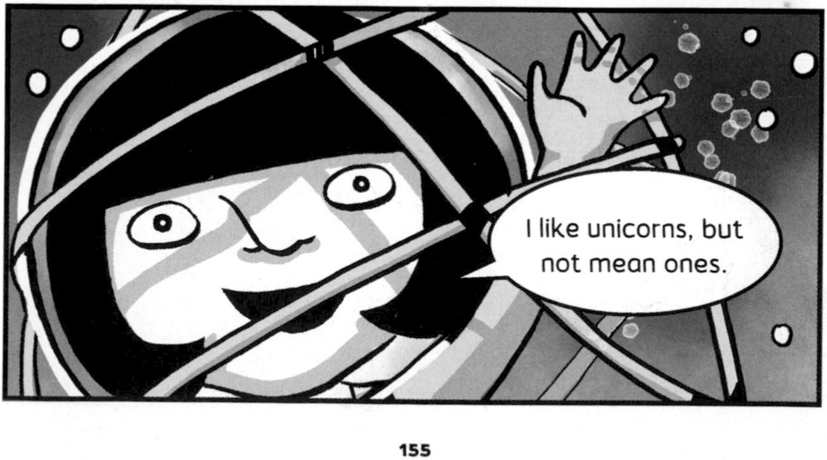
I like unicorns, but not mean ones.

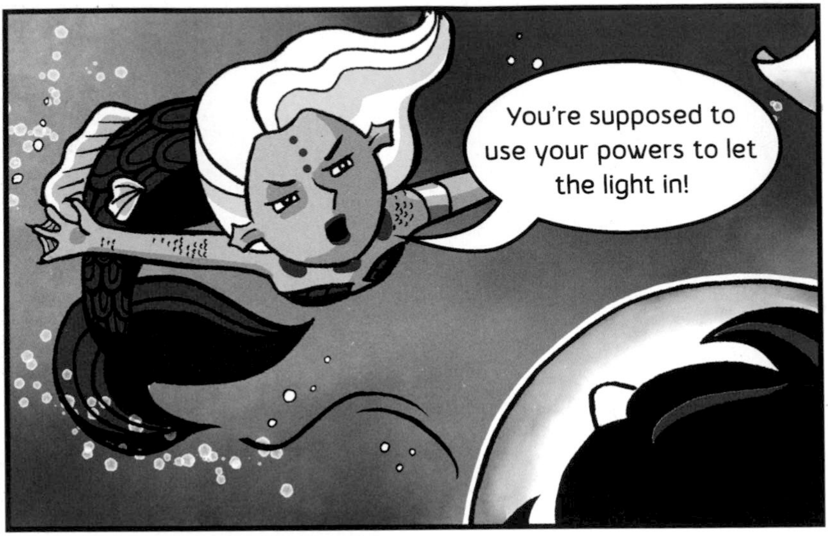
You're supposed to use your powers to let the light in!

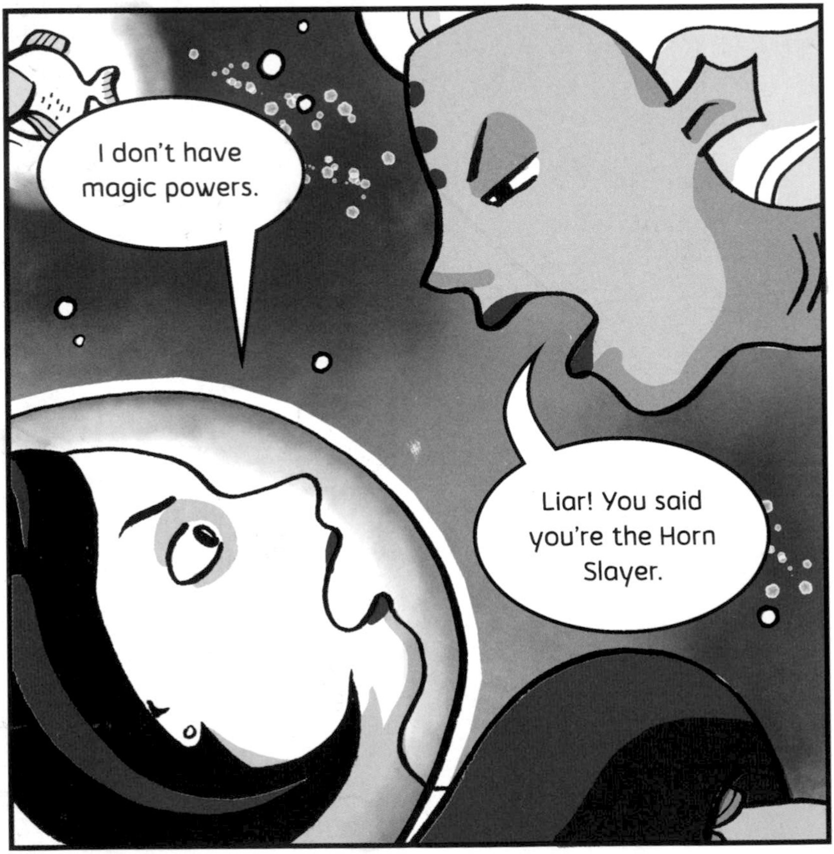
I don't have magic powers.
Liar! You said you're the Horn Slayer.

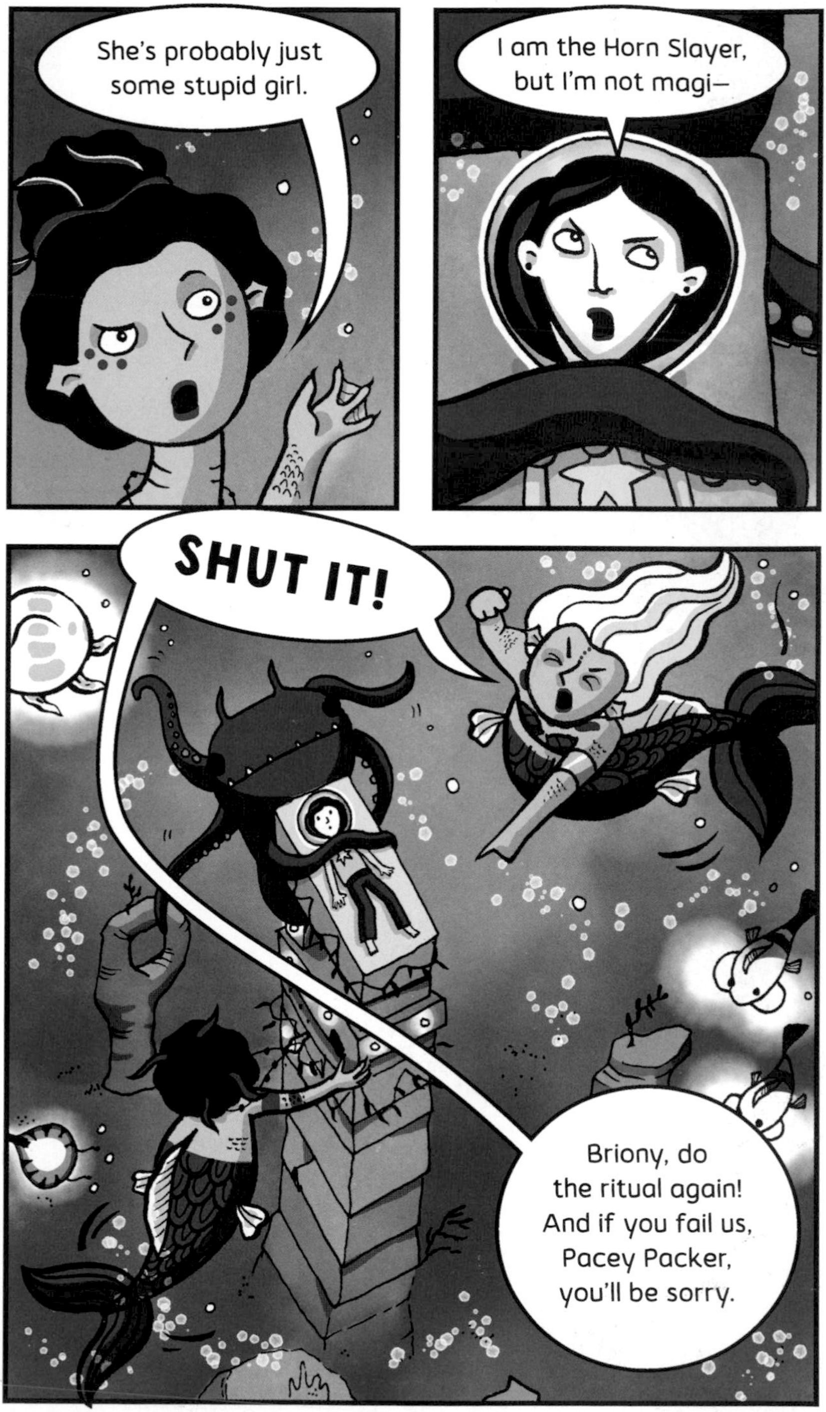
She's probably just some stupid girl.
I am the Horn Slayer, but I'm not magi–
SHUT IT!
Briony, do the ritual again! And if you fail us, Pacey Packer, you'll be sorry.

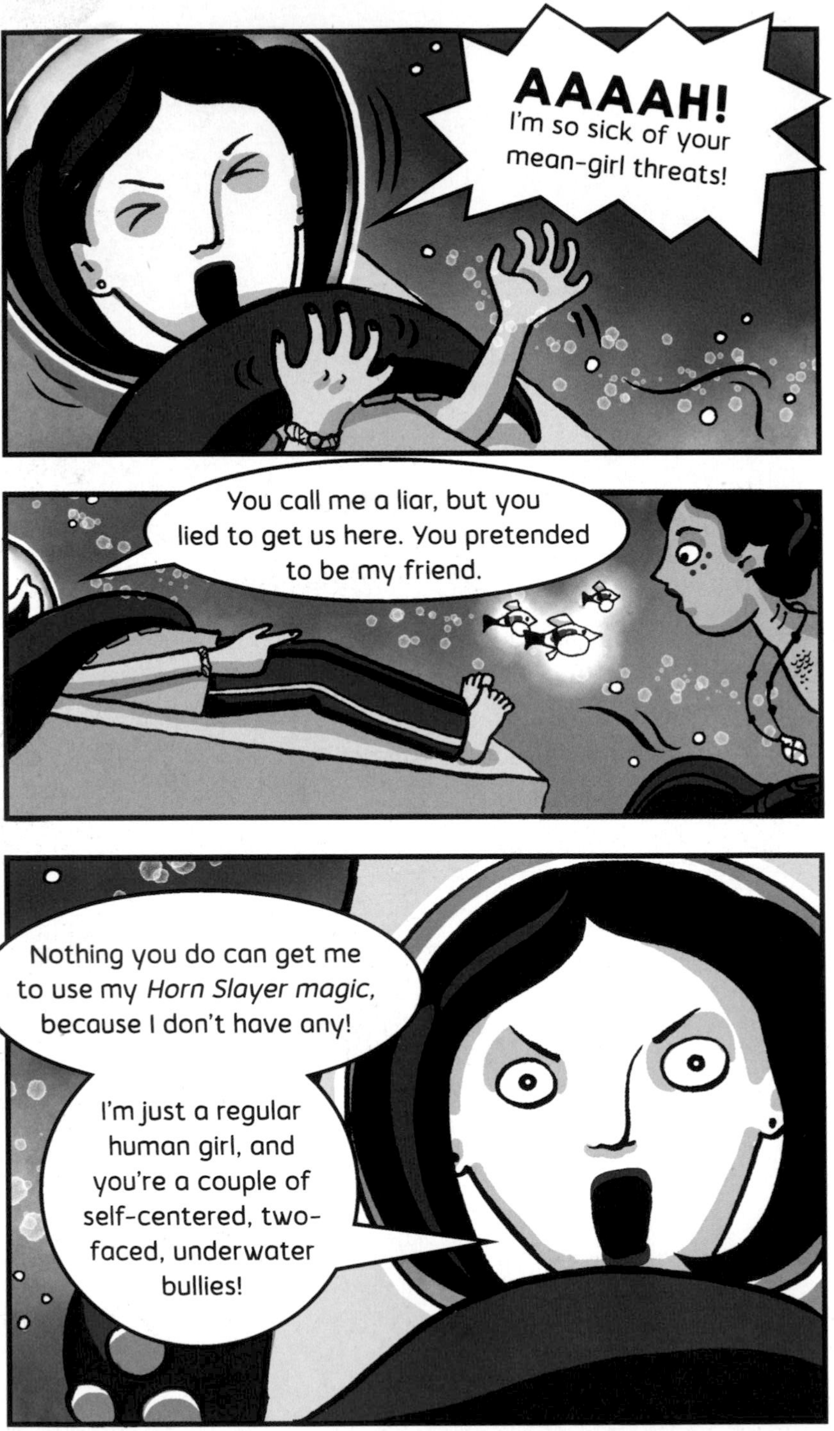
AAAAH!
I'm so sick of your mean-girl threats!
You call me a liar, but you lied to get us here. You pretended to be my friend.
Nothing you do can get me to use my *Horn Slayer magic,* because I don't have any!
I'm just a regular human girl, and you're a couple of self-centered, two-faced, underwater bullies!

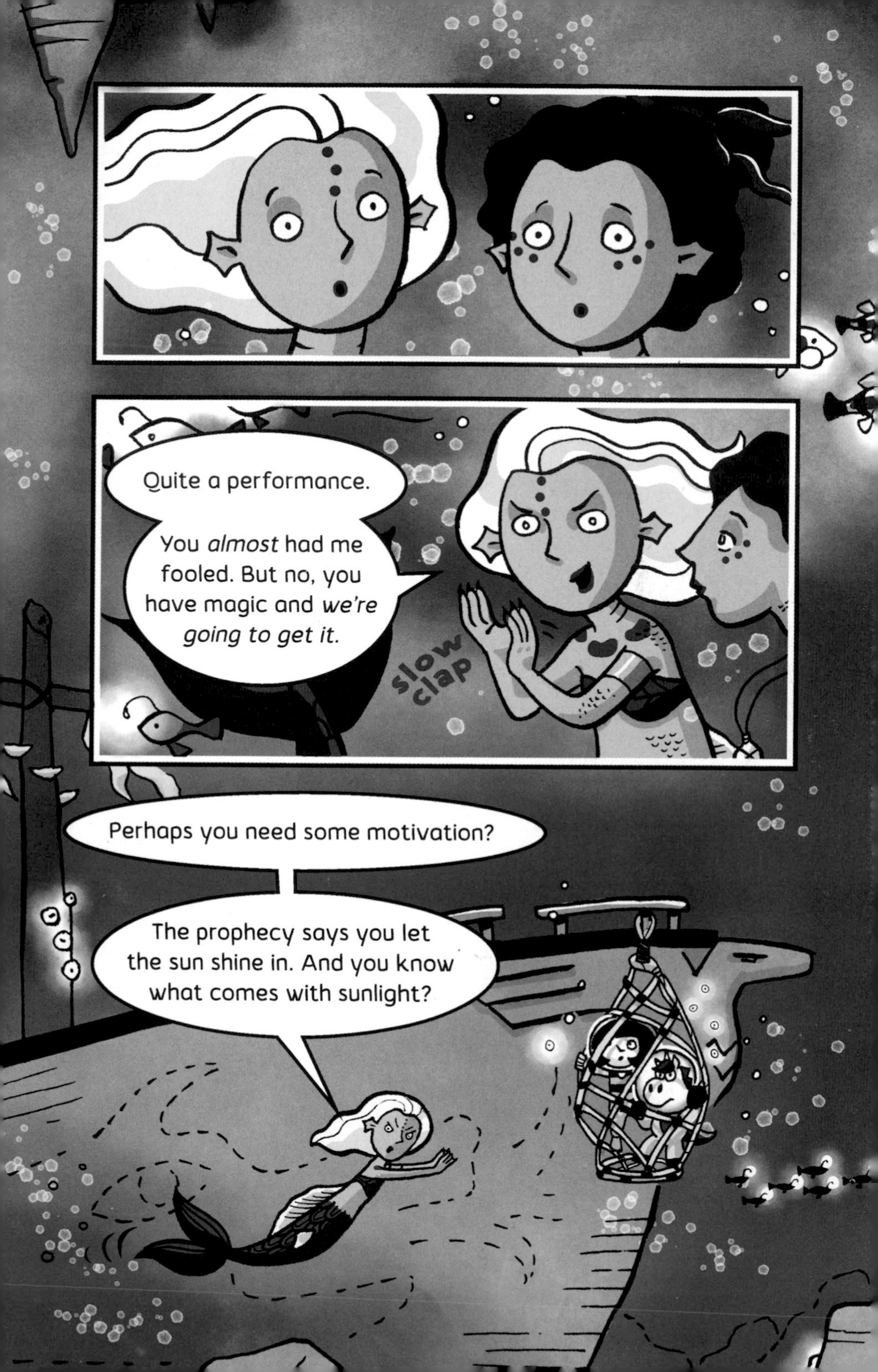

Quite a performance.
You *almost* had me fooled. But no, you have magic and *we're going to get it.*
slow clap
Perhaps you need some motivation?
The prophecy says you let the sun shine in. And you know what comes with sunlight?

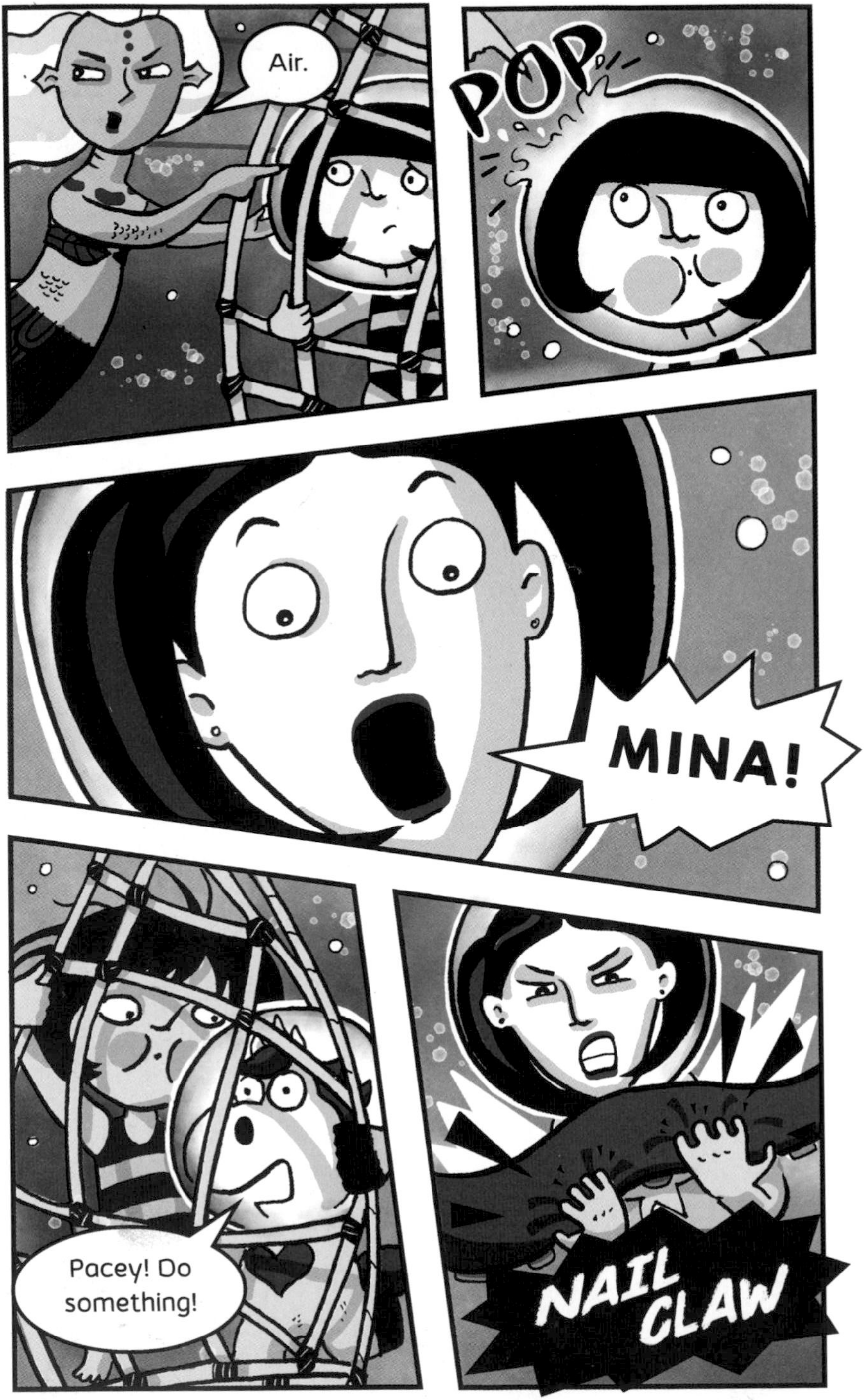
Air.
POP
MINA!
Pacey! Do something!
NAIL CLAW

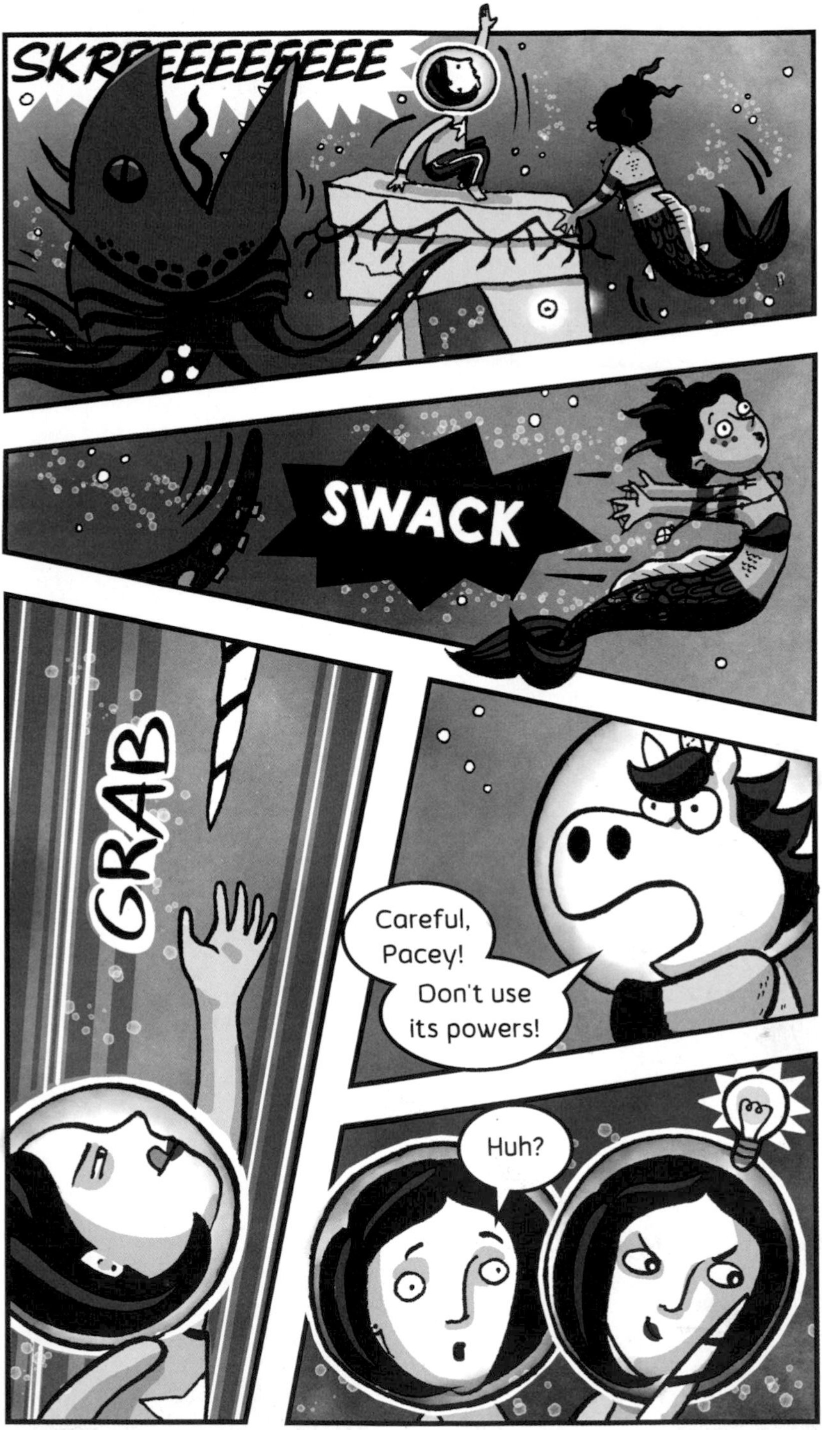
SKREEEEEEEEEE
SWACK
GRAB
Careful, Pacey!
Don't use its powers!
Huh?

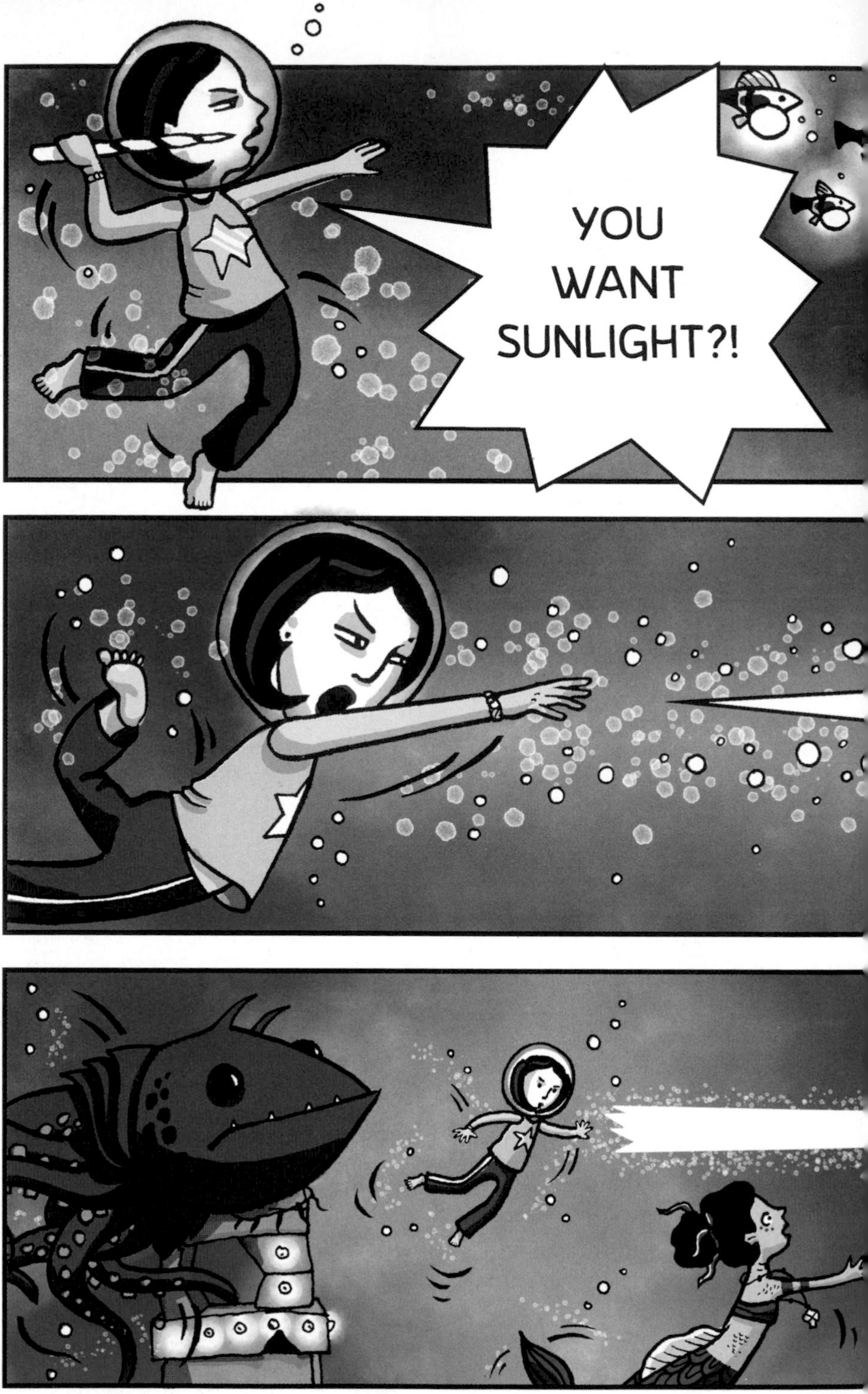
YOU WANT SUNLIGHT?!

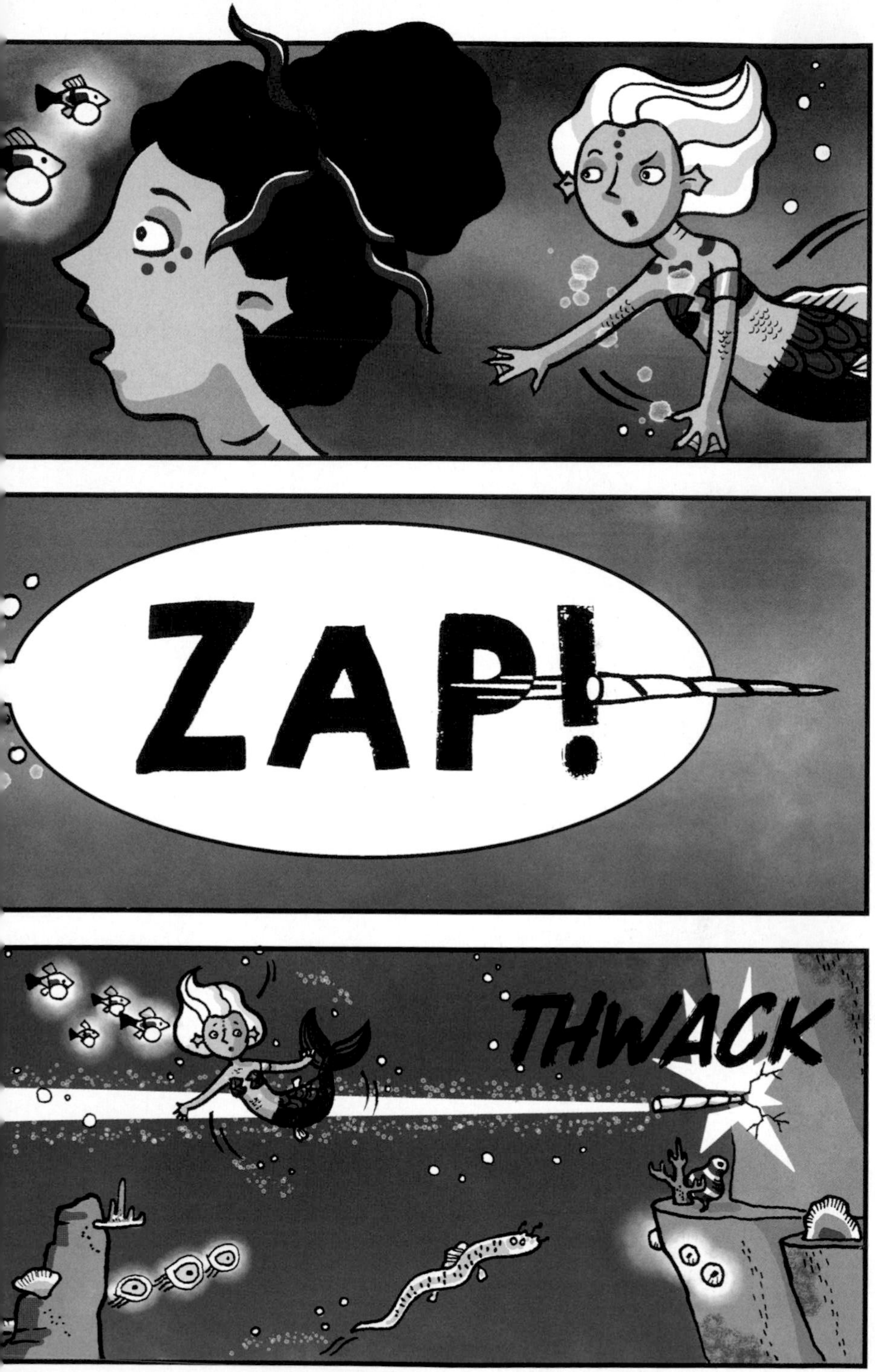
ZAP!
THWACK

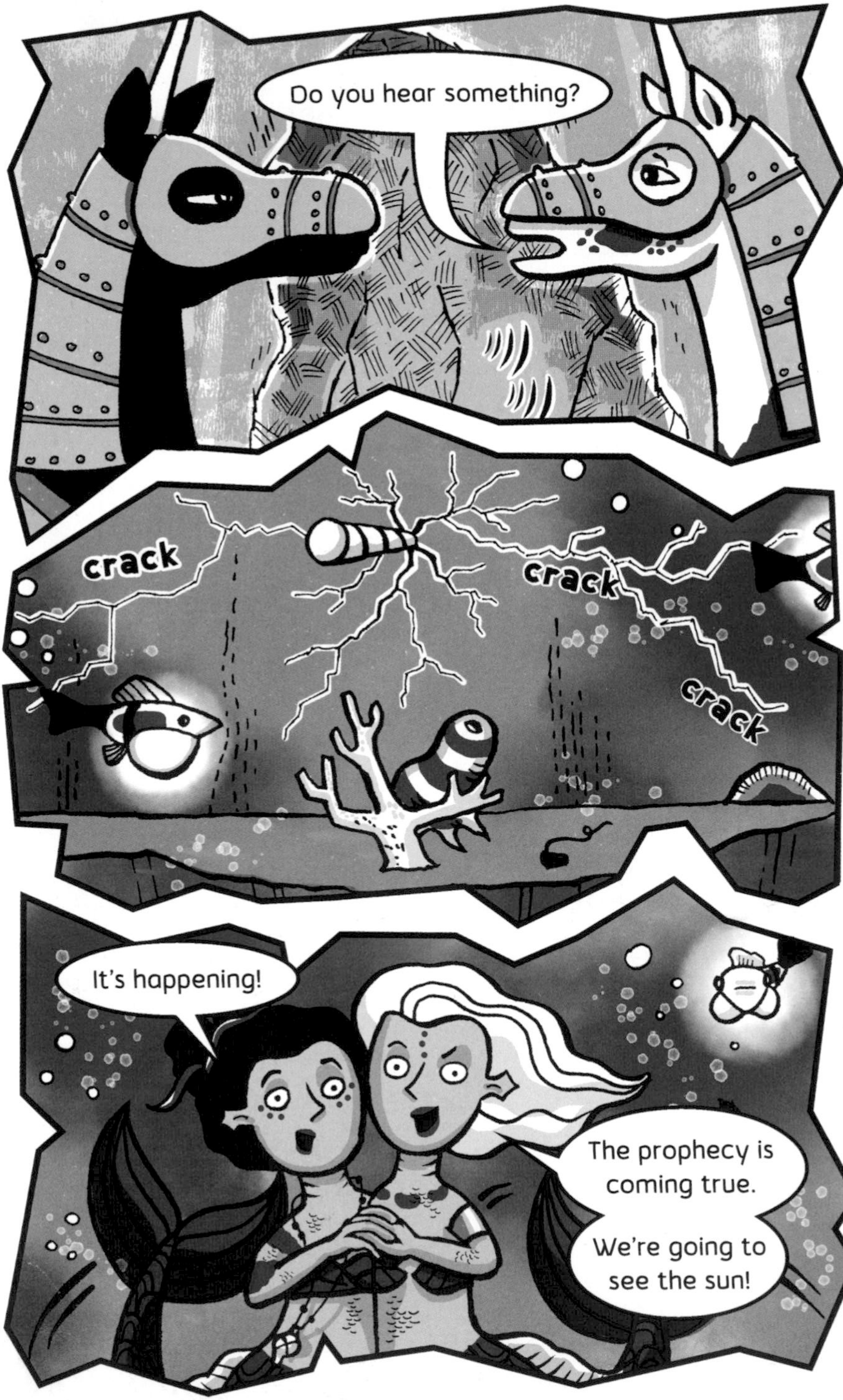
Do you hear something?
crack
crack
crack
It's happening!
The prophecy is coming true.
We're going to see the sun!

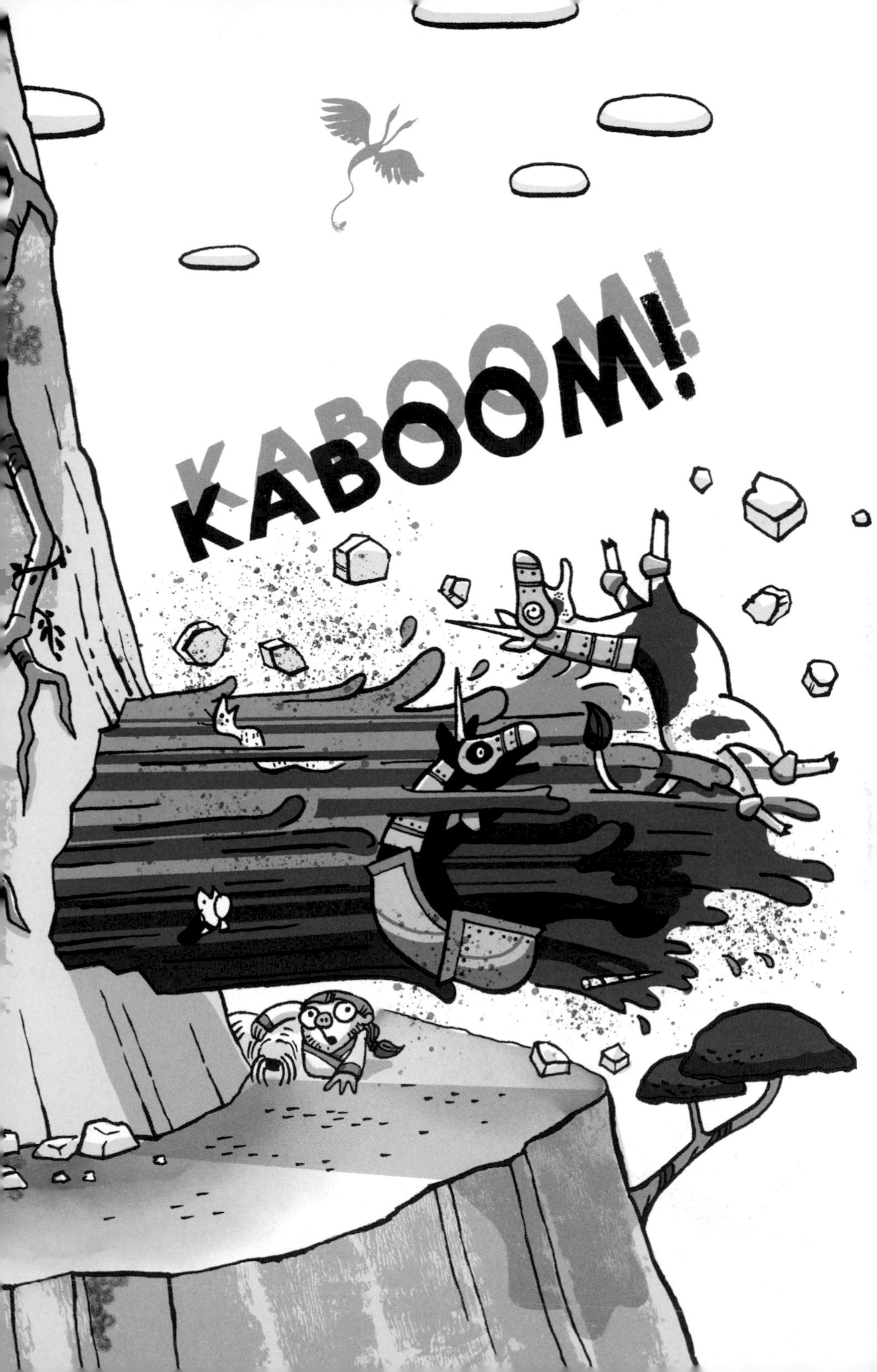
KABOOM!

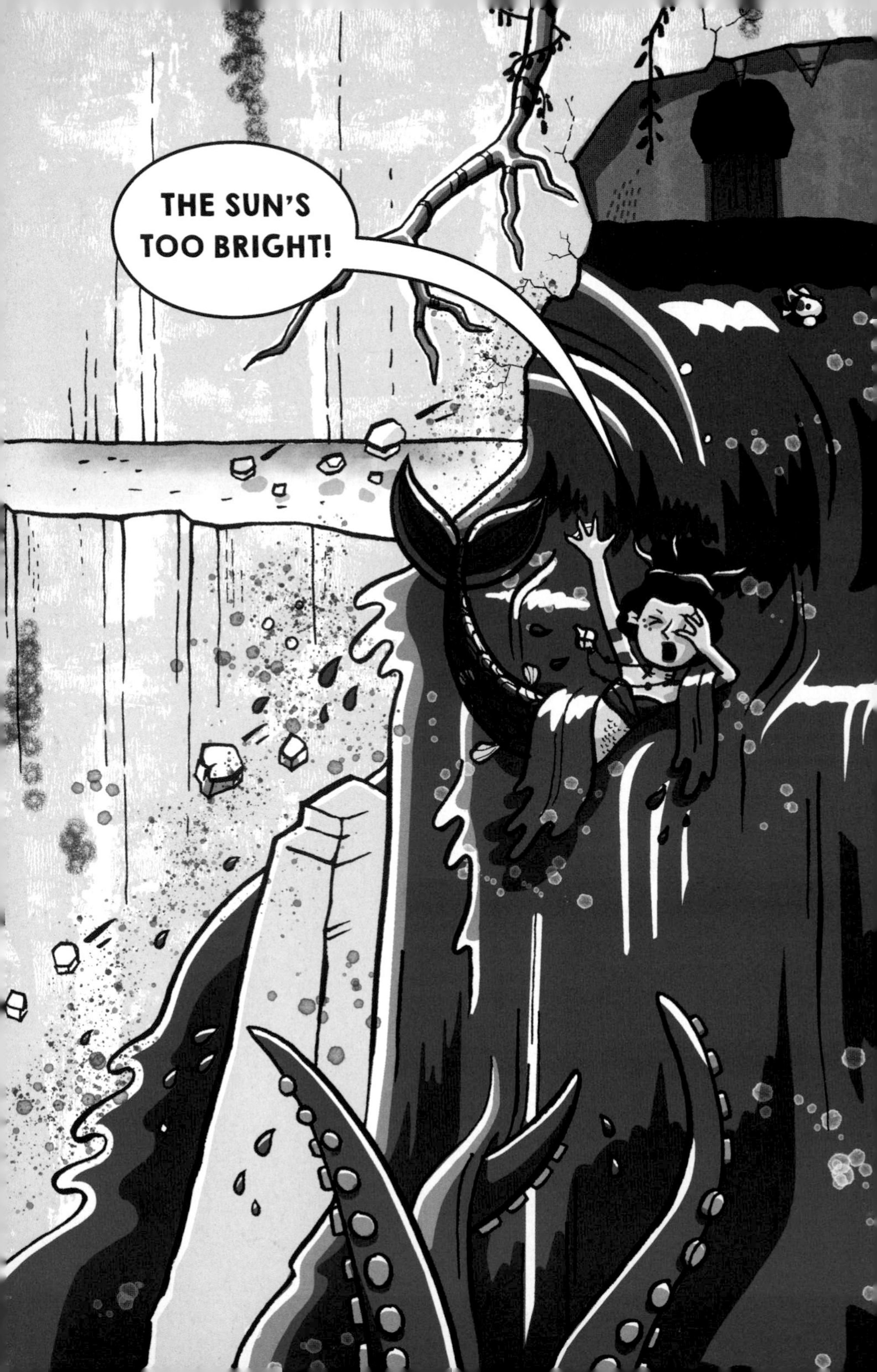
THE SUN'S TOO BRIGHT!

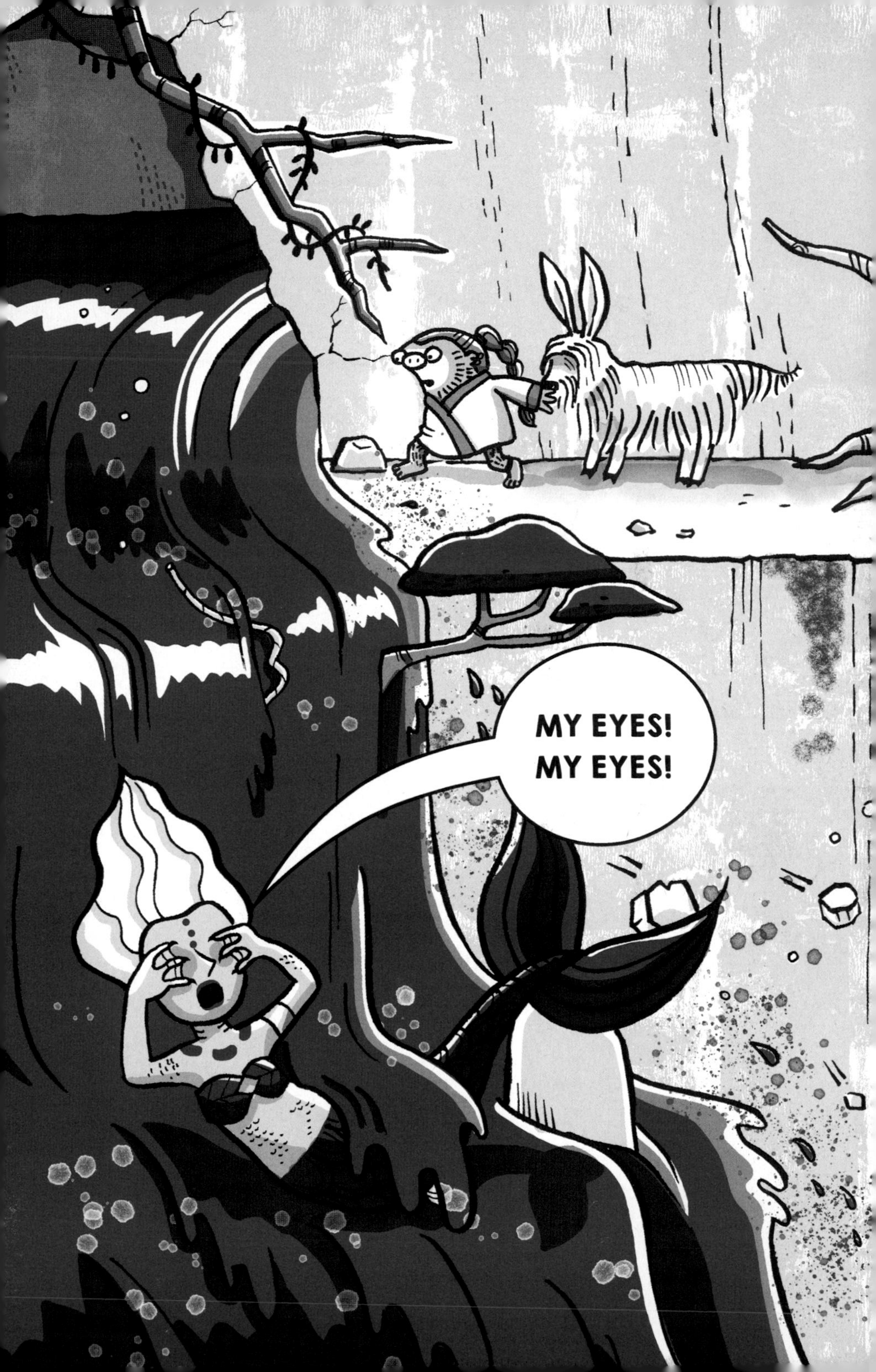
MY EYES!
MY EYES!

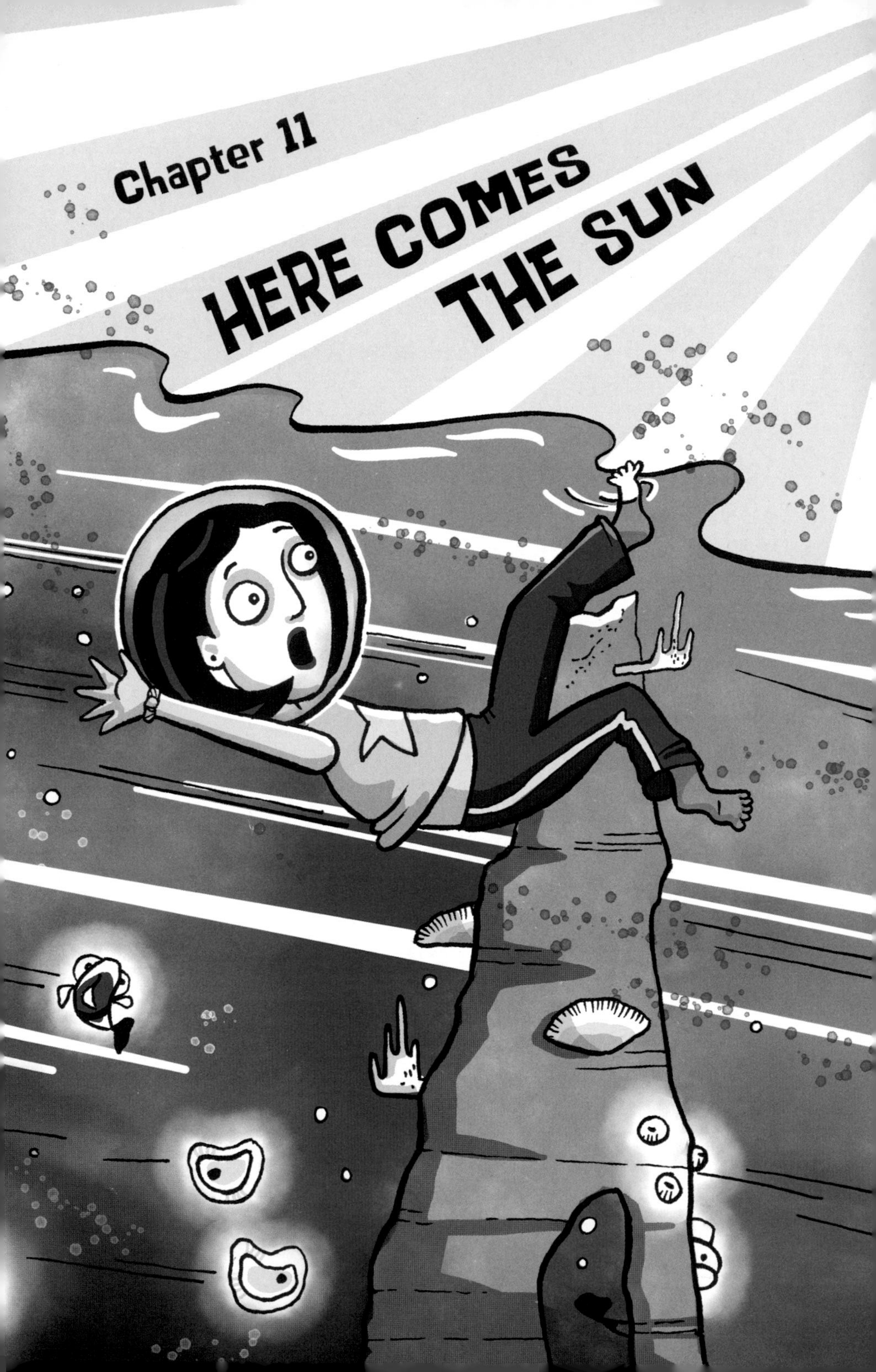
Chapter 11
HERE COMES THE SUN

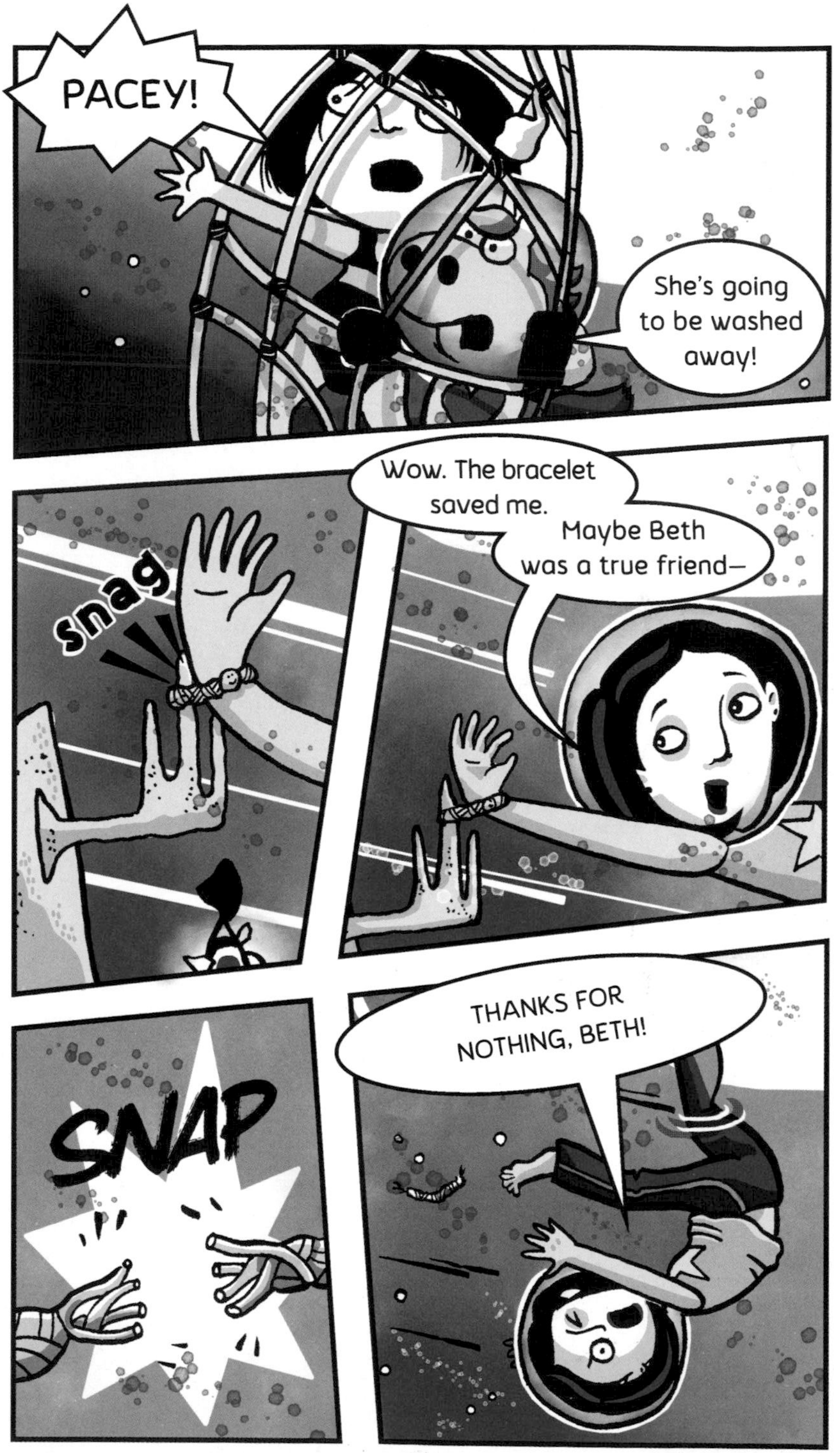
PACEY!
She's going to be washed away!
Wow. The bracelet saved me.
snag
Maybe Beth was a true friend—
SNAP
THANKS FOR NOTHING, BETH!

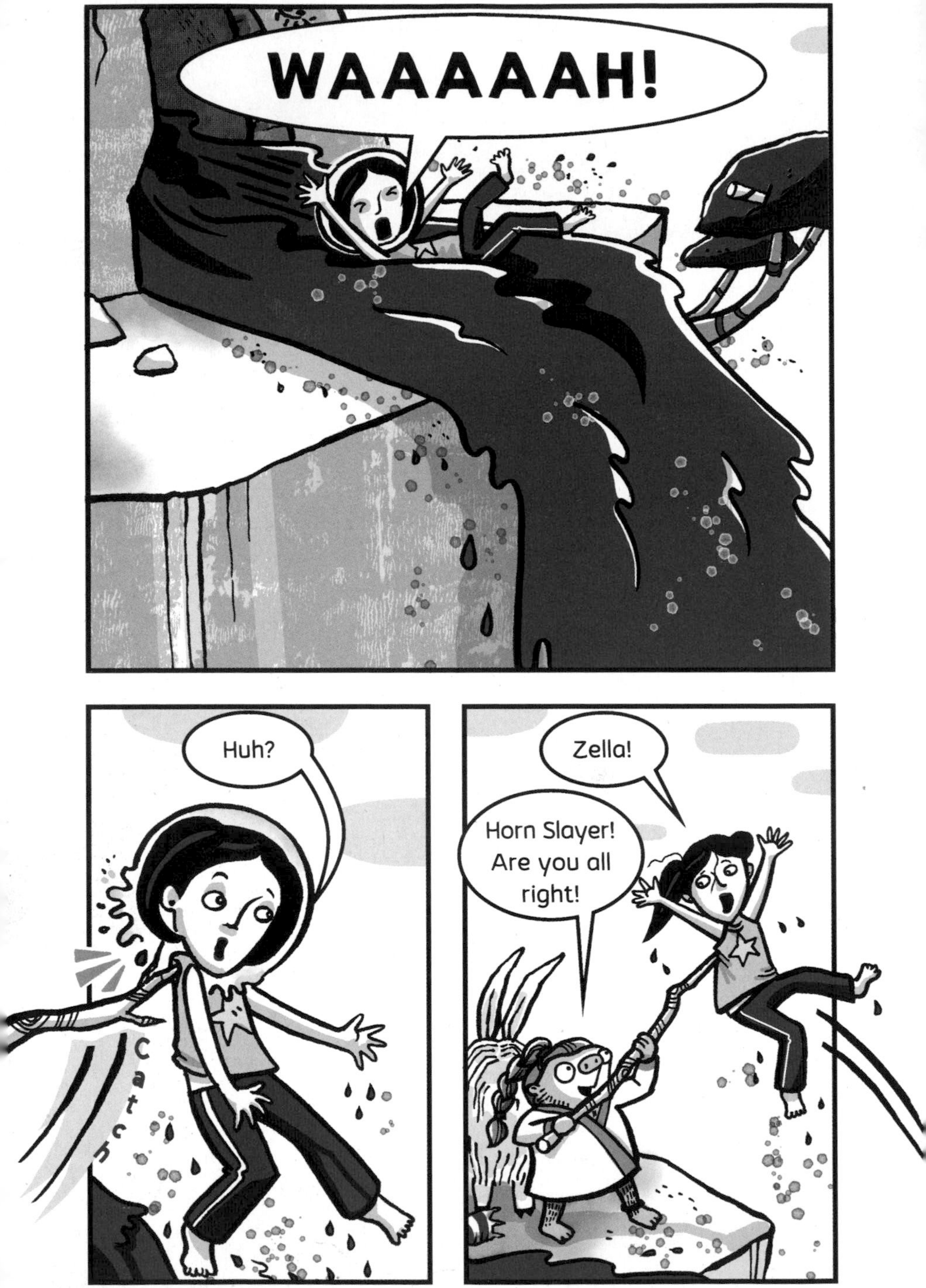
WAAAAAH!
Huh?
Catch
Zella!
Horn Slayer! Are you all right!

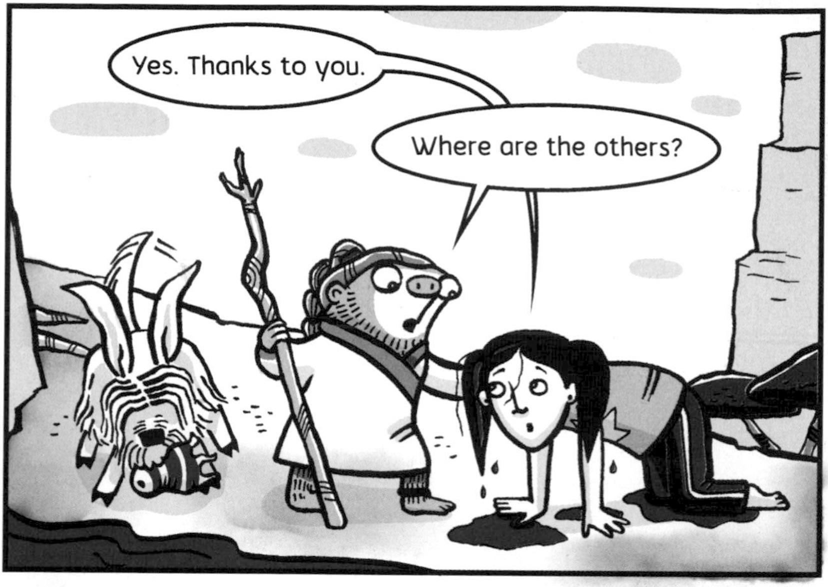
Yes. Thanks to you.
Where are the others?

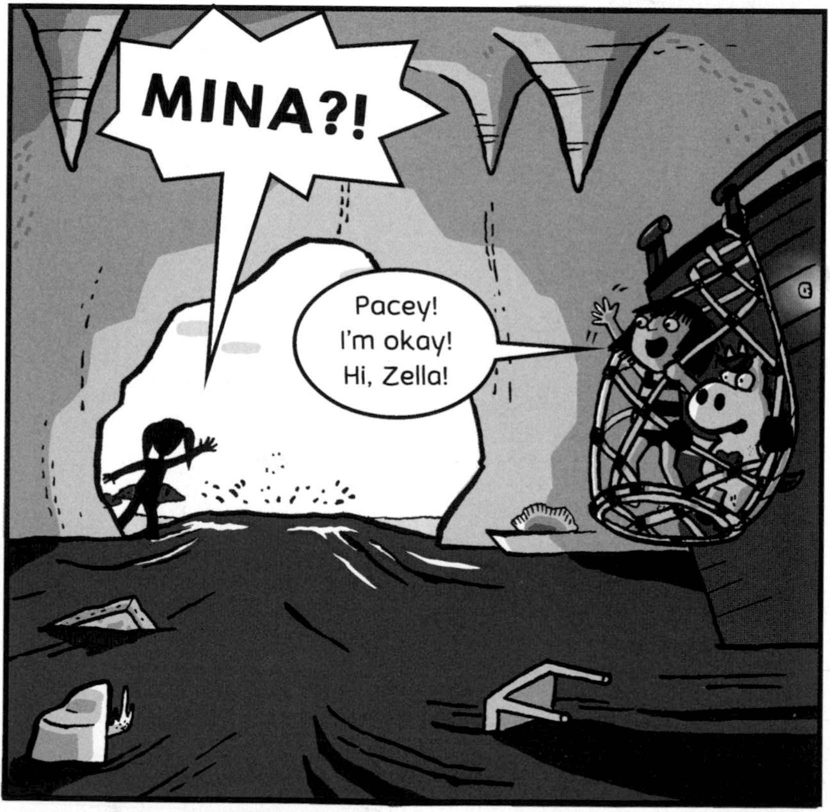
MINA?!
Pacey!
I'm okay!
Hi, Zella!

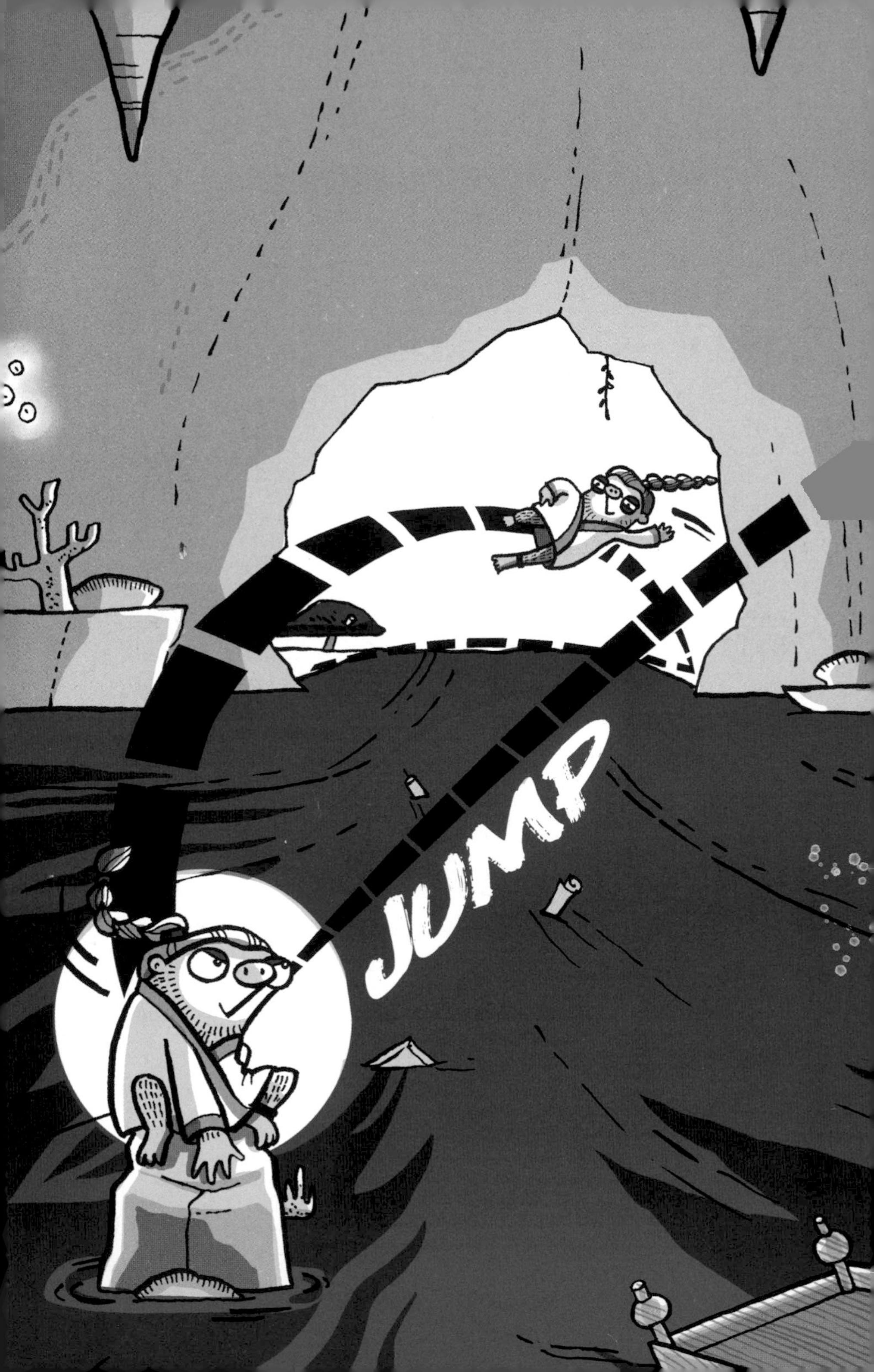
JUMP

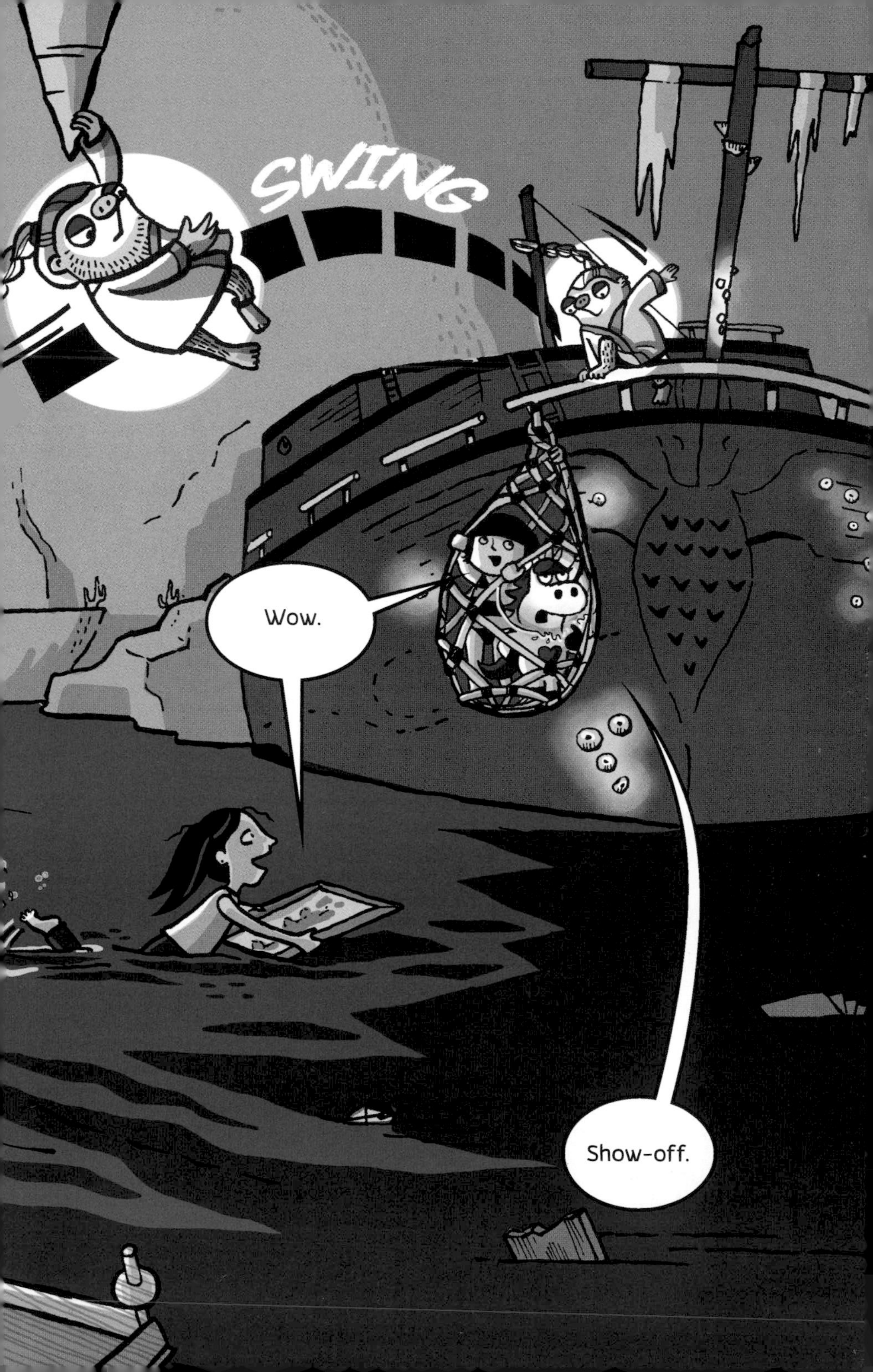
SWING
Wow.
Show-off.

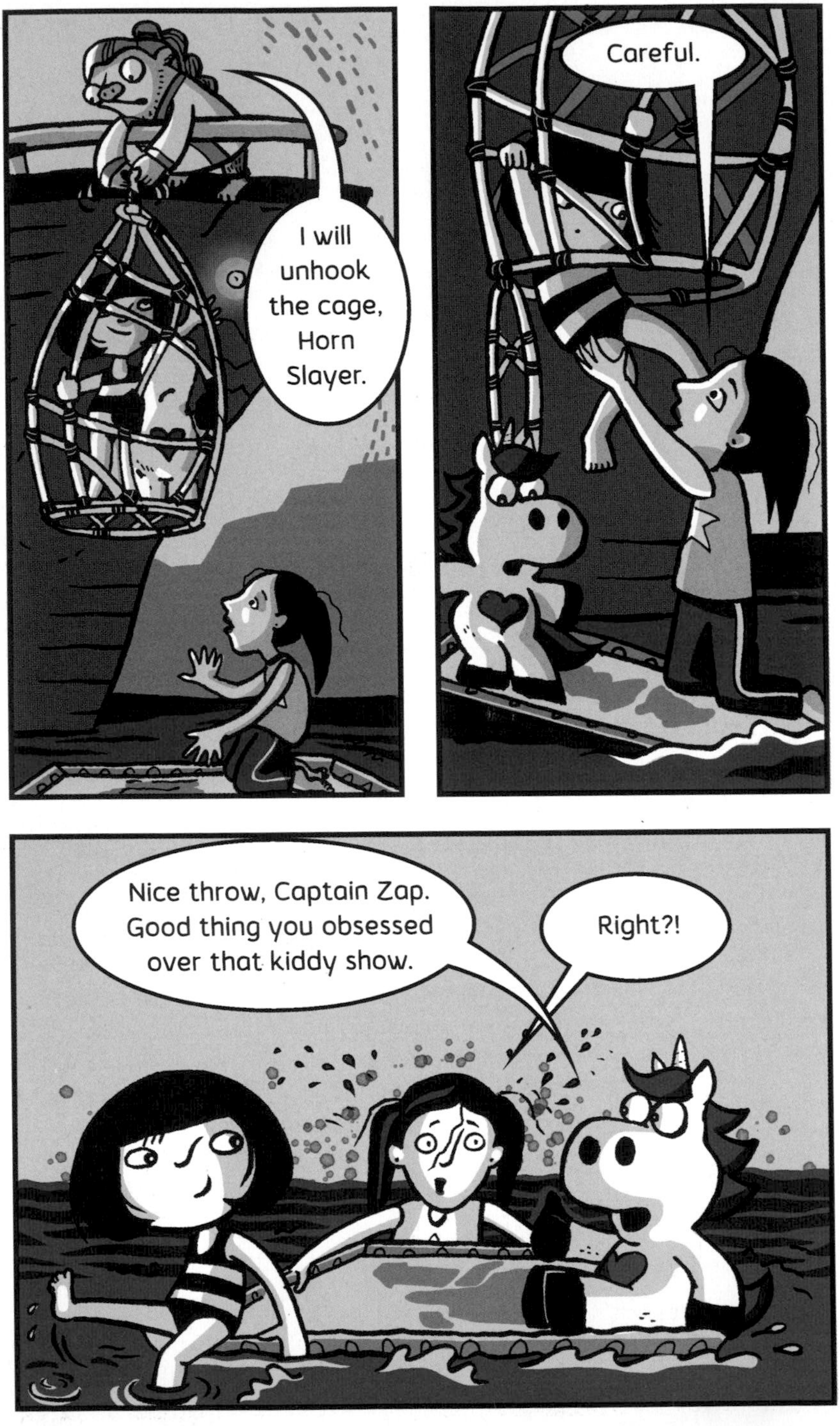
I will unhook the cage, Horn Slayer.
Careful.
Nice throw, Captain Zap. Good thing you obsessed over that kiddy show.
Right?!

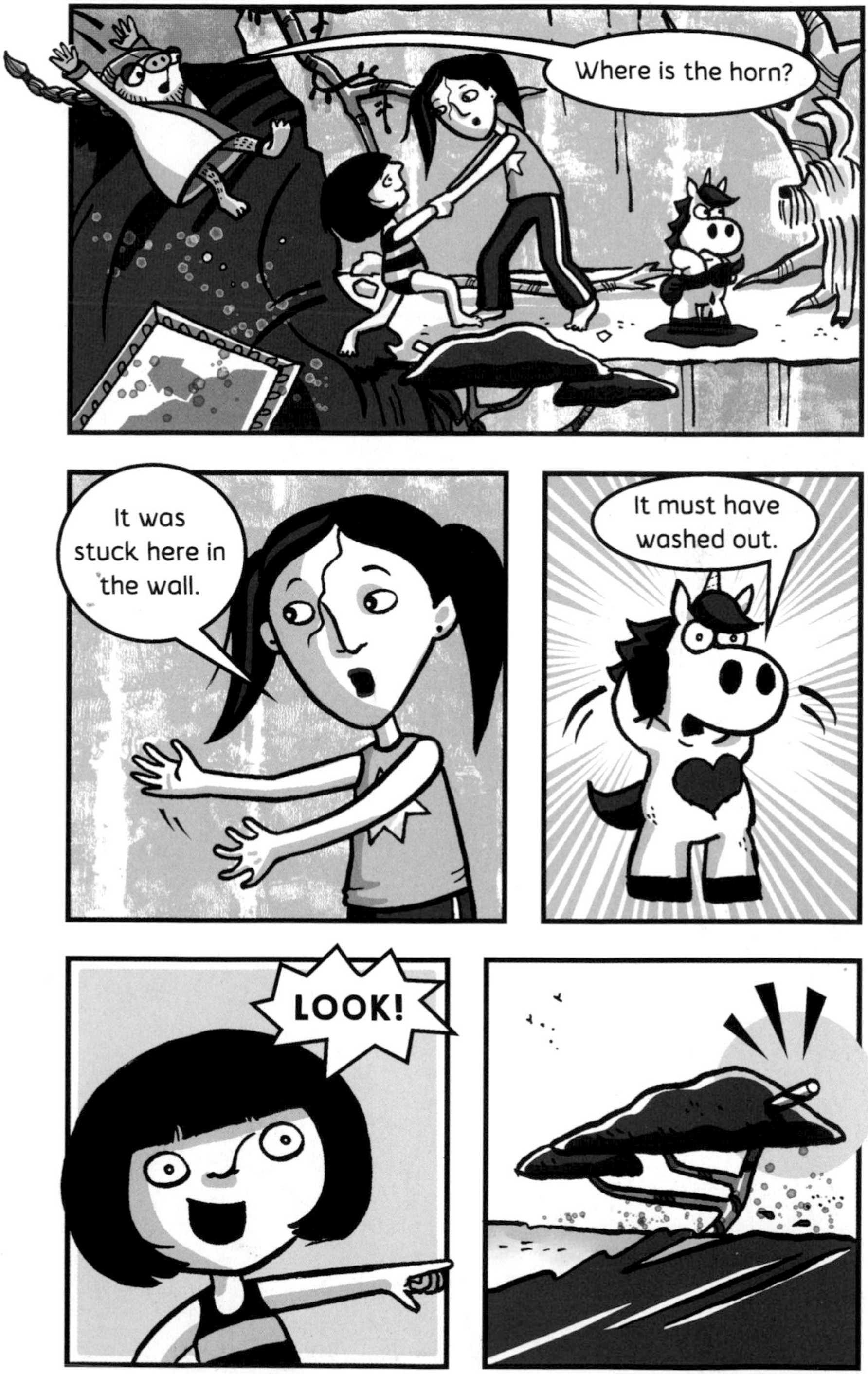
Where is the horn?
It was stuck here in the wall.
It must have washed out.
LOOK!

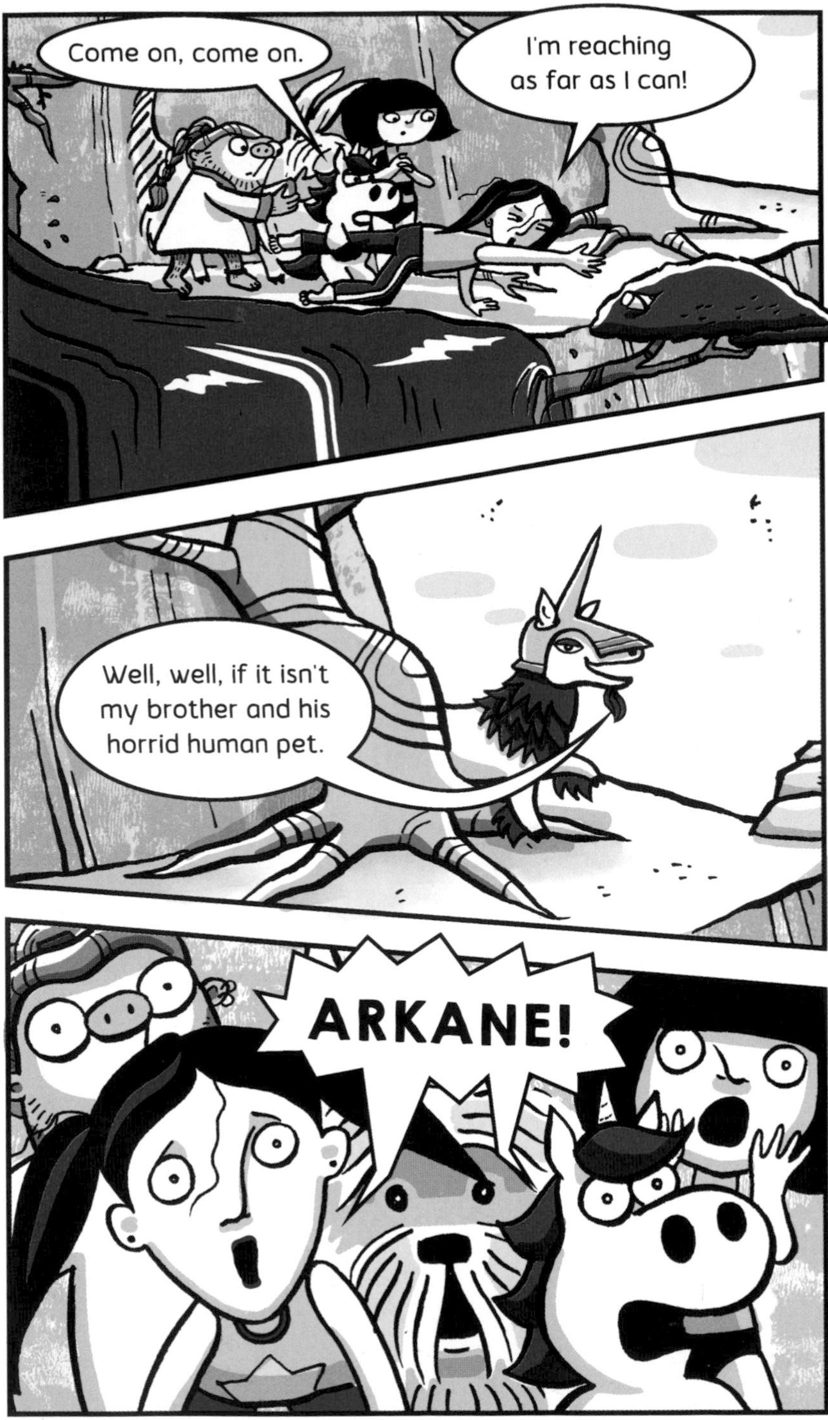
Come on, come on.
I'm reaching as far as I can!
Well, well, if it isn't my brother and his horrid human pet.
ARKANE!

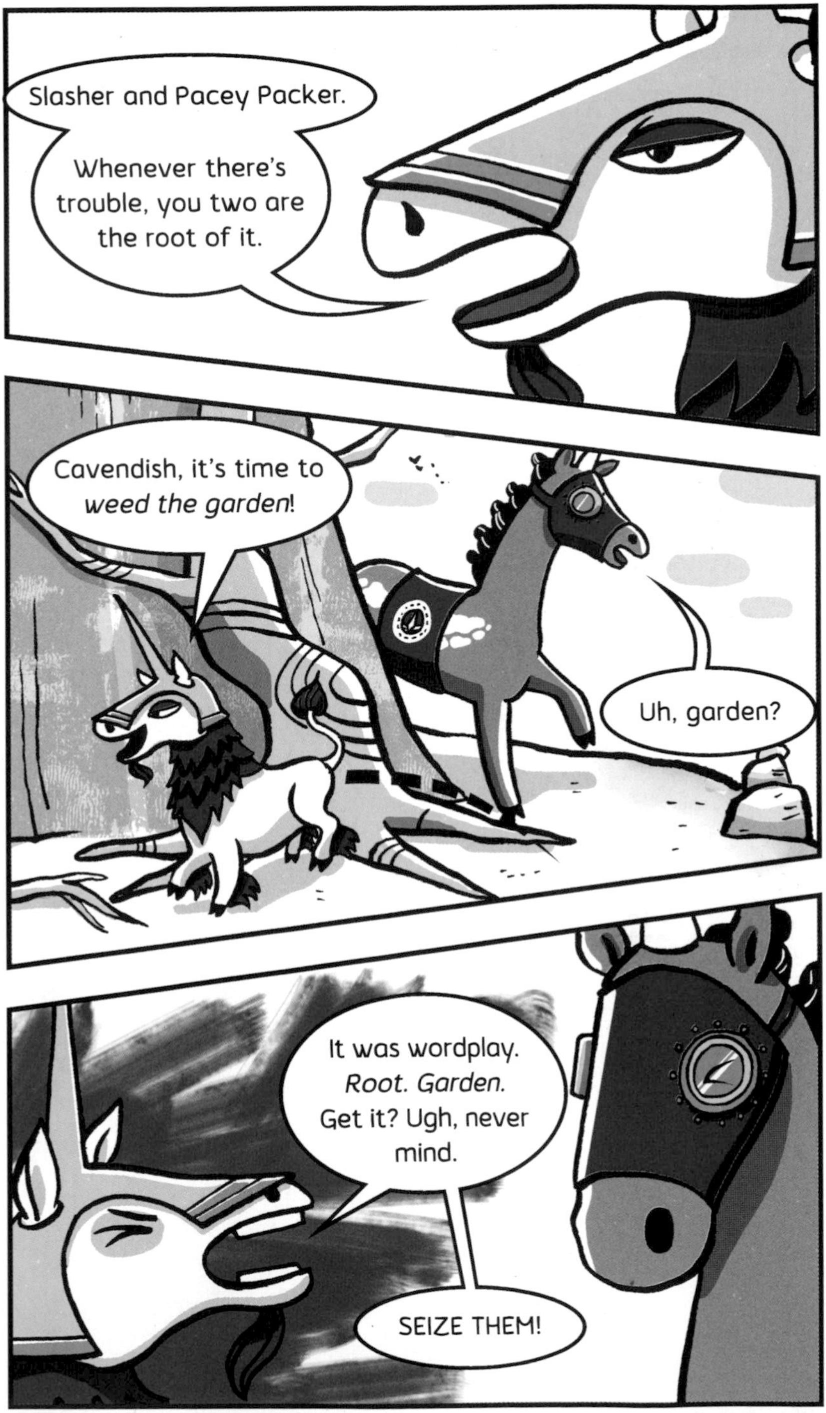
Slasher and Pacey Packer.
Whenever there's trouble, you two are the root of it.
Cavendish, it's time to *weed the garden*!
Uh, garden?
It was wordplay. *Root. Garden.* Get it? Ugh, never mind.
SEIZE THEM!

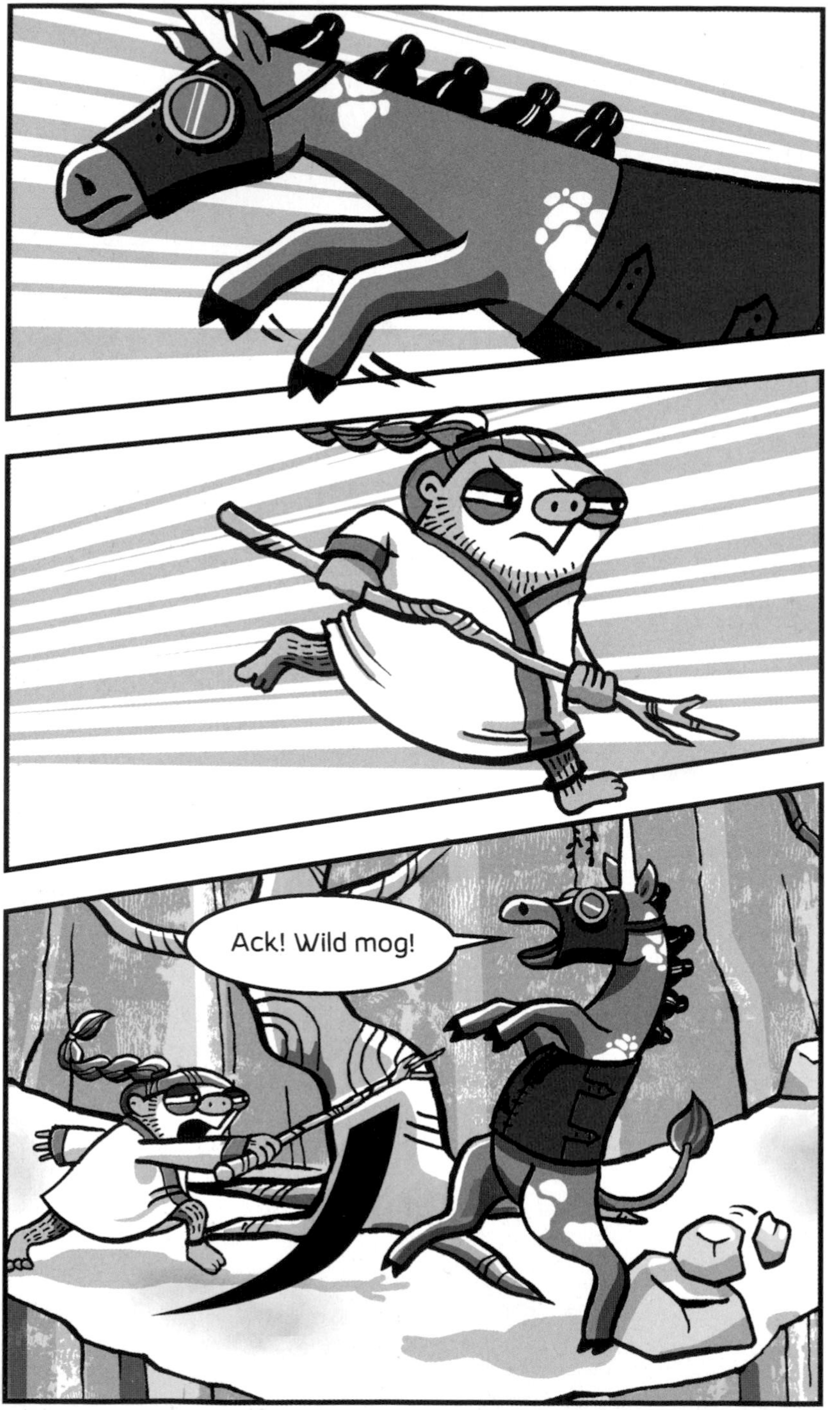
Ack! Wild mog!

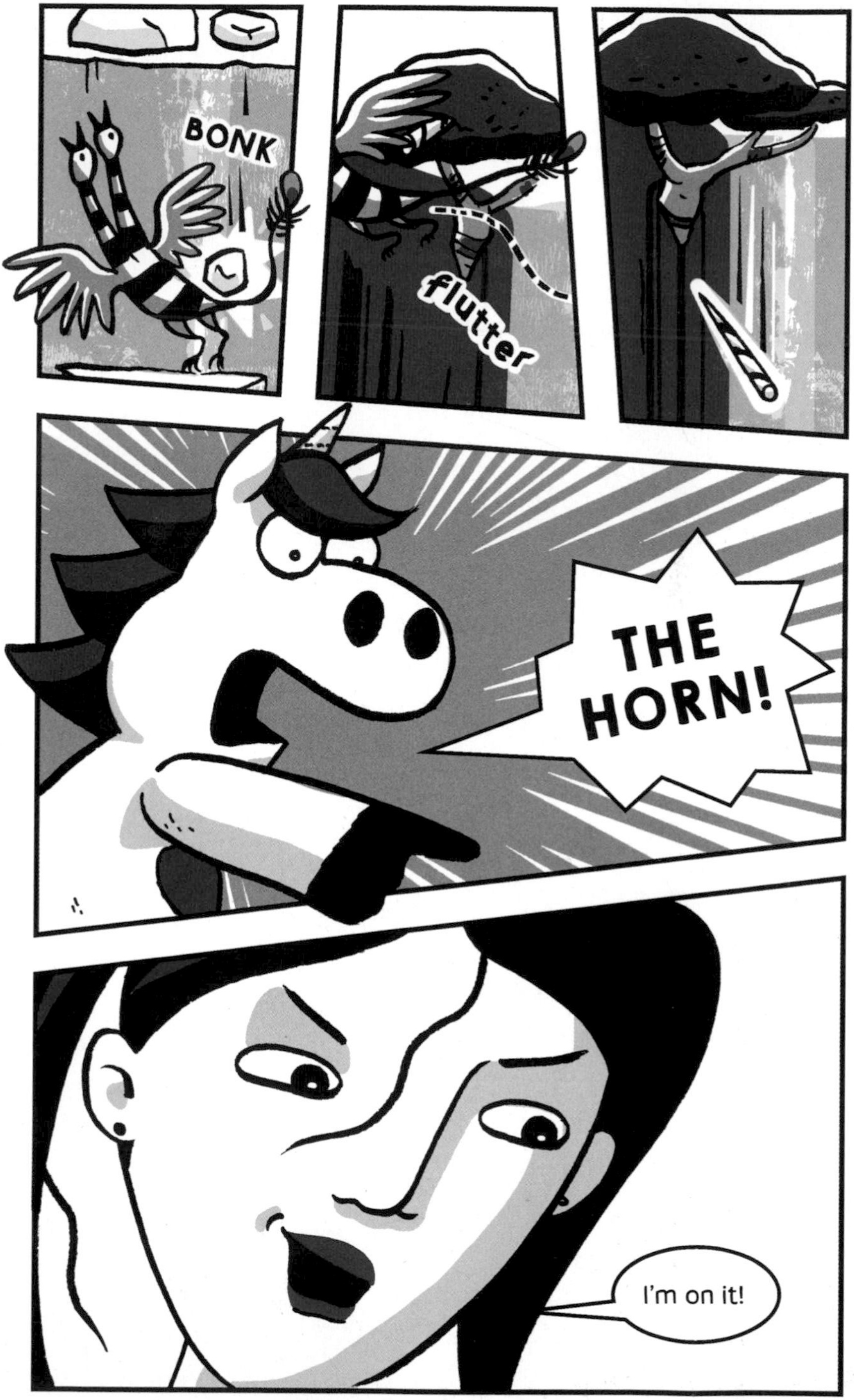
BONK
flutter
THE HORN!
I'm on it!

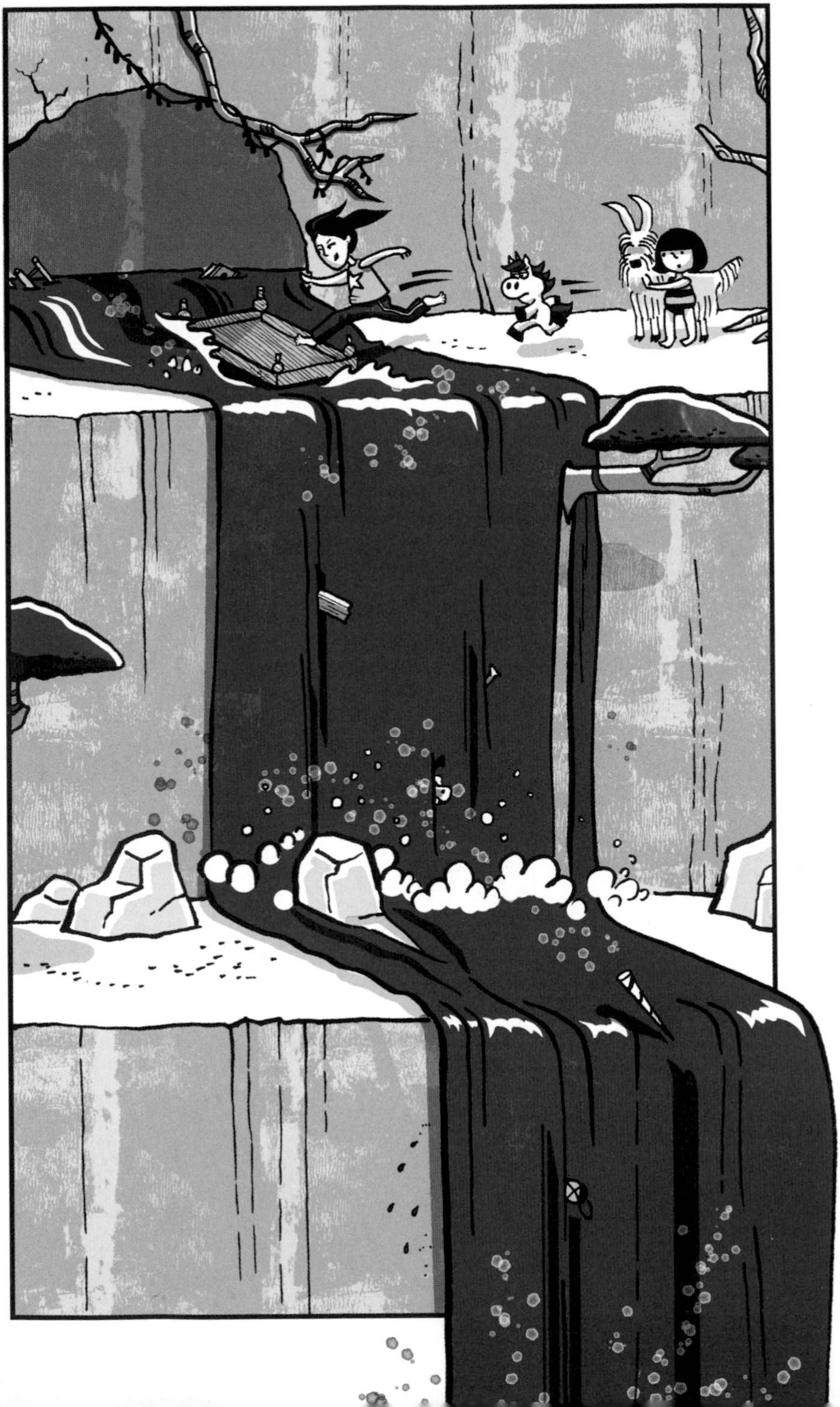

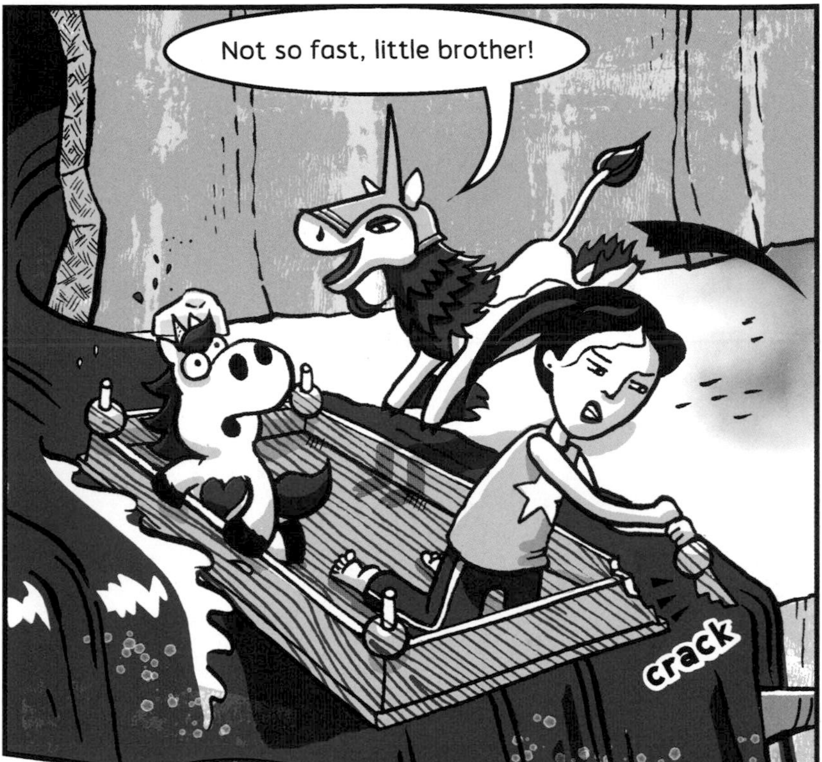
Not so fast, little brother!
crack

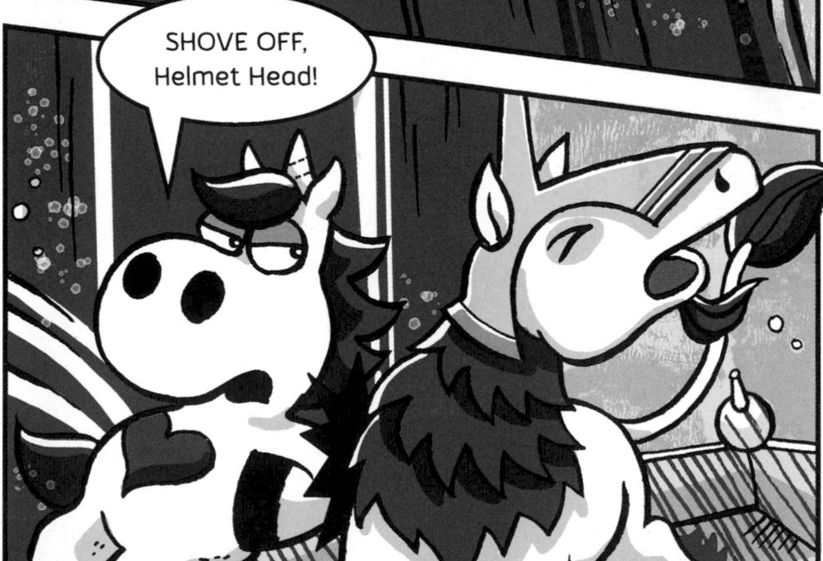
SHOVE OFF, Helmet Head!

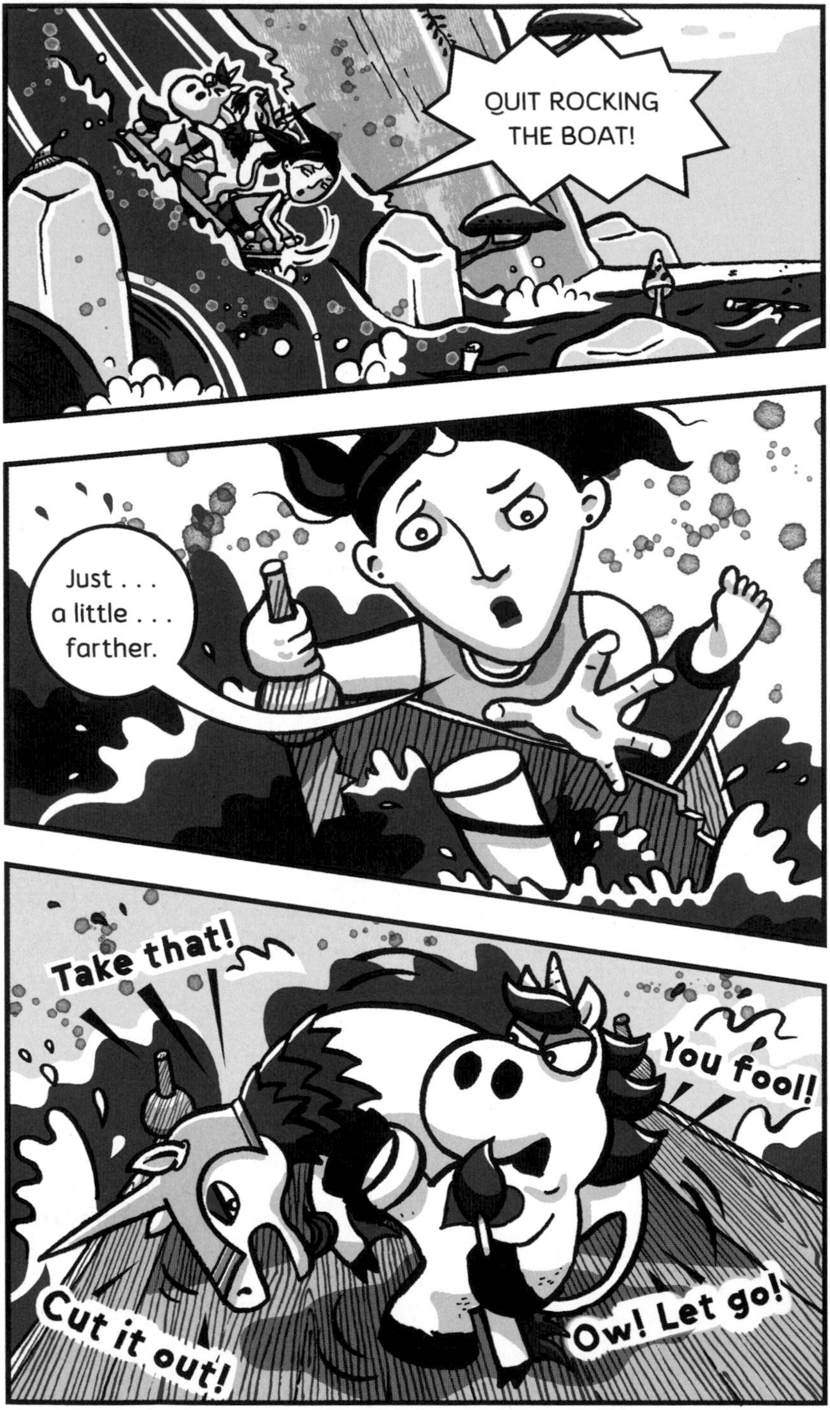
QUIT ROCKING THE BOAT!
Just . . . a little . . . farther.
Take that!
You fool!
Cut it out!
Ow! Let go!

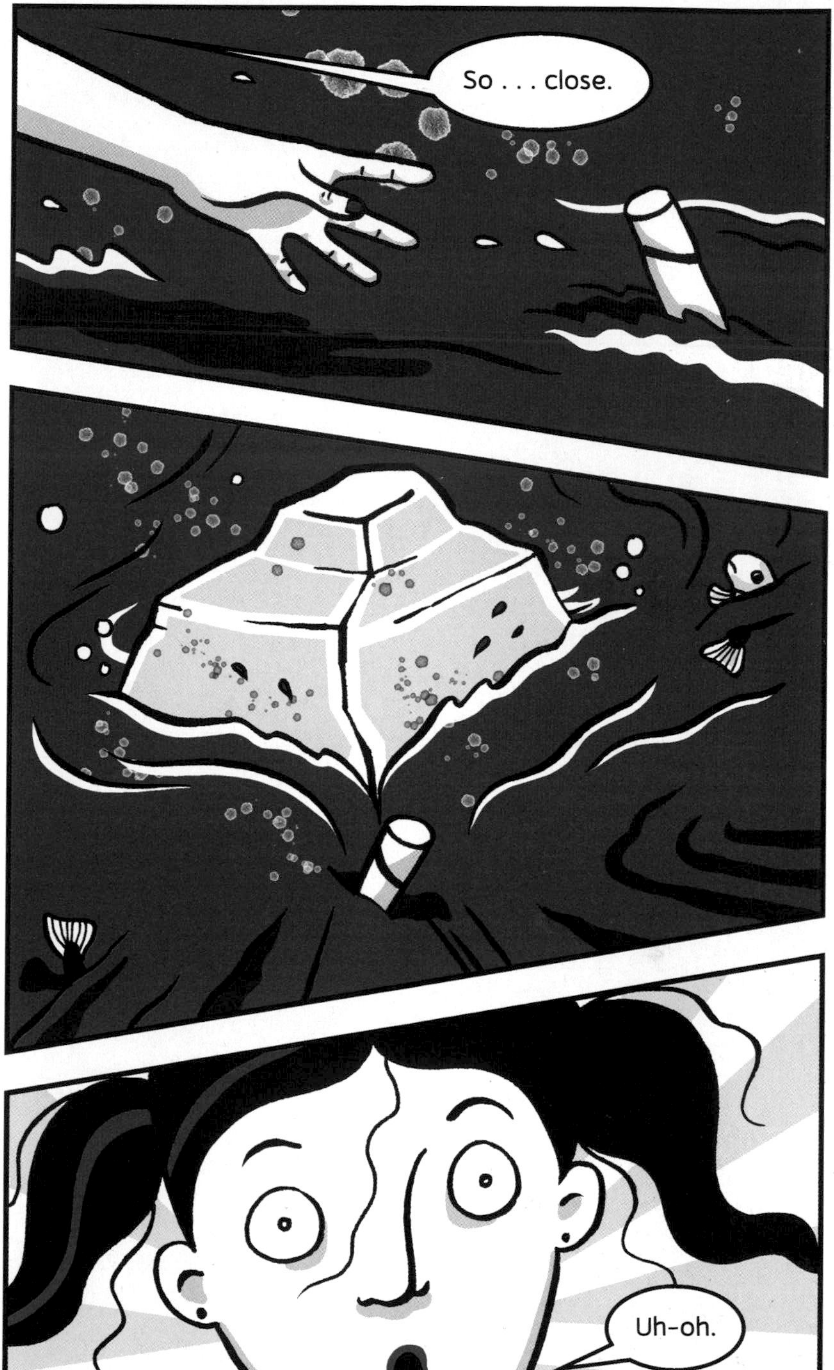
So . . . close.
Uh-oh.

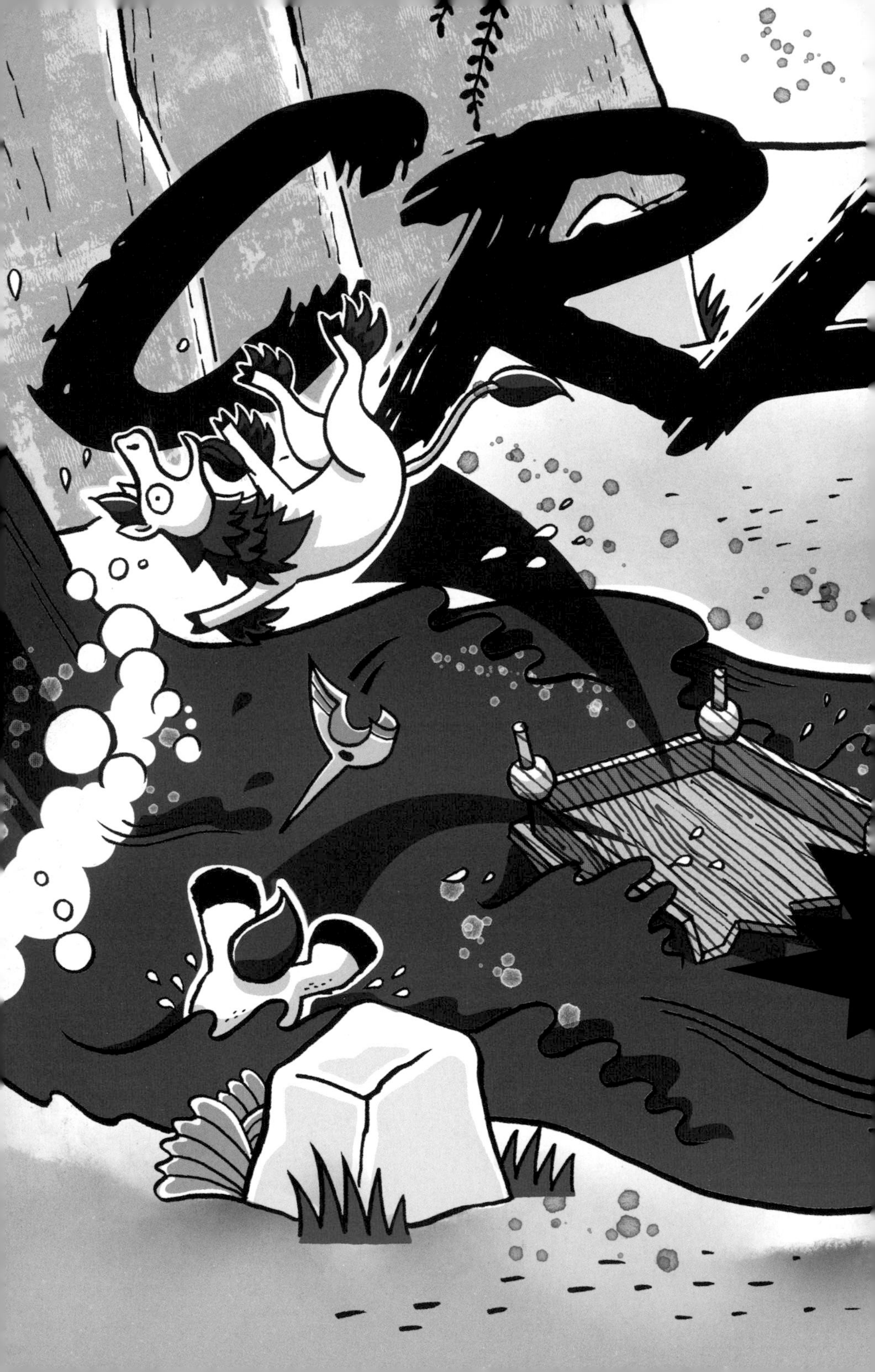
CRA

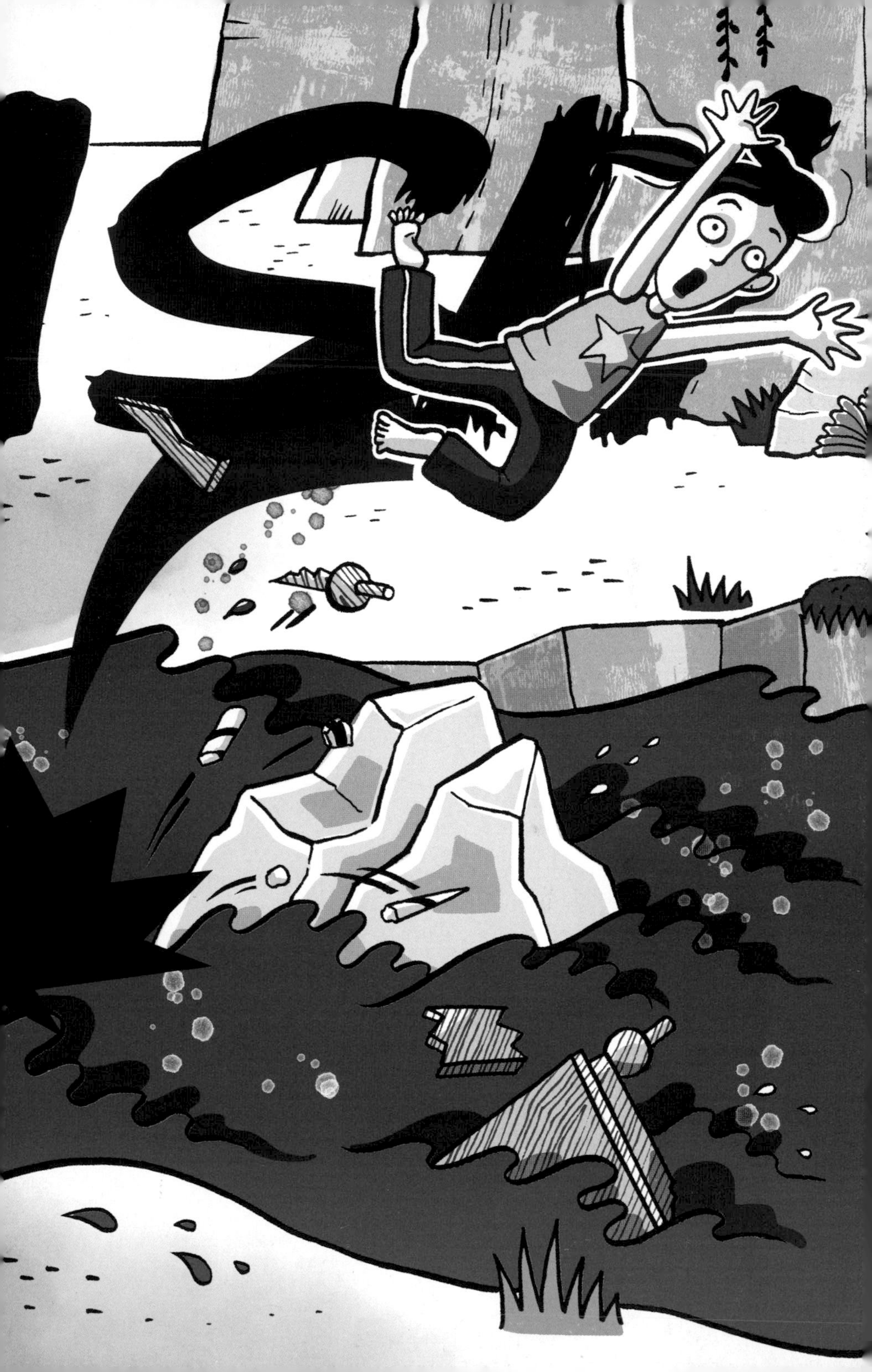

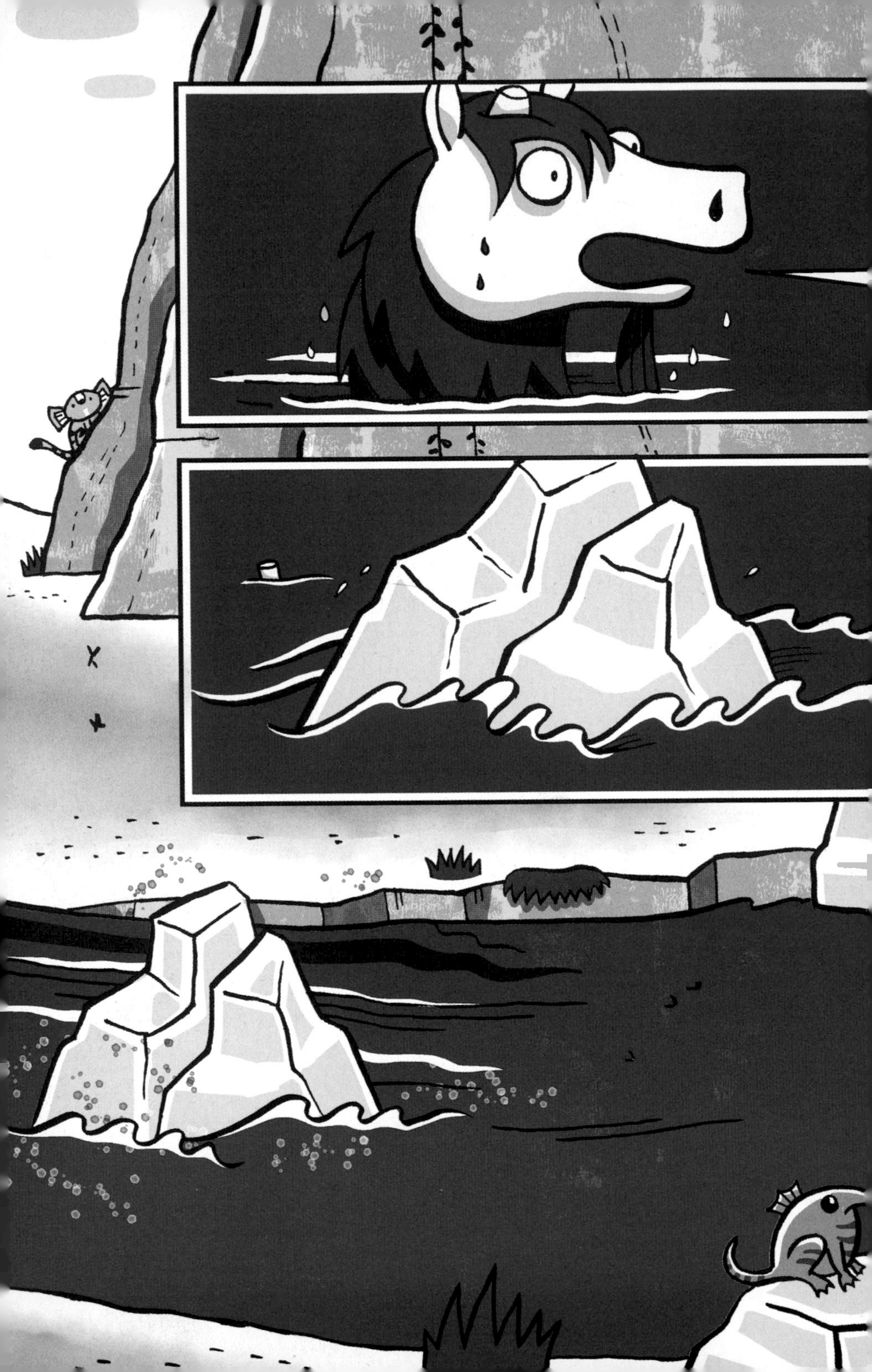

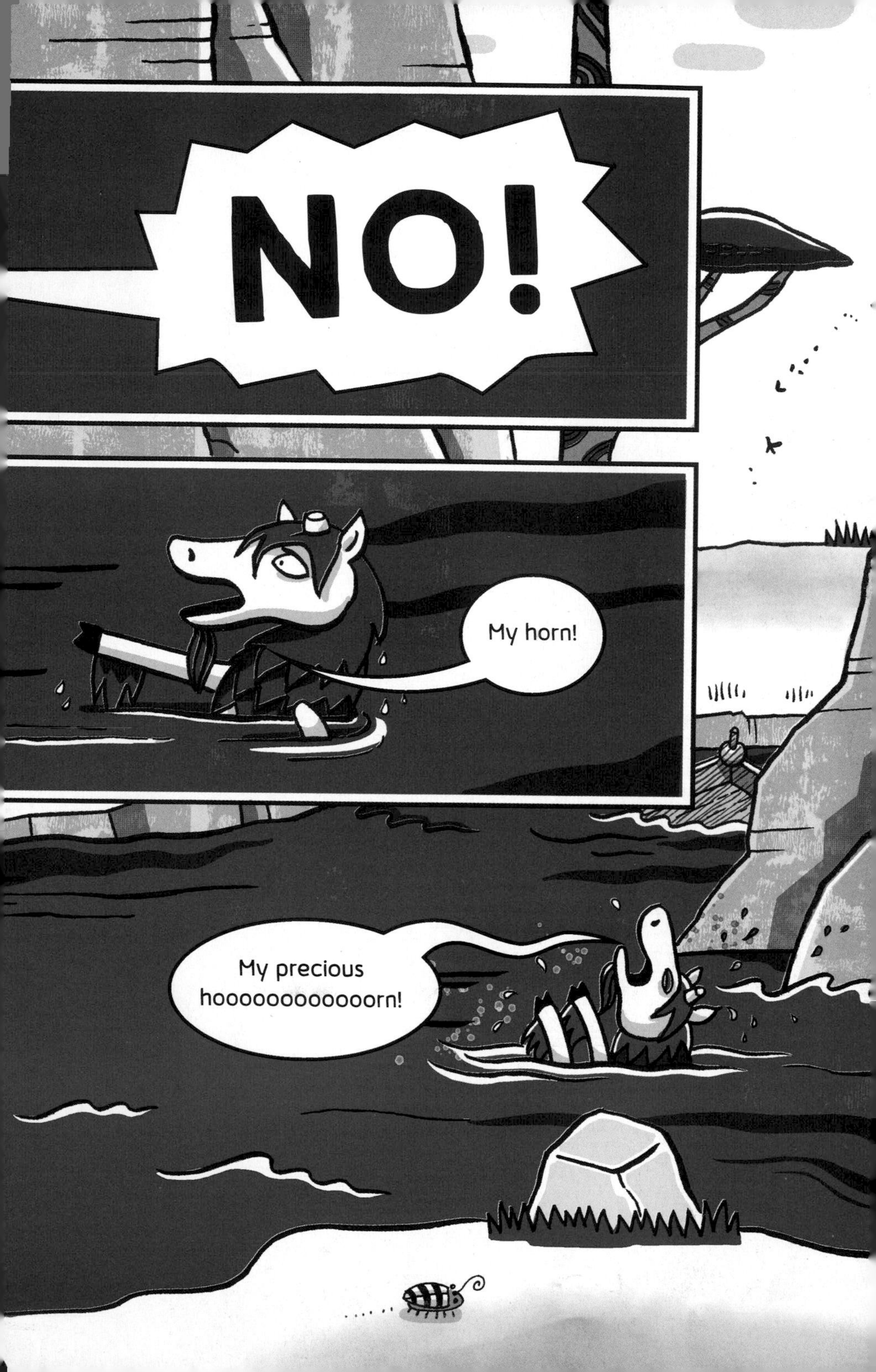
NO!
My horn!
My precious hoooooooooooorn!

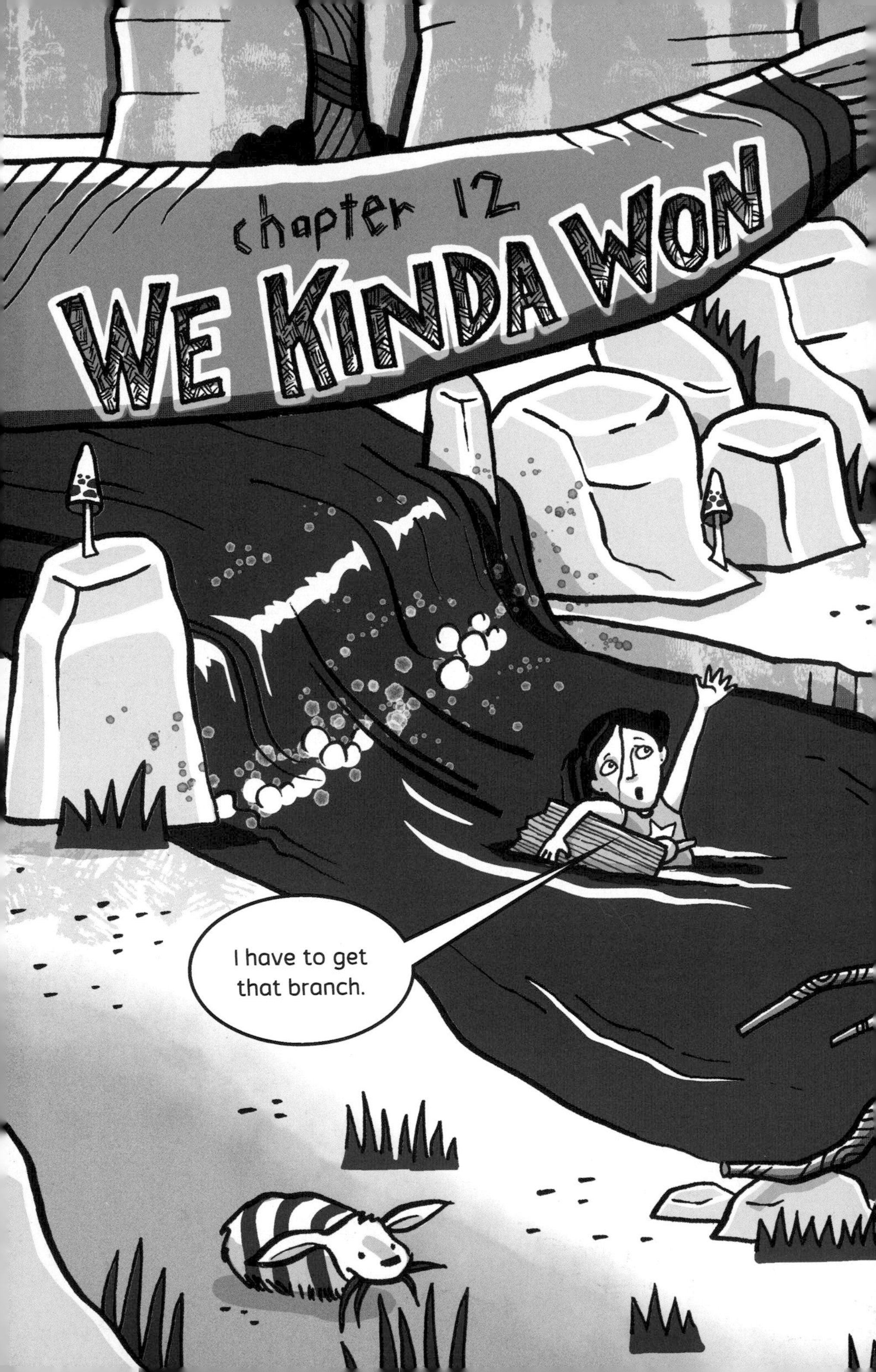
chapter 12
WE KINDA WON
I have to get that branch.

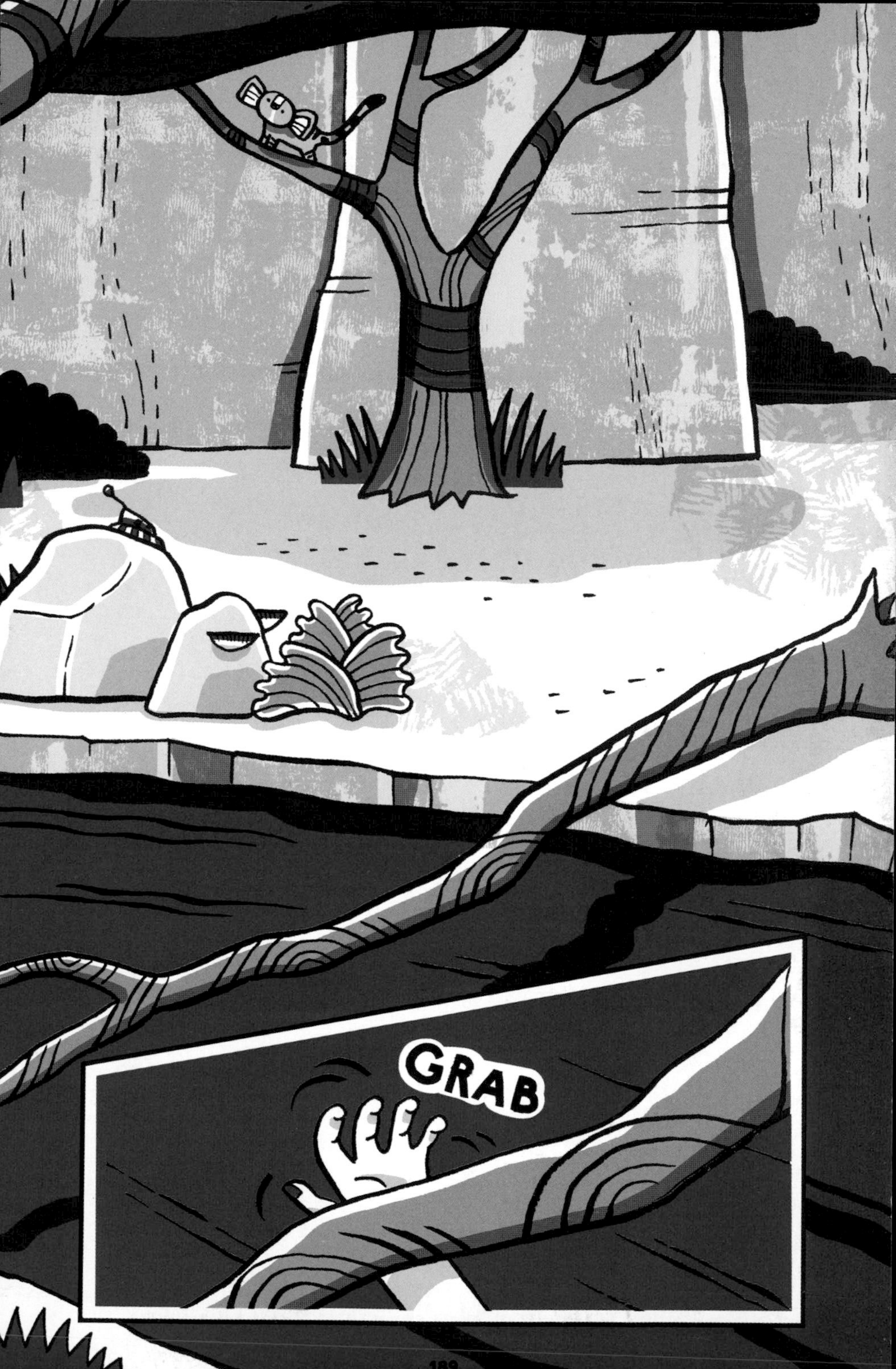
GRAB

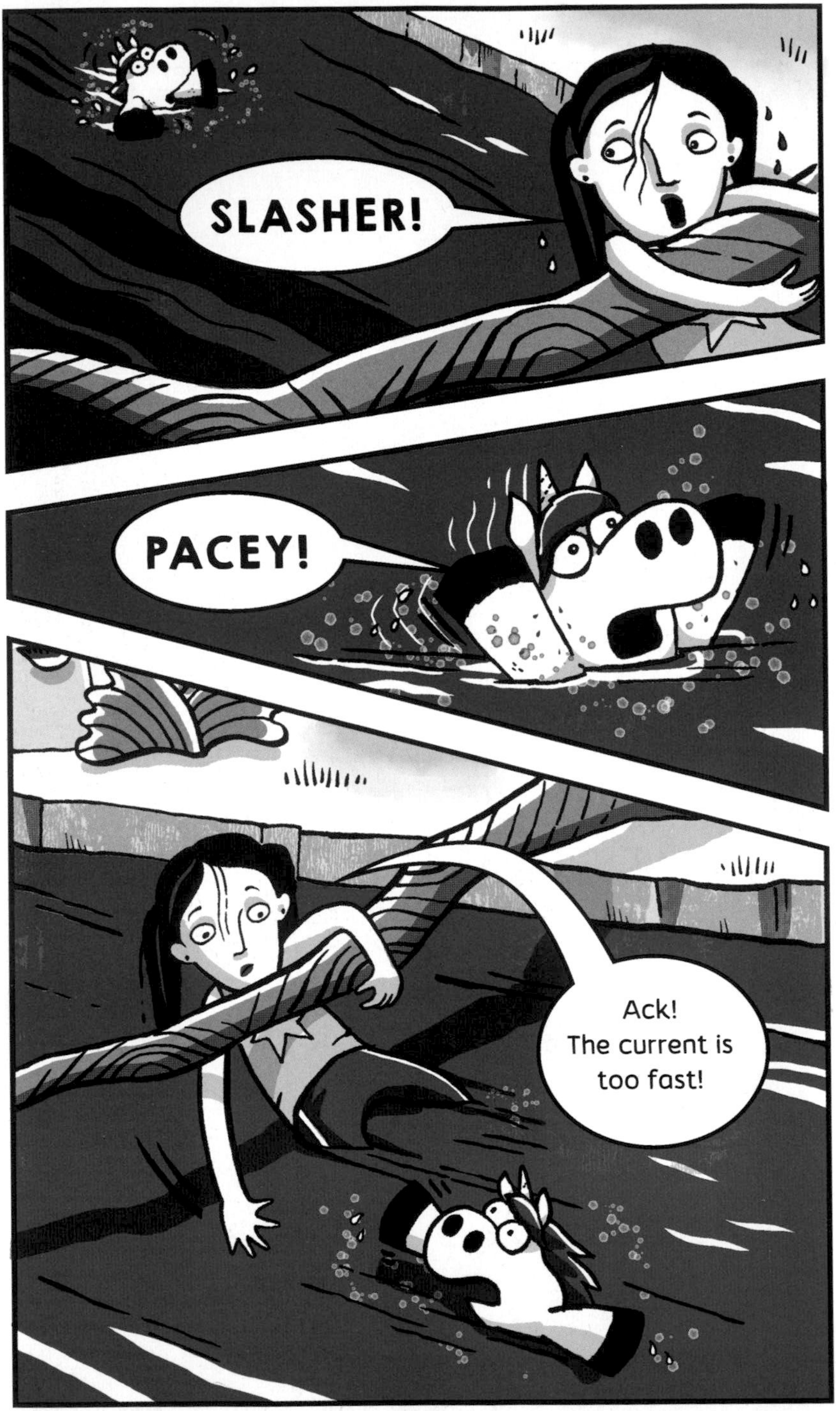
SLASHER!
PACEY!
Ack!
The current is
too fast!

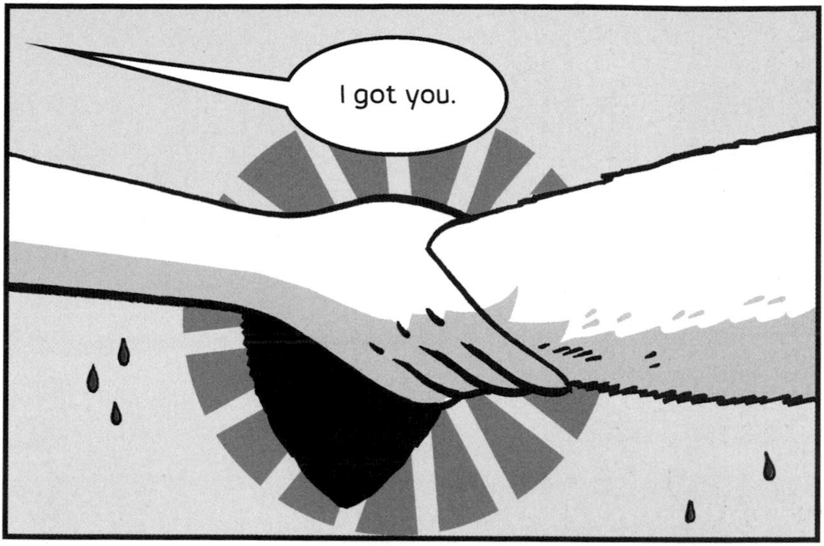
I got you.

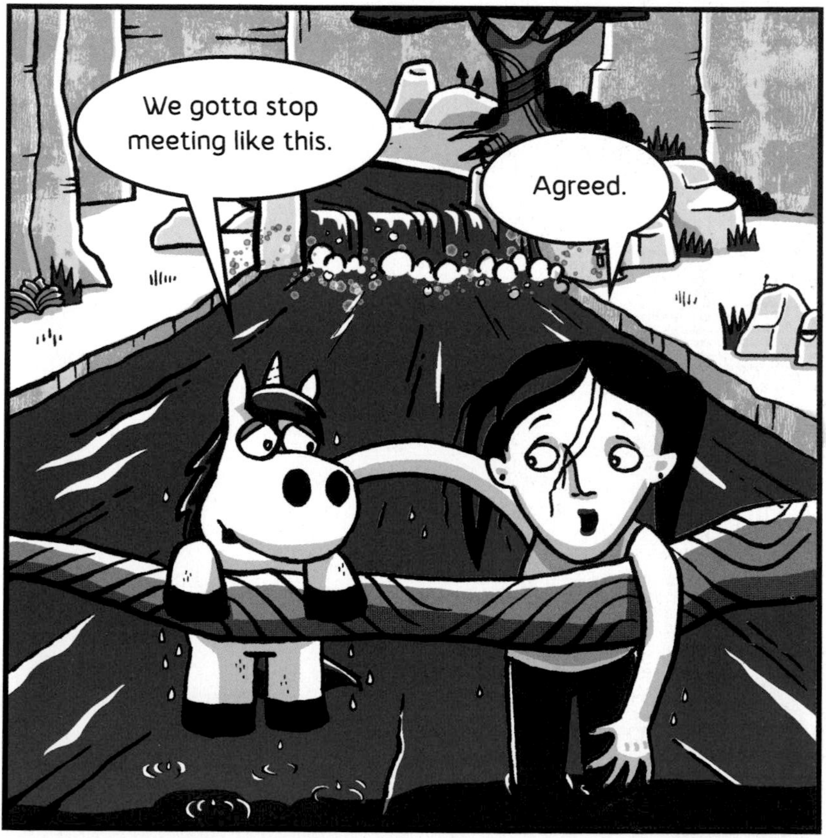
We gotta stop meeting like this.
Agreed.

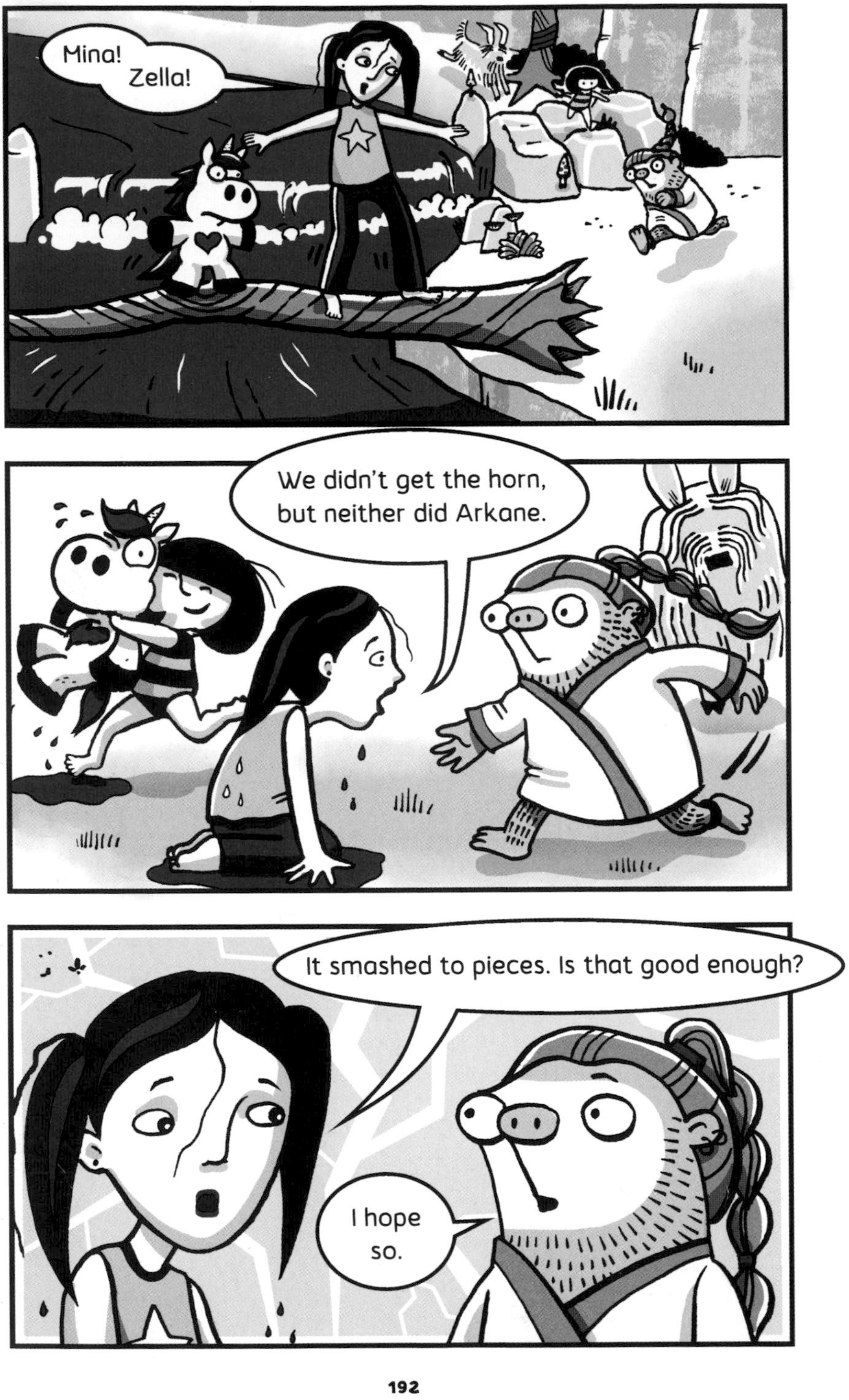
Mina!
Zella!
We didn't get the horn, but neither did Arkane.
It smashed to pieces. Is that good enough?
I hope so.

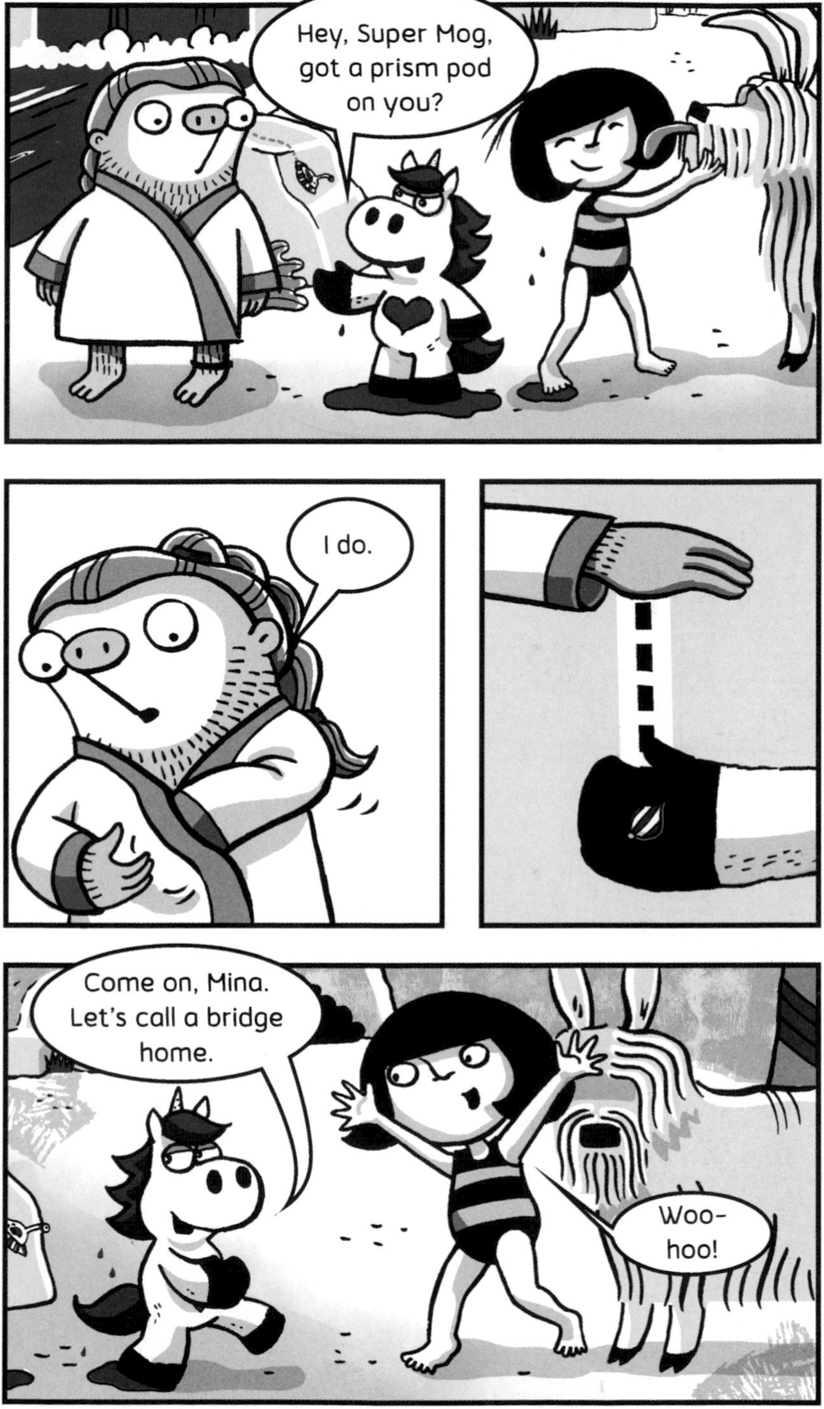
Hey, Super Mog, got a prism pod on you?
I do.
Come on, Mina. Let's call a bridge home.
Woo-hoo!

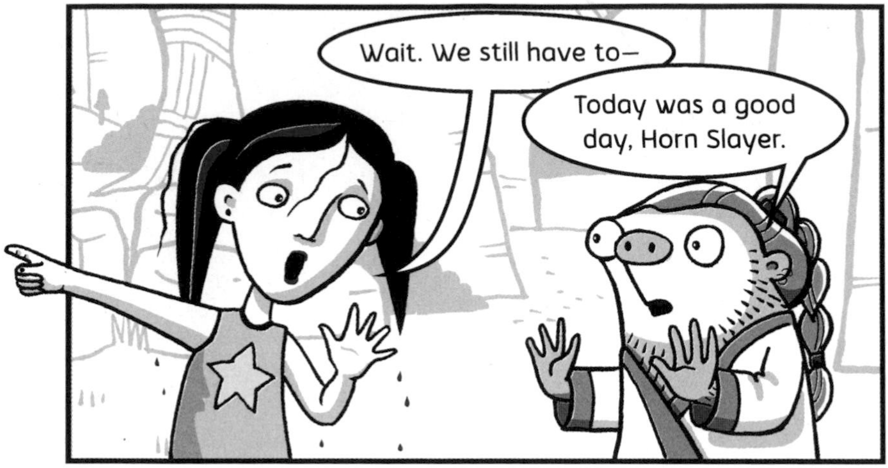
Wait. We still have to—
Today was a good day, Horn Slayer.

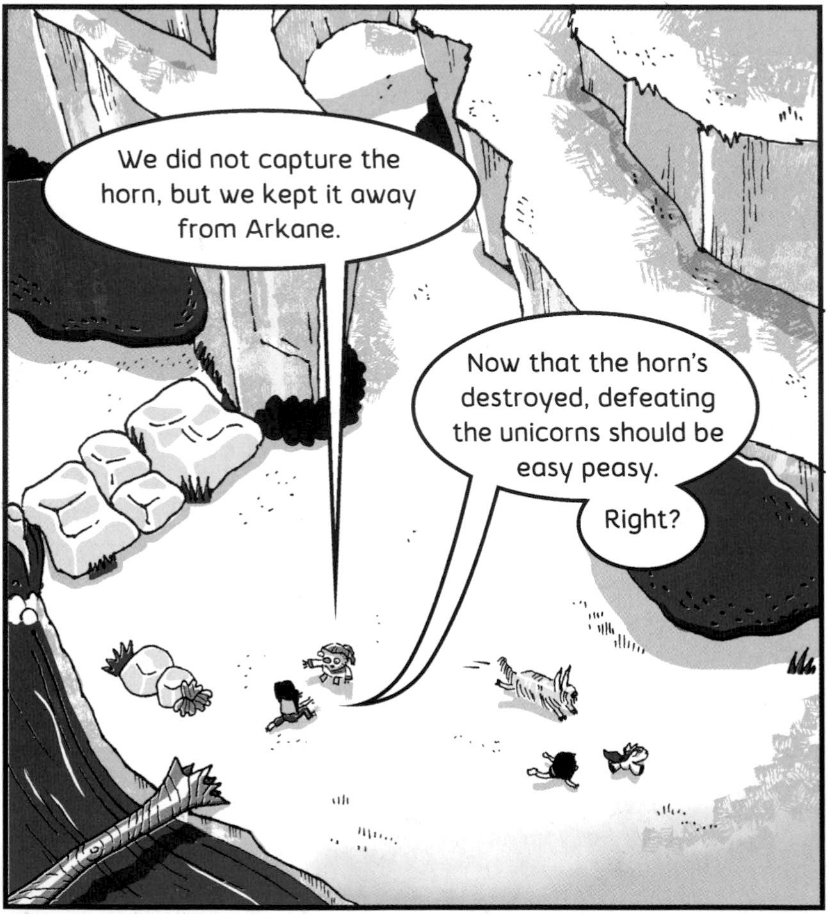
We did not capture the horn, but we kept it away from Arkane.
Now that the horn's destroyed, defeating the unicorns should be easy peasy.
Right?

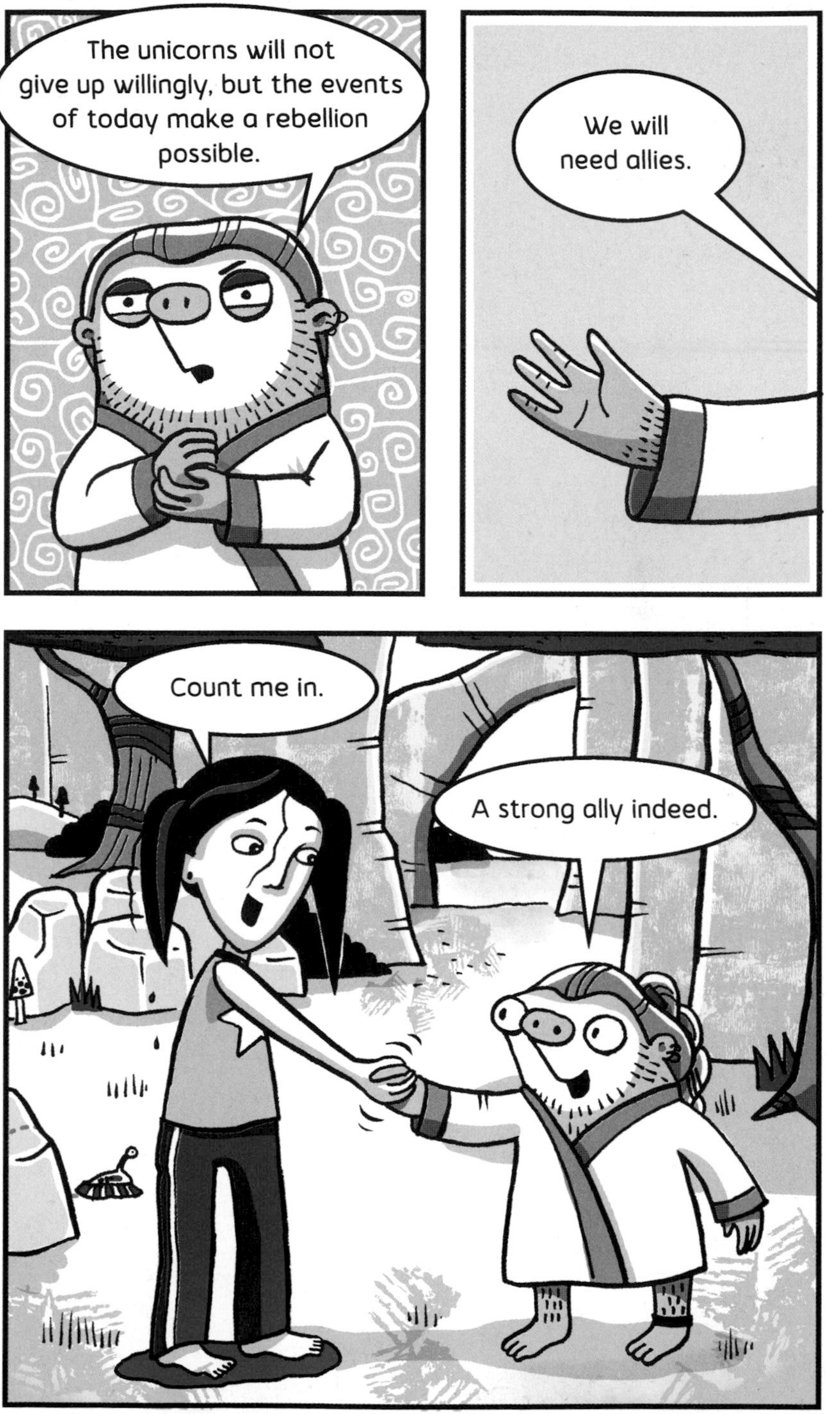
The unicorns will not give up willingly, but the events of today make a rebellion possible.
We will need allies.
Count me in.
A strong ally indeed.

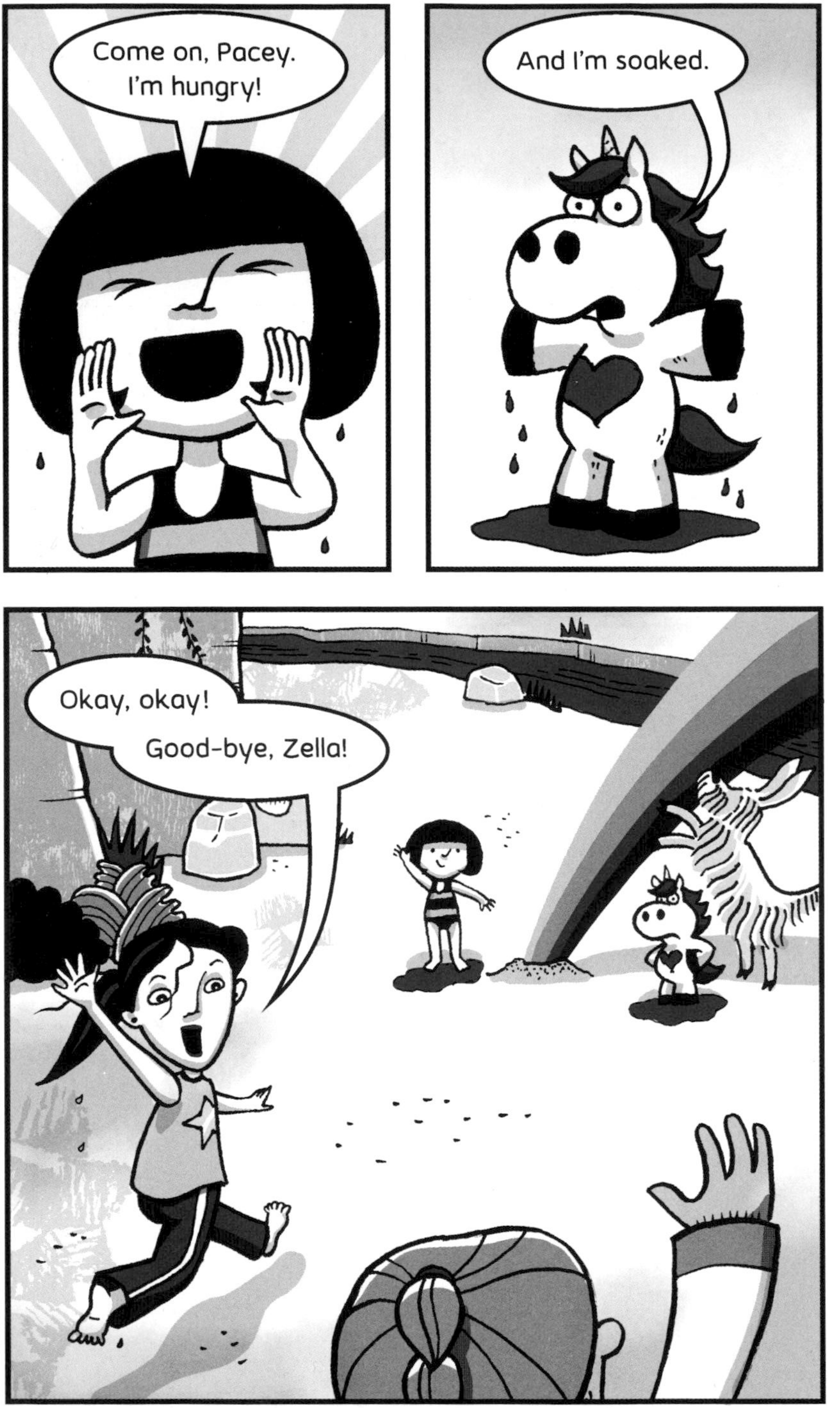
Come on, Pacey. I'm hungry!
And I'm soaked.
Okay, okay!
Good-bye, Zella!

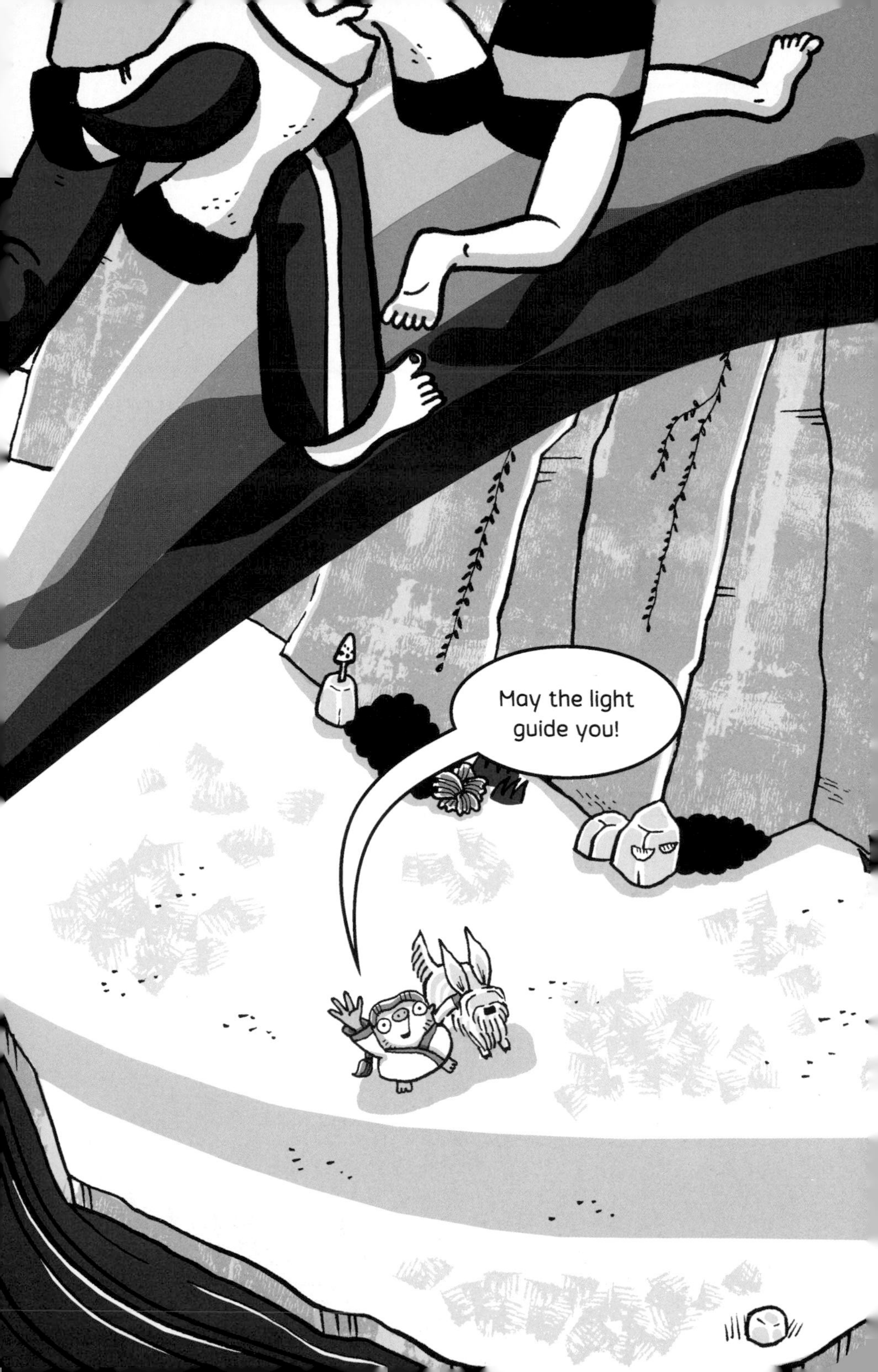
May the light guide you!

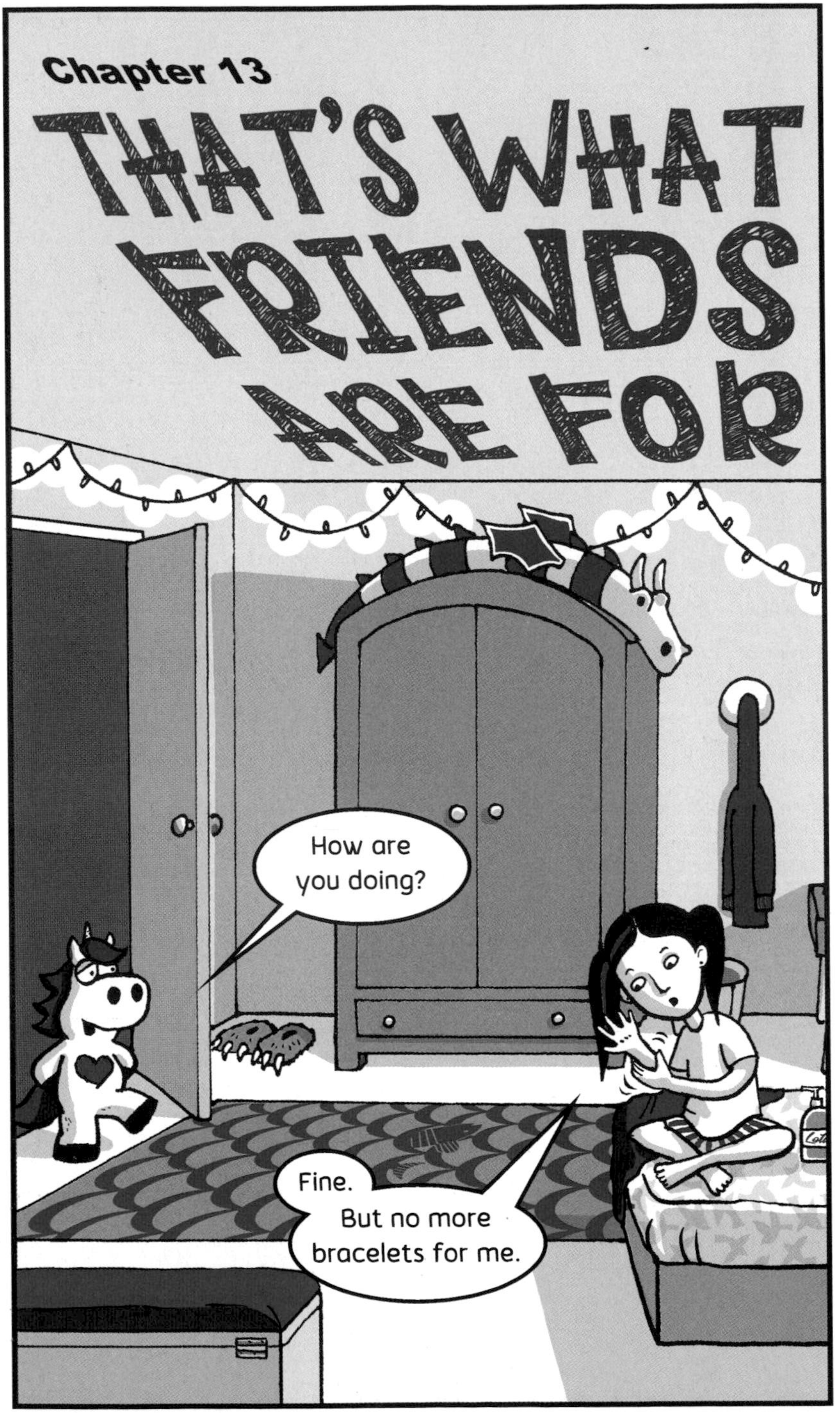
Chapter 13
THAT'S WHAT FRIENDS ARE FOR
How are you doing?
Fine. But no more bracelets for me.

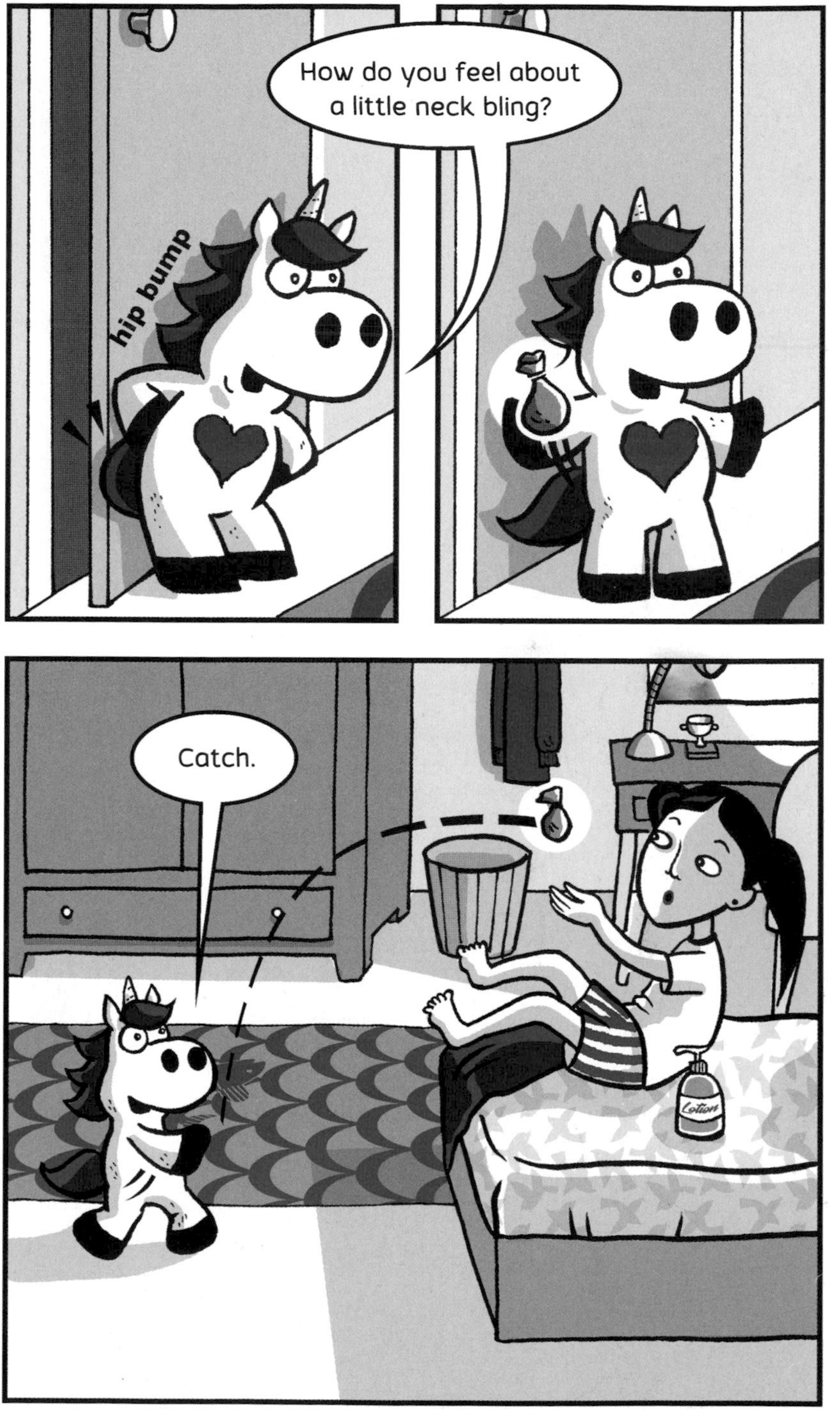
hip bump
How do you feel about a little neck bling?
Catch.
Lotion

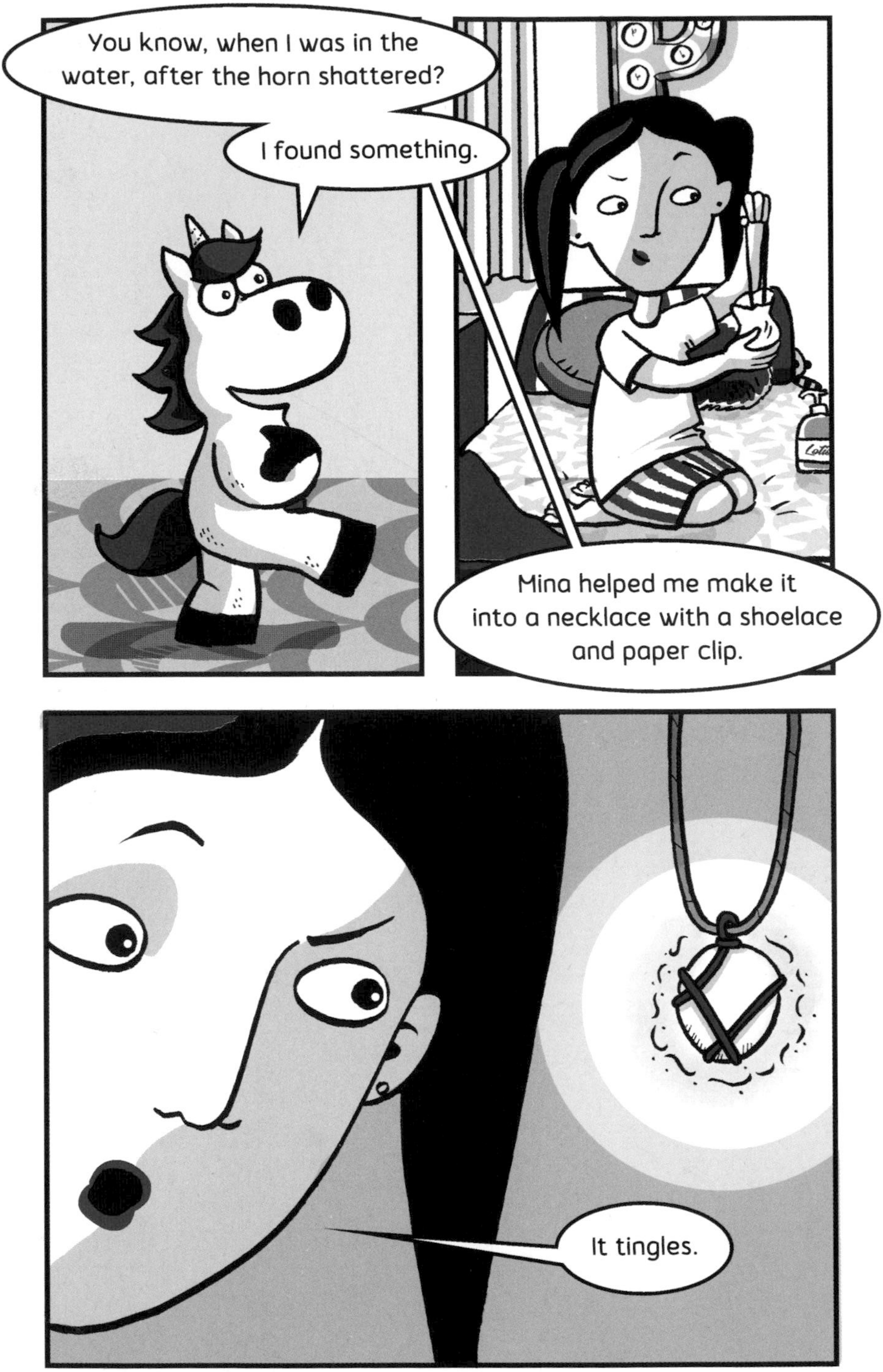
You know, when I was in the water, after the horn shattered?
I found something.
Mina helped me make it into a necklace with a shoelace and paper clip.
It tingles.

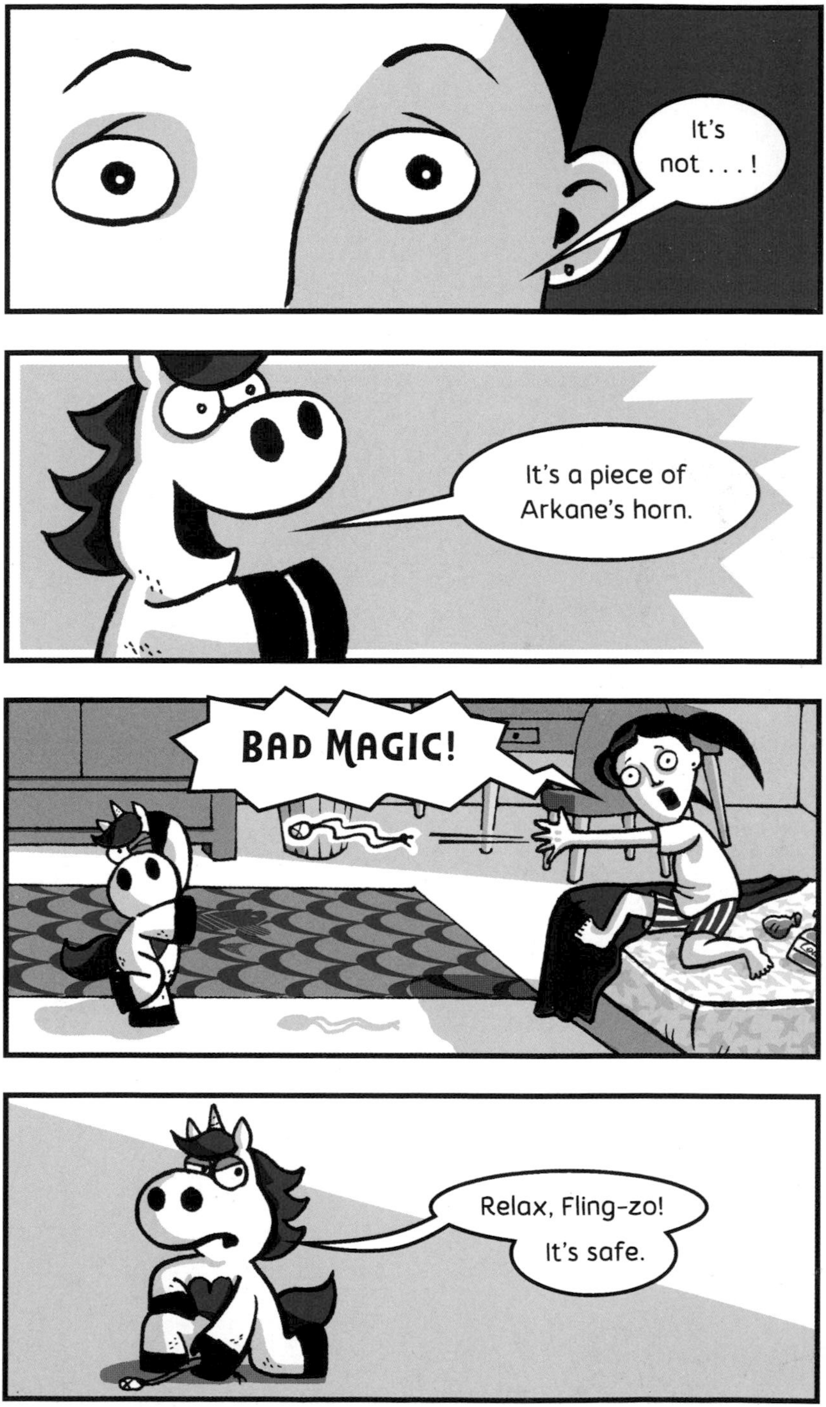
It's not . . . !
It's a piece of Arkane's horn.
BAD MAGIC!
Relax, Fling-zo!
It's safe.

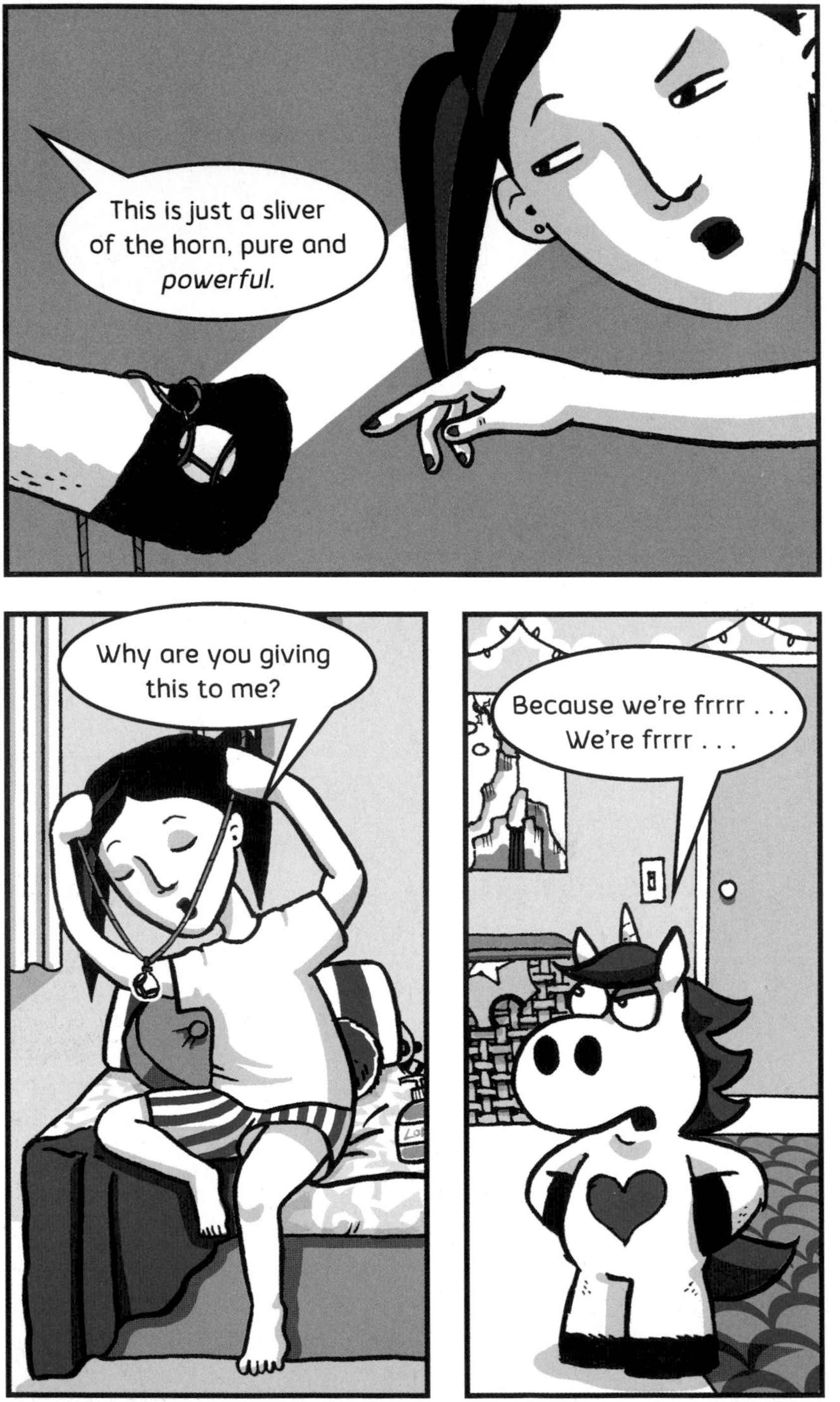
This is just a sliver of the horn, pure and *powerful.*
Why are you giving this to me?
Because we're frrrr . . . We're frrrr . . .

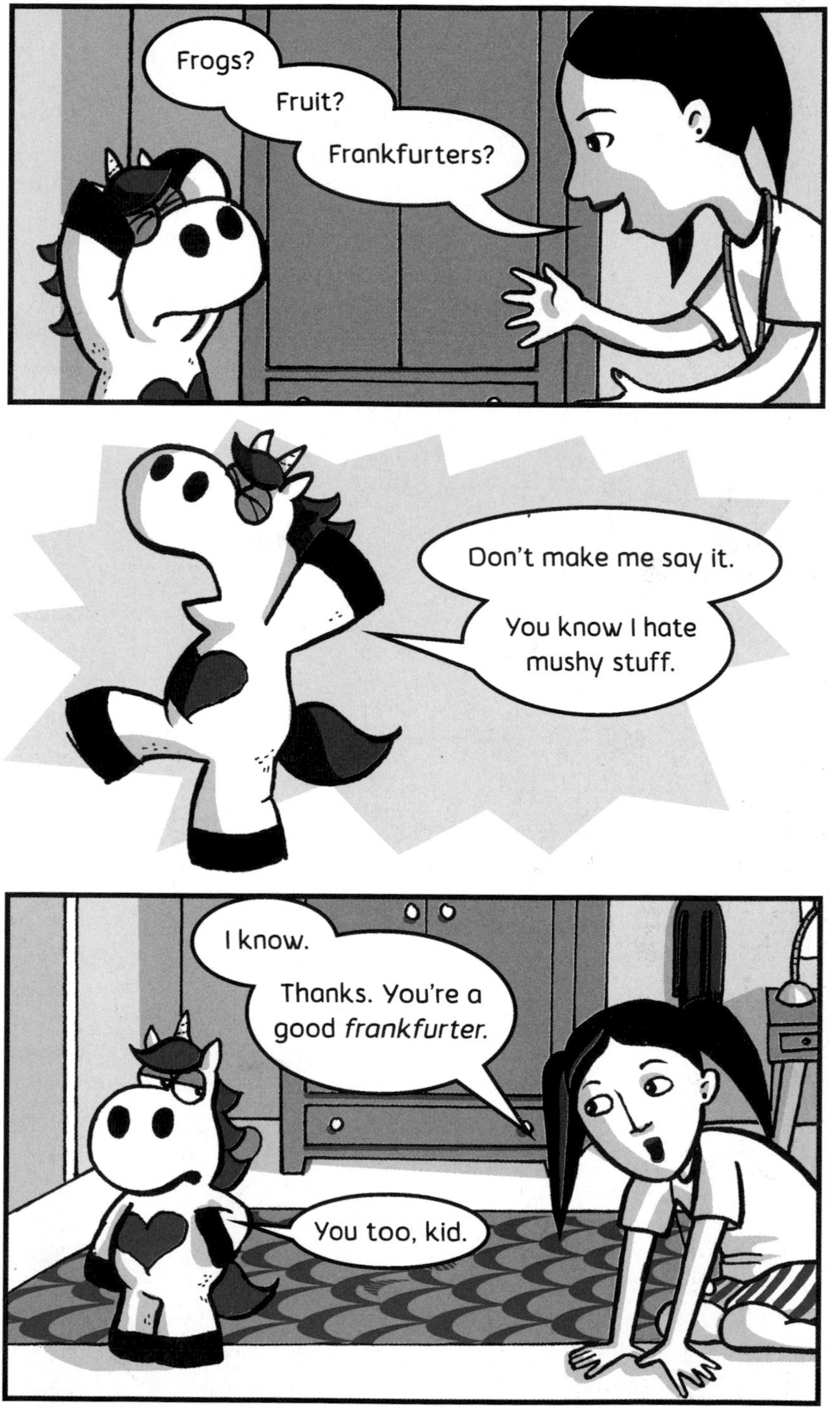
Frogs?
Fruit?
Frankfurters?
Don't make me say it.
You know I hate mushy stuff.
I know.
Thanks. You're a good *frankfurter.*
You too, kid.

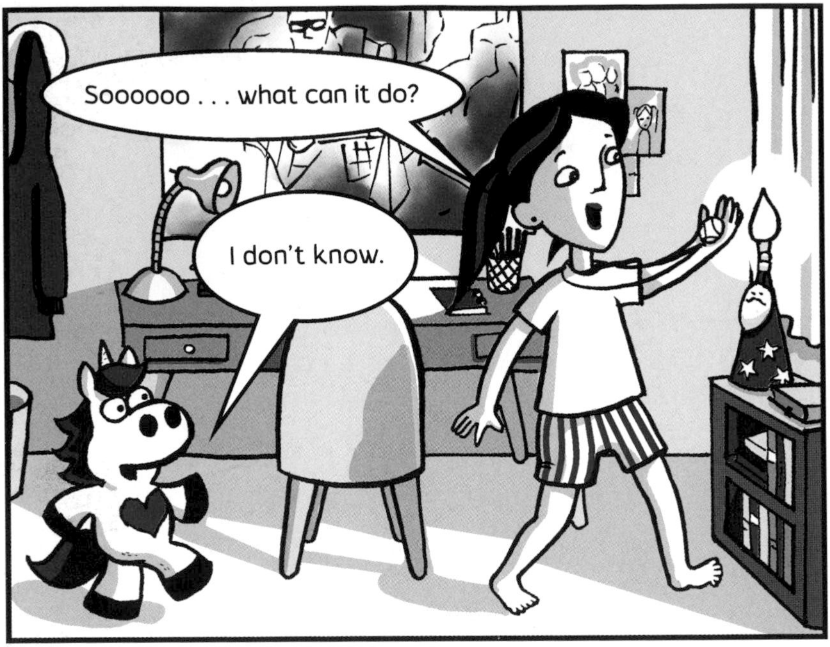
Soooooo . . . what can it do?
I don't know.

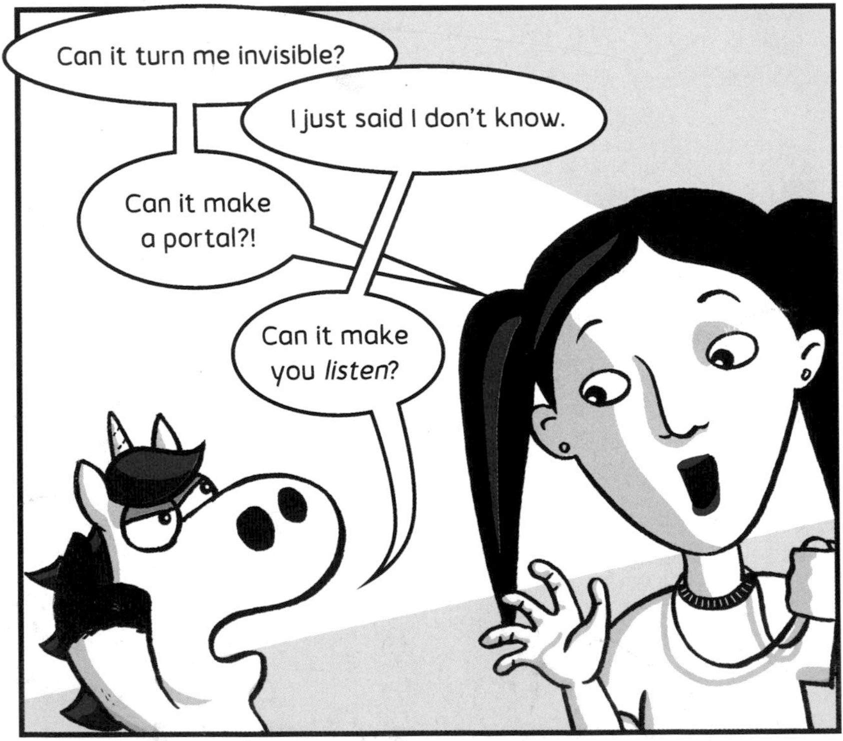
Can it turn me invisible?
I just said I don't know.
Can it make a portal?!
Can it make you *listen*?

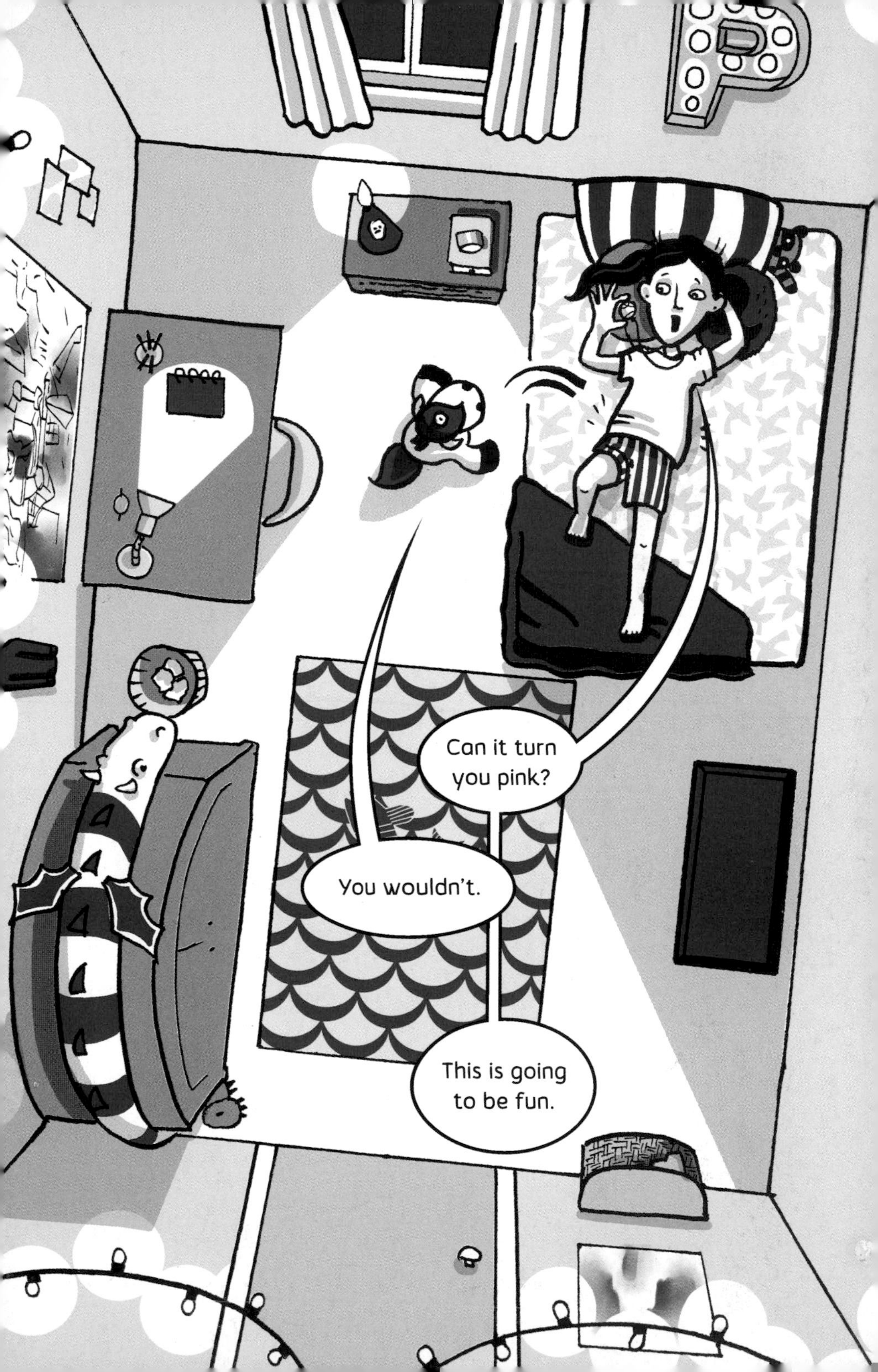
Can it turn you pink?
You wouldn't.
This is going to be fun.

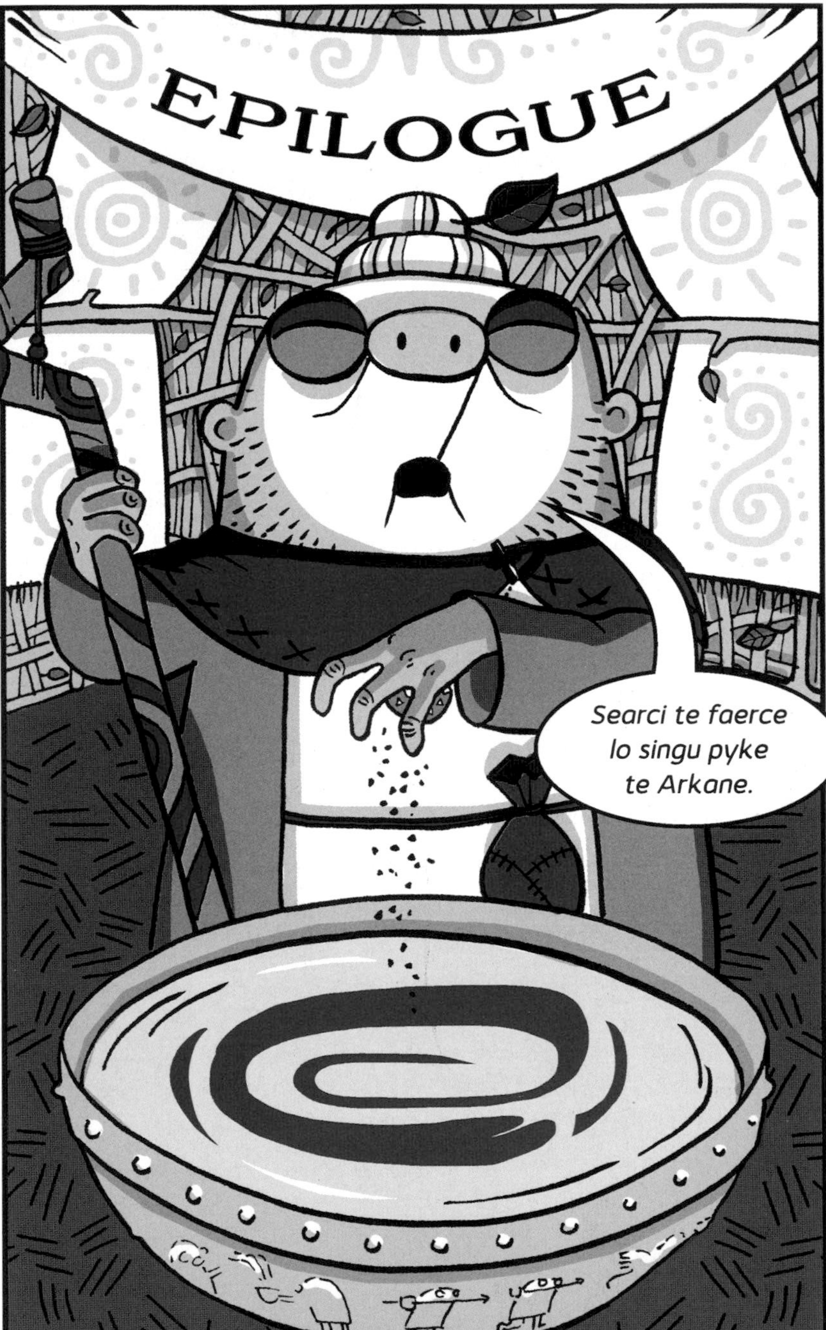
EPILOGUE
Searci te faerce lo singu pyke te Arkane.

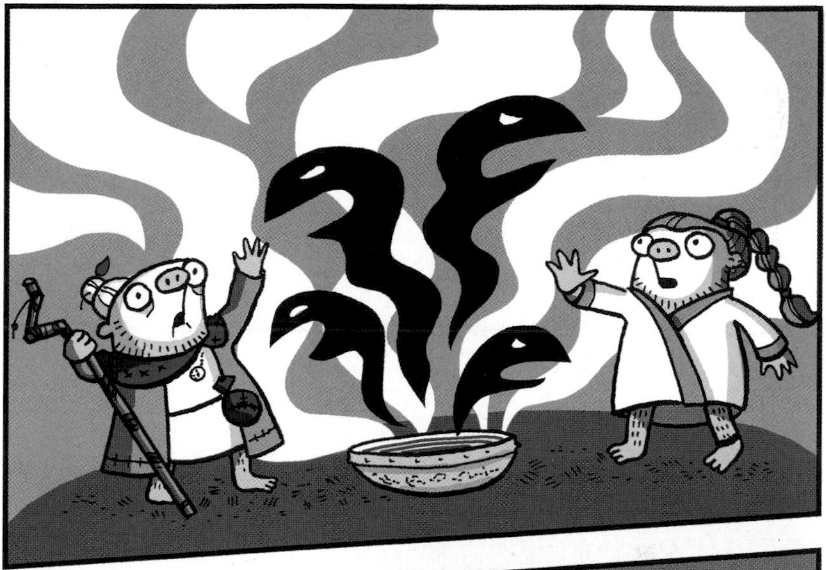

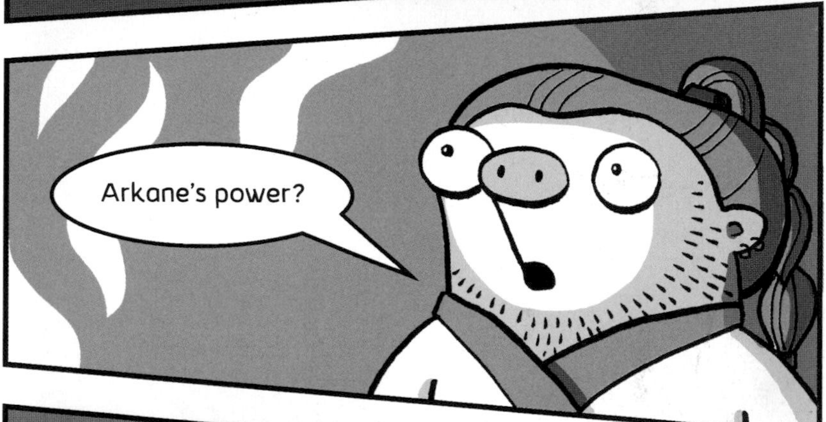
Arkane's power?

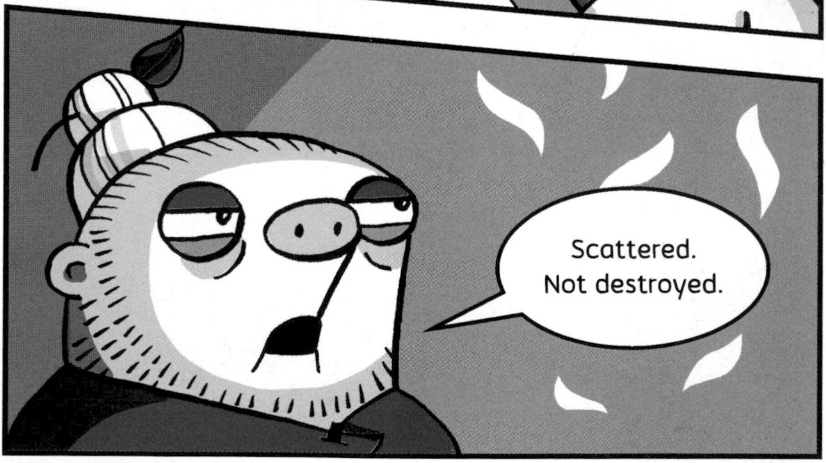
Scattered.
Not destroyed.

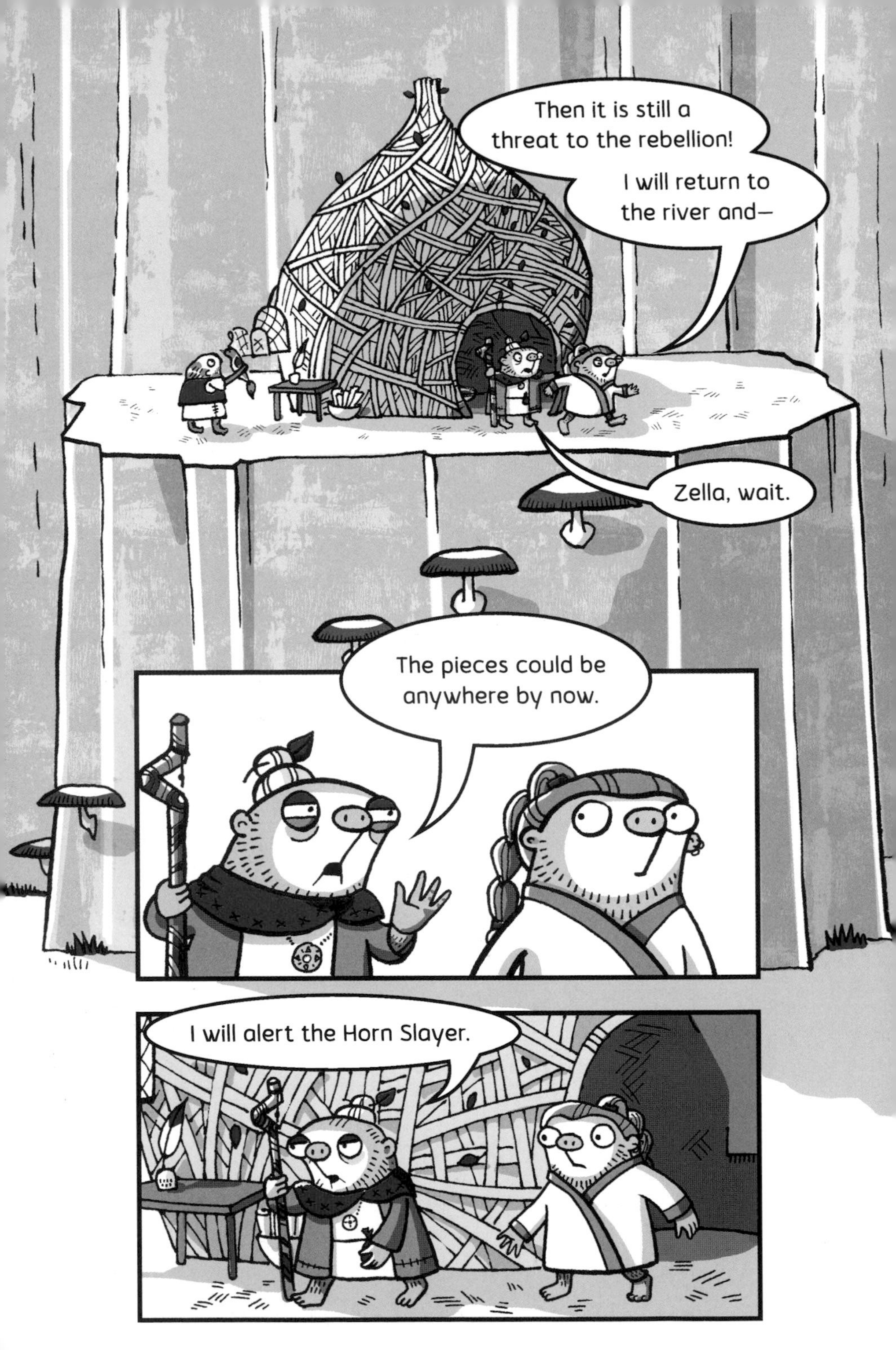
Then it is still a threat to the rebellion!
I will return to the river and—
Zella, wait.
The pieces could be anywhere by now.
I will alert the Horn Slayer.

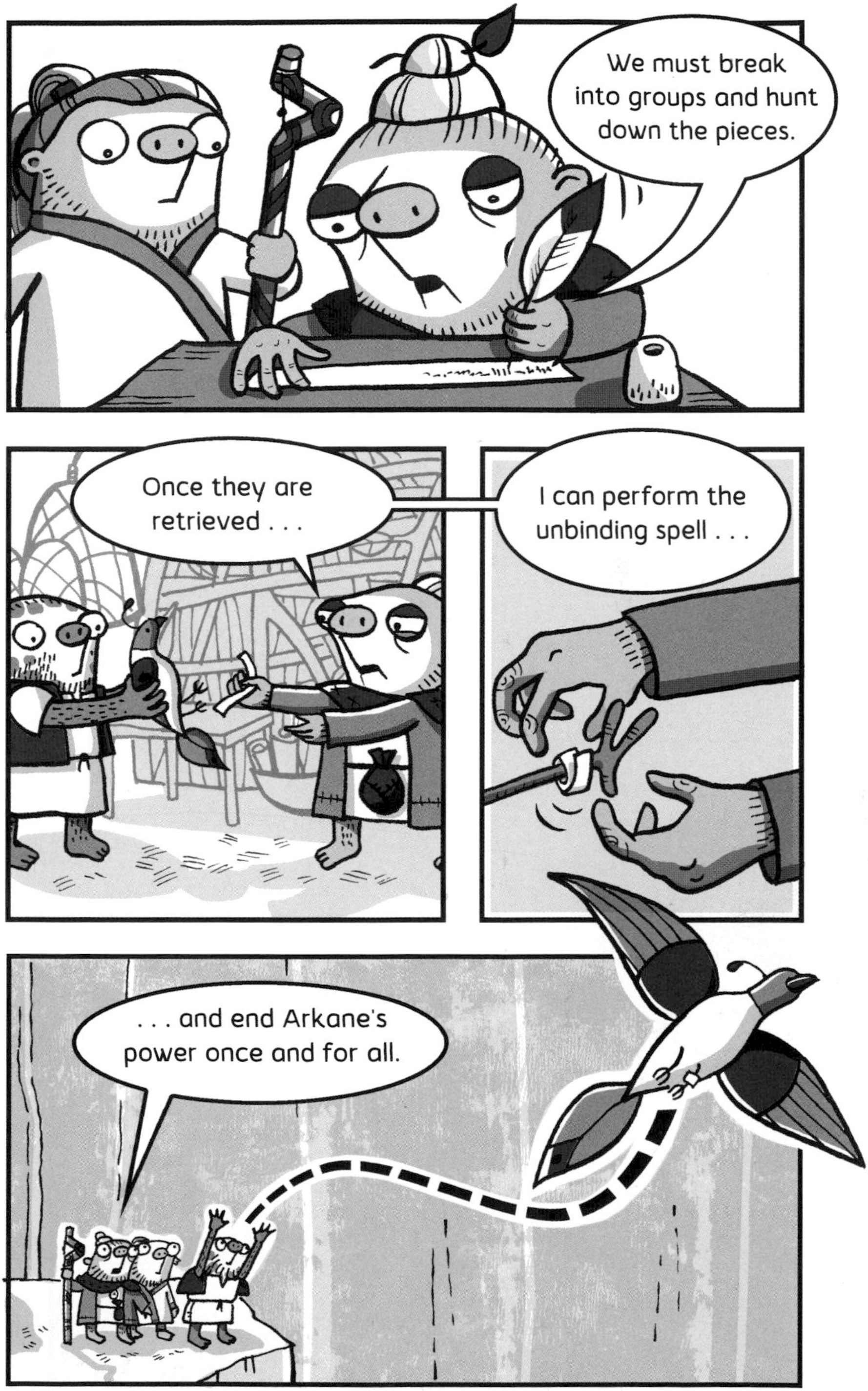
We must break into groups and hunt down the pieces.
Once they are retrieved . . .
I can perform the unbinding spell . . .
. . . and end Arkane's power once and for all.

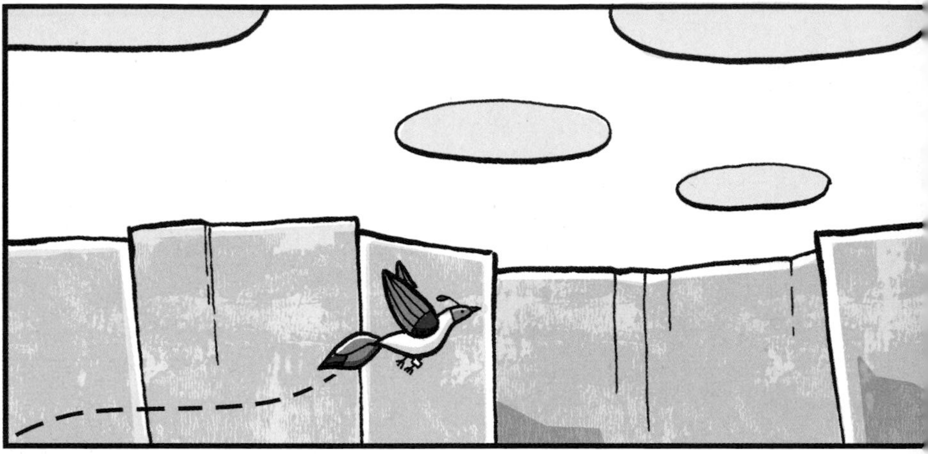
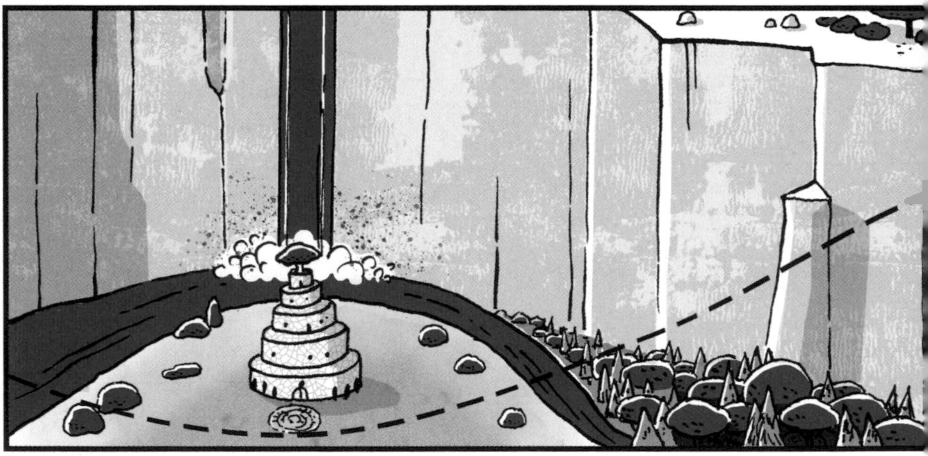
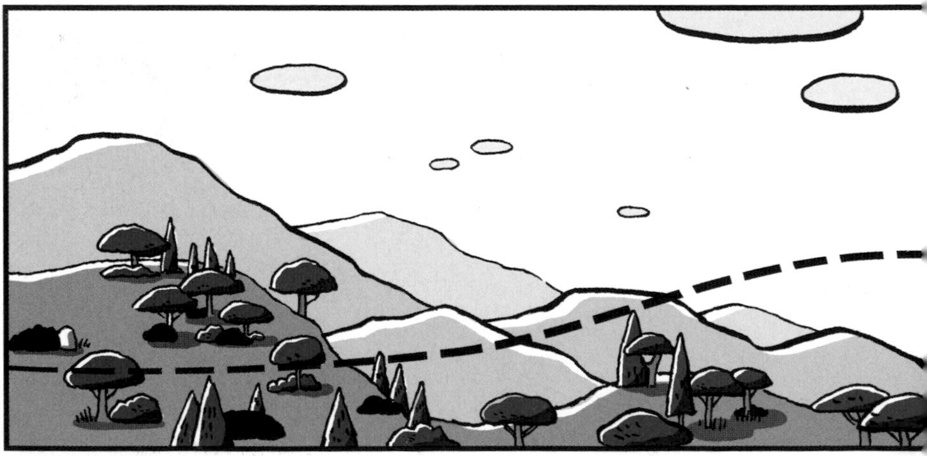

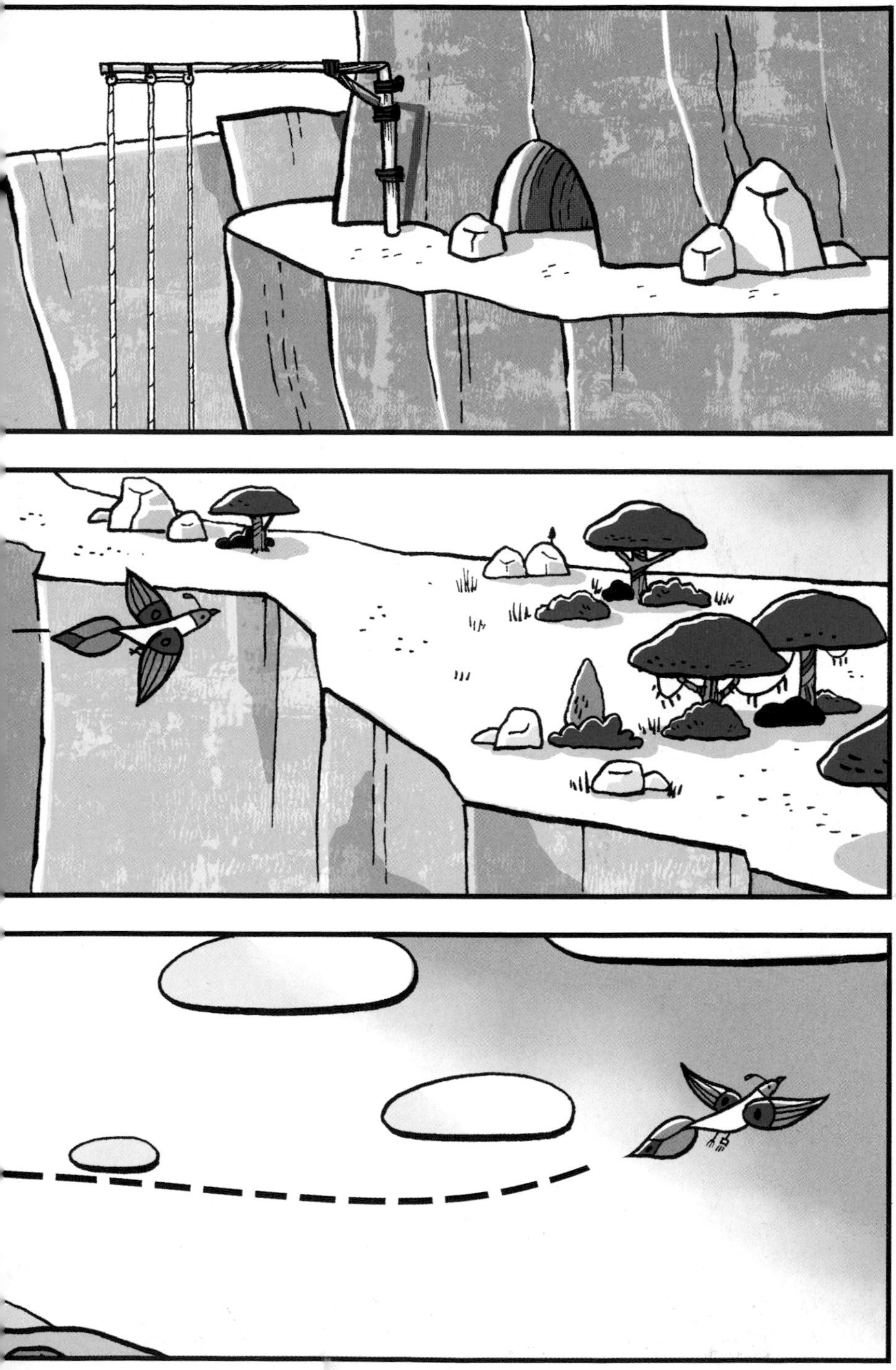

END OF BOOK 3

THE ADVENTURE CONTINUES IN

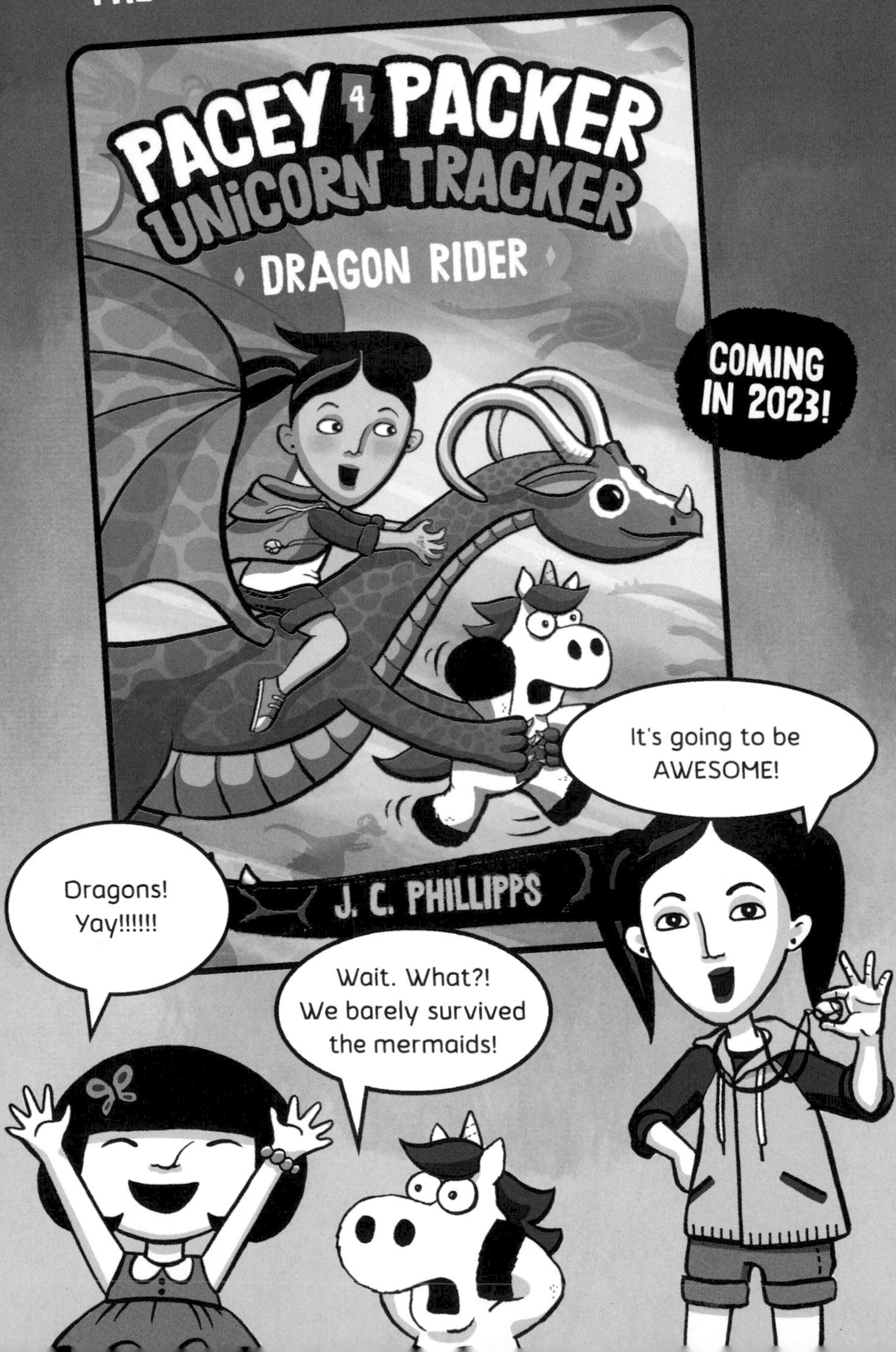
PACEY 4 PACKER
UNICORN TRACKER
DRAGON RIDER
J. C. PHILLIPPS
COMING IN 2023!
It's going to be AWESOME!
Dragons! Yay!!!!!!
Wait. What?! We barely survived the mermaids!

DRAW IT! BRIONY

1

With a pencil, draw a round oval.

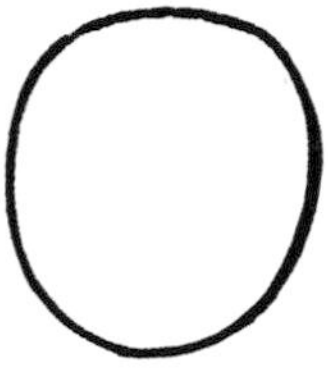

2

Draw ears, hair, and seaweed hairband.

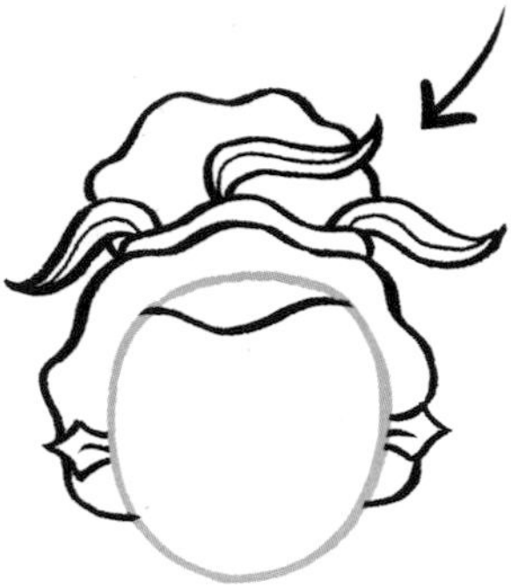

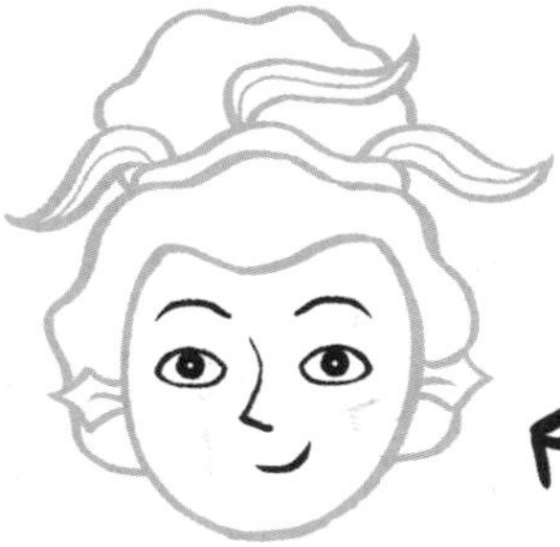

3

Draw Briony's face. Notice that her nose is pointy.

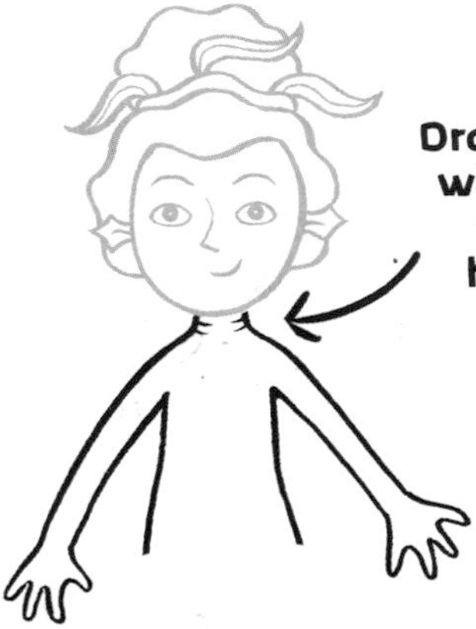

4

Draw the neck, with the gills, the arms, hands, and waist.

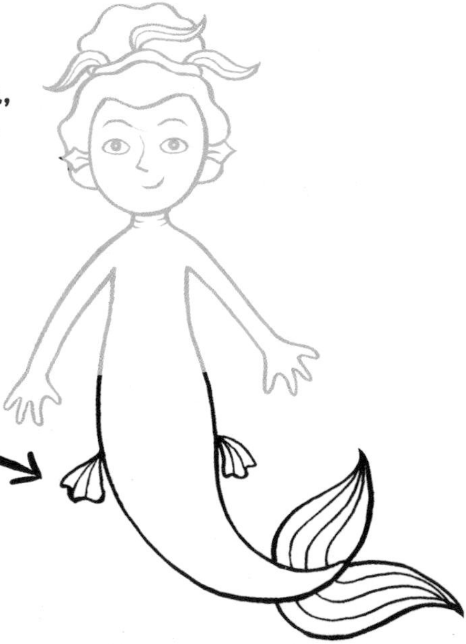

5

Draw the mermaid tail. Add the side fins and all the lines in the tail and fins.

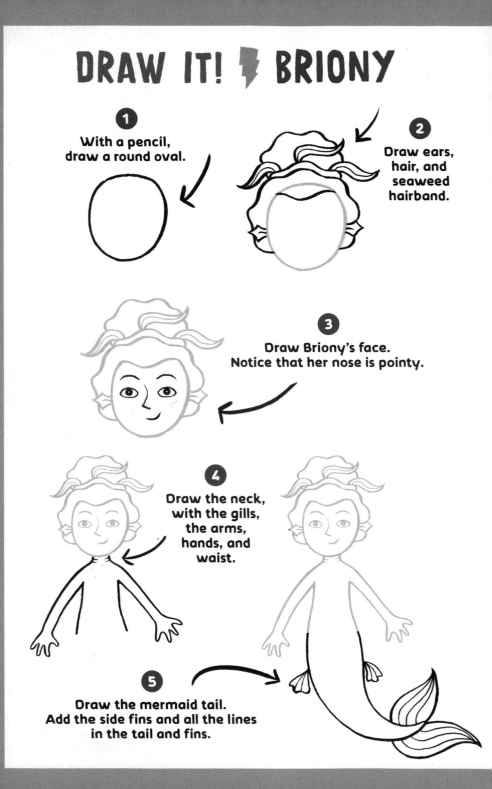

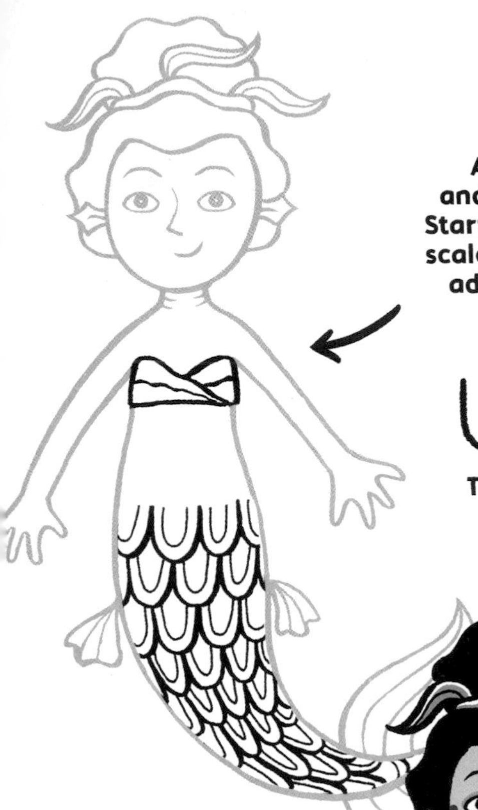

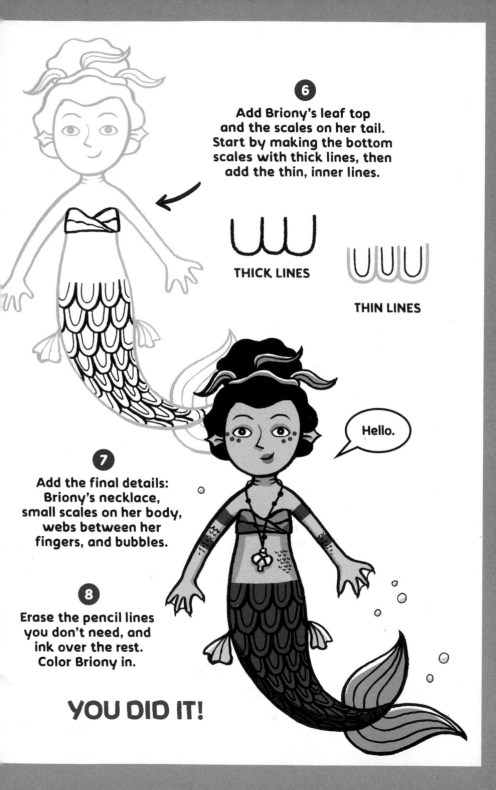

6

Add Briony's leaf top and the scales on her tail. Start by making the bottom scales with thick lines, then add the thin, inner lines.

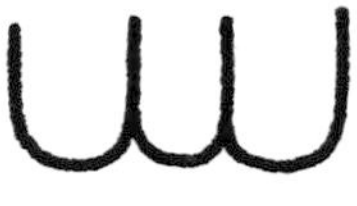

THICK LINES

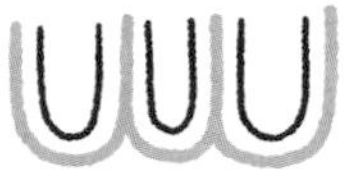

THIN LINES

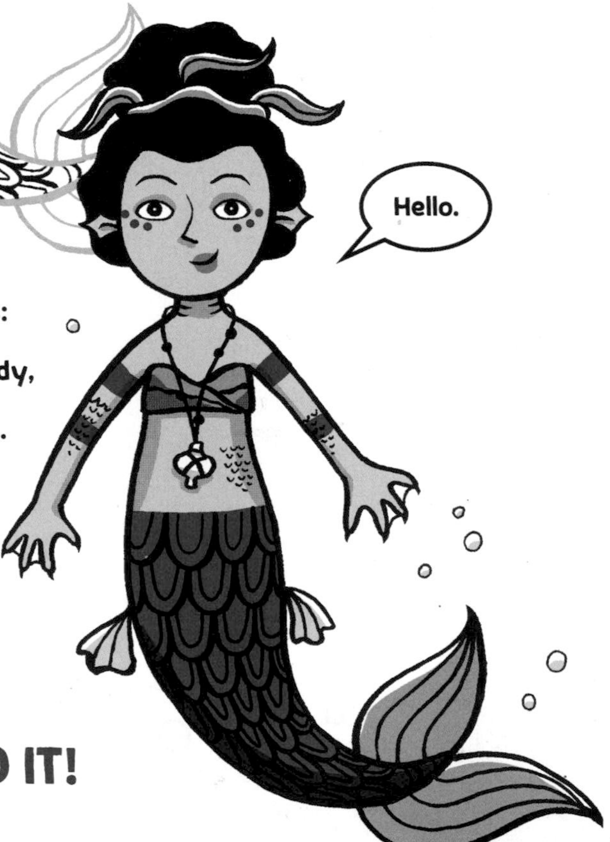
Hello.

7

Add the final details: Briony's necklace, small scales on her body, webs between her fingers, and bubbles.

8

Erase the pencil lines you don't need, and ink over the rest. Color Briony in.

YOU DID IT!

ACKNOWLEDGMENTS

Since Pacey's story arc involves knowing who your true friends are, I'd like to thank the wonderful women in my life: Adrian, Jackie, Heather, Angela, Darlene, Annalisa, and Kristine. You are all amazing women who bring so much laughter, support, and encouragement to my life. Special shout-out to Stefanie Marco Lantz, who has so much enthusiasm it's bursting out of her pores. And to Staci Granzetto, everyone should have a friend as funny, kind, smart, empathetic, and open as you. I am lucky indeed.

Sending big love to my fabulous editor, Shana Corey; my designer, Michelle Cunningham; and all the wonderful people on Team Pacey at Random House. High fives to my agent, Michael Bourret, for always being so supportive and calming when I go full freak-out.

Over the last year (it's April 2021 as I write this) I have spent A LOT of time with my husband and son, both of whom are smart, lovely, funny men who embrace the super-weird dork that is me. I love you both. (And love to Boris and Natasha, my cats, who will not read this.)

And a final thank-you to all the young readers, teachers, and media specialists out there who have shared your Pacey Packer art, compliments, and enthusiasm. It always brings a smile to my face! Thank you.